GHOSTS OF ALDA

THE OBSCURED THRONE TRILOGY
BOOK 2

RUSSELL ARCHEY

5 PRINCE PUBLISHING

Published by 5 PRINCE PUBLISHING & BOOKS, LLC

PO Box 865, Arvada, CO 80001

www.5PrinceBooks.com

ISBN digital: 978-1-63112-309-2

ISBN print: 978-1-63112-310-8

Cover Credit: Marianne Nowicki

05222023

To my wife and kids, who are always supportive and encouraging.

To all the readers, for taking the time to enjoy all the work that goes into every story, setting, and character.

ACKNOWLEDGMENTS

A very special thank you to Bernadette at 5 Prince Publishing for taking a chance on a writer of the weird, fantastical, and terrifying.

Thank you so much to my editor, Cate, for making my ramblings more presentable.

ALSO BY RUSSELL ARCHEY

The Seven Spires

Ashes of Alder

Ghosts of Alda

GHOSTS OF ALDA

THE GROVE

An elf-kind sat in a chair within a grove. On a table fashioned of one block of pure quartz sat a cup that held swiftly-cooling tea. The elf-kind smiled as he watched a couple of fox kits tumble just outside the tree line. His chair was simple, carved of wood and without a cushion, and greatly mismatched against the elegant table, but he was comfortable. The afternoon sun was almost unnoticeable behind the western edge of the canopy; its warmth was still quite present, however.

He tended this grove. He was its keeper. This was no ordinary grove but a cluster of the precious aldyrs revered by his people. They were not held in the same respect by dwarves or humans, but their importance was not lost on the other races, regardless. Since the first days of their world, Alda, these trees represented the blossoming, eternal spirit of every continent. They were the world's soul, connected to Alda and everything living on it and within it. Elves ensured that all their forested lands grew strong and withstood the grasping fingers of industry and expanding cities but being a grove of aldyrs, an elf-kind of noble-birth and not directly in line for succession was allowed to tend to it. His particular bloodline was known for its longevity, even among the long-lived elves. He was perfect for the role.

Most grove-tenders went about their work and then returned to the elven cities within the forest. This elf-kind preferred to stay among his trees, his aldyrs. He sat for hours at a time, watching the creatures of the morning hours—elk, rabbits, and birds. He'd watch as the fog hid them within its chill obscurity and allowed them to eat in safety. He watched in the afternoon, like today, as the kits played and squirrels ran up and down the trees in their frenzied work. Even in the evenings, when he stayed late and the tea was switched out for wine, he listened to the owls call, and the crickets and frogs sing an off-key melody. The larger animals of the night revealed themselves as their eyes caught the moonlight.

Visitors would come to speak of casual things and of elf-kind business. They would sit and drink with him and bring him food, insisting he needed more to subsist on than aldyrfruit.

Such was the way of things for many, many years.

One day, the grove became quiet. No songbirds called. No animals skulked or skittered about their business. Even the air felt different. The wind was deathly still, and the grove-tender felt on edge. Something was wrong.

An ear-splitting sound cut the air. A moan, like that of a massive, dying beast, followed immediately after, thrumming through the grove-tender and sending a panicked shudder along his bones. Something was very wrong.

After several moments, his skin stopped trying to crawl from his body, and the panic ebbed. He felt different, though. A tiny pin-prick of hollowness ached within his soul. He breathed through it, taking deep, calming breaths. What had just happened?

He sat in his chair, sipped on his tea, and listened for the sounds of the grove: the animals and the wind. All was still silent and unmoving. He was so preoccupied with looking through the trunks of the aldyrs for any sign of life that it took him several hours to look up to the sky. A purple welt, laced with thin streaks of lightning-like exposed, pulsating veins, ran the length of the view above the canopy.

He stood quickly, haphazardly, rocking the table and knocking over the cup and its lukewarm contents. This grove was deep within the forest kingdom of Athil'glyn, on the eastern side of the north continent. Trees ran for a hundred miles in any direction. A gap in the canopy in the midst of these aldyrs provided him a window to the sky. He looked up at the hole in the canopy at what was once a brilliant blue sky staring back like a still, serene pond among the blossoms. Now, the pond ran red like blood, with an angry, bruise-colored streak slashing through it.

Athil'glyn was quite isolated, the closest other sovereignties being a few human towns and a small dwarven kingdom all near or in the western Belgallant Mountains. Beyond that, the Blackwood Forest and then the cold, northern-most city-state of Kalthav. This great rupture in the sky must have stretched even further, all the way to the western end of the continent by Carnelia.

An ill feeling overtook the elf-kind, sending a wave of debilitating nausea to well up from his gut into his throat. He fell back into his chair. His vision began to blur, then darken. Strange sounds and dark shapes came from within the forest all around him. He thought these were the animals panicking. Birds took flight in screeching flocks from the trees. Small animals were crying out and scurrying into their burrows. Wolves were running with their tails between their legs, and bears were growling in anger and fear.

His head lolled to the side, and as he tried to straighten it, to force himself to stay conscious, it merely flopped to the other side. His muscles had all the strength of limp saplings, his mind growing foggy as the riverbanks in the dawn hours. All that remained of his vision was a blurred, narrow tunnel. The frenzied silhouettes of the animals still darted between the trees in that narrow tunnel. Sometimes they looked at him, and their eyes gleamed with something other than fear. Perhaps it was the abyss of unconsciousness closing in, but the dark outlines no longer looked like any animals he'd ever seen.

THE FIRST SENSATION he recognized was his skin tingling. His eyes were slow to open and felt heavy. His head pounded. He felt intoxicated. A subtle wind kissed his arms where the sleeves of his robe had pulled up from his weak flailing. The tingling sensation was the chill kiss of that wind, too cold for the season. His mouth was dry and bitter. Moments passed as he tried to remember where he was. Trees surrounded him; white blossoms covered the ground in a light blanket like early winter snow. He was in his grove, surrounded by his aldyrs.

But why were the blossoms falling? They never fell. Not in fall or winter. Whether in the heat of summer or the bitter cold of winter, the blossoms and leaves never fell. He blinked his eyes, wiped the residue of sleep from them, and looked again. He wasn't dreaming, and his vision wasn't failing. The aldyrs were dying.

In his bones, he recognized this truth. His own body felt suddenly frailer. The weight of encroaching mortality weighed on him. Approaching one of the sacred trees, he placed his hand on its trunk and took a deep breath. He needed to tell those in the city.

A low noise came from behind the trunks of the trees before

him. It sounded like a growl, angry and cautionary. He retreated, stepping back into the grove. The oaks and ash trees were closer on this border, and their boughs were still full. The shade they provided was thick, and past the aldyrs, he saw something there. Something slouched behind one of the broad trunks.

The elf-kind called out to them, but the shape didn't move. He couldn't tell if it was animal or elf-kind. He called out again and took a few steps toward the grove's edge. The shape came out from behind the tree. It skulked like a goblin from the swamps, only taller and lankier. Its four-fingered hand splayed out on the trunk beside it as though it hesitated to leave the shelter. Another one of them came from behind the next tree. They lurched slowly in his direction, hissing and growling like wounded cats.

His breath caught, and he stumbled backward. An exposed root caught the back of his heel, and he fell bodily onto the ground, the white blossoms exploding around him. The creatures stopped when they reached the aldyrs and stared at him. They began circling around to another side of the grove. He watched in horror as their ungainly, unnatural movements took them further away as the band of aldyrs grew thicker; they appeared to be repelled by the trees. He also noticed, as they walked, the grass and bushes below their feet wilted, turning yellow, then brown, then black as decay took them in moments.

The other sides of the grove were no different. Everywhere the elf-kind ran to try and escape, to make it back to the capital of Athil'glyn, there was something waiting. Either more of the wretched, gangly creatures or other shapes of various sizes, all unrecognizable and all wrapped in shadow.

He was trapped.

Moving the table to the center of the grove, along with what supplies he had, the elf-kind waited. The days and nights turned into a different kind of wretched cycle. The days felt cold and strange. All manner of unnamable and unwholesome creatures waited patiently behind the broad trunks of the trees. The aldyrs, standing like fatigued sentinels against them, continued to shed their blossoms a little more each day; every sunrise brought them closer and closer to death. In the evenings, the setting sun, now more visible through the thinning canopy, caught the eyes of the creatures and reflected a hateful glimmer. After nightfall, an entirely new world took over. The moonlight seemed to cast their shadows even deeper. The things waiting on the outskirts of the grove were even more visible in the darkness of this new, strange night. Stars the elf-kind had never seen before shone through the open space above the grove. Now, instead of a pool of blue during the day and shimmering black at night, it felt like an eye, watching and judging. Instead of offering a sense of serenity, it made him feel exposed. As though something were watching from far away.

The weeks passed, and no one came to his aid. The wine ran out after a few days. Thankfully, the empty bottles caught enough rain to survive on. The food also did not last long. The aldyrfruit fell just as the leaves had, and for the first time in his long life, he saw them begin to soften and rot on the ground. It brought him to the verge of tears, but he ate them for as long as he could. After a few weeks, desperation set in, and his standards for what he could consume lowered significantly.

The aldyrs continued to wither. Their branches became stiff and dry. The blossoms on the ground turned to shades of ashen gray and brown. They crunched under his feet as he circled the grove, listening to the angry, whining growls of the things with the presence of decay and the shadowy creatures that darted between the trees. As the aldyrs slowly died, the creatures pressed closer to the border of the grove.

The elf-kind new no magic and carried only a small dagger, a family heirloom, for protection. He'd never once had to remove it. It seemed so trivial to carry that he left it under the ornate table, only carrying it back and forth between the grove and the city. He withdrew it from under the table and pulled it from its sheath, the sharp blade catching the dappled light of the sun. He looked at it forlornly, feeling the cold steel with his fingers. Hearing the throaty, gargled noises from outside the grove, he placed the flat edge against his wrist, felt the cold weapon against his skin. He turned the blade to its sharpened edge and felt the cold work its way into his soul.

The growling seemed to intensify. The creatures were watching him, goading him. He hesitated; his thoughts went to his family back in the city. He had no children, but his brother had several. He wondered what had become of his beloved nieces and nephews these last few weeks. Life is sacred to elf-kind, those long-lived stewards of the longer-lived forests. Suicide, they believed, brought a curse onto whose who took the precious gift of life from themselves. Elf-kind believed that upon death, their souls became a new aldyr. Taking one's own life, however, doomed one to walk the world forever until one became a vengeful specter for eternity.

His eyes went from the blade to the creatures in the woods. They were even closer now. Any day could hold the moment they broke through and came for him. The darkness of their presence and the shadows of the creatures around them never lifted even as they stood with their feet just outside of the grove's border.

His grip weakened as he saw the grisly creature at this closer distance. The knife slipped from his fingers, and he stood from the table. He walked closer, each step bringing a larger pang of horrifying realization to his already stretched mind. The whining growl from the creature reached a ghastly new pitch. It splayed a hand over the tree next to it as though it would spring on the grove-tender but was still held back by a thin row of dying aldyrs.

The elf-kind stood, his breaths escaping in sharp, broken rhythm from his open mouth. A tear finally escaped his eyes as he saw the creature up close for the first time. Though many of their features were shrouded in unnatural darkness that fell from their bodies like a rancorous mist, a small pendant on a chain could just be seen behind the cloying miasma that clung to the thing. It was of distinctly elven design, as was the clothing that could be seen; the point of their ears was also unmistakable.

A second creature stepped out from behind them as though from the miasma itself. This one had the features of a female in elegant dress. They both stared at him with a hatred that defied description. The one bearing the pendant placed a splayed hand against an adjacent tree as though it would launch itself at the elf-kind.

The grove-tender turned his back on them, hearing their growls pick up again. He walked, trance-like, back to his table at the center of the grove. Sitting down, he picked up the dagger again and clutched it tightly. No help was coming. The pendant on the thing in the woods bore the symbol of Athil'glyn. Something happened there when the sky opened, and the world cried out.

He would never know the fate of his people. Whatever the things outside the grove were, lurking in the unnatural darkness they brought with them; they were not his kin any longer. The shadowy things that skulked at their feet, darting amongst the trees where the forest creatures once lived, were not of this world. These were grotesque revenants of what should have been; ghosts of the world before the rupture that brought on the events of the last weeks.

The elf-kind sat in his chair at his table. He took a slow drink from the last bit of rainwater that his wine glass caught. The rainy season was ending. The fruits of the trees were rotted. He held the knife but refused to use it on himself. Maybe the revenants in the woods were the ghosts of those who couldn't bear the new world and took the same way out he had considered. He couldn't become one of them. He would simply wait and watch the last blossoms fall from the aldyrs.

TITAN'S BOG

VICTOR HAD TWO CHOICES WHEN HE DEPARTED FROM THE Trifold; head north to the Greenshores and find a boat to the perilous woods of Athil'glyn or head south to where the weakest arm of the Brindlecrag Mountains cut into the eastern continent and would allow him access to the city-state of Felkirk. Heading quickly north grew less enticing. The maps and notes he had been poring over before he departed stated that the large, haunted forest-kingdom would be the least of his potential problems. The mountains of the Belgallant range had collapsed in on themselves during the Rupture, making for a slow, hazardous trek. The Wilting Groves, formerly the Blackwoods, waited beyond that. Some dark goddess held control over those woods now, and he didn't dare risk traversing Her territory. That left the southern option.

In the chaotic days following the rupture, when magi were blamed for the calamities that befell the world and were hunted like fugitives, sanctums like the Trifold were built in isolated, self-sustaining locations. It would take several days to travel to the nearest town, whatever was left of it.

Victor made a point to keep a lookout for any type of shelter he could find near nightfall, as traveling past dark was not recommended, even for a mage. He was lucky at first, finding abandoned hunting shelters or outbuildings. Once, he had taken a rest in a barn early one afternoon to pore over some of the books he'd brought when he heard a noise outside. A group of brigands, by the looks and sounds of them, were making a raucous noise on a nearby road. Victor stayed all through the night in that very spot until the next day.

Victor eventually made his way into a sleepy town on the border of a small stretch of woodland known as Carmeline. The sun was beginning to set, the sparse clouds turning shades of orange and yellow. He'd asked around for a local inn and received mostly suspicious stares or, at best, a silent nod motioning him down the road. So, Victor followed the nods. He soon saw the sign for the *Traveler's Tryst* hanging from the frame of the only building in town with windows glowing with a welcome light.

Inside, a fire crackled within a soot-covered mantel. The few patrons sat alone with heads down or in pairs speaking in low voices. The fire was the main source of light, but candles on the tops of the rustic tables also cast their meager light on the building's unembellished furnishings. Other than a few hunting trophies, some ripped tapestries, and a faded coat-of-arms hung on one wall, so old that even a learned man like Victor didn't recognize it. The tavern comprised of plain brick, old wood, and age-clouded windows.

Now, Victor found himself in a half-empty tavern in a half-empty town.

Approaching the end of the long bar nearest the door, he shrugged off his backpack, feeling the ache in his shoulders from carrying it for a day and a half. He only brought a couple of the most important texts he could think of out of all the libraries that the Trifold had to offer. It's all he could carry when including the provisions and other supplies he needed for a long trek on foot.

Victor sat quietly at the bar and waited for the gruff-looking man behind the counter to notice him. He didn't want any added attention from the rancorous townsfolk, just a drink and possibly some of whatever food he could smell wafting from the back. This held his tongue, though his hunger and thirst were quickly getting the better of him.

The barkeep noticed him, finally, as a set of tired eyes under bush-thick eyebrows focused on Victor. The man turned, revealing a broad frame that was equal parts muscle and fat. With his long, deep brown hair and thick beard that hid his lips, he looked like a tall dwarf. He made his way slowly to Victor. When he stopped, he bent over, leaning on one trunk-thick forearm, and eyed the young mage.

When it became clear Victor wasn't going to offer up any words, the large man spoke: "What are you having?"

Victor froze under the piercing gaze. It had been over a year since he spoke with anyone other than his master at the sanctum. And none of the prior magi had been built like an intimidating stone giant.

"Um..." Victor mumbled, trying to think of what to order. He wanted wine but thought that he should probably order an ale. Then he also wondered what the food was so he could ask for some but had trouble placing the smell. It led to him fumbling for the words to say.

"No loitering," the man grumbled, his voice like an old oak tree.

"I..."

"I'm fucking with you, son," the man said with a smirk. "You're not from around here. People from around here don't take much to people *not* from around here. But if you're paying, we're on good terms."

Victor nodded, sighing and relaxing. "Food and something to drink. I'm sorry, I don't know what you have."

The barkeep stood, pointing to the door. "*Traveler's Tryst*. You know what a tryst is?"

Victor's eyes looked around nervously, not knowing where this question was going. "Yes?"

"You're the traveler. Just need two more things for a tryst. Here, that's a pint and a partridge."

He smiled again, the only sign being his mustache curling like he hadn't had the opportunity to share the meaning behind his tavern's namesake in quite a long time.

"What do you take for payment, barkeep?" Victor asked. He assumed that coinage from the old world was no longer viable.

The barkeep's mustache twitched, and his throat rumbled. "What do you have?"

Victor reached into one of his pockets and pulled out a ring. It was thin, made of gold, and lacking any precious stones but engraved with ivy leaves. It would make a wonderful gift and should be plenty for a meal and a room for a few nights.

The large man leaned down and took a long look at the ring. He took Victor's hand in his own, his thick fingers turning Victor's hand back and forth to see the light glint off the metal surface. He stood back up and nodded. "That's good for a few meals. My wife will like that quite well, I think."

"Is it also good for a room for the night?" Victor asked.

The barkeep shrugged. "Don't have any rooms ready, truth be told. Not a lot of travelers this way lately. But, I can make you a room up. Nothing fancy, mind you."

"As long as it's warm, barkeep," Victor said, setting the ring on the table.

The barkeep picked it up, lifted it in salute to Victor, and placed it in his pocket. "I'll get your ale and food. Name's Gustaf.

If you're going to be staying here, might as well not call me 'bar-keep' all night."

Victor returned a smile. "I'm Victor. Thank you for your hospitality."

Gustaf delivered Victor's ale quickly. The partridge followed soon after; hot and seasoned with herbs, it was the best meal the weary mage had eaten in days. He took his time with the food and drink, savoring it, before pushing the plate and mug aside. Pulling one of the books from his pack, Victor opened it to the page held by the thin silk ribbon. He began reading quietly in his secluded corner of the dim tavern.

Sometime later, quiet but heavy footsteps approached him. He only half-heard them due to the depth at which he was engaged in his study. Gustaf stood quietly, wiping a plate with a clean cloth.

"Room's ready when you are," he said, casual and quiet.

"Oh, thank you," Victor replied, head still buried in the book.

Gustaf continued to wipe the plate, despite it being as clean as it could get. "Not many people read around here; don't know many that can. What's it called?"

Victor finally broke from his trance. "It's, well, history. Some folklore and such thrown in here and there."

"History?" Gustaf scoffed. "Who gives two shits about history anymore? The kings are dead, councils are dead. We're all that's left, and no one here gives a damn where they came from anymore. Just what they're going to eat and what's trying to eat them."

Victor was quiet for a moment. He didn't remember a time of monarchs and banners. No one alive, in fact, would be able to remember it, nor their fathers or grandfathers.

"I still have some answers I'm looking for," Victor said, looking at the written lines but unable to read them. The shadow of the tree trunk named Gustaf now proving a distraction.

"Like what?"

"Old history. The oldest...origins and creation, like the First Kin."

"Thought you said history, not old religious nonsense."

"It's not nonsense, I'm afraid. At least, I really don't think it is. I need to find every parcel of information I can about them and the origins of..."

Victor paused, nearly letting slip a very dangerous word in such a cloistered, suspicious place.

"Origins of what?" Gustaf asked with genuine curiosity.

"Everything, I guess," Victor said hesitantly.

Gustaf stopped cleaning the plate. He sat it down on the table and crossed his arms, gripping the rag in his fist. He squinted his eyes, letting them pierce into Victor. "These dry old bastards around here are all I ever see, but I still deal with people every day, the best and worst at their worst and best. I can tell a liar."

Victor's mind ran. He tried to think of a spell he could prepare in the event he had to make a quick exit. He looked up at Gustaf and returned the barkeep's hard stare. He quietly answered, "I'm trying to find what I can on the origins of magic."

He left out the details regarding, specifically, the Fifth Sect.

Gustaf lowered his arms and glanced over his shoulder. His patrons were either silently moping or busy with their own hushed conversations. Victor's fingers twitched as he awaited the man's response. Gustaf leaned over and rested his forearms on the table, getting close enough to Victor that he could smell old liquor in the thick beard. "Where are you from, Victor?"

The question stalled Victor's thoughts. Now, he was the one glancing over Gustaf's shoulder. The patrons' eyes weren't paying attention, but their ears might be.

"A few days from here," he said, being as vague as possible.

"You're a mage," Gustaf stated matter-of-factly.

Victor's eyes flicked to the patrons, the tavern door, then back to Gustaf. His silence was his answer.

"I wouldn't mention that to anyone here. Or pretty much anywhere. You'll get a lot of attention you don't want."

It appeared that Gustaf wasn't going to inform the town of Victor's secret. That, at least, was enough to make his heart slow down from its rabbit-like pace.

"I hear it was once not too friendly for those like me. I'm assuming by your tone that sentiment remains."

Gustaf stood straight again but remained close so as to keep his voice low. He grabbed the clean plate and continued to wipe it down, appearing busy.

"It does. Last mage we had through here was when I was a boy. Came with a few soldiers in armor. Had a tree on the breast-plate. The town rallied against them and ran them out of town. Only way that mage survived was because no one wanted to take on the soldiers."

The conversation suddenly became quite interesting to Victor. Another mage who also traveled with well-equipped soldiers could help immensely in his search. They may have come from an area where civilization held together throughout the ruination dealt by the Rupture, or they'd rebuilt in spite of it. The possibilities were invigorating.

"Do you know where they came from? The tree must have been a sigil for their city." He continued to speak low, but his tone became more energized. Gustaf looked around nervously.

"No, no one does. The townsfolk saw a man in green robes asking about a sanctum, then everything went to shit from there. At least, that's how the story goes. I wouldn't take the risk on anything."

"What religious nonsense do you know about the First Kin?" Victor asked, pressing Gustaf with his quietly spoken questions.

The bushy mustache crinkled on the sides. Victor assumed he was grimacing.

"Mum used to tell me all kinds of stories to go to bed at night. Heard some of the same ones at the little temple that used to be on the other side of the village. The first men, dwarves, and elves all used to look alike. Then, they defeated the god of evil, created magic, and settled in the mountains, forests, and plains, where they turned into what we are now. More or less."

Victor's head dropped. Gustaf was wrong, more or less. All of his teachings were, as he put it, religious nonsense. Save for the idea that all the different peoples of Alda were once the same. Victor would find no further help from Gustaf. He doubted there was much more to be gathered from the village altogether, but he needed the rest.

The wide shadow of the barkeep still loomed over Victor. He looked up to see Gustaf looking around somewhat nervously. The large man turned slightly sideways and stepped even closer to Victor. His next question came in a harsh whisper.

"Is there a sanctum nearby? Is it really full of other magi?"

Victor's eyes lowered, stopping at the book that was one of the last remnants of his friends, peers, and lover. An ache developed in his chest, and he suddenly longed for more ale.

"Not anymore."

"That's a shame," Gustaf said gruffly. He returned to standing normally and not looking quite as suspicious.

"Yes, it is," Victor replied, his voice thick with sadness.

"Sorry, Victor. I wasn't thinking." Gustaf said. "Why don't I get you one more ale, and you can turn in for the night?"

Victor nodded and offered a weak smile. Replacing the silk ribbon to mark his place, he returned the book to his bag and sat for a moment in contemplative silence. Heavy footfalls announced Gustaf had left, but he returned a few minutes later with another ale. He sat it down gently on the counter in front of Victor.

"Feel free to take this to your room; just bring it back up front in the morning." His mustache turned up slightly in a small smile.

"Thank you," Victor replied quietly.

"One more thing, if you don't mind," the barkeep began, hesitating, then continued, "You're a mage. Not a priest. I don't believe you're just looking for the origins of 'everything'. What exactly are you searching for?"

The only sounds were the barely audible mumblings of the other patrons and the wind that had risen outside since Victor's arrival. He looked at Gustaf and pursed his lips, then turned away, thinking of his next words. He was alone in the world, this terrible place it had become, and unloading his burdens was quite tempting.

"It's...a little more than that," he started. He mulled the explanation over, letting it coalesce into something more than a rambling ambition. "I want to find the origins of the Fifth Sect of magic. Do you know what that is? The Fifth Sect, or any of the sects for that matter?"

One bushy eyebrow raised as Gustaf replied, "Not really, no. Magic is magic to me."

Of course, it is. Victor thought sardonically. "Magic is as complex as any other trade: metal-working, art, masonry. There are five sects to my trade, each focusing on a different area of magic."

"This is already confusing," Gustaf moaned.

"Think of it like...alcohol," Victor clarified as he eyed some appropriate comparison for the barkeep. "You have ale, beer, wine, spirits, and mead. They're all alcoholic, but each is also different in its own way. The five sects are similar. The First Sect uses raw, arcane power. Something like this," Victor took a quick look to see if anyone was watching. Then, he made a subtle, fluid grasping motion with his fingers and whispered the word *vul*. Gustaf's rag slipped from his belt and into Victor's hand. Gustaf's eyes widened. It may have been the first time he'd ever seen magic. Victor slid the damp rag across the countertop back over toward Gustaf.

"No sparks, no flame, nothing that looks fancy or complex, but the power is there. The Second Sect involves the elements like fire, ice, lightning, and such. The Third is alchemy: the imbuing and manipulation of physical objects with magical power."

The next words carried more weight. Victor's tone changed swiftly. "The Fourth Sect is forbidden. Many thought it was just necromancy and similar dark practices, which would be bad enough; however, it's so much more than that. It was to our own damnation that we didn't find out sooner. That vile practice is directly connected to our current fate. But, the Fifth Sect...that could save us."

Victor began diving into his own thoughts again, ruminating on the letter Nethara had written before her passing. He went so deep into his contemplations that he'd forgotten about Gustaf, who'd crossed his arms and raised his brows expectantly.

"Sorry, I've been on my own for a while. I drift off like that sometimes. The Fifth Sect is the rarest and most difficult to control or even learn. I was the only one in my sanctum with the ability to use it. It was just as misunderstood as the Fourth Sect. The Fifth wasn't just about healing and rejuvenating powers; it was the magic connected to the soul of Alda itself. It was about life."

Victor gained a spark in his eyes. He pushed the mug of ale to the side, much to the barkeep's chagrin, and continued to speak faster, his tone lifting, and his eyes staring straight through Gustaf's torso as he played out his words in his mind.

"I have a theory. The first worship of the gods didn't show up until several hundred years after the earliest mentions of the First Kin and the Obscured Throne. I think that the gods are basically magic given sentient form—"

"Wait," Gustaf interrupted, "the obscure what?"

Victor's eyes lost their luster. He blinked, having been jerked back to the harsh present by the question. "The Obscured Throne. The 'great darkness' or 'living evil' or whatever religion you grew up with that the First Kin defeated in the stories. The thing they fought, no matter the source, was always the same: the Obscured Throne."

Gustaf winced. He felt a dark hole in his gut when the name was mentioned. "What is it?"

"I don't know. I don't think anyone does, not even its followers. I'm hoping if I find out more about it and the Fifth Sect, I can, perhaps, do something about all this," he said out loud.

"All this?"

"The world, the Rupture, the things that have taken Alda and made it their plaything. There are too few people left and no civilization at all that I know of. It's probably hopeless, but that line of thinking does nothing for anyone." Victor sighed heavily, tapping his fingers on the counter.

A shadow fell over Gustaf's face as it turned downward. The light caught against the wrinkles in the skin exposed between his dwarf-like hair and beard, making the creases stand out. He gave the impression he was older than Victor already, but now the lines on his face spoke to those extra years being very harsh.

"You ever hear of the Battle of Godscrown?" Gustaf asked, his voice gruff.

"Yes, of course," Victor replied, running his fingers through his short hair. Weariness began to seep into him, aided by the alcohol.

"Then you know not even an army, two of them even, can stop whatever 'they' are. Not the big ones, anyway. The nasty beasties that make stone drakes and trolls look like children's pets, those vicious shits tag along like ticks on a dragon. The big ones—those are the dragons. Those are the new gods, boy, and it's best to let them be and live your life as far out of sight and out of mind as you can until you die. Then, best hope that Sheemra, Dynus, or one of the other gods our ancestors worshipped found a cosmic rock to hide under and will take you in."

That statement caused another set of wheels to spin in Victor's mind. He pushed away the new line of thought that threatened to pull him into another bout of speculation. He'd had enough of that for one night. Standing and gathering his things, Victor informed the barkeep he'd be heading off to his room for the night. Gustaf nodded and reminded him of where his bed waited.

"Oh, and welcome to Summer's End," Gustaf quickly added with a gesture of his hand, providing Victor with the name of the village where he found himself.

The small room, or, rather, large storage closet as it revealed itself to be, had a small bed with a disheveled blanket, rickety night-stand, and a candle all tucked into a corner. The accommodations looked ragged. When Gustaf said he'd throw a room together for Victor, the barkeep meant the words literally.

He put his things underneath the old bed and caught a breath of the dust and age wafting from beneath. Coughing, he sat on the bed that felt little more welcoming than a moss-covered rock. At least the blanket seemed somewhat comfortable. He lit the candle and sat there in silence for several moments, taking in the mundane items stocking the shelves:

bags of flour and grains, dusty bottles, barrels, and other such things. This was quite unlike the Trifold Sanctum. No bottles, scrolls, tomes of old magic, or herbal ingredients lending their various odors to the air.

Victor removed his outer layers of clothing, folding them and stacking them neatly on the floor. He blew out the candle, casting himself into near-pitch blackness in the storeroom. He lay in the dark, listening. No noise made it into the room. No insects of the night sang to him. No laughter or hum of conversation came from the main room of the tavern just outside the wall. Not even the orders of Gustaf or his servers could be heard. All was quiet and still. It was troubling at first, but then Victor realized he might as well take in the peacefulness of it, as who knew what tomorrow would bring when he returned to his journey.

VICTOR WOKE to a stillness equal to the night before. The room had no windows, so he knew not what time it was. It could as easily have been midnight or noon the next day. He pushed the blanket aside and sat up, tossing his legs over the edge of the cot. It must have been at least morning, he assumed, as even though sleep still lay heavy on his eyes, he felt his body and mind waking more with each passing moment. Thoughts, plans, and ideas began to blossom, and his muscles began to call out to move.

He yawned, yearning for some water and possibly breakfast. He'd have to check his pack to see what he could trade for such things, or perhaps Gustaf's wife liked the ring enough he could possibly get a small meal before taking back to the road again.

The door swung open, halting his thoughts, and Gustaf's wide shoulders filled the frame. His eyes were wide with alarm.

"Victor, I need your help," he said urgently. "Please, come with me."

Victor stood, embarrassingly conscious of being in only his smallclothes, and dressed quickly. Gustaf turned his head.

"What's wrong?" Victor asked, concerned.

Gustaf looked behind him, shuffled his feet, and coughed uncomfortably. "Someone...we think someone's died."

Victor was in the middle of slipping into his overcoat when Gustaf's words stopped him. He held one arm half-in the sleeve and looked up to see the barkeep looking at him with a creased brow.

"You think?"

"Please, just come with me."

Victor finished putting on his coat and reached under the bed to grab his belongings.

"I don't think you'll need those," Gustaf said quickly.

Victor pulled out the bag and threw the straps over his shoulders. "This goes everywhere with me," he added matter-of-factly.

They both left the tavern in a rush, the big man much quicker than he looked. The tables were empty, and Victor saw the weak light of early morning coming through the windows. The chilly room smelled of wood and old smoke, as not even the fire had been lit yet.

They exited onto mostly empty streets. A man pushing a cart of large sackcloth bags, half-filled with things unknown, nodded to Gustaf and ignored Victor. The barkeep walked quickly across the street, swung left to another, and then ducked into an alley. He didn't once look back during this frantic half-run to see if Victor had kept up.

They arrived at a door in the middle of the shadowed alley, never a good sign as far as Victor was concerned. He gripped a dagger he kept tucked in a reachable spot on his pack just in case. Letting loose a spell here would give him away and endanger him even further. If trouble arose, it would be better to end this quietly or even just run.

Gustaf laid a heavy fist on the door. One hard thump followed by a shout: "Naydor!"

After a few moments, the door slowly opened, and an aged but handsome-looking man stood in the crack of the door. His stern eyes landed on Gustaf, then moved quickly to Victor. Silently, he turned back to Gustaf and lowered his head just slightly, obviously unhappy.

"We're here about the swamp," Gustaf said, his voice low and gruff.

The man nodded. "Come in."

Victor entered behind the barkeep, his arms looking like they were merely crossed in order to conceal his hand still resting on the dagger.

The inside of the building was both home and workshop. Simple furniture and sparse decoration indicated the living space while the smells lingering in the air gave away that this individual's home doubled as their place of business—at least of some kind. A closed door at the side of the current room led to spaces unknown; however, Victor knew the smells that hung in the air. This man practiced magic.

"You bring a stranger into my home, Gustaf." The man said with the slightest interest. "And you say it has to do with the swamp?"

Gustaf lowered his head and placed his hands on his hips. His shoulders slouched slightly. He took a deep breath before speaking. "Some lads disappeared last night. Old lady Caufa said they took off while she slept and never came home."

"How does she know they went to the swamp?"

"She said she scolded them just the day prior for talking about heading out there to look for the titan."

The man's face scrunched. His eyes focused on something as he delved deep into thought. When he looked up, it was at Victor.

"And why did you bring this young man? What does he have to do with it?"

Gustaf cleared his throat. "This is, uh, this is Victor. Victor, this is—"

"Naydor, as you heard Gustaf call out," the man interjected.

"Well, he's...I figured he could help." Gustaf's words came hesitantly.

"A stranger looking for some missing local boys?" Naydor returned with obvious doubt.

Gustaf looked back at Victor, who simply stood quietly watching the two. "He's a mage," Gustaf said quietly, as though someone outside was listening.

Naydor's eyes lit up, his brows raising. "Indeed? What sects have you studied?"

Victor panicked at first and gripped the dagger tightly. Gustaf had just exposed him to this stranger; a stranger to Victor at any rate. Naydor did mention the sects, however, and that made Victor curious himself. He thought carefully about his answer.

"Mainly the Principle Triad," he answered. Best to keep it vague and not mention the once-maligned Fourth Sect and the still-mysterious Fifth.

Naydor nodded. "Even those who study the primary sects are hard to come by, nowadays."

"We're a dying breed," Victor added.

Naydor pursed his lips. "I understand why Gustaf brought you here."

He motioned for Victor and the barkeep to sit. Removing his pack, Victor set it next to a cushioned chair and sat, sinking into the soft furniture. This chair was more comfortable than his cot by far. He settled in and allowed himself to relax for a moment.

Gustaf took a seat as well, although he seemed far less at ease. His shoulders were still tight, his eyes sad.

"I'm getting older. My powers are still strong, but they've been waning of late. The nearby swamp has been a local legend of sorts for decades. Most townsfolk avoid it. Some, like the boys in question, it seems, either don't believe the stories or are too morbidly curious and want to see for themselves. The latter always ends badly."

"What are the stories?" Victor was suddenly intensely curious.

Naydor filled three mugs with a dark, opaque liquid. He handed one to each of them and kept one for himself. Victor waited for Gustaf to drink before he took a hesitant sip. It tasted earthy with a hint of sweetness. He wasn't sure if it was meant to be ale, tea, or some mix of both. Naydor then took a seat himself.

"The creature of Titan's Bog. Started up a few decades ago, like I said, and it's been whispered about ever since. A creature walks the swamp now and again, but no one knows where it came from. Not surprising given the time we live in. Those that venture out there don't come back, except once when a hunter managed to straggle back into town. Died of his wounds within hours but told everyone of a dark, hulking monstrosity that killed and ate his horse, then came for him."

Victor noticed that Gustaf lowered his head and stared at the floor.

"What do you think?" Victor put forward the question plainly.

Naydor shrugged. "I think he met up with some form of alligator, maybe a swamp drake. The townsfolk tell stories because there's little else to entertain them, and they don't know any better. It's not even a bog, as the name suggests. It's a swamp, as we've been saying. Although I suppose the misnomer is due to the first stretches of the swamp that has little trees, so it does look more like a bog."

Victor offered a half-hearted smile. "I suppose 'Titan's Bog' does sound more ominous."

Naydor chuckled. "Regardless, the swamp *is* dangerous. It's best avoided one way or the other. However," he sighed heavily, as though slightly annoyed, "if curious folk go missing, someone needs to go look for them, and that's usually me. We only have a handful of armed men willing to put themselves in danger for the village, and we don't want to waste them on foolish myth-chasers."

"And you'd like my help to find them," Victor concluded.

"A little more than that," Naydor replied. "I need you to go find them. I'm getting too old to venture out there alone anymore. If you hadn't been here, Victor, those boys would likely be left to their fate."

The last words were spoken softly, regretfully. Naydor took a drink from his mug and shook his head. "Will you help us?"

Victor was quiet. He looked into his mug and watched the light flicker off the amber liquid. His journey had barely started, but he only had so many ideas on where to go and what to do. He didn't want to leave the boys to die in whatever gods-awful place they'd gotten themselves into, but he was unsure of how much he could actually help.

"Why is it so important that a mage go?" Victor asked suddenly. The question came out of his mouth before he had a chance to consider it.

Naydor was quick with his answer. "I told you, the able-bodied men in the village refuse, and, let's be honest," he smirked at his next point, "we mages have much more potential to survive."

Victor tilted his head and popped his eyebrows up in silent

agreement. Then, another question came to him. "How long have you been hiding the fact you're a mage? Have you always lived at Summer's End?"

"Easy enough. The locals are simple folk," Naydor replied nonchalantly. Gustaf raised an offended brow. "According to them, I've always been an apothecary. As long as I keep their illnesses at bay, they leave me alone."

"And Gustaf?" Victor pressed, gesturing to the "simple folk" sitting in the room with the two mages.

Naydor smiled. "He's quite good with people, as I'm sure he's told you."

Naydor plopped his mug down on a table nearby and stood. "I tell you what; I'll give you something to help. If you bring the boys back, you can keep it."

He went to one of the closed doors and slipped inside the other room. When he returned, he was holding an amulet. He lifted it by the chain to show Victor. At first glance, it appeared to be a snake eating its own tail, but as he looked more closely, Victor saw that the tail had turned into a laurel. It was made of brass and silver, and Victor could feel the essence of magic radiating from it.

"What are its properties?" Victor asked, intrigued by the item. "I can feel the Third Sect radiating from it."

Gustaf gave Victor a quizzical glance. "You can feel something? I just thought it looked shiny."

Naydor was grinning from ear to ear. "Very astute. It will ward off many poisons for a time, make breathing in heavy miasma easier, and keep mosquitos at bay. I hate mosquitos."

"Very helpful to have in a swamp," Gustaf noted.

"It is," Victor added. He still hesitated with his answer, however.

"I also put a small contractual sealing spell on it. Should you try to take the amulet and run, it'll grow heavier the farther you get from the village until it weighs you to the ground. You can take off, but the amulet will stay. And if you ever came back, you would be quite unwelcome."

"Fair enough." Victor quipped. As he continued to think over his response while watching the amulet glisten in Naydor's hand, the other mage grimaced.

"Very well. I also have quite a collection of tomes I've collected over the years. You can peruse some of them before you depart from us if you bring the boys back."

Victor suddenly became very intrigued. To access another mage's collection of books was too good to pass up.

"We have a deal," he said with conviction. They both shook hands, and Victor noticed Naydor wore fine silk gloves. A peculiar quirk in a town that so far seemed only filled with farmers, masons, and other hardworking folk.

"Very good," Naydor said with a smile. "I'm sure Gustaf would have no problem giving you food to last the trip and a place to stay upon your return, yes?" He looked over to the barkeep, who sat up straight in the chair.

"Done," came Gustaf's stiff reply.

"And done," Naydor added. "The day is early, Victor. Gustaf, get our young mage his supplies so he can find those boys."

The mage and barkeep quietly left the house that was so carefully tucked away from prying eyes. As they made their way back to the tavern, the old barkeep asked in a gruff tone, "So, how you plan on going about finding them?"

Victor pondered the question quietly, seeming as if he almost ignored it. It wasn't his intent, but he slipped away once more into his internal problem-solving process. He certainly couldn't go exploring a possibly alligator-infested swamp or drake's nest with no direction on what to look for. Gods forbid, if the boys did run into such creatures, there was likely nothing left.

"I need something that belonged to one of the boys. Clothes, tools, toys, anything. Naydor didn't even say how old they were."

"Oh," Gustaf grumbled. He sighed and said, "Young men. Early twenties, one of 'em was a big lad. I'll go speak to the boy's mother and get you something while you're packing for the walk."

"Walk?" Victor replied incredulously, looking up and raising a brow at the larger man. "Can I not at least borrow a horse or a mule to get me there a little faster? I might possibly be facing a drake; saving my strength would be more conducive to coming back alive."

Gustaf chuckled. "Yeah, we can get you a horse."

When they returned to the tavern, cantankerous patrons were haranguing Gustaf, who shushed them with a few stern, choice words. He unlocked the door, let everyone in, and asked Victor to take a seat while he got a few rounds going to keep the customers quiet. Afterward, he retreated into the back kitchen and returned with a satchel of goods for Victor. The barkeep had packed him a healthy supply of food that would survive the road: jerky, traveler's bread, and dried fruit and nuts. He also refilled Victor's leather canteen with water and provided a flask of whiskey. "No drinking wine out of these; it's sacrilege," he'd quipped.

There would be no leaving his books and other belongings behind, that Victor had made quite clear. Gustaf huffed at his stubbornness and informed him he'd return shortly with a horse and something belonging to one of the missing boys. Victor spent the time sorting what would stay on the horse and what would be most helpful when he inevitably had to trudge into the swamp on foot. Snakes and alligators would be the most likely hazards he'd come across, but he'd need to be prepared for the worst. A swamp drake would require spells he'd only used in practice. Though, in all honesty, most of his spells had only been used in practice.

By the time Gustaf returned, opening the door and once again casting off the verbal barbs slung at him by his regulars, Victor had somewhat of a plan formulated. The sorting of his belongings, both borrowed and otherwise, was complete, and he'd thought through his defenses for dangers, both small and large. He felt the amulet around his chest, almost forgetting it was there, and he was grateful for that bit of help, as well.

"Here's one of the boys' shirts," Gustaf said, setting a large, crumpled ball of brown cloth down on the top of the bar before Victor.

After unfolding it, calling the owner of this shirt a *boy*, was quite a stretch. The person who wore this must have stood as tall as Gustaf. It was stated they were in their twenties, and boys was obviously a term of endearment for these young men of the village. Victor held up the shirt by the arms and looked at Gustaf quizzically.

"Are you sure this isn't yours? Am I being played for a fool here?" Victor wasn't sure if he intended for it to be a joke or not.

Gustaf pursed his lips, obviously still troubled by the missing owner of the clothing. "No. This was Calub's. That big lad I told you about. Body of a troll, heart of a lamb, that one." Gustaf shook his head.

"I see," Victor said softly. "I'll set out immediately. If I don't find them by sunset, I'll return with any news I have."

"If you don't find them and will consider looking for 'em again tomorrow, I'll have dinner and a bed ready when you get back."

Gustaf looked at Victor with big brown eyes that reminded him of a large dog that once lived in the sanctum. Boris was his name. A large, brown-and-white ball of fur that ate twice his body weight daily, that everyone loved. The large barkeep very much reminded Victor of every time that dog begged for his dinner scraps.

"I'll think about it," Victor said, smiling inside.

Gustaf nodded. "Horse is outside waiting for you. Name's Gilfoyle," he said with a motion toward the door.

Victor gathered his various satchels and packs and made for the door. As he opened it, he heard Gustaf call out from behind him.

"Victor—good luck."

The mage turned, his packs rattling, and saw a look of sincerity coupled with fear in those eyes now. He nodded his head and pursed his lips, then left to meet his absurdly named horse waiting for him outside.

"GILFOYLE," Victor said aloud. The packs on the horse jostled and rustled as he rode in the fields leading to Titan's Bog. The horse took to him easily, and the trip so far had been rather pleasant. "Can I call you Gil? That seems like less of a mouthful."

The horse had made nary a wicker since they left. It was a beautiful dark brown with a white mane. He didn't know anything about horses, but it looked like a rare breed if he had to guess. Victor wondered if anyone in Alda still bred horses or if it was another relic of the past world and the only horses left were those that anyone could tame on their own.

They had no horses at the sanctum when he left. The last was taken by fellow magi on other sojourns; they had never returned. Their disappearance and the sudden lack of pack animals resulted in a restriction on all travel unless absolutely necessary.

The thoughts of his lost fellows led Victor to another question: why had they never returned with information on Summer's End? Surely, all the years the magi of the Trifold Sanctum had been journeying out into the world would have led them to the small town on the southern road.

Victor's thoughts were yet again wrenched back into the present by Gilfoyle snorting and tossing his head. The horse became uncharacteristically stubborn and fought against further travel. Victor tried spurring the beast on, but it whinnied and snorted more, then finished its tirade by stamping its feet and moving no further.

Pausing for a moment to take a good look ahead and squinting against the sunlight, Victor saw the empty fields stretch before them a bit more before he saw the reflection of the sun off broken patches of water. Beyond that, patches of dark trees sat like a gloomy palisade. It was Titan's Bog, but there was nothing present that Victor could see that should be a cause for concern.

"What's got you so worked up?" he asked, stroking Gil's muscled neck. The horse gave a deep whinny and side-stepped nervously.

"Let's try this again," Victor said in a low, exasperated voice. He gripped the reins with both hands and dug his heels in just a bit to get the horse's attention. Then he said in the most commanding tone he could muster, "Come on! Hya!"

Gilfoyle whickered at first, then neighed loudly in protest. The horse even reared up slightly, and Victor feared he'd be tossed to the ground. He looked around ashamedly even though he knew no one was there. He felt foolish and very likely looked preposterous. He sighed, then dismounted the stubborn animal.

The handler that had waited for Victor outside of the *Traveler's Tryst* repeatedly told him to hitch Gilfoyle to something so the horse wouldn't wander off or be frightened away. In this particular instance, there was nothing to hitch the horse to. The fields before Titan's Bog were empty save for bushes and wild-flowers.

Victor sighed again, heavier than the last, and walked up to Gil to stroke his snout.

"If you leave me...well, there's nothing I can do about it, but I will be very, very upset."

Still petting the nervous animal, Victor looked at the bags and packs hanging from its sides. His rations and other belongings, arguably more important to him, were all right there. If Gil ran off, who knew if he'd actually return to the town. If the horse insisted on staying here, with no place to secure it, Victor decided he had to remove all the packs and set them aside. At least if the horse took off, he'd have his belongings.

Not all of it could be carried with him into the swamp, so Victor had to make a choice on what would serve him best. He rearranged the items so that he had a single pack to carry with him as he searched for the boys. Food, water, some warm clothes, a dagger he carried just in case (for all the good it would do him), and the whiskey. He preferred wine, but if he was to slog through the grime of a swamp, he might need the alcohol.

Giving Gil one more pet on the nose and pleading, one more time, for the horse not to leave him stranded, Victor slung the straps of the bag over his shoulders and began his walk to the swamp. The firm ground of Summer's End's outskirt fields grew soft as the shimmering, scattered patches grew closer. Soon, he had to watch his steps lest he sink knee-deep into the first dark pools. The strong stench of stale water and wet vegetation heralded his arrival on the outskirts of Titan's Bog.

This stretch of wetland appeared much like a bog or a fen, which Victor found ironic. Once he reached the trees, it would no doubt become a proper swamp and, therefore, much more troublesome to traverse. Finding solid, mostly-dry footing was still possible here. Once inside the swamp, he had little hope that he would remain completely dry.

Meandering his way through the patchy ground and grasses, Victor felt the chill of the shadowed tree line brush over him. It felt unnatural, like the cold breath of a corpse sighing at seeing him. He stopped midstride, his feet straddling a murky patch of grasses, and felt his breath catch. What were the boys doing out here?

When the first trees came within reach, Victor found himself grateful for the ability to lean against something for balance. Perhaps he was being too prim, but he desperately wanted to remain as dry as he could. He leaned against the sturdy bole and caught his breath. He looked around at the edge of the swamp. It was much as he imagined. The density of the trees increased rapidly, and underneath their sad canopies, little light was to be found. The smell alone was deterrent enough, but he could see the sturdy species of maple and oak that lined the edge of Titan's Bog changed to feeble willows and the occasional cypress further in before shadow obscured the rest.

He continued to scan the edges of the swamp, looking for the best way in and chuckled in relief when he saw a slim arm of dry ground cutting into it. The awkward, dance-like steps to get there felt as long as the trip from the town itself, but he eventually made it. The ground here was so firm it felt as though he were back in the fields again; he could once more walk with steady footing.

Crossing through the threshold of the swamp seemed anticlimactic at first. There was no dark mouth surrounded by sinister trees beckoning him like in stories. No fog or mist crawled about the wet ground in a menacing fashion. Despite quickly growing darker as the trees became denser and the incessant chirping of insects, Titan's Bog appeared to be a typically wet, miserable swamp.

Victor recanted this impression after walking further in. The moist, still air was permeated by something else. Something that didn't belong. Something magical. He stopped, took in the permeation, and let it crawl about his senses. Each of the five sects' residual effects had its own particular ways of presenting itself to a mage.

The back of Victor's throat tingled, and he lost his sense of smell for a moment. Tickling sensations ran up and down his arms in waves. These were resonations of the Third Sect. When his arm began involuntarily twitching, as from a muscle spasm, Victor knew these were very strong resonations. Someone had been at work in Titan's Bog for some time. That, or very powerful alchemical practices or magical imbuing, had occurred here. There was something else there, too, tugging at the front of Victor's head, pinching his mind like a vice. Was there another sect lingering here, as well?

Question after question came to Victor. Not only was the possibility of two magical resonations here, but why would strong Third Sect power be manifesting in a swamp? He couldn't imagine a gathering of elf-kind hiding out here, lacing the willows and cypress trees with their magic to create a home. Could it be the legend of the creature haunting Titan's Bog was the work of some wayward mage creating an illusion and binding it to the swamp to keep out trespassers? That would mean that a fellow mage might be in this swamp. Or, on the other hand, a warlock, necromancer, or other dangerous practitioner. Victor's interest was instantly renewed.

He forged ahead on the dry path that grew narrower as it snaked deeper into the swamp. The presence of magic remained fairly stable until he reached a point where the dry path ended. As the firm soil fanned into a spongy but still traversable patch of swampland, so did the magical permeation swell until Victor felt his body flinch as though brushed by a chill wind.

Very strong magic here, Victor thought.

He took a few hesitant steps onto the soft, wet ground. His feet squelched into the gray-green carpet as a thin layer of water pooled around his feet. He looked around and saw shallow pools of various sizes amid the dispersed trees. The sounds of the creatures—insects, birds, and frogs—became ominous. Victor didn't know if this was due to the presence of the magic, the purpose of which, yet unknown, made him uneasy, or if his imagination was beginning to toy with him.

Something sloshed into the water nearby. It was quiet; had Victor not been standing still, he may not have heard it at all. He held a hand up, prepared to use his skill in the First Sect to defend himself if need be. He walked slowly, hearing the long, slow *squish* of his boots into the soggy ground. His head turned slowly in both directions, and he asked himself again: *What the hells were those boys doing here?*

A very disturbing sound, like a hiss mixed with a growl, caused Victor to swing to his left.

"Shit!" he shouted.

A very large, very angry alligator lay half-out of one of the larger pools. Its jaw opened, exposing a red throat surrounded by many sharp teeth.

"*Ifworrd*," Victor said, making a grabbing motion with one hand and a shooing motion with the other. The alligator hiss-growled again as it was pulled back into the water several dozen feet away. It sloshed lazily in the pool and thrashed about momentarily before submerging. A log-shaped head rose from the water and watched Victor, making him uneasy.

"Are you the creature of Titan's Bog?" Victor asked aloud, trying to humor himself. Naydor did mention such a possibility. It would be much easier to deal with than a drake, certainly. The head began slowly moving back toward him.

"Oh no," Victor said to the beast, chiding it like one would a child. "*Ifworrd-crif.*"

Victor repeated the incantation and gestures, except he pushed with his one hand rather than the previous gentler motion and added an enhancing phrase. The alligator was dragged through the water forcefully, but not violently until it broke the surface and landed with a wet thud next to another pool.

"I don't want to hurt you, but I'm not becoming dinner."

With another angry, guttural noise, the alligator began a waddling run toward Victor. It was frightening with a touch of humor. Victor repeated the spell, pushing the beast back into the second pool, then said sharply, "*Flal,*" and swung his forearm up and towards his body, followed by a flick of his wrist. A spray of water, mud, and sodden grass flew off to the side of the beast like the ground had been struck by a whip.

"*Yto,*" Victor said, repeating the motion but to his right this time, on the opposite side of the beast. The same effect occurred, and it appeared the alligator had enough. It hissed, a deep, throaty sound, and turned away to disappear into the waters of the swamp.

He sighed, hoping that was the worst he had to face and that the missing boys didn't cross this same creature's path. His hopes were quickly doused. When he turned to continue on his course, something stood between the trees. A black shape, large and broad and humanoid, stood in the shadows deeper in the swamp. Partially concealed behind a large cypress, the shape didn't move. Heavy arms hung limp at its sides. Something else draped over its body and hung in ragged strands from its hunched frame—tattered clothing or unkempt hair, perhaps?

"Calub?" Victor called out, remembering the large young man Gustaf had mentioned. "Calub, is that you?"

The figure continued to stand still, making Victor wonder

for a moment if he imagined things. After a confrontation with a massive swampland predator, maybe he saw things as more sinister than they truly were. This could be a large tree stump covered in moss, for all he knew.

Then, the shape charged him. It moved so quickly that Victor couldn't react. The shadow-coated monstrosity raced toward him in a way that was only vaguely reminiscent of a human gait. It was broken, displaced, and wrong.

Panic-stricken, Victor turned and bolted for the edge of the swamp. To his surprise, the trees and sunlight marking the entry to the murkier parts of Titan's Bog were gone. He appeared to be surrounded on all sides by darker and more menacing terrain. The entrance had disappeared and left him in some strange, new location, likely deeper in the swamp.

He turned, terrified, expecting to see whatever the human-like shape was to be bearing down on him. Instead, he was staring into a chest of rotten flesh and exposed bone. The smell hit him then, and he fell back in fright and disgust.

Murky water, inches deep, greeted him as he landed, soaking through his clothes. Sodden earth pushed between his fingers. He began to crawl backward as fast as he could. The figure before him was human, or used to be, but was covered in moss, mold, and vines that grew in and out of its gray flesh and between exposed bones. The tattered things Victor saw from a distance were a mix of dangling flesh, tree matter, and rotted clothes. Atop this viciously disgusting frame was something that perhaps could once have been called a human face. It had rotted down to little more than a skull with broken teeth, patches of brown-rotted flesh clinging in some places, and one milky, deflated eye laying in a yellowed socket like a demonic egg sac.

Victor froze. He wanted to scream, but the sight before him stole all manner of movement from his muscles. Even his drive to flee or will to live sank before it. The moment must have been no more than seconds, but time stood still for a long, horrifying eternity. Just enough for Victor to see what would kill him.

The creature of Titan's Bog dropped to four legs like an animal and sprang at Victor. Its hand outstretched, Victor saw the shredded skin of fingers that exposed sharp bones sure to rip the flesh from his body in bloody, painful strips. However, the creature stopped, itself frozen as if suddenly paralyzed. Victor's breaths came heavy and quick. Tears streamed down his face. The rancid odor emanating from the decayed throat and mouth inches from his face threatened to make him vomit.

The creature wasn't staring at Victor, at least as much as one in its state *could* stare. It was staring at the amulet. Even as Victor sat unmoving, waiting for a horrid death that didn't come, his chest heaved with each breath. The creature didn't move in any sense; it didn't even breathe.

He swallowed hard and took what felt like the largest risk since leaving the sanctum. He moved backward. Slow. Painfully slow. The swamp was so quiet he could practically hear when one of his hands moved back and settled into the water. The creature lurched forward suddenly, its joints cracking awfully and unnaturally. Victor gave a slight gasp, but the dead eye continued to focus on the amulet. Victor cautiously moved one hand up to grasp its chain. He feared losing it, wondering for a moment if it offered some sort of protection against the creature. A wet, guttural sound came from within the decayed chest and throat. Victor removed his hand.

Nothing happened.

It continued to stare at the magical jewelry. Maybe that was all it wanted? Victor carefully began to pull the amulet from his neck. Just before slipping it over his head, he closed his eyes and prayed to whoever was listening.

The creature, lightning quick, snatched the amulet from Victor's grasp with clawed fingers. The terrible haunt of Titan's

Bog stood and walked morosely away. Victor stood and stared, dumbfounded, as the soft light appeared in the shadows of the boughs of the trees. The edge of the swamp reappeared. The creature walked within an inch of the light's border...and dropped the amulet.

Victor's breathing slowed, only for his mind to begin racing. The creature walked off in the opposite direction of the swamp's entrance and the abandoned amulet. Victor watched the creature enter the shadows towards the deeper parts of Titan's Bog. He ran up to the amulet, keeping an eye behind him, and picked it back up. When he turned to look, drawing currents of sparkling energy into his hand to prepare a bolt of lightning that would, hopefully, crack the creature in half, there was nothing there. The shadows quickly grew thicker, but he should have still been able to see the hulking monstrosity. It was gone.

There would be no finding the boys with that thing stalking the swamp. If that was truly the creature of Titan's Bog, they were likely dead. He couldn't leave without finding out, though. And he wouldn't be caught off-guard again. The chain on the amulet was broken, but he tucked it into a pocket within his long coat. That thing seemed interested in the amulet, but once it had removed it, left Victor alone.

Victor sloshed his way through knee-deep water and viscous, slimier areas for hours. He no longer cared about alligators, wet clothes, or anything else. He needed to find that creature and discover whatever had happened to those boys. Though he liked to think that his determination would help him through this, he still found his current situation incredibly disgusting.

The air grew cooler as the day progressed closer and closer to the evening hours. Being stuck in the wet, gloomy confines of Titan's Bog's dark boughs gripped Victor with a different kind of cold: fear. The thought of that thing being out there in the dark nearly sent him back toward the comforting embrace of daylight and dry fields right away. As he pushed each thought away, another rose to take its place, and he didn't like it at all. There was a sure way to get the creature's attention.

He pressed his hand against the outside of his longcoat over the pocket where the amulet rested. If he put it on, he would be summoned to wherever the creature likely attacked him last time. However, if he removed it, he should be back by the entrance again. All this was assuming he lived through another encounter.

"Here we go again," he sighed to himself.

He slipped the amulet out of his pocket and went to one of the numerous tree stumps. He put his pointer and middle finger together, then, using the tip of his middle finger, made a near perfect circular motion on the rough surface of the stump.

"*Forgus Incantus Minorii,*" he chanted softly. A red circle appeared, glowing softly on the damp wood. Using the tip of his pointer finger, he tapped three spots in a triangular pattern while softly repeating the words, "*Incantus. Incantus. Incantus.*"

Victor placed the amulet the alchemist's circle he'd just conjured with the Third Magic. He made sure the broken links were touching and placed his hand over them. This particular enchanting circle was too small and not powerful enough to do much, but it would be enough to repair the necklace.

Victor uttered a few more words, felt the heat in his hands, and uncovered the amulet to find the links fixed, although it was noticeably poor and quick work. A wave of his hand with another muttered word and the circle disappeared.

He placed the amulet back over his head and gritted his teeth. He felt a strange sensation around his feet and looked down. The water had receded from his knees to his ankle. He looked back up and saw that, though the general area was the same, he was in a different part of the swamp. Different than the time he encountered the creature and different from where he had just previously stood.

A large, black shape was wandering, slowly and aimlessly, about a few dozen feet away, its shoulders slumped. It turned, looked in Victor's direction, and stood to its full height, its shoulders sweeping back and the creature now appearing intensely focused. It was only a matter of seconds before it came for Victor again.

His first thought went to casting a crackling bolt again, the air qualities of the Third Sect being his specialty in that particular field and what he considered a potent offensive spell. He remembered he was in ankle-deep water, however, and would need something less lethal to himself.

The creature took one step forward. If Victor didn't catch it now, the thing would be on him in seconds. He concentrated as much heat into his hands as he could muster. Flinging one of his hands outward, he channeled all that energy into a ball of flame that roiled toward the creature. Victor lost sight of the monster as his spell lit up the swamp like a dozen torches and set the scattered waters to shimmering like fireflies as it exploded against the giant of rotten flesh and bone. The creature had already begun its sprint towards him, though. The fire dissipated, and the creature of Titan's Bog barreled toward him with bits of plant and clothing singed and glowing with faint embers.

Victor immediately began to cast another spell when the creature, yet again, stopped within inches of him. Victor took an involuntary step back but found the thing was still not going to harm him. Now, he smelled cooked rotting flesh and did, indeed, vomit.

What is going on here? he thought to himself.

The creature stood there, unmoving. Though, as Victor looked the thing over for a sign of any helpful information, he saw that the foul hands twitched. Occasionally they would raise slightly, as the thing wanted to reach for him but couldn't.

"You want this amulet, don't you?"

The creature made no sound, no movement except for the occasional cracking of bones and joints. Was it suffering? Something like this would certainly require powerful necromantic magic, but he didn't feel any the presence of any such permeations. This wasn't the work of the Third Sect, although there was something strange about the residual magic when he first entered the swamp.

"I'm going to end this for you. I'm sorry; I wish I knew who did this to you," Victor said, hoping that somehow whoever this once was could feel how sincere his words were.

Victor raised his hands and parted them, positioned as though he were about to grab something. He let out a long, sad sigh. Despite the gruesome appearance of the thing before him, it was once a human being. "I'm sorry," he said one last time.

"*Stenn-crif,*" he said, clasping his hands together firmly. A disgusting squelching and crunching sounded as the creature of Titan's Bog was smashed into a heap of dead flesh from both sides. It fell in a crumpled pile into the shallow water.

He now had to find the boys or whatever remained of them. Pulling the large shirt from the pack, he spoke the words to a fairly common First Sect invocation. Combined with the energy hopefully still present in Calub's shirt, Victor could try to track him down.

Holding out his fist, with thumb, pinky, and forefinger placed outward in three prongs, he saw a small point of blue-white light appear between them as he finished the short incantation. The light would grow brighter as he drew closer to the intended target. He turned slowly, waiting for the light to show the first signs of intensifying, signaling where he should go. When the glow brightened, he began walking slowly.

He expected the light to grow slowly and was prepared for a trek through the swamp to hopefully find survivors. It came as a great surprise when the light grew suddenly and reached an apex no more than a few steps away. Confused, Victor turned around and moved away, letting the light dim again. He walked in circles, tried recasting the spell, and all with the same results. The spell was leading him to the body of the creature crumpled in the water.

Victor looked down at the remains, the revelation dawning on him and making his head swim in confusion. The shirt belonged to this creature, long-rotting and dwelling in this swamp for possibly decades. Was this actually Calub? The boy who had only been missing for a matter of days at most? His eyes focused on something caught by the light of the spell, furthering this mystery.

The crushing spell he used had broken the creature every which way, opening the chest cavity as well as spilling what was left of the stomach's contents into the water. In the brownish-red stain that spread across the cloudy surface, Victor saw what looked like two stones covered in viscera inside the fully dead thing.

Pulling them from the nausea-inducing entrails, Victor washed away what he could. These were no ordinary stones. They were two halves of a circular-cut tablet covered in runic etchings. His spell must have broken it in half. This is what ultimately killed the undead titan.

What the hells is this?

He turned away from the rancid remains, unable to bear the stench, and squatted on his haunches, avoiding the cold, murky waters and with no dry space to return to. The titan of the bog might yet hold clues to its origins and purpose; therefore, Victor hesitated to remove the amulet and return to the outskirts just yet.

The tablet halves were stained red from their many years embedded in the stomach of the poor creature, despite Victor being told the boys had only been missing for days. Runes ran in rings around the tablet. They appeared in two different scripts. Some with sharp angles that could almost fit together like puzzle pieces confirmed what Victor already knew: powerful Third Sect magic. It was the second type of script that caused his insides to grow cold. Spidery, thin lines with seemingly no pattern at all that appeared to be etched by a man half-dead with delirium—the sinister work of the Fourth Sect.

The more horrible of the two types of runes were carved in the center of the tablet. That the dark etchings were in the heart of the spell was not some poetic gesture. This was part of the spell itself. The mage responsible made it part of a secondary spell to hide the use of the necromantic conjuring and suppress the residual permeation that would follow. Two powerful sets of runes from two different sects. Victor's forehead scrunched in confusion. He needed to piece this together.

It's probable that dark magic could decay a body quickly. Why someone would do that is the question. The titular titan could be a guardian of some sort, and Victor's circulating logic brought him back to the idea that perhaps someone wanted to hide in the shadowy confines of the swamp. He decided his next best option was to investigate the swamp a bit longer before returning.

After another hour of wandering the swamp, looking for any signs of habitation and finding none, Victor concluded he needed to leave in order to return to town before dark. He'd discuss his strange findings with Gustaf and Naydor and possibly return tomorrow to find out more.

He removed the amulet and waited for light to show through the gnarled branches. Many minutes passed, and he continued to wait, turning circles and looking for a sign of the relief that was the end of the swamp to appear. He clutched the amulet, wondering what was amiss. He couldn't wait long, as night was coming. Even with the creature dead, a dark swamp was no place to stay after sunset. To his great chagrin, he didn't know exactly where he was. His hopes to return had rested entirely on the amulet functioning properly.

It took hours more to find his way out of the swamp, fending off mosquitos the size of apples and dodging snakes slithering through the water and muck. Thankfully, he was visited no further by any alligators or other large predators. When he finally saw the barely perceptible rays of light through the tangled branches of the swamp's outer wall, he nearly fell to his knees in relief.

The last rays of daylight hung on the horizon as though they waited specifically for him. He followed the wet edges of Titan's Bog until he saw a faint dot out in the drier fields: Gilfoyle stood very much where he had been left. Victor approached the horse, who stood neck-down, grazing lazily and hugged the magnificent beast. He attached his bags and rode—wet, cold, and miserable—back to Summer's End. The day had been dangerous and mystifying; a warm bed and hot food would make everything better.

Sunset came well before Victor arrived back at the town. Doors were closed, windows were shuttered, and not a soul walked the unlit streets. The *Traveler's Tryst* looked dark, as well, when he rode up and hitched Gilfoyle outside. The door was locked, which struck Victor as odd, even in his exhausted state. He pounded on the door with a closed fist. After several minutes of silence, he tried again. Inside, muffled thudding foretold of a heavy-set barkeep that had been roused from sleep and was stumbling his way to the door.

"...we're closed for the night, gods-damned," came a slurred, gruff voice as the door opened. "Oh, Victor, it's you."

Gustaf's eyes livened up at the sight of the mage covered in swamp-filth with eyes barely staying open. He looked around nervously for a moment before inviting Victor in.

"Surprised to see me?" Victor asked, somewhat rhetorically.

"You're back late, is all. Feared something might have happened to you at worst, or maybe you decided to camp out by the swamp."

Victor grumbled a half-hearted reply and slumped into the chair by the cold, unlit fireplace. "I'm sorry, Gustaf, but I'm exhausted and could do with some food if you have any. I need to speak with Naydor, but I need sleep even more."

"Aye, aye...let me see what I can get you."

He lurched off to the back kitchen and returned a while later with some cold soup, bread, and a mug of ale. When he plopped it in front of Victor, the sound of the bowl hitting the table shocked the mage from his half-sleeping state.

"It's all I could gather up for you at this hour, Victor. But it should hold you over."

Victor nodded, mumbled a quiet but heartfelt thank you, and devoured the soup and bread. He stood, placing his hand on the table for support, and told Gustaf he'd take his ale back to his room.

"Of course," Gustaf said, nodding and putting a hand on Victor's shoulder. He helped the mage return to his room.

Victor practically fell onto the bed. He sat there, shoulders slumped, and said with sudden vigor, "My things; they're still strapped to Gil."

"I'll get them, don't worry." Gustaf left and returned quickly with all of his packs, piling them onto the floor for Victor to sort later.

"Now," the big man stated, "down that ale and get some sleep. We'll go see Naydor first thing tomorrow."

Victor nodded and thanked Gustaf for everything. The

barkeep went to leave the room, stopping momentarily to look back at the exhausted mage sitting on the edge of the bed. He left, closed the door, and left Victor in the silence of the dark room.

Groping in the dark to find the handle of the mug full of ale, Victor let his hand rest there momentarily. He decided he was far too tired to even drink at this point and fell back onto the coarse sheets; they felt like clouds. He slept fitfully but didn't know for how long. He attributed part of the problem to the smell that seeped into his clothes from the swamp, but it was too late, and he was too tired to bathe. The other issue was the tablet.

The magic sewn into it troubled Victor deeply. Giving up on sleep, he got out of bed and pulled the cold pieces of stone from the pack he placed it in after finding Gilfoyle. It was still damp and smelled terrible. The runes could still be clearly made out, though.

He studied the parts belonging to the Third Sect, as they comprised most of the writing. Spells upon spells were woven among each other. Victor couldn't just focus on one sect at a time. The full purpose of the tablet was complex and multi-layered; the Third and Fourth Sect runes and spells intertwined with one another; the grotesque aspects infecting the more technical ones like mold growing on fruit.

The tablet bound a subject to a specific area. Not only that, but it would resurrect the subject to a smaller area should they die. The titan would continue to return if killed so long as the tablet remained intact. The tablet kept the titan alive.

The majority of the runes belong to the Third Sect. They granted a boon of strength and speed to the bearer of the tablet, accounting for the titan's vicious, unnatural swiftness. Thankfully, Victor had been spared an example of the thing's supposed grotesque strength. More runes near the center and the spindly writing of the Fourth Sect suppressed the aura of the darker magics. This must have also created a mental block when discerning the evil magical saturation.

An interesting section of runes was carved apart from the others: a separate set tying the tablet to another object. The runes appeared to be those of binding magic that drew the tablet to an object once it was worn. An amulet. The wearer of the amulet would be brought to within a certain distance of the tablet.

Naydor...you shit-peddler.

Anger set Victor's blood to boiling. He felt energized as adrenaline coursed through him. His eyes went over every nick and scratch of the blood-stained tablet in his hands.

The necromantic inscriptions were self-evident. They kept the victim alive beyond their natural years, revived them upon death, and held their soul in thrall. They also obliterated the victim's self-awareness, conscience, and memories.

Did Gustaf know about any of this? Victor's anger against Naydor faded as his focus shifted to the big, friendly barkeep. The one who brought him the shirt and told him about the missing boys in the first place. Was he also a pawn of Naydor's?

The sound of a door closing caused him to blink back to the present. Sounds of muffled voices came from outside his door. Victor stood on unsteady feet. The voices stopped, and he waited by the door, pressing his ear against it to listen. The voices faded as though walking away.

He slowly opened the door, trying to ensure the hinges didn't creak. He walked softly down the hallway, where he heard voices coming from the main room of the tavern. A weak light reflecting off the stone walls indicated a candle burned softly around the corner.

Victor recognized the low, gruff voice of Gustaf.

"Why didn't you bring him directly to me?" The other voice said, apparently irritated. It also sounded familiar.

"I didn't know what to do. This has never happened before." Gustaf sounded distressed.

"No, it hasn't. And I'd like to find out why immediately. You gave him the shirt?"

"Yes!" The answer was a hoarse and whispered shout.

"Gods damn it," Victor whispered to himself, Gustaf's involvement and betrayal no longer questionable.

"Calm down. The amulet should have worked, too. The titan should have torn him to pieces...I don't understand."

Victor recognized the scholarly tone and youthful voice of Naydor. They had both betrayed him. But why? They were quiet for several moments. Naydor finally spoke, whispering pointedly. "I need to know why the creature didn't kill him. Grab a weapon. We're waking him."

"No, we aren't. I slipped something into his ale to keep him asleep."

Victor looked over to the mug of ale that sat undrunk on the stool. His heart began to race, and his face felt flushed.

"I wasted my time coming over here if he's drugged unconscious," Naydor said with open disdain.

"Again, I didn't know what to do," Gustaf replied tersely.

"Bring him to me first thing tomorrow. Do not let him think anything is amiss. Understand?"

"Yes," Gustaf answered, sounding downtrodden.

The next sound was that of the door to the tavern closing with Naydor's departure. It sounded like Gustaf remained in his seat. Victor heard a muffled thump, like a fist on wood, and the muttered words, "Damn it. Damn it!"

Victor slipped out of the door when he heard the sound of a chair scraping against the wood floor, echoing in the empty building. He saw Gustaf stand from the table—possibly deciding to check on the mage that should've been sleeping down the hall. The barkeep's eyes stared at the floor, his focus apparently on the current situation rather than the hall in front of him.

When Gustaf looked up, Victor's eyes met his. The mage stood like a haunting at the end of the hall. The old barkeep jumped, making a sound like a startled hound. Just as his mouth opened to surely cry out some number of obscenities, Victor's hand rose, and he spoke a short, sharp word. A quick flash of bluish-green light flickered in Gustaf's eyes before they closed, darkness overcoming him as he dropped to the floor like a very large sack of flour.

Victor drew his knife and placed it on the fat of Gustaf's neck. He spoke a counterspell and made the required motions with his free hand. The barkeep's eyes fluttered open, his mouth slightly ajar and his breathing steady. Realization dawned in the eyes tucked above heavy folds of wrinkles. Victor put a finger to his mouth, suggesting the barkeep stay quiet.

"What's going on, Gustaf?" Victor asked flatly.

"What are you doing, Victor?" Gustaf asked quietly, afraid to speak too loudly with the knife pressed so hard against his flesh. His lips were the only thing that moved on his entire body. His eyes remained locked on the mage.

"I overheard your conversation with Naydor. I didn't drink the ale, by the way. Too tired. I'm curious what was going to happen if I did, if I wasn't here holding a knife to your throat."

"Why didn't you just kill me?"

"Because I spent the better part of a day trudging through a swamp and nearly getting killed by an abomination, thinking I was trying to help some strangers and come to find out they were trying to get me killed. I want to know why." Victor had never felt such a cold resolution in his life.

Gustaf stared at him for a few moments. Victor wondered if

the barkeep was thinking about using the excuse, *I don't know what you're talking about.* However, judging by the soft sigh the big man gave, he had decided against it.

"I just help the man. I don't have much choice." Gustaf's gaze broke from Victor's. He stared off into the distance.

"Why? How powerful a mage is he?"

"If it were only him, we could probably manage. But he's not alone. He's the only one of them here in Summer's End, but others come from time to time."

"Others? Like a group of mages? Rogue magi? Are they strong-arming the town?" Victor asked, wondering if there was some sort of collective of mages acting like brigands and forcing tribute from nearby towns.

"He's been here a while. The one before him left. She was old, and they wanted a fresh face to replace her. Other townsfolk don't know anything. They want to keep things secret."

"Who's *they*, Gustaf?" Victor asked, his patience growing thin.

"The black-robed ones. Worship some kind of diamond shape. Evil fucks; gravitated to my family's tavern because it would serve them best."

Victor could see the defeat on Gustaf's face. He suddenly looked very old and very tired.

"How involved in this are you, Gustaf? Did you know what waited at the swamp?"

"I told you, the town is unaware of what's really going on. The legends in the bog are just that to them. I'm the one that has to work with them. All I know is, if a mage shows up, I take them to Naydor and do as he says. The ones that have visited tend to go off to the swamp and don't come back."

"Why?"

"I don't know, and I only asked once. I learned quickly not to ask again."

Gustaf didn't look like one who took sadistic glee in murdering travelers, but he had lied quite skillfully. Victor went back and forth on the prospect of the barkeep being pressed into service to Naydor. He'd have to deal with that later. Naydor would have many more answers than Gustaf, at least the kind Victor was after.

"I'm going to speak with Naydor. I'll come back, and we're going to have a long talk," Victor said with a piercing look at Gustaf.

The large man's expression turned grim, but his next words were spoken with sincerity. "I won't make no excuses for my part in this, lad. But that man is evil. And there is nothing any of us in this town can do against a mage with his powers. I root for you, I do...but I ain't holding my breath."

Victor had practiced magic against the other magi of the sanctum for years; however, that was only practice. His first few days outside of the safety of the Trifold would test his abilities against a true opponent in their arts. He wouldn't admit it, but Gustaf's words shook him somewhat. He'd had no time to study his opponent or learn of his abilities. His options were to face Naydor blind or flee. The second option seemed safest, but Victor simply couldn't bring himself to do it.

"We're both going to learn a few things today, it seems," Victor said quietly, both to Gustaf and himself.

Placing his hand on the barkeep's head, he muttered a short phrase and felt the large body go limp. The sleeping spell would keep Gustaf out of the way, but given his words about Naydor, he would likely want to see the dark mage defeated as much as Victor.

Not wanting to give Naydor any time to prepare, Victor left the bar in a rush. He could only partially lay out a plan of attack, not knowing what awaited once he reached the apothecary's home. He could try to bait him out into the open, but who knew what would happen when villagers awoke to a mage duel in their streets. They'd likely gang up on and kill both of them.

The dull, hazy light of predawn tinged the skyline as Victor looked down the alleyway leading to Naydor's door. Death or deliverance lay beyond that simple wooden feature. He steeled his nerve and walked down the dirty, worn street. He hesitated at the threshold; it occurred to him that Naydor believed he was still in a drug-induced sleep. The other mage may have decided to rest himself. For all Naydor knew, Gustaf was bringing the hapless newcomer to him, and Victor, himself, was unaware that anything suspicious was happening. The first plan was to blow the door open with a burst of magic, hopefully throwing Naydor off-guard. Now, there may be an alternative.

He reached out for the door handle, prepared to slip in quietly. His conscience then struck him. Was he prepared to murder a sleeping man? It was also possible that he was opening the door to a quite conscious and dangerous individual waiting for him. Gripping the handle, he resolved to find out one way or another.

The door opened with the slightest moan. The first thing Victor saw was the soft light of a candle flickering against the stone walls. Then, Naydor turned from his seat against the wall, and their eyes met. An eternity passed in that moment to Victor, but both men truly had only a brief time before reacting as a result of their delayed human reflexes.

Naydor shot from his seat, his hands already in motion, and an incantation begun before he was on his feet. The shadows deepened fleetingly, appearing drawn into his outstretched hand and splayed fingers. Black strands leaped from his hands, their needlelike points streaking toward their target.

"*Tyryn,*" Victor spat reflexively, twisting his hand and making a fist. The air before him blurred and swirled. The black, needle-tipped strands bounced off his magical shield and careened in multiple directions embedding into the floor, walls, and ceiling.

Now standing, Naydor whipped his other arm around, speaking in a language strange even to Victor, and the shadows of the room enveloped the lying mage. He disappeared, wrapped in the darkness. There would be only seconds to react before another spell would claim Victor's life. His mind raced. He focused on the flickering candle, knowing others were in the room. He snapped his fingers and lit every other wick available. Over a dozen candles blossomed to life and expelled most of the shadows from the room.

On the opposite side of the room where Naydor once stood, an inky stain bubbled and stretched between the stones and a bookshelf. It was him. He was trying to sneak up on Victor. The light of the candles gave him little shadow to work with, and his partly corporeal form was struggling to maintain the spell.

Drawing on the chill of early morning, the clear sky, and the still-visible moon, Victor drew in the power of cold and, with a flourish, unleashed it in the shadow's particular direction. A layer of hoarfrost followed in the wake of a cold blast of air. The crystalline rime covered everything in a sweeping layer before Victor. An echoing cry came from the roiling black shape on the wall. A human-like head pressed out from it, crying out in pain. Naydor's body fell from the shadow like an oil-covered babe newly-born.

He shivered, cursing Victor, and spoke a quick word in that awful tongue once again. His fists closed violently, and every candle in the room winked out. Victor was night blinded and saw nothing but pitch black and pinpoints of light from his eyes' memories.

"Shit," he said reflexively.

"Indeed," Naydor replied somewhere in the dark, his voice shaking from the cold.

Then, Victor heard the guttural sound of another spell being cast. It felt like spiders crawling in his ears and maggots squirming in his brain.

This must be the Fourth Sect, he thought, as fear began to take hold of him. I can't see...I can't see...

He fought the urge to flee, as Naydor would certainly kill him before he could leave. "Nos Ilyg," he said, recalling a spell to see in the dark. His vision returned, but all was shaded in grays and blues. Shadows were deeper, and objects lost their depth, but he could see. The foul man in the room with him had just finished his spell, and Victor saw a dagger, curved and wicked, form in his grip. It was made of more than darkness, appearing to be a black spot in existence. Naydor, himself, walked in a cloud of wispy black strands that surrounded his person, his eyes standing out like gray orbs of fiendish light. This wasn't normal for the spell. Something was amiss with this vile mage.

Naydor approached like some sort of assassin, knees bent and body ready to pounce, the void-dark blade held up, ready to end Victor and continue the trail of deaths in Titan's Bog. He must not have heard Victor recite the night vision spell or, less likely, didn't know of it. So, Victor decided to play the part. He looked to the right, then the left. Then, he moved to the right, where more room would be available, continuing to appear like he couldn't see. His heart throbbed in his ears. Naydor moved without making a sound. Victor purposefully moved more loudly, though only barely so.

Victor saw a smile spread across the would-be-assassin's face. None the wiser that his every move was being followed by his target. Naydor probably thought he had the hapless newcomer right where he wanted him. It would only be a few more steps now before he made his move. Slowly, he stepped toward Victor; each step calculated and silent. His confidence was threatening, but the fact that he had no idea Victor followed and analyzed his intent was slightly amusing to Victor.

Squeezing his hand into a fist, Victor prepared a spell for the incoming strike. He would have only a moment to cast it, and if his timing was off, Naydor would drive the blade into his heart and finish his journey here in this dark room.

Naydor sprang, a slight grunt the only noise escaping his mouth. Victor turned at the waist, shouting the words that unleashed the spell from his fist. The blast should have been enough to propel his attacker away, possibly even knock him unconscious, but his aim was off. The energy caught Naydor on his left shoulder, propelling the dagger forward. It struck early, driving through Victor's shoulder and sending a cold, shocking wave of pain throughout his body.

Shrieking in pain, he threw the surprised assailant off of him. His hand grabbed the dagger embedded in his body to the hilt. Numb waves reverberated through his fingers upon grasping the black handle. He pulled it out, seeing dark blood, tinted blue in his vision by the spell, pour from the wound. He threw it away, but it dissipated into nothing before landing on the floor. Scrambling to his feet, Victor stretched out his good arm and pointed his still-numb fingers in Naydor's direction.

"How—how are you still alive?" Naydor asked, his pale lips contrasting against the pitch black of his mouth in Victor's arcane night vision.

"You missed," Victor replied, pain causing him to take rapid, wheezing breaths.

Naydor shook his head slowly. "It shouldn't matter...that blade..."

Victor had never been stabbed before, admittedly. He wouldn't know exactly how it should feel, but he imagined the numbness radiating from the wound belonged to some sort of magical imbuement rather than a gash from a common blade.

"How?" Naydor pressed, his confused expression clear on his gray-blue face.

Victor tilted his head, "What did you try to do to me, Naydor?" he asked with an edge to his voice.

The stunned mage's chest heaved from exertion and confused shock. He refused to answer.

"Poison? Dark magic?"

"Much more," Naydor said, his eyes boring through Victor's. "That cut should have torn you apart, ripped you into fleshy strips."

Victor repeated the spell that lit the candles and dispelled the one altering his vision. The surroundings were more natural and put him slightly more at ease. The usual earthen tones and the soft glow of the candles cast the despicable man before him in a different light, both physically and metaphorically. He appeared as a frightened, middle-aged man holding one arm up to ward off any magic likely coming his way.

"Who are you?" Victor asked, his voice without pity or patience. Naydor stared back at him, his fear refusing to make him relinquish any answers. "Is Naydor even your real name?"

Sparks flickered between Victor's fingers, and Naydor flinched, his lip curling into a snarl. "Yes, that's my name."

"How is Gustaf involved? What are you using against him?"

Naydor chuckled. His arm lowered, and he leaned back, very slowly, to get more comfortable, but didn't dare attempt to stand.

"A barkeep, that's all he is. I needed his tavern for my purposes, and that's that."

Victor shook his head. "Not good enough. The creature in the swamp, the magic used for it—I don't feel such powerful magic here. That wasn't even your work, was it? You have someone else."

The proud mage huffed. He may have helped produce the tablet, but the powerful spells woven into it required very advanced skill. Naydor didn't put up enough of a fight against Victor to wield such potent magics. The dark mage's skills were certainly strange and unlike anything Victor had seen or studied, but not of the level inscribed on the tablet.

"What makes you so sure?" Naydor said, insulted.

"To be honest, I came here not quite sure I would walk away. There's some very powerful work integrated into that stone; however, what I see from you doesn't quite measure up to it."

Naydor's eyes flashed, and he momentarily considered lunging at the mage. After a few moments, he turned away and stared. Likely, he was calming himself before he made a stupid mistake.

"What was the purpose of the creature?" Victor asked.

Naydor's lips moved, like he was chewing on something, but he didn't reply.

"What was the titan's purpose?" Victor pressed, his pitch rising with his irritation.

When no answer came, another method was needed. This man had tried to kill Victor and had successfully killed many others. He was going to have to do something regrettable to get any answers before Gustaf woke and came for him. Victor spoke a quick succession of words, each one sharp and purposeful. A flurry of hand gestures and a smattering of arm movements accompanied them. The cloth covering a table next to Naydor's cushioned chair was yanked as though by invisible hands, then twisted itself into the tightest possible rope. It wrapped quickly around Naydor's neck before he had a moment to react and pulled him upwards. The strangled mage began smacking his hands against the ground in a desperate attempt to find purchase, lift himself up and breathe.

When the spell eased at Victor's command, Naydor choked and wheezed, gulping in air before shouting, "What the fuck are you doing?"

"Let's start over," Victor returned with a loud command. "What's the purpose of the tablet and the creature?"

"No," Naydor choked out, "I can't—"

Victor squeezed his hands and pulled downward, the rope following his command and jerking Naydor off the ground. He gave a painful croaking sound before thumping back onto the floor.

"Mages..." he croaked, "...looking for mages."

"Why?" Victor barked.

"Our reasons," Naydor continued, his voice returning, "are manyfold. See how many are left, their powers, and to..." he hesitated, his eyes darting away to avoid Victor's. The rope shifted, reminding him of the penalty for not talking.

"To kill any with certain abilities," he finished.

Victor's brows furrowed. "Special abilities?"

The Fifth Sect, he thought. *They're looking for mages gifted in the Fifth Sect.*

Naydor looked back at Victor and said, "If you came back from that swamp, with the tablets at that, you certainly have what we're looking for."

"Who's we? And stop being cryptic before I string you up and leave you here." There was no mirth in Victor's statement. Naydor grimaced.

"The Black Gnarl. Fifth Sect magic. We need mages who use it. Others died in the swamp or came back. Then, they joined the Gnarl or died."

"You've made this a recruitment center," Victor thought aloud, making his disgust obvious.

"Recruitment. Research. Execution. We have to be multifaceted to survive."

Victor stared at the Black Gnarl follower on the ground, his thoughts racing over the events of the last few days. Something else came to him, and he felt a wave of anger and pity at once.

"You gave Gustaf the shirt."

"Yes."

"I used a tracking spell on it to find the owner. I thought it belonged to one of the missing boys. Who did it really belong to?"

Naydor's eyes flicked away for a moment, then looked back to Victor. "The missing boy."

Victor's mouth curled in anger and his shoulder flinched as he prepared to tighten the tablecloth rope again. Naydor's eyes widened in fear as he shouted, "It's the truth!"

The rope slackened, and he looked at Naydor to continue —quickly.

"The creature is a young man named Calub. My predecessor used him when a mage killed the prior one—"

"How long ago was this?" Victor asked, cutting him off.

"About thirty years or so..." he trailed off for a moment, "give or take. We needed another, and it had to be the largest and strongest person we could find. The story keeps the locals afraid and superstitious, and the tablet...fits better in a larger vessel."

The last words were spoken hesitantly, as though Naydor knew what effect they would have. Victor's gut turned on itself. The callousness and evil of this mage and his predecessor were unthinkable.

"Who's your predecessor? Where are they now?" Victor said, his rage burning on his tongue.

Naydor dropped his head and shook it slowly. "Kill me now. I turn on the Black Gnarl and they'll do worse than that."

He lowered his head just enough so he could still glare at Victor. "You've seen as much."

"A name," Victor said sharply.

"No," Naydor said in a low voice.

"A name," Victor repeated more firmly. Naydor lay there, silently staring.

Victor's hands moved with amazing swiftness, the rope whispering harshly as it tightened around the wicked mage's throat. He swiftly beckoned for the other half of the rope to tie itself around one of the beams. Naydor's feet hung in the air, kicking wildly as he choked and pulled at the tablecloth around his throat.

"I know you didn't make that tablet and I want to know who did," Victor shouted, his hands balled into fists in front of his chest, holding the spell in place. "I will leave you to hang here and die, you sick bastard!"

The next few moments each seemed like paintings stuck in time, passing like a fresco. They also happened so quickly that instinct and reaction were all that could be managed.

The sound of the door slamming open behind him caused Victor's head to jerk around. He saw a large man coming into the room. He recognized Gustaf just in time to hear Naydor's feet thump to the ground. The distraction had broken part of the spell holding him in the air and tying the tablecloth to a beam, leaving enough room for the dark mage to land on his feet. Victor wanted to yell, at both Gustaf and Naydor at the same moment, but a blur of motion registered in his periphery.

Turning back, he saw a silk-gloved palm opened in his direction. Attempting to duck the incoming magic, whatever it may be, Victor drew his hands down with him. The tablecloth, still imbued with the spell, followed suit. Naydor was ripped up into the air with a loud grunt and a sickening crack, but not before he'd spat out the word to his spell.

A burst of energy jumped from his open palm as his arms jerked wildly from the tablecloth pulling him up. The spell missed Victor, who felt his coat lash against him as it passed within inches. However, it caught Gustaf in the face, whipping his head backward and slamming him into the wall.

"Shit...shit!" Victor cursed under his breath. The room fell into a deep, sudden silence. Naydor swung slowly from the makeshift rope around his neck, his arms and legs hanging limp. His feet dragged on the floor. Victor stared at him for long moments, making sure he was dead before approaching or turning his back on him. Seeing his eyes open, staring blankly and his parted lips already turning blue, Victor went to check on Gustaf.

The blast had finished slamming the door closed, and next to it, sitting slumped on the floor was the big barkeep. His eyes were barely open, but a slight wheeze escaped his lips. He was barely alive. Dust and bits of stone littered the area around him where his massive frame collided with the wall.

Victor looked up to see a red patch of blood where Gustaf's head hit the wall. It was so thick it had begun streaming in thick rivulets down the stones. The man, barely beyond a stranger, had betrayed him; it was by force, but he did take part in attempting to have him killed. He and Naydor succeeded with many others. He still felt pity for the man. It tore at him to consider what he could possibly do for the man now.

The barkeep's eyes, wet and fading, looked up at Victor with agonizing slowness. The wheezing became softer by the moment. "Can't feel anything," Gustaf said quietly, his lips barely moving.

"I don't know what I can do," Victor replied apologetically.

Gustaf's eyes lowered, his breath all but gone. Then, barely audible, he whispered, "Just...wanted to help you..."

One of his big hands twitched, and he was gone. Victor lowered his head and shook it. He stood to his feet and took in the room around him. Two dead men, both killed by accident, and one at his own hands. He wanted—no, needed—information from the Black Gnarl cultist. Naydor wasn't leaving him much choice. The heinous situation he'd created in Summer's

End caused Victor to make rash decisions. Now, Naydor hung from his own tablecloth.

This looked, for all intents and purposes, like a murder-suicide. A pang of guilt coupled with a sickening pit in his stomach struck Victor for even considering leaving them both here, especially Gustaf. The light of morning had already broken, however, so there would be no safe way for him to move and bury the bodies. They would have to remain this way and Victor couldn't tarry here much longer. The supposed apothecary could go hidden for days, but people would come looking for the barkeep.

Returning to the road would require supplies that he no longer had. He was also still filthy from the swamp. Checking the room, Victor found some food that would last him a while without spoiling, especially when helped along with his magic when needed. A few canteens and flasks were around that he could fill with water. He also found a bottle of wine; this he would definitely need.

He stopped for a moment before entering the room behind the lone closed door in the domicile. Naydor was a follower of the Black Gnarl. There's no telling what awaited behind that gateway. He took a deep breath and opened his palm, summoning a small dancing flame to light his way. He assumed it would be dark. He wasn't wrong.

The room inside was pitch black, unlit by any candle, torch, or magical means. The shadows teased of things that Victor shuddered to see in full light. Spotting a candle, he lit it with his hand-held flame. More light came into the room, but not enough. The candle illuminated a nightstand and bed, both of fine, but not opulent, make.

He walked slowly by the bed, looking for other sources of light. It was as if some heavier darkness lingered in the room, fighting against any light to expose what Naydor really was.

Another set of candles appeared at the edge of the flickering available light. The closer Victor came, however, the slower he walked. These candles sat in a trio, each of different heights and use. Their purpose was growing clearer. Next to them, symbols were written in a black fluid on the desk upon which they sat. He lit them, as well, and covered his nose and mouth at the sight in front of him.

A barbed diamond, the symbol of the Black Gnarl, was drawn on top of the desk in the same foul black ichor as the symbols surrounding it. Naydor had also written other symbols and invocations on the wall in blood, which had dried almost as black as the strange ichor on the desk.

After lighting the other candles he could find, and there were several spread haphazardly around the room, the darkness mostly abated. The shadows still weighed heavily, fighting for every inch of the room they could gain. The ghastly contents were fully laid bare, and he found himself in what was surely some demonic study rather than a room of rest and contemplation.

Ignoring the more grim aspects and items, Victor found a few tonics, oils, and tinctures that could prove helpful. Numerous books on illicit magical practices caught his eye, as they could provide insight into the Gnarl's workings. Unfortunately, there was no correspondence providing names or locations, especially in regard to Naydor's superior who crafted the tablet. The knowledge he'd gathered would have to do.

Victor was more than ready to leave the dark mage's home behind. With a final look of pity at the still body of Gustaf, he departed into the alley.

The morning was still very young and cold. No citizens walked the streets yet. Victor strapped his packs to Gilfoyle, took care of one final issue in Summer's End, and mounted his new traveling companion. The sound of the horse's hooves echoed in the fiery colors of dawn. He continued south on his journey into Alda, hoping never to return to Summer's End.

BACK IN THE TOWN, a crowd began to gather around the side of the *Traveler's Tryst*. Hushed murmurs grew into a larger chorus as more and more came to witness what the others were discussing in such fervent but quiet tones. Sitting against the side of the tavern were two pieces of stone—rounded, stained red, and smelling of the worst rot and decay imaginable. A beautiful amulet hung from one sharp corner of a broken edge of the stone.

Above this odd display, a note was stuck to a beam of wooden bracing with a note. This was the greatest source of the crowd's interest. Written in large, clear letters were the words, "The Titan Is Dead."

THE HALLS DARKEN

LIGHT SPLIT THE DARKNESS IN A PERFECT BEAM. THE SHARP EDGES of stark white gave way immediately to deep shadow. Dellig looked up and saw a slender t-shaped line of light at the top of the beam. Looking down, he saw the same at the bottom. He stepped back, feeling at any moment he could plummet backward into an infinite abyss. The beam shrunk slowly in his vision until it became a large 'I' of perfect white light. The beam narrowed further and further until there was a resounding, thunderous peal accompanied by total darkness.

Dellig's eyes opened. His breathing was steady, but his heart pounded. Sweat beaded on his head, cold and clammy. The rough-spun sheets of his bed clung to his body. Sitting up, he rolled his neck first. No cracks or creaks this time. He lifted his arm, rolling his shoulder, and realized all the soreness and joint crackles had decided to take up residence there. He evicted them with a groan. His muscles turned softer by the day. At least, those in his upper body did. He stood from the bed on legs still hard as iron. His stout dwarven frame comically split in half at the waist from the softening of age in his upper torso to the scout-hardened physique of his lower body. If not for a generations-long food shortage, he'd no doubt have a paunch at this rate.

He turned and looked for a moment at the crumpled sheets behind him. The sting of their emptiness still remained but grew a little less every day. He went to his dresser and pulled out a dull gray set of trousers, a white shirt, and cotton vest. After dressing, he sat back on the bed to pull on his boots; old leather things, once tough and dark as coal, now faded and nearly supple as cloth. He needed a new pair, but animal hide was a valuable commodity. He didn't have enough favors to trade right now. Dellig stood and went to leave but paused, remembering his bed was in disarray. Grunting, he let it be. When *was* the last time he made his bed?

Dellig's house was located in a lofty cavern of carved, natural stone. Like most dwarven mountain cities, Stendenbrock's entire borders lay within a mountain, in the roots of the earth, as Dellig's people liked to say. The streets were chiseled right where they lay. The houses were built of stone from the very walls of the mountain. Some even carved right into massive stalagmites protruding from the floor of the cavern. Most domiciles were single- or two-story structures. The roof of the cavern where the residential district was located rose a hundred feet above his head, but dwarves always preferred to be economical in their designs. This inclination had increased exponentially in the last few generations. An underground stream ran through the district, splitting it in half. Dellig's home faced the stream. He found the sound of it gurgling through the stone calming. A supply of clean, stone-filtered mineral water was also nice. Stendenbrock, though, was also a gate-city. One of a few locations where the inside of the mountains gave way to the outside world; however, this was no longer the case for this place. The gate was sealed, and Stendenbrock was now just another mountain fortress of the dwarven people.

Dellig gave a weak wave at his neighbor, who passively nodded in return. Like every morning before, Dellig needed to check the stores of mushrooms in the next district over. He passed several glum or disinterested faces on his walk. He didn't blame them, but to see his society, once so close-knit and family-oriented, reduced to cold indifference caused him to ache. Again, he couldn't cast stones at them. More and more houses were shuttered every year. The empty windows, locked doors, and entry ways heavy with dust and unswept sediment stared back at him as he passed one after another.

The residential district ended abruptly and opened into a wide avenue once used by many ponderous beasts of burden to cart supplies and resources to other districts. The beasts were fewer, but the creaky turning of wheels still echoed on the main thoroughfare throughout the day. The stream flowed back underground here, right where the avenue began. Staring at him from across the worn stone street, a windowless building with the words "Food—No Trespassing" chiseled into the side, waited. The markings hadn't always been there. The building was once a community center. Without much of a community, it was repurposed to hold additional food. When the food began to run out, it was handed over to Dellig to put what food he could into it. He was always reminded of his duty and the sourness it caused as he walked past that front wall and saw where, a few years ago, the carvings had been defaced with the word 'no' written above 'food.' No one had bothered to remove it.

The job of gathering additional food was given to Dellig because he was a resourceful dwarf. He'd been a valued member of the council when there was one, and it was because of him that there was even a need for additional space to hoard food. When most dwarves returned to the mountain cities, they realized that food would become a priority. There was no farmland in a mountain, and keeping livestock would be challenging at best. The fear following the Rupture caused his forebears to slam shut the great doors to the outside world permanently. The dwarven lords were confident they could return to life as their religion had told them they once lived ages ago: strictly within the halls of the mountains. Alda's purest castles. Alda's oldest children.

Dellig groaned out loud. The old beliefs may have saved them for a time, from what reports of other cities had told them of the horrors outside, but quite possibly doomed them in the long run. Infighting and political bullshit struck first. You can take the dwarf out of the outside world, but you can't take the outside world out of the dwarf. Then, real problems arose. Shortages of food and medicine, disease, revolt. Worse things in the dark belly of the mountain they never expected. But, the doors were closed. Dellig first posited the idea of using the flattened areas of cliffs to build small farms, the aptly named Sky Gardens. It would take a lot of effort to find usable soil, but ideas were formed and, soon after, troops of dwarves were sent to locate and return with soil. The other issue was that these flattened stretches of mountainside were half a day's trek from the walls of Stendenbrock. The dwarves, of course, never thought they'd need to grow anything within their own mountains.

A sharp, pungent smell greeted Dellig upon opening the door to the food warehouse. He cleared his throat, coughed a little. The torches on the wall revealed a depressingly depleted stockpile. The sight made his stomach grumble. The only foodstuffs available in this storehouse were various mushrooms and clumps of lichens. Most of them consisted of two flavors: earthy and bitter. Not unlike the people they helped sustain.

These two simple foods were once plentiful, but unwanted. They once grew in patches all along the rough, uncut halls of the mountains. They were the last things to be eaten, being both distasteful and undesirable even for the hungriest dwarven families, but in lean times, their consumption became more prevalent and often required. Unfortunately, they were also the least nutritious. Trips to the Sky Gardens became harder and more dangerous. Things in the deeper reaches of the mountain were working their way up from the world's belly. Things best not interacted with in any way.

Dellig shook his head, closed his eyes, and forced the dark thoughts out. He'd have to prepare for a trip to gather more food soon. Actually, it would have to be today. The longer the trip, the more the stores would be eaten up while he was gone. Most of the stock that was in here was already molding and turning.

Before leaving, he turned and looked back at the empty, shadowy room. Ghosts of a happier past still echoed there. In the chairs and tables once circled for conversation and debate that were now pushed against the wall and stacked with empty boxes. Boxes that once held food and supplies. In the dais near the front where dwarves would once share their ideas for keeping the community going and the families prospering in dark times. All these things, these ghosts, haunted his memory with every visit. He blinked his eyes, heavier now, and turned to leave.

DELLIG'S GEAR for his trip hadn't changed in probably twenty years: backpack, pouch belt, rope, grapple, sword, knife, torch, dried mushrooms, and some dehydrated minnows from the stream. He took a quick look in the mirror to see if he might catch something he'd forgotten. He never did, but it was a habit. Dwarves were creatures of habit, sometimes obsessively so. As he departed his home, he once again turned and looked at the bed, the sheets still crumpled and unmade. The pang itched at his insides once more. Speaking of habits...

The route to the outskirts of town took him in the opposite direction of his previous trek. This time he walked south, towards the center of the mountain. A few old dwarves were playing a game of chess at a stone stump of a table by the stream. A few children splashed water at each other. It seemed relatively normal, making Dellig smile just a bit.

A sharp pain shot through his foot, curdling his smile and causing him to yip in pain. He looked down, standing on the tip of his toes with one foot, bouncing reflexively on the other to distract from the pain. Hobbling over to an empty table, he leaned against it. He plopped down on a stool to take a look at what was causing his foot to now throb in pain. A sharp piece of stone stuck into the bottom of his foot, piercing right through the ruined leather of his boot's sole.

Son of a bitch. He cursed to himself. There would be no question now. He needed new boots. There is no trek into the deep tunnels with ruined footwear that you come back alive from. Luckily, he was already near Craftsmen's Nook, where said craftsmen hold all their shops. It would also be nice to see Broche again.

"You alright, son?" One of the old dwarves called. He looked at Dellig from under thick, bushy brows. His tone was flat, but his eyes were soft with concern.

Dellig nodded in return, his frustration at the situation still simmering in him.

"Might wanna get that looked at," the other old dwarf added as he moved a piece on the board.

"I've been through worse," Dellig responded.

"Tell Broche we said hi," one of them said as Dellig passed, but he wasn't sure which. He simply waved in response as he continued on.

The Craftsmen's Nook was as busy as it ever was. Which was to say it wasn't busy at all. People did keep to themselves more, with not a lot of work to go around. A few hammers *clinked* in a few shops. Small gatherings of dwarves stood about discussing business and orders, some even casting glances Dellig's way. Broche's shop could be smelled before you found it. Leather-work was dirty, odiferous, and not the most respected job among dwarves, at least traditionally. Dwarves believed metalwork was what dwarf hands were made for. Broche disagreed. Leather strapped the plates of armor together, kept mail from rubbing a dwarf's muscles raw, and even "held one's god damned pants up," he'd once insisted. The tannery was located on the outskirts of the Craftsmen's Nook for the sake of all nearby. The scant number of dwarves thinned even more so until the streets were practically deserted by the time he found his old friend's doorway.

After two quick knocks, Dellig waited patiently for Broche to answer. Gods knew what a craftsman could be doing at any time. Dellig liked to provide some courtesy. It didn't take his old friend long to come to the door. Must've been a slower day than usual.

The door swung open, and Dellig recognized Broche's sharp green eyes and wiry red beard staring back at him. A wool cap covered the younger dwarf's auburn hair, a difference from his beard that always struck Dellig as odd. Or unique, as he always told Broche, who was quite sensitive about the subject.

"No solicitations," Broche grumbled.

"Fuck you. Let me in." Dellig growled back, smiling.

Broche chuckled, a low rumbling sound, and pulled the door open, motioning with his free hand for Dellig to enter. Broche led him to the usual spot. A seating area for waiting customers sat off to the side of Broche's desk, which had a few papers spread across in a disorganized fashion. Dellig sat down and Broche left into a back room without a word.

Dellig took in the room around him. He hadn't seen his friend in months. Before that, it had been years. In all that time, nothing in his shop had changed. The same samples for customers, the same smell of cured leather, the same tinge of dried incense, meant to mask the more unpleasant smells that resulted from Broche's profession, which had sat for years and was almost gone. Dellig smiled to himself. Dwarves are stubborn people. Always have been. It's what had kept them going for so long, long after the main doors to the outside world were shut permanently—sealed forever by that same stubbornness.

Broche returned with some ale for the two of them. Dellig took a pull from his mug and winced. Ale brewed from what was available in the mountain halls was not entirely pleasant.

"So, how have you been?" Dellig asked, wiping his mouth.

Broche looked at him with furrowed brows, the skin around his eyes as wrinkled as old laundry.

"What's it been...months?" Broche asked.

"A few, yeah," Dellig mumbled, taking another hesitant sip from the mug.

"You still keep track of time?" Broche scoffed.

"Some of us still do."

An awkward silence hung in the air for a moment. Dellig swirled the drink in his cup and watched as bits of froth clung to the inside walls of the mug.

Broche sighed. "What did you come here for? I know you need something. I can smell the guilt on you."

It was true. Dellig hadn't visited in some time, and now he came hat in hand to his friend needing something without much in the way of payment. He crossed his legs, throwing the foot with the ruined shoe up on his knee.

"Fuck, that looks painful," Broche grunted. He saw the dried blood on the bottom of Dellig's boot surrounding the smooth edges of a hole in the bottom. "That sole is paper-thin. You go on foraging trips with that? Why didn't you come to me sooner, you moron?"

Dellig shrugged. "Leather's pretty scarce nowadays, at least I imagine so."

A smile spread underneath his friend's red mustache. "Well, it's limited but not quite as scarce as it used to be."

It was Dellig's turn to scrunch his face at Broche. "What are you hiding?"

Broche threw his arms open wide. His smile dropped, and his eyes softened in mock offense.

"I ain't hiding shit, friend. You just haven't been around to see what's what."

"And what is *what*?"

Broche plunked his drink on the table next to them, slapped his legs with both hands, and stood. He beckoned Dellig to follow. They entered the back area to the workshop, where the younger dwarf earned his wages. The rancid smells of curing leather hit Dellig like a physical slap to the face. He was able to shrug it off when he saw several skins stretched on frames. All of them were various colors of robbe pelts. Small, lean beasts, robbes were sometimes called 'cave rabbits'. In more plentiful times, they were considered pests and not worth bothering with, let alone hunting and eating. These days, they were a main source of protein for the mountain-dwelling dwarves.

"Where did you get all this?" Dellig asked, incredulous.

"Found me a little community of the buggers," he answered with a smile. "About half a mile in the south tunnels. They've something to subsist on that keeps 'em alive and breeding. I give 'em a season, got a fresh batch I can go after."

"And the meat?"

Broche's mustache on his upper lip bristled. "Not too much on them, but I get some good stew for a while and smoke the rest to last me and do some trade."

Dellig crossed his arms and raised an eyebrow at his old friend. "And the meat?" he repeated.

"Oh, for fuck's sake, you just have to ask."

Grumbling under his breath, Broche left momentarily and came back with a handful of dried meat. Dellig nodded in thanks, taking one of the dried, thin pieces. He gripped it in his teeth. The bite pulled away fairly easily. The meat had little flavor itself, but the smoky flavor was pleasant.

"It's good," he said, still chewing. "Now, I owe you even more."

Dellig could practically feel the cold stone of the floor through the hole in his boot. He flexed his foot, feeling the dull pain of where the stone had cut through his flesh.

"Turns out," Broche paused and swallowed his bite, "you could do something for me that would cover the boot and the meat."

"And what's that?"

"I need an escort to make another run to the south tunnels. 'Bout time I check the snares and check on a few other things. Need someone to watch my back."

It was a sad fact of life. Once, a foraging trip into the Old Halls surrounding Stendenbrock to reach the gardens or hunt for the timid robbes could be undertaken alone. Not so anymore.

"I've already got boots that should fit, and I'll bring food for the trip," Broche continued. "May even be able to help cart some of those mushrooms back."

Dellig grunted. He didn't like the idea of having a friend come along to the Halls. It's true that other dwarves never go alone these days, but Dellig wasn't one of them. He preferred to travel light, fast, and alone. The stout, heavy-iron-wearing soldier-dwarves of old were gone. The remnants were left to guard the walls and crevasse protecting the town's borders. There were no outside threats anymore. No elves getting their silk trousers in a twist over border disputes at the mountain forests. No more bandits raiding along the valley roads. No longer were the temperamental mountain drakes a concern here within the mountain walls. Now, all the spears and shields faced toward the inside of the mountain where much worse than elves and bandits and drakes stared at them with unblinking eyes and rancid, ancient breath.

A loud thump brought Dellig back, snapping his consciousness into the unpleasant smells of the tannery. He blinked a moment, his eyes dry and his mind reeling from the echoes that threatened to bring other unpleasant memories to the forefront.

A new pair of boots sat on the table in front of him. The gray, smooth material had a faint lavender hue—the tell-tale sign of robbe hide. Dellig grabbed one of the boots and ran his hands over the leather. He put a hand inside and felt the support and quality of it.

"Well, try 'em on." Broche snipped.

Dellig took the boots and sat on a stool nearby. He flopped his old, loose ones off and went to put the new ones on when his friend spoke up.

"Hold on there, let's fix that cut. You could get an infection in your foot, and that's not good considering your old ass is responsible for some important stuff around here."

Dellig pursed his lips and nodded. After sitting down, he realized his foot was throbbing.

Broche went to fetch some bandages and salve, leaving Dellig momentarily alone with the stench of the tannery and, worse, his listless thoughts. Thankfully, his friend returned in mere moments.

"I use this a lot more than I like to admit," Broche grunted as he knelt down to get a better look. "Gods, you cut yourself pretty good. I hate to say it, but we might want to hold off on that little trek."

"No time," Dellig replied. "Food stores are too low. Just the 'shrooms and lichens left. Too many mouths to feed with that pig feed."

Broche tightened the wrapping and slapped his hands together as he stood. "There, now put 'em on. No stones cutting through my shoes any time soon."

"Thanks," Dellig said. It was more a grunt, but genuine all the same.

"Call it a downpayment," Broche said, smiling.

"You're paying me, now?"

Broche sniffed. His mustache twitched. His friend did this whenever he was uncomfortable. Broche had these tells for as long as Dellig had known him. He just let the question hang until his old friend decided to answer.

"Well, I know you don't like having a partner on your outings since...you know."

"We don't talk about that. Or her."

There was an edge to Dellig's voice, like a growl from a guard dog. Broche had quickly learned to heed this warning. He raised his hands in a manner of surrender and tilted his head to the side in submission.

"I'm just saying, I understand why you're hesitating, old friend. But I need to make this run as you need to make yours. Let's go together and return just the same."

The older dwarf nodded. He closed his eyes and breathed. Whenever he thought of that empty space on his bed, a name echoed in his mind: Veerka. Sometimes, he heard her name in the resonating peal that woke him from his fitful dreams of the pillar of light, the last remnants of his memories when the great gate to the outside shut forever. He quietly stood from the stool. "Get your things. We leave as soon as you're ready."

Despite his discomfort, the old scout agreed to let his friend come along to gather his supplies. He knew the stubborn dwarf would go regardless. It'd be safer for Broche, at least, if Dellig was there. He wouldn't be able to move as quickly, but the second pair of eyes and ears, along with another axe, would be welcome.

"I'll be outside," Dellig called out, hearing his friend clanking and rustling through his gear in the next room.

He stepped out the door and listened to the quiet. The tannery wasn't far from the gate they'd exit to head into the Old Halls. Dellig took a deep breath. The air felt stifling. He'd never say this out loud. To a dwarf, to breathe in the still air in the mountain is to breathe in the breath of the world itself. Something didn't feel right, though. The darkness of the mountain roof stretched overhead, where the lights of torches faded to the barely perceptible glow of iridescent fungi glowing like faint stars and, finally, to pitch black. It should have been comforting: the dwarves' own eternal, quiet night. Instead, the darkness felt heavier. Unnatural. The stillness of the mountain air stirred with...something. He grunted aloud to himself, not sure what to make of this ill feeling.

The door behind him groaned, signaling that Broche was joining him. He heard his friend step up beside him, but Dellig's eyes remained on the spectral dots of fungi at the edge of the cave's blackness and the city's torchlit glow.

Broche glanced over and saw the older dwarf's face scrunched. The bushy, salt-and-pepper brows were furrowed over his dark eyes. Normally sharp and piercing with an intelligent gleam, they were now squinted in some unknown, tumultuous pattern of thought complete with sleepless, wrinkled bags beneath.

"So, uh," Broche began, unsure how to rouse his companion from thought-induced catatonia, "thinking about..."

He wanted to say "her" but immediately let the word catch in his throat. Dellig wouldn't take kindly to a second mentioning of it. Broche just sniffed and completed the question with, "never mind."

"It's nothing," Dellig replied. "Let's get going."

The two walked toward the southern gate in relative silence. Dellig enjoyed the simple pleasure of new, comfortable boots while Broche quietly attempted to bolster his courage for another trip into the treacherous Old Halls.

The southern gate was one of only two remaining entrances into the city of Stendenbrock. With the large doors to the outside world sealed off, that left the western and southern entrances, which both led deeper into the mountains. The western door led to mines, which ran parallel to the side of the mountain facing the world beyond and all its horrific splendor. These mining tunnels were relatively safe and still in moderate use to gather materials for tools, construction, and repairs. This led to its appropriate name: The Metal Passage.

The southern gate was a different story altogether. Where the Metal Passage ended, a cavernous trench began that ran the length of Stendenbrock's border with the mountain's interior, save for a long stretch of hard stone walkway to the Old Halls on the other side. Watchtowers were constructed not long after Stendenbrock's founding to protect against cave trolls, goblin raids, and the occasional tiff with other dwarven kingdoms. The chasm provided ample protection as no threat from the mountain could jump a three-hundred-foot gap with no visible bottom. After the doors were sealed, an unexpected problem arose: criminals. Having been cut off from former trade routes and with limited space, the dwarves of Stendenbrock had to come together as a community for survival, let alone any form of prosperity. This made any crimes against the community all the more grievous. Feeding and housing those who broke the law and threatened the safety of those who remained was out of the question. The only remaining option was banishment.

This was essentially a death sentence these days. The Old Halls ran far and deep. Most dwarven cities on any given continent on Alda were all connected via the ancient hallways built by the first dwarves. They were still very far apart, however. Criminals were forced through the southern gate and across the natural stone bridge with naught but the clothes on their backs. If they could survive to the next town or city, they might be able to find a place in that community, though it was unlikely. Their guilt would be evident upon their arrival, what with nothing to their name and a likely haggard and half-starved appearance.

This led to desperation on the part of most of these outcasts. Many suicidal attempts were made to cross the chasm. Some, having survived for extended periods of time, banded together to try and return. This led to the construction of the city walls and a proper gate between the watchtowers. The attempts to return to the city stopped altogether, and the imposing structure received a new moniker: The Dead River Gate.

This ill-named feature of their city leered at Dellig and Broche as the two dwarves approached. The dark iron of the gate dully reflected the light of large torches burning on either side. The cold, carved stone of the walls stood as a harsh reminder of what lay on the outside.

"I never liked this place," Broche whispered. "It's so close to my home; I can feel it looking at me."

"You always feel like something's looking at you," Dellig replied flatly.

"Where are ye headed?" An armored dwarf called out from atop one of the three-story towers.

"The Sky Gardens," Dellig shouted back, "Returning with a cart-full of goods in a day or two."

"Aye, is that you, Bornmason?" A separate voice asked as another helmet came into view.

"It is," Dellig replied, answering to his surname.

The two armored figures disappeared. Dellig and Broche looked at one another quizzically. After a few moments, the small door to the tower clicked and two guards emerged. Their armor clanked and jingled. Their spears thumped as they came to a stop. Dellig vaguely recognized one of them through their open-faced helmets.

"Glad you're making a run for the gardens," the familiar dwarf said. "My son's been grumbling about mushrooms lately."

"He's not alone," Broche said sardonically. Dellig grimaced.

"You're armed, yes?" The other, taller guard asked. His tone wasn't as cheerful as the first guard's.

"Always," Dellig answered, but he raised an eyebrow at the guard who asked. Said guard then looked at Broche, who had a bow slung over his shoulder and a skinning knife hung on his belt. "I hope those are good for more than just hunting."

"It's just..." the familiar guard began but trailed off. The two guards passed a quick look at each other. "Things have been strange over the chasm lately."

The tall guard shuffled his feet and thumped his spear nervously.

"Strange, how?" Dellig asked. "Outcasts having at it again?"

"Maybe. There've been no attacks for a few years now, and not even a sighting of an outcast in the last year. There's been some movement on the other side of the chasm the last few days, though. Just shuffling in the dark near the entrance to the Old Halls."

"Hmm," Dellig grumbled, his mind starting to go to work.

"And...noises." The second guard added, his voice low. The familiar dwarf pursed his lips and looked to the ground. "I swear, I think it's growling."

"No, not growling, but definitely some damned guttural noise. Like a bark or a gargle. Or both, maybe?" the other guard added.

"Trolls? Maybe goblin packs?" Broche thought aloud.

The tall guard shook his head. "Never heard anything like that from a troll or goblin. Haven't seen any of them in a long time, either. Besides, we've seen some of 'em here and there." His words trailed off to a whisper, and Dellig swore he saw the dwarf shiver.

"Too short for a human or elf but too tall for a dwarf," he continued, his voice hoarse.

The familiar dwarf shrugged. "Maybe a troglodyte, with the way the light hit their eyes."

"Aye, maybe." The other guard followed, his voice breaking slightly.

"The job's been right boring of late, actually. Almost like the mountain's insides have been completely abandoned. Except the last few days." The familiar guard explained. "Just be careful. All's we're saying. Everyone needs that food."

Dellig nodded firmly, saying, "We'll be back in a day or two."

The guards nodded, shook their hands, and returned to the tower. The door clicked after it shut, and the sound of cranking gears and chains accompanied the rising portcullis. In front of Dellig and Broche, the narrow natural bridge stretched like a stone strand of a spider's web across the dizzying blackness of what Stendenbrock's residents had come to call the Dead River.

Dellig looked left to right. The city wall ran right up to the edge of the perilous chasm. From this angle, the walls looked meager compared to how they appeared from within the city. In front of him, the narrow bridge seemed thinner and longer, like the depths on either side were black teeth grinding it down.

"So...you first?" Broche said, his question brusque. Stepping forward, Dellig gave him a sideward glance that was more of a glower.

The crossing was brief. Their footsteps echoed as they reached the opposite side of the chasm. Broche turned back to look at the city from this viewpoint. He rarely left, even to hunt the robbes. He always had the same thought when he looked back at the large arch leading to the Old Halls.

"It seems so small," he said, referring to Stendenbrock.

"We all are, in the heart of the world," Dellig replied without looking back. He was focused on the dark mountain corridor before him. The upkeep on the halls had lessened over the last year until not so much as the torches were lit. Now, there was only darkness and crumbling stone.

Broche turned back to gaze down the hallway with him. "Too bad trade stopped from the other cities last year. The halls would be lit and probably safer."

"Think the outcasts had anything to do with that? Too many raids?"

The question sat unanswered for a moment. They both knew that no final word had ever come from connected mountain cities. The trade caravans just stopped.

"I doubt it." Broche finally answered. "Some starved criminals overrunning too many armed caravans? I bet everyone else is just turtling up," he explained hesitantly, "Closing the gates. Everyone trying to protect their own."

Dellig lit an oil lantern that he took on all his excursions. Broche took an unlit torch from a sconce on the wall and sharply struck two pieces of flint together until the sparks created a decent flame that quickly grew into a roaring light.

The plan, to Dellig, was as rote as it was important. The Old Halls were large, imposing, but impressive. They were also dug to allow travel within the mountains, not outside of them. That was the purpose of gate-cities. When he found the natural rising path that led to an open, exposed surface, it created a fine spot for building the Sky Gardens. It did not, unfortunately, allow for easy transport of the harvested crops. Too few could be carried back down the narrow passageway, which was also ill-fit for restructuring and broadening. More scouting expeditions found an area below the designated farming surface that would allow closer and safer access for individually-pulled carts to make fewer trips and gather more food. A lift and pulley system was built to lower the harvested crops down to a receiving dock that was created after digging a more structurally-sound tunnel to the lower area. This receiving dock was also conveniently closer to the city geographically. The combined feats of dwarven engineering coupled with a "blessing from the mountain," as the priests had put it, created a life-saving solution to their food problems. It just required a strong back, as mules and oxen were too difficult to maintain under a mountain.

This resulted in the situation Dellig and Broche now found themselves in after an hour's walk: passing the carved archway on their left that would lead to the receiving dock where a locked storehouse waited with the carts. The path that wound its way up to the gardens themselves was another several hours away. There, a guarded post would allow them entrance.

Until then, they had to traverse the abandoned halls of their once-great society. Stone floors, columns, statues, and simple, abandoned outbuildings carved right from the natural stone showed the cracks and wear of age and lack of upkeep. They journeyed on until toppled columns became more prominent. The carved statues of dwarven leaders and heroes were missing limbs and heads, which lay broken at their feet until, further down the halls, nothing but the feet of the statues even remained. The crumbling structures became so derelict that exposed unworked, natural stone of the mountain showed through the craftsmanship. The sharp yellow glow of the lantern and the flickering flames of the torch created chaotic shadows and played havoc with their minds. Their steps echoed in lonesome dirges as the two walked alone—small, insignificant fleas in the heart of the world—leaving long, empty shadows behind them.

A sudden, sharp sound drew their attention to a darkened corner near some fallen columns. Dellig's heart jumped. The darkness and adrenaline combined and threatened to wake something in him that he kept pushing down. Waves of panic rolled over his skin as he gritted his teeth and faced the lantern toward the noise.

"Was that a scream?" Dellig asked, his voice so low Broche barely heard him.

The fiery-bearded dwarf readied his bow, drawstring creaking, and aimed the shimmering tip of an arrow at the shadowed corner where the sound seemingly came from. Sharp breaths huffed from his nose as he stared, eyes wide and fearful. The same sound came from some rubble, a result of a tumbled column, and two plump creatures lazily half-hopped into his line of sight. Dellig must have heard them too, as a soft "fuck" merging with a sigh of relief came from behind him.

"Well, there's your first catch," Dellig said with a wave of his free hand.

Broche shook his head. "Nah. One of 'ems with kits. Need the population to stay healthy. My traps'll be full when we get there, I'm sure."

Their journey continued into the cloying dark of the halls. Soon, there was little evidence left of the dwarves' presence at all. It was as if the mountain itself was reclaiming what the mountain people had cut into it.

So much for the elders' ideas of dwarves and the mountain being of the same soul, Dellig thought sardonically.

They may have been about half an hour from the guard post that would take them to the gardens when Dellig stopped abruptly.

"You smell that?" he asked Broche.

It took the other dwarf a moment, but his hands soon curled into fists. "Aye," he replied softly, "I know that smell."

They drew their weapons. Adrenaline flowed into them, sharpening their senses and intensifying the foul stench that grew worse with each step.

"Gods..." Broche said in an exhale as the light of their torch and lamp fell upon a horrid sight.

Dark splotches, thick with viscera, spread over the cracked floor before them. Bits of armor and broken spears littered the floor. A hand attached to part of a forearm lay on the floor, fingers curled up toward the ceiling.

The dwarves were speechless. Dellig looked around, taking in the details of the grisly scene. Kneeling down by the arm, he saw ragged strips of flesh and shredded muscle trailing behind snapped bone. The limb hadn't been severed with a blade. It had been torn off. One of the spears was covered in a black, tarry substance that smelled like sulfur and dead animal. Even more concerning was the state of the metal tip. The smooth, sharp edge had become wavy, uneven, and thin. The tip was rounded, and smooth bits of metal clung to the flat side like candle wax. Whatever this substance was had melted the forged steel.

"Dellig," called Broche in a hoarse voice. "You need to see this."

Dropping the broken shaft, Dellig stood and wiped his hands on his pants. The strange substance left him feeling corrupted and dirty. He turned to Broche and saw his friend standing there holding the torch at arm's length in the direction they were headed, his eyes wide and jaw clenched. Several wide red trails on the floor led into the dark.

"They were dragged somewhere," Dellig concluded, his tone flat but his heart thumping.

"By *what*?" Broche shouted, his voice echoing.

Dellig glanced back down at the spear and the strange substance that had warped its tip. "I couldn't say."

"No shit! We should go back, tell the elders and bring more soldiers."

"What if the rest of the guardpost needs our help? We're close—"

"Not close enough," Broche cut Dellig off. "If the outcasts are doing this, they've completely gone tits up. And they're getting closer and more desperate."

"This wasn't outcasts. No half-starved dwarf could tear another's arm off," Dellig returned, pointing to the pale appendage on the ground. "And the guards would've just killed any one of 'em that tried to get to the food. These guards were running from something. And I've no idea what that black stuff is."

The older dwarf motioned behind him at the broken spear, for he was casting the light of his lamp on the red smear trailing off toward the precious garden and its guard post and staring into the darkness beyond.

"How're you not pissing yourself right now?" Broche asked, getting more worked up. "I'm going back."

Dellig held the lantern up. He continued to stare at the darkness, tried to stare through it. He swore something caught in the furthest reaches of the light and reflected back at him. "Don't, Broche, give me just a moment."

Squinting, Dellig continued to look for the reflection again. Sometimes, he thought he saw it but couldn't be sure. He moved the lantern light around slightly, hoping to spot it, when he heard Broche begin to speak, or maybe it was a gasp. Regardless, the manner in which it rose so sharply and then suddenly stopped sparked an acute and terrible reaction in the old scout. Dellig turned to find nothing but shadow and dried viscera.

"Broche?" Dellig called out. His friend had utterly disappeared. Not so much as the light of his torch could be seen. "Broche?" he called again, louder.

A distant scream echoed from somewhere in the cavernous halls. It was indistinct, but Dellig knew it was Broche. He knew it in his soul. That hoarse, horrified sound belonged to his friend. It was heading further away. The sound almost appeared to come from near the ceiling, perhaps along the walls.

His eyes were drawn upward. No torches lit up the horizons like back home. Only the dim, bioluminescent fungi separated the dark hall floors and walls from the ceiling. The faint, bluish-green lights peppered the darkness in a wide band. The ghostly lights calmed him, if only for a moment. Within those cold cave-stars sat something hot and hateful. Dellig held up his torch again, thinking he could see the faint reflections his lantern had caught before, but the longer he stared, the more he realized it wasn't a reflection. Multiple pairs of yellow-orange orbs glowed among the fungi like seething, burning coals.

They didn't move. He tried to rationalize to himself, thinking that perhaps they were a new kind of fungi, simply glowing a different color. It was futile, however, as the sets of orbs moved together. Those eyes, as he knew they were, belonged to haunted memories he shoved down deep into a repressed lockbox in his mind. The lid on that box blew open and images of blood, sounds of screams, and the smell of seared flesh flooded his mind and drowned it in fear and self-loathing.

"Fuck it," Dellig growled, his eyes beginning to grow warm and wet, and he took off in a sprint back to Stendenbrock.

He heard the worst kind of guttural croaks, growls, and spits come from behind and above him. His feet pounded on the stone, the new boots from his now-damned friend carrying him swiftly through the dead halls. Something flashed in the light of his lantern in front of him. He recognized the reflection of light on metal. His frenzied rush hadn't taken him far, but hope lit up his heart for a moment as he briefly, ever so briefly, wondered if it was the guards from the post at the gardens. Or, perhaps, a patrol from the city?

This hope was burned away almost instantly as multiple sets of those unblinking, cavernous eye sockets stared back at him. One set after another appearing like the ghost-lights of hell. Dozens of creatures stalked slowly out of the darkness into the light of his lantern. They had that same vague familiarity he remembered from over a year ago. He hadn't gotten a good look then, but he could see them clearly now.

They were dwarves. At least, they once were. The hellish lights glowed from where their eyes should have been, the sockets of their skulls clearly visible. A few hands reached out to him, but many of them were barely covered in any sort of living flesh. Most of the fingers, hands, and forearms were badly burned. In many places, the bones were exposed, but they looked different. Instead of the white skeleton and red sinew, his lantern reflected off of a black, rough-surfaced material that only looked like bone. It looked, for all intents and purposes, like rough pig iron. The flesh that was present sizzled where it met the blackened metal.

The leering faces that stared at Dellig were in the same state. Skin tore in places, revealing rictus grins of steaming black iron, with bits of molten metal dripping from exposed ribs and throats. Clinking and croaking sounds accompanied the mouths that opened and tried to speak. Ear-splitting shrieks came from hoarse throats and torn lips that covered angry, gnashing metal teeth. What remained of their clothes and armor was covered in soot, in some places smoldering with bright embers.

Why did they not attack?

"You don't recognize me," a voice said from somewhere in the wicked throng. It was guttural, unwholesome. It was female. It was familiar.

"Veerka..." he said, barely above a whisper, the word carrying on a hushed breath.

"You left me."

"No, I didn't...I mean, I didn't mean to..."

Dellig babbled, his throat hoarse and eyes growing warm and wet as he watched a figure emerge from within the crowd, which had grown chillingly still. The exposed, iron bones creaking. The frayed and torn clothing smoldering. The flesh searing and smoking. The eye sockets glowing and the mouths opening, closing, gaping. The one that stepped to the front had longer hair. Most of her features were intact, though her eyes were long melted away, a fiendish, forge-yellow glow coming from them like all the others. Some of the flesh had been torn from her arms, exposing the horrid bones of black iron beneath. It was his wife, Veerka. The one he thought he'd lost.

"It's ok," she cooed in a hoarse whisper. "I'm better now. I've been purified in His forge."

"His forge?" Dellig asked aloud. "Igni's forge?"

He didn't know what to think. Was she referring to the great forge of the dwarven smith-god? Dwarves had multiple gods in their pantheon, but the smith-god was revered above all. Dwarves believed that Igni would take all worthy dwarves and reforge their souls after death, creating the purest forms of themselves to feast in the warm hearths at the heart of the world for eternity. Veerka had given up on that belief, and all the others, many years ago. Dellig wasn't far behind.

"The dwarven gods are nothing. The elven gods are nothing. The human gods are nothing. Only That Which Dwells Below. The Baleful Forge. Your dwarven gods are engulfed by the bottomless glow, remade to serve in the endless molten sea. Every throne needs a master smith. Every smith, a forge. Every forge, ample coals. Every coal, a pitiless fire."

Veerka had no connection to the old beliefs. It made her

reckless and stir-crazy within the mountain's halls. She would come on every outing with Dellig to the gardens, sometimes sleeping outside between the rows of vegetables. Then, there was the trip roughly a year ago. Dellig shivered, accustomed to pushing the memory down and deep, but the images in his head were no longer ghosts. They stood before him in reeking bodies of burnt flesh and metal bones.

"They pulled me away. Took me. You ran." Veerka said, her tone matter-of-fact and without accusation. Dellig felt a year of repressed guilt blossom in his gut.

"I had no choice; I tried to save you!"

"I no longer need saving," she said, gesturing to the crowd around her.

Dellig looked out over the sea of eyes behind her, glowing in the dark. There are so many more than there were when he and Veerka encountered them. He no longer wondered where all the outcasts had gone or why the trade caravans had stopped. A more horrifying thought occurred to him: this was much closer than where he had lost her. They were getting closer to Stenden-brock. Then he noticed something else. Through tears in his eyes, he saw something that dulled the ache in his chest.

"I panicked. I'm sorry, Veerka. I didn't know what to do."

She held her hand out to him. "No more apologies."

When she answered his question, Dellig made sure to watch those around her. Those with jaws intact and lips to speak moved them in tandem with her words.

"You are no longer my wife," Dellig said, a tear making its way down his wrinkled face. His expression hardened, as did the hollow vestige of his lost wife.

"*She is one coal among many that feed the forge.*" The crackling voice that came from her still sounded like the woman he remembered, but it was different, somehow. Like a replica of a fine blade or a duplicate of a good painting. Familiar, but flawed in the most horrific way. *"Many souls feeding the flame of the Throne's vicious forge. More are always needed."*

Her hand hadn't moved. It continued to be held out for him as though he should welcome this fate. Dellig put away the gods of his ancestors, thinking they had forsaken them, if they even existed at all. Whether real or otherwise, the wretched master of these former dwarves had filled a void in the heart of the mountain. Possibly every mountain. It had been filled with fire and iron and pain. He needed to tell the elders.

Turning to run back in the direction of the city, Dellig saw the burning eyes close around that passage like a tide of angry lights, steam from their bones warping the air above them. He clenched his teeth painfully. Drawing his weapon, the guilt in his gut turned cold.

"Stay with me," he heard Veerka's voice say from behind him just before many hands grabbed him. Some were tough but fleshy and dug into his clothes and flesh. Others were iron-hard, and these were the ones that hurt abominably. The heat burned through leather and cloth, searing his skin.

Dellig screamed, his mind trying to listen to the voice of his wife behind him but picturing her as she was before. The pain wracked his body, and the hands lifted him from the ground. He felt himself being carried deeper into the gut of the mountain. These dwarves—outcasts, caravaneers, guards, his friend, and his beloved—all cursed to feed some unholy god's forge, carried him to the same fate. They were close to the city; it seemed they were getting closer all the time. He wondered, somewhere amid the searing pain, if all other dwarven cities and kingdoms were falling victim to the same awful deity. He cried again, but this time not for her.

CANDLES

THE BALANCE OF LIGHT AND DARK BECAME LESS DISCERNABLE AS time marched on. Hope and fear. Mercy and damnation. They changed hands so often that, sometimes, they even became hard to distinguish. The former could come at the most surprising moment, whilst the latter would strike when it was most desperately unneeded.

Father Marcus finished chiseling the last of the stones for now. The rest would hold for a while. He made sure not to move any and that one always touched the next, just as he was instructed. He looked into the overgrown streets and saw the broken statue in the empty pool down where the old village center sat in shadows cast by the large oaks circling its perimeter. He thought he saw something flicker but put the thought aside. It was too early.

He went back to his chapel on the hill overlooking the village below. Nothing out of the ordinary save for a lone traveler walking on the dirt road up the outskirts. A small smile crept across his face.

. . .

THE VILLAGE APPEARED a safe harbor to Allek, at least on the surface. The houses were neither in ill repair nor in pristine condition. Children busied themselves in the field while farmers tended crops and others went about their daily business. All in all, it was a great improvement over what remained of the other decrepit locales. People regarded him with a measure of curiosity, but he didn't get the feeling he was being watched with any ill intent. All save for one; a younger man with shaggy, curly hair and a sour scowl. This man's eyes followed him everywhere he went.

He asked about a place to take him in for the evening, putting the one sour inhabitant out of his mind. Each person answered him the same: there was no inn or tavern in this small hamlet off the beaten path. Hopefully, someone would take him in, but none so far had agreed to such. One kindly old woman pointed up the hill and told him to try the chapel.

"Father Marcus is quite agreeable," she said with a smile composed of mostly missing teeth.

His eyes followed the dirt road winding through short green grass and patches of wildflowers. A small bridge stepped over a river before twisting up a hill to a stone building. The chapel looked comforting and inviting, much like the one his mother took him to when he was younger.

The walk was enjoyable enough, the day being cloudy but without wind or rain. Only a slight breeze rustled through the grasses, creating an almost ethereal feel once Allek reached the chapel. Two heavy wooden doors stood out against the light stones that comprised the building. It looked several stories tall, but each floor became smaller and smaller, giving the impression of a beehive made of squares and sharp angles.

Wooden sigils were carved into the doors; or, rather, burned into them, given the scored and blackened nature of the images. The symbols belonged to Auchmeer, an obscure god that Allek recognized in name only. He was unfamiliar with the practices of the god's followers and knew it to be from the pantheon of the old world.

Allek knocked, a few polite but firm raps. They were indeed made of heavy wood, the sound of his knuckles fading immediately upon hitting the cherry-colored wood. He waited a few moments, knowing he'd never hear someone coming from inside.

One door creaked open and a man's face appeared. He smiled behind a black beard, clean and neatly trimmed, with solid gray streaks to either side of his mouth, revealing his age. He wore robes colored the burnt orange of torch embers trimmed in yellow.

"Welcome," he said with quiet warmth. "I'm Father Marcus. Please, come in."

The priest stood to the side and gestured for Allek to enter. Returning the smile, Allek walked past the priest slowly, conscious of his dirty appearance from days on the road. The inside of the chapel was plain and unassuming but well cared for. Pews lined one half of the room, while stools, tables, and shelves made up the other half. A red banner, hand-made by the look of it, bearing the symbol of Auchmeer, hung on the far wall behind the pulpit: a candle atop a crossed wheat stalk and dagger.

"Have a seat, young man," Father Marcus said, placing his hand on one of the simple wooden chairs.

Allek smiled, hoping not to offend. "I'm sorry, but I'm quite dirty from my travels."

Father Marcus waved his hand. "We'll get you a basin to clean up. What's a chapel for if not the weary and filthy?"

Don't have to tell me twice. Allek thought. He sat down in the offered chair and sighed, happy to be off his feet. "I'm Allek."

"Where have you come from, Allek?" the priest asked, walking around to the other side of the table.

"Kolstrom," Allek answered, setting his bags on the floor.

The priest whistled. "Near Kalthav? That's a ways north. And cold. Do you travel alone? I saw you alone, but Kolstrom's dangerous lands to walk by oneself."

"You saw me?"

"I was out front of the chapel earlier. Saw someone making their way to us from the north road."

"Ah, yes. I do travel alone." Allek leaned back in the seat, staring at the ceiling. "And every land is dangerous anymore."

Father Marcus looked down at his clasped hands. "Too true. How long have you been on the road?"

"Several days. Most other towns are empty or unwelcoming. When I came close to your borders and no one rode out to run me off, I was surprised. When I actually walked into town and none accosted me, I thought I was dreaming. Maybe even died on the road."

The priest chuckled. "You're quite alive, I assure you. We're a bit off the beaten path, but we manage on our own."

"That is the best news I've heard in many months," Allek sighed, leaning forward on the table and resting his head in his hands. "I really could use a secure place for just a day."

Father Marcus stood and walked over to the weary traveler, placing a comforting hand on his shoulder. "You won't have any worries here. We struggle like any others during these times, but this chapel has a bed for you for the night. I'll have some dinner ready later, as well. For now, go to the room in the corner, there," he pointed to a door to the right of the pulpit, "and there you'll find a small place to rest your head."

"I appreciate it, truly," Allek said, leaning back in his seat.

"I have some business to attend to for a while; we have a festival beginning in a few days. Your timing is fortunate."

His eyes furrowed as he looked at the priest, who was smiling back with genuine mirth. "A festival? What kind?"

"The Festival of Candles," Father Marcus answered warmly. "I'll be happy to explain later, but I have a baker waiting for me. Get some rest, for now."

The door leading to the village closed softly as the priest left the room. Alone in the interior of the small place of worship, Allek didn't feel the presence of the gods, Auchmeer specifically. That isn't to say he felt unwelcome. He simply no longer felt any kinship to the powers of the former civilization, like many others. Men, elf-kind, and dwarves made their own choices that led to this state, tempted by the strength of magic. Playing with powers they didn't understand. They had doomed everyone with their hubris; if there were gods, they either did nothing to stop it or were powerless to do so. In either case, he felt no piety toward them.

The room did, however, feel safe. There was something comfortably simplistic about it. He went to the room offered by the kind priest and slipped quietly inside, feeling like any noise in the silent chapel would be heard by the entire village.

The room wasn't large and contained a simple bed, a flat-topped dresser that doubled as a nightstand, and a simple painting of the symbol of Auchmeer in a crude frame hanging on the wall (likely produced by the priest himself). To Allek, it may have been a palace. He slid his hand-made leather travel bag off his shoulders and onto the floor. He untied the string strapping his waterskin to the side of it and pulled an apple from inside the bag. Getting comfortable on the bed, he ate, drank, and let his worries melt away for a moment.

He should have been tired. He should have fallen fast asleep in the warmth and safety of the small room and comfortable bed. Instead, his mind wandered. Memories of the past months on the road and the trials they brought beat in his head until it throbbed. Perhaps some time out in this village and, hopefully, seeing some friendly faces would help.

As soon as he set foot out of the chapel, Allek was greeted by one of the villagers. His stomach sank when he recognized it was the one that had been staring at him incessantly upon his arrival.

"You're not welcome here," the young man said.

Allek grimaced.

"You don't mince words, do you?" The question was obviously rhetorical.

The man appeared like a common worker, not any sort of fighter or troublemaker. With the exception of his perpetual snarl, he seemed wholly unremarkable. Then, he spat on the ground.

"How 'bout the lads and I take you for a tour?"

Two deep brown eyes bore through him. The man's jaw clenched, the lower half jutting out slightly. Allek felt this tour might be one you don't come back from. So much for the priest's talk of no worries here. He should've just stayed in the chapel.

"Sten!" came a shout from toward the village. "Leave him alone."

Sten's shaggy brown curls wobbled from the force of his head, turning to see who addressed them. Allek looked past the hostile villager and saw Father Marcus coming up the way. A grumble escaped the scolded man's throat.

"You know better," Father Marcus continued as he came up to them. "We welcome guests here. Always. What are you doing?"

Father Marcus came to a stop and Sten turned to face him, leaving his thin back turned to Allek. "We have a hard enough time managing on our own, Father. We don't need no additional mouths to feed or hands to hold!"

Sten's tone was one of frustration and justification rather

than outright aggression toward the priest. Even the violent ones in the village held Father Marcus in high esteem, apparently.

"*All* are welcome, Sten. If food was so hard to come by, we wouldn't be building up to our annual festival, would we?"

"We've all worked hard for that, Father. This one just up and arrives beforehand to take part in the fruits of our labors."

Father Marcus placed his hand gently on Sten's shoulder like he had Allek's earlier. The tension seemed to ease, if only momentarily. The priest's words came as gentle as ever.

"The festival is to celebrate Auchmeer's blessings and his teachings. That a tired wanderer found our village so close to the festival seems like divine providence, does it not?"

The irate villager turned to look at Allek. Though the fire of his hatred had lowered, the embers still burned. Sten appeared to chew on many words, debating on whether to speak. He finally turned back to Father Marcus and said, "I best go keep preparin', then."

As he stalked away from the two of them down the path to the village, the priest gave Allek a smirk. "Sten, take Allek with you. He can help with the preparations."

Allek's jaw dropped, his eyes widened, and no doubt Father Marcus saw the protest coming. Before he could get one word out, the priest walked past him and gave him a swift pat on the back.

"Auchmeer says nothing about guests not helping their hosts, young man. You're sturdy and healthy; you can do some good down there. Meet the villagers."

There was some mischievousness in the priest's tone. Allek had no issue offering to help his hosts, but certainly Father Marcus didn't have to send him with the one villager who openly despised him the most. Or perhaps the priest saw this as an opportunity for them to make amends or even, gods forbid, bond.

Allek caught up to Sten, who walked with long steps to carry him quickly away from the unpleasant situation. He walked just behind the villager, hoping to keep some distance. However, it would make for a long afternoon if he didn't attempt to ease the tension between the two of them.

"I'm not here to eat you out of house and home," Allek said. Sten continued walking in silence, his shaggy curls bobbing. "I am truly grateful for the rest. I'll work for my part; I don't expect any handouts."

"It's not handouts that concern me, *stranger*," Sten emphasized, still facing forward as he walked. "Our village has enough tragedy in its history, especially from folk who come along that road. If it wasn't for Father Marcus, we'd all have likely chased you off."

Allek scrunched his face at the assumptions. Sten was the only one who had shown any open hostility so far. He'd just have to interact with some of the other villagers, himself, and let them make up their own minds about him.

The conversation was left there for the time being. The village was alive with people of all ages working and preparing. Banners with the candle symbol of Auchmeer were being sewn and hung on houses and shops all along the streets. Tall candelabras of wood, brass, iron, and other materials were being placed outside of homes and along streets. Red candles adorned all of them.

Someone is going to have a lot of work to do, Allek thought. It would take an hour just to light those present already. He assumed there were going to be many more.

They stopped at an open field of grass between buildings. Long tables were being arranged with stools and benches. Some already had tablecloths and others were sitting at awkward angles, waiting to be lined up with the others.

"Go help with the tables," Sten said with no small amount of irritation. He walked off in another direction, not deigning to look at Allek.

Another middle-aged gentleman was maneuvering a few circular tables into place. He smiled and nodded, waving a hand to summon him over. Allek walked up and patted the table.

"Need some help?" he asked the villager.

"Moving some of these bigger ones would be a lot easier with two," the man replied.

Twelve large and heavy tables later, they both sat on one of the benches that still had yet to be paired with a table. Sweat beaded on Allek's forehead, but it felt good to be helpful. This village might not be such a bad place to linger in.

"Thank you," the man said, catching his breath. "I'm Trevin."

"Allek," he replied, offering his hand to shake. His palms were sore and rubbed raw. He discovered Trevin had heavily calloused worker's hands. Likely everyone in this village did, come to think of it.

"Greetings, Allek. I saw Sten dropped you off here. He's a friendly one, isn't he?"

Allek chuckled. "Can't be everyone's favorite, I guess."

"He's always been a troubled one," Trevin explained, his tone becoming sad. "Parents left years ago, been on his own since then. He and some of the other younger ones in the village get restless sometimes. You think they'd welcome new people, maybe find it a break from the dull day-to-day. But they don't. Our young folk are getting more insular. Untrusting."

Looking around at the banners, candles, and other festival preparations, Allek realized the village was a small pocket of normalcy in the darkness of the world. Could he truly blame them for wanting to protect it from that darkness?

"I suppose I'll just have to earn their trust. Or leave. I'd rather not, though."

Trevin patted his shoulder. "We haven't had too many travelers lately. Some new blood in town, another hand to work the fields or watch the cattle, would be nice. See how you like the festival, and then we'll talk."

"About this festival," Allek began as he looked at one of the god's symbols hanging on a nearby door front, "I'm not a religious man. I know Auchmeer by name and his symbol, but that's all. What's this festival about? What's going to happen?"

"Well," Trevin leaned on his knees with his elbows, then pointed to one of the streets lined with candelabras, "The candle is his biggest representation. Auchmeer is the patron deity of travelers and those who keep them. The candle guides travelers to safety, and the wheat and dagger remind us to feed and protect those who come to us in need. We set out all the candles to give thanks to Auchmeer, and then we eat from our recent harvests. Any guests who arrive during the three days leading up to the festival are meant to be taken in, treated well, and allowed to join the festivities. In the old days, the candles tended to draw curious people from nearby, merchants and such, so it helped keep them coming in despite Edgewick being off the main roads."

Allek couldn't help but think about the reception he'd received from Sten. "And if you don't?"

"I don't want to go about pissing off any gods, do you?" Trevin smiled. "We take the festival seriously, though. Sten's been warned in the past about his behavior, and those warnings have become sterner. If he keeps it up, well," the villager shook his head and shrugged, "I don't know what kind of punishment he'll be in for. They could kick him out of town, I suppose."

Banishment was a tough penalty nowadays. As good as execution or, given what Allek had heard from others on the roads, worse. He made himself stop lingering on the belligerent young villager and asked another question of Trevin, his curiosity leading him to another line of thought.

"It seems funny that a town called Edgewick has a chapel devoted to a god who is celebrated with a candle festival."

Trevin snickered. "I think it fits real nice. From what I remember being told growing up, the chapel was here first. The town came after, so you can figure there were no creative types at the first meeting. That was the old village, though. We don't...talk about that much. Just old wives' tales at this point. Father Marcus can probably tell you more about such things, though."

"The old village? This is a new one?" Allek asked incredulously.

"Uh," Trevin hesitated and rubbed the back of his neck, "As far as I know. I was born right here; the old village has been uninhabited for a long time. I don't know much about it and never asked. Never needed to. It's forbidden to go there and no one wants to. We have it good here, from the tales we hear from folk like you, so we don't go messing with things."

"And your priest didn't think to tell me this?"

"Have you even had a moment since you arrived to go prying around?"

Allek nodded. "Good point. I'll definitely ask Father Marcus about it," Allek said. Forbidden ruins or not, if this quiet hole in Alda's moldering wall was a place he could wait out the rest of his years, he genuinely wanted to know more about it.

He helped with what tasks Trevin asked of him. By the time they were done, pots of food were brought out to the tables and a few barrels of ale were rolled out; drinks in wooden mugs were administered to all who asked and in whatever quantities they desired.

A man and woman, whom he later learned were husband and wife, came out to a hastily-built stage. The woman began playing a faded-looking, well-used lute while the man accompanied her on a wooden double-recorder. They were both quite talented, and when they began playing, the festival started in full.

People began talking and laughing amongst each other. Children played and ran among their mothers' hems like pups. Trevin brought Allek a mug of ale for one hand and a wooden cup of savory-smelling stew for the other.

I'm starting to like this Auchmeer, Allek thought to himself.

He looked around for Father Marcus and saw him talking with a group of older people. They all wore yellow clothing and carried small candles, already lit. They must be devout followers receiving an impromptu lecture from the priest. Father Marcus glanced up and he smiled and nodded when his eyes met Allek's.

Allek lifted his mug and found a quiet spot at a table to enjoy his food and drink. The comfort was short-lived, as he also noticed Sten glaring at him from across the crowd. A few of Sten's fellows, both men and women, turned to look at Allek. Though their eyes didn't contain the same level of revulsion that Sten's did, it was clear they aligned with their friend's opinion of Allek.

He stayed a while longer, drinking more ale and partaking in more of the food but mostly the alcohol. The villagers he spoke with seemed friendly enough, but he couldn't be sure if it was the festival or their own share of too much drink talking for them.

Not long after sunset, the effects of the drinking began to blur his vision. His lips felt numb and he knew this was a sign to call it a night. The festivities would continue tomorrow, according to Trevin's explanation of the festival, so he'd be happy to return then. Perhaps, he could even speak with his new friend tomorrow and begin to find where he would best fit in this town for the foreseeable future.

The walk back to the chapel was peaceful, even with the

raucous sounds of laughter and celebration coming from the village. Candles lined the path all the way to the front door, stretching out before him like fireflies guiding him to a warm bed.

A rustling sound caught Allek's attention halfway to his destination. He stopped and listened. Tipsy though he may be, he wasn't drunk enough to be imagining things. He looked around, but the pathway the candles illuminated was narrow, and their light in such close proximity glared in his vision and prevented him from seeing further out into the dark of the unlit fields.

When he heard more rustling, he stepped outside the candlelight, off the path, and could see more clearly. In the cold, natural light of the moon, there was indeed something there. Next to a copse of trees, outside the glow of the village festival, a few figures stood. It was difficult to make out how many. Horned humanoid silhouettes gathered together and watched him.

Allek's heart pounded. These were the types of stories travelers shared over campfires and tavern tables. None of them ever ended well.

He took off in a sprint for the chapel. Not because he felt any particular deity would protect him, but for the protection of someplace, any place, with walls and locks. His feet pounded on the ground and he never looked back.

The chapel doors were, thankfully, unlocked. He ripped the door open and practically fell inside. He looked frantically for any sort of locking mechanism and found one—a double iron rod that slid through similar iron loops on both doors. Allek's eyes darted around the room in search of anything to protect himself. He had a knife in his bag, but fear overcame him and his hands ached for something to hold right now. He grabbed a tall candelabra, the ones in the chapel being made of heavy iron, and held it in front of him with both hands.

His breaths came loud and heavy, his head pounded, and his chest felt like it would burst. The chapel was silent and warm, so Allek focused on that. After several moments, he finally felt his breathing slow down. He tried reasoning with himself. Maybe he *was* seeing things. Maybe the alcohol, combined with the weariness of the day's work and the dancing candlelight in his vision, caused him to hallucinate.

He had just placed the candelabra back on the floor, one hand still gripping the cool metal when a knock came at the doors. He gripped the iron tighter, feeling his knuckles crack, and froze.

Another knock.

"Allek?" a voice called out. It was muffled, coming from behind the heavy wooden doors, so he couldn't discern who it was.

"Allek, it's Father Marcus. Are you ok?"

He cautiously approached the door, once again holding the makeshift weapon in his hands. He paused at the threshold, unsure if the person waiting on the other side was truly Father Marcus.

Another series of knocks. "Allek, please unlock the door."

The concerned tone sounded genuine, but he hadn't made it this far in life by not being overly cautious. He used the butt-end of the candelabra to slide the iron prongs from their resting place. They clattered to the floor, echoing among the empty chapel like a banshee's shriek.

The door opened slowly, and Father Marcus walked cautiously through, only opening it halfway. He closed the door and replaced the two-pronged lock. Allek set the candelabra beside himself, too distraught to put it back where it belonged, not even thinking about doing so. He let his fingers slip from the comforting iron.

The priest turned, his face scrunched in concern. "What's wrong, son? What happened?"

Allek looked past the priest to the door where the horned shadows watched him near the celebrating villagers. He couldn't remember how many there were, not a large number but more than a few. His eyes moved to look at Father Marcus, who was staring back with a mix of fear and concern.

"Did you see them?" Allek asked breathlessly.

"See who, Allek?"

Allek stopped, looked to the ground, and shook his head. Nothing sounded crazy anymore, did it?

"The shapes," he began, slowly, trying to find the words, "there was something, some things, out in the fields. I saw them on my way to the chapel. I couldn't tell how many; they looked like humans with...horns."

Confusion joined the emotions brewing in Father Marcus' eyes. His face scrunched just a bit further. "Horned humans. I have no idea what you mean, Allek. There's never been any trouble with such creatures here. Auchmeer has protected us for generations."

"I saw them, though, right next to the trees outside the village. They started running toward me!"

The hairs on his arms prickled at the memory of the fiendish silhouettes in the night. He grasped at words, but they all slipped through like water, splashing into his stream of thought and lost in the current. Finally, the eddies caught and dredged up what Trevin told him earlier.

"There's another part of Edgewick nearby, isn't there? What's there?"

Father Marcus didn't look very surprised or caught off guard. He simply nodded and replied, "Yes. A part of town I've yet to talk to you about."

"Would those things I saw have anything to do with it?"

The priest's eyes softened and his face dropped. "No," he said with dismayed conviction. "They wouldn't. I truly don't know what you saw, but I'll go look for myself."

Before Allek could stop him, the priest had already turned and opened the door. His eyes widened and he wanted to shout at the priest to stop, thinking the creatures were waiting at the door, ready to enter and tear them into bloody shreds or worse.

The night beyond the threshold was chill and quiet. No screams or evil shadowed figures accompanied the opening of the chapel doors. Only the faint flicker of multiple candles beyond the priest's back, lining the path to the village below the small hill.

"There's nothing here, Allek; come and see."

He approached the door slowly, his heart beating a little faster with each step. Father Marcus stepped aside; he stepped up to the empty, dark space and felt the wind brush his face. The sound of laughter and music still filled the village. Hundreds of yellow dots flickered among and around the simple wood and stone buildings.

Hesitantly, his head turned to a particular patch of trees, turned to a sinister black blob against the moonlight that contrasted heavily against the joyful, bright village next to it. There was nothing there, nor anything in the fields around it. The creatures had disappeared.

"I...I don't know what I saw, but I know I saw something," Allek said, his words breaking as he doubted his own sanity at the moment.

As he tended to do, the priest placed his hand on Allek's shoulder and gave a gentle squeeze. "You've been drinking, it's late, and you're likely exhausted. Get some sleep, and tomorrow I'll tell you about the other part of Edgewick. I promise."

The priest's hand squeezed just a little tighter. "You're safe here," he emphasized. Allek wasn't so sure, but the temple could be locked, he wouldn't be alone with Father Marcus around, and whatever he saw didn't follow him in. He would happily sleep this all away and let the nightmares go back into the dark where they belonged.

THE SMELL of food woke him, along with the sound of his door closing gently. Allek sat up in bed and saw steam rising from a bowl of porridge on the nightstand. Two apricots sat beside it, along with a mug of water. He drained the mug in one go, his throat parched from the night before, then ate his breakfast just as eagerly.

He brought the dishes out of his room and found Father Marcus sitting silently and reading from a book on the dais. The priest offered Allek a warm smile as he closed the book and rose from his chair.

"How are you feeling this morning?"

Allek looked at the door, recalling the previous night's events with some embarrassment.

"Better now. I'm sorry, I must have had more to drink than I thought."

"It's quite all right. In these times, we must be more forgiving of mistrust and fearful outbursts."

Allek shook his head. "I've seen much and heard much more on the roads. Maybe it's beginning to wear on me; turn my head to dark imaginings."

"I doubt there's any corner of Alda that doesn't bear some dark secret anymore," Father Marcus said in a low voice, his eyes sad. "Follow me, won't you?"

The priest led him through the chapel's front doors, the only way in or out of the building. The village lay in the thralls of post-night revelry. Few people stirred. The multitude of candles unlit, the candlesticks still plenty tall to be burned again this evening. Someone had the unenviable task of snuffing them all before retiring for the night. The copse that had been so menacing the night before was utterly unremarkable in the daytime, appearing no different than any of the other patches of trees surrounding the village.

Allek's gaze lingered on the trees for several moments before he turned to follow Father Marcus around the corner of the chapel. Behind the building, the river that ran in front of the chapel's hill made its way back here, like a horseshoe. It emerged from a line of trees to the right of the hill that shielded the fields from sight.

At the edge of the row of trees, sitting among the last of them behind the river, was a gathering of old, dilapidated buildings. Most were still standing with dark, empty windows that glared out of the shadows like skulls in the weeds and grass. At least one building had collapsed, the remains charred and black.

"That is old Edgewick," Father Marcus said softly.

"Does anyone live there now?" Allek replied in a low voice.

"No. Not for a long time. No one sets foot on those streets anymore," Father Marcus turned to look at Allek, who met his gaze, and the priest's eyes bore into him. "And neither will you, understand?"

He turned back to look at the ruined village. It was off-putting at first, but now, painted by the priest's dark tone, the buildings looked outright evil. Their appearance changed in an instant.

"I, uh, don't plan on it," he said firmly. "May I ask why?"

"Of course. Most of the villagers don't care for the details, some having heard stories from their folks. Right or wrong, it keeps them away and that's all that matters. Every town has its secrets, remember? Ours is...not so secret to those who live here, though the details may change."

Allek nodded. He understood how things were. Half the stories he heard in his life were probably mostly bullshit superstitions, but there was always a kernel of truth to them. From the origins of the world to a ghost haunting the manor where he was murdered for fucking the nobleman's wife. Most often, it was the worst parts at the hideous core of the tales that remained correct. And secrets always got worse.

"Those old buildings," the priest pointed towards them like he was telling a story to a child, "used to be the village. Cobblestone streets, a nice plaza that even had a statue in it, right next to a well-traveled road."

If he squinted, Allek could see the remains of a road leading around the left side of the hill below the chapel to another small bridge. The road was overgrown and barely visible, the bridge crumbling and looking ready to collapse into the tiny river at any moment.

"The original chapel to Auchmeer is over there, too. One of my predecessors, long ago, was well-liked among the people. He had many loyal worshippers that attended his services to our god of travelers. Took many weary ones in."

The priest was quiet for a moment. The wind blew softly, rustling the grasses. When he continued his story of Edgewick's secret, his voice was heavier.

"It came to light that the Auchmeeran priest actually followed another being: Subiri. Have you ever heard of her?"

Allek shook his head. "Can't say I have."

"It doesn't surprise me. She didn't have a large following. Some called her the Goddess of the Night Flame. The opposite of Auchmeer in every way. The former priest of Edgewick found it ironic and pleasing that he used the house of a god of warmth, welcoming, and light for sacrifices and rituals to a goddess of murder. Regardless, his actions were discovered when he became prideful and careless.

The village elders discussed at length how to stop him. His magic alone was dangerous and his inner circle would, and had, killed for him. They eventually sent one of their own to a nearby academy to request the assistance of one of their own mages. The academy magi couldn't have cared less who he worshipped, but readily accepted the opportunity to detain a practitioner of dark magic.

They sent a number of their own to bring the wicked false priest to justice, and on the eve of the festival at that. And, of course, he refused to acquiesce. His followers fled, but he stood his ground at the desecrated chapel. He fought the other magi but was quickly overcome. There wasn't enough of him left to bury."

Father Marcus pointed to the charred remains at the edge of the other buildings. "The chapel, the one there that's collapsed upon itself, is what remains of the battle. Everyone assumed justice was done. The activities that took place in the cellar of the chapel gave the place a reputation, so it was never rebuilt and none wanted to touch the rubble."

"They thought it was cursed," Allek assumed. He'd heard plenty of such tales.

"Indeed," Father Marcus nodded. His eyes continued to stare toward the village. "One of the magi stayed behind for a few days. She mentioned that there was a strong resonance of evil energy resonating from the chapel. The elders told no one this, for fear of a panic, but urged her to do what she could."

"How do you know this?" Allek interrupted.

"That mage was my ancestor," Father Marcus replied matter-of-factly. "They discovered a strong resonance, indeed. Whether via a curse, angered goddess, or something else, once the false priest's sanctum was destroyed, something was set loose."

Allek's heart sank. Thoughts of horned silhouettes returned

to haunt his memory and prickle his skin, despite Father Marcus saying he'd seen nothing of them.

"That next year, during the annual festival, few people were in the mood to celebrate. The chapel remained in ruins, and the mage, having taken up residence to continue studying the issue, hadn't found a way to remove the stain of the dark magic that was a blight on our village. That evening, a great tragedy struck.

From what remains of the accounts, some thought the festival began again. Many villagers saw lights outside their windows. As folk began stepping outside, screams could be heard. It was horribly disorienting, and none could believe their eyes at first. Skeletons, their bones held together by some wicked magic, were tearing into anyone they could get their hands on. They stripped the people of their flesh and brought them back as similar revenants right in front of witnesses' eyes. Through the mage's intervention and the bravery of a few armed men, they protected what was left of the village."

Allek grimaced at the imagery. That didn't sound like the things that chased him the previous night, but awful nonetheless. "You said there are accounts of this? Are they still written down somewhere? Or just old stories?"

"Places like these, the stories are better than the written word," Father Marcus answered with a half-hearted smile. "My ancestor's experiences have been passed down in our family as though it was the word of the gods themselves. And, yes, she wrote letters. She was a mage, after all."

"Oh," Allek chirped, surprised.

"Everyone spent the night in a few barns belonging to one of the farmers. None wished to stay where grotesque piles of bones and strips of flesh lay scattered along the streets. The mage kept them safe with some arcane wards, but the next morning everyone met to discuss what to do. Many left, some not even gathering their belongings for fear of returning to the village.

My ancestor asked for a few hours to investigate, and she was quite horrified by what she discovered. Some of the original revenants still wore clothing from before they died. She recognized some that belonged to villagers she'd known. The Subirian priest was not only murdering travelers but using the bodies of those that died in the village and were given funeral rights in Auchmeer's chapel."

The muscles in Father Marcus's jaw clenched beneath his beard. His hands clenched in memory of the unfathomable defilement and sacrilege.

"It's believed the Subirian cast a curse just before his demise, his power that he held over the skeletal revenants collapsed and freed them, or perhaps the saturation of the Fourth Sect magic he used continued to build until it pulled the creatures back to some sort of mockery of life. All those are possible, according to my ancestor, but none can be confirmed.

She assured the town she could keep the creatures at bay but not destroy them outright. She informed them she would stay to protect others from the village's lingering evil. A few decided to stay with her, this being the only home they'd known. Inspired, most of the village chose to stay and they rebuilt around those barns, which were eventually torn down. Edgewick has grown into what you see today. Still humble and persisting despite the darkness at its roots. They rebuilt the chapel, and she just happened to marry the new priest at some point. My lineage is the result and we now take the tenets of Auchmeer and the festival quite seriously. Most of us, anyway."

He likely clarified his point to include Sten and his ilk.

"And the old village...what did your ancestor do about the creatures? The revenants?"

The priest pointed again, this time leaning his head toward Allek. "Look at the border of the old village, by the river. Do you see the stones?"

Allek peered in the direction indicated. The small river, no more than a few dozen feet wide, flowed quietly next to the village. Tall grasses grew along the banks, obscuring his view. The buildings could be seen, but not any stones, such as those Father Marcus mentioned.

"No, I can't see anything."

"They are just beyond the river. The reeds and river grasses don't grow too near them, but I suppose they're not easy to spot. They circle the entire old village, but likely the trees and bridge hide them from this viewpoint, as well. They're all roughly the size of melons. Quite smooth; I believe they were taken from the river itself. Etched into each one are runes of binding and protection. My ancestor, in her notes, said the flowing river helps reinvigorate the magics bound into them. The creatures can't pass the threshold. At first, the village made it their duty to watch over the old village and ensure no one entered. After the Rupture, as the roads emptied, we became mostly forgotten."

No more words were spoken for several moments. Allek tossed the next question over in his head multiple times. He was curious but also afraid of the answer. Finally, he broke the calm silence between them.

"Have you seen them?" Allek asked, his voice low as though he'd not yet fully made up his mind to ask the question.

"Who?" Father Marcus asked, still staring at the village.

"The revenants. Have you seen them in the old village?"

The priest's head lowered. His face dropped, and he sighed deeply. "A few times."

He felt guilty now after asking. Father Marcus' head turned slowly to him, still bowed. His eyes bore a grave look that flickered like the candles beloved by his god. "You cannot go there, you understand? Under any circumstances. Travelers recently have come and gone within a day. Since you've remained here—and I'm happy you have, truly—you know what waits within those stones and you must abide by the most important law we have. Stay out of that village."

The weight of that warning wasn't lost on Allek. The calm, kindly priest spoke with a gravitas very uncharacteristic of him. He waited for a response, and Allek managed only to nod his head.

After such heavy conversation, it seemed important to clear the air. Father Marcus asked if Allek could help prepare for the second night of the festival. There was less to do, so he might be assisting with lighting the numerous candles. This seemed appropriate; if he was going to make a home here, then lighting some symbolic candles of the village's god could be a good omen for his new beginning.

That night, the festival continued in a manner similar to the night before: eating, drinking, music, and dancing. No new travelers arrived to join the festivities, of course. Although, it may have been for the best. Sten and his fellows kept to themselves for the most part, save for a few sideways glares. There were three men and two women that kept the angry young man company. Knowing their faces would probably save a lot of hassle in the future.

Allek preferred not to drink this night, so his mind would be clear for the return trip to the chapel. He had a feeling in his gut that whatever he saw the night before was not an isolated occurrence. However, Trevin and other villagers were quite insistent that he take full advantage of Auchmeer's hospitality. The second night resulted in more drinking than the first.

When his lips became delightfully numb, it was a sign that the next luxury he would indulge in was a warm bed. Well-wishes were given and cheers shared as Allek left the festivities that showed little sign of slowing down. His foot caught on something that came out of nowhere and he swayed to catch his balance.

The chapel called to him and the trail of lights leading its path blurred slightly in his drunken vision like a dream. His wanderer's cares and fears melted away in a comforting blanket of community and normalcy. This would make a good home. Perhaps he'd even attend services for this Auchmeer. A god of friendship and hospitality was quite a contrast to the world outside Edgewick.

Nearly halfway up the dreamlike, candlelit path, a nightmare coalesced before the chapel doors. Allek remembered, through the haze of alcohol and celebration, that Edgewick had sharp, bloody shadows. The horned figures waited, all in a straight line side by side, blocking him from the chapel. Some stood, some crouched, but all faced him, their hideous details still obscured by shadow. One of them flexed their fingers, nearly making a fist before relaxing them again.

Allek began breathing heavily, panic threatening to root his feet to the ground. The agonizing moment hung in the air. No sound came from the creatures and most were completely still, black statues of death and terror. He risked a glance at the copse of trees where the figures lingered the night before. No more were there. They were bolder, waiting right here for him. At least, now, there was no doubt they existed. This was no hallucination caused by flickering light and darkness enhanced by drink. He'd been drinking again this night, and doubly so, but fear-induced sobriety was taking hold along with the rising panic.

He turned the fear from freezing to fleeing; turning on his heels, he made a frenzied sprint down the path back to the village where the sounds of the festivities continued. Where light and people and safety were within reach. The sounds of multiple other feet pounded behind him. The creatures gave chase. He didn't turn, didn't think, and didn't stop. He urged his legs to carry him faster, prayed his drunkenness didn't cause him to stumble and fall to be torn into pieces and become one of the cautionary tales told around the campfires.

Everything was a blur. Dots of candlelight became thin yellow lines as he rushed by the candelabras. The music melded into his harried breathing and the sound of so many pounding footfalls.

Something crashed into him. Allek felt the impact and nearly fell off his feet. Reaching out, he grabbed something in his fist that kept him standing and realized it was not some*thing* but some*one*. He reared back his free hand in a fist, ready to drive his knuckles into the face of what had caught him.

"Allek! What are you doing?" a voice shouted.

His head swiveled around in both directions. The light and sound disoriented him, but he soon realized he was back in the village. His hand clutched someone's collar tightly.

"What's wrong, son?" the voice asked again, deeply concerned. "It's me, Father Marcus!"

Still breathing heavily, his chest heaving, Allek stared at where the voice came from, and finally, his vision cleared. The priest looked at him with wide eyes, his hands up in surrender.

His frenzied thoughts coalesced and congealed back into something recognizable and untainted by blind fear. His fingers unfurled and he lowered his hand that was once raised to strike blindly at whoever or whatever was in his way. Shame blossomed in his stomach, and he released his grip on the priest's orange robes.

"I'm sorry..." Allek began, but excuses and reasons evaded him.

"You look terrified. What happened?"

It took a few moments before he was prepared to tell the priest the truth. He knew he was no longer imagining this. He was certain of it.

"I saw them again; the horned figures came back."

The priest's brows furrowed.

"This time, they were waiting for me at the chapel."

"They were inside?" Father Marcus interrupted, his voice a garble of outrage, concern, and an attempt to not let others hear.

"No, they waited outside. They chased me back here, but I don't know where they went."

Allek's head swiveled and his eyes darted about. His voice broke as he tried explaining more. He was quickly shushed as Father Marcus put an arm around his quaking shoulders. His hands shook as the adrenaline drained from his body, and the sights, sounds, and smells of the festival took over.

Laughter and music sounded strange after the frantic beating of his heart coupled with the horrid footfalls so close behind him. The smell of food, wine, and incense contrasted bitterly with the taste of blood in his mouth; he must have bitten his tongue whilst charging down the path from the chapel.

Father Marcus guided him to a nearby seat; a simple log stump near the festival grounds, but it would suffice. Allek didn't care to be near many people at the moment, but numbers would feel safer. He didn't notice Father Marcus waving over someone and was startled when he heard another man's voice talking above him.

"Maurice, watch over Allek for a moment. I'll be right back."

Allek turned to see where Father Marcus was going and saw him heading straight for the outskirts of town toward the chapel path. He walked with clenched fists and purpose. Allek began to protest, but the man named Maurice stopped him with a few gentle words.

"Ol' Marcus is tough. He'll be fine," Maurice assured him.

His mind raced the entire time the priest, his closest confidant in years, was gone. He didn't know for how long. He jumped at every flickering shadow cast by torches and candles caught in the wind. He clutched his arms around his chest at first but eventually relaxed little by little. Maurice brought him a drink and some food, though Allek had no appetite to speak of. The ale he drank readily, however.

At one point, he looked up to see someone approaching and thought the priest was returning. He saw the glowering face of Sten instead.

"The hell is your problem?" the crude youth asked. "Our food and drink too much for you?"

Allek looked up at him, not in the mood for the belligerent young man's antics. Allek quietly returned the stare, waiting for his frayed nerves to be pushed just one more time.

"Back to the festival, Sten. This isn't the time," Maurice chided harshly. Sten sniffed derisively and walked away back to his waiting fellows.

"Fuck him," Allek heard one of the others say, their voice just audible over the noise.

Father Marcus finally returned and thanked Maurice for keeping Allek company. When his babysitter was out of earshot, the priest began speaking in hushed tones.

"I saw several footprints on the path to the chapel but nothing else. However, that path is traveled all the time." He shook his head. "I don't know what to say, Allek. I don't know what you could be seeing."

"It's real," Allek insisted in a harsh whisper. "They were right in front of me."

"I'm not saying they aren't real; I just don't have any other answer for you. I can assure you, however, that you are safe in the chapel. Why don't we go back together? I'll take you to your room, lock the door for good measure, and we'll both get some sleep and see what we can find out tomorrow?"

Allek leaned his head back and looked to the sky. The stars flickered above like candles of their own, millions of them. The fresh alcohol began to calm his nerves and his face felt warm.

Having a priest escort him back would be much more agreeable.

He sighed and said, "Alright. I definitely need some sleep."

They returned to the chapel, bypassing the activities of the second night of the Festival of Candles. No horrible creatures watched from the trees, the fields, or anywhere else. They disappeared yet again.

The inside of the chapel was warm and inviting as ever. The candelabrum lit the interior more brightly than those outside. They bid each other goodnight, and when Allek closed his door, a soft click of a lock on the other side followed soon after.

He removed his clothes and sat them next to his bag. His eyes lingered on his dagger strapped to the side for several moments. He finally untied the rough cord holding the sheathed blade in place and tucked it under his pillow. As he lay in bed, he wondered if he could truly stay here. Fear clawed at his stomach as it occurred to him that should he leave Edgewick, the creatures may follow. Were they tied to him or the festival? Or the chapel? No one had mentioned the horned figures before and Father Marcus acted like they simply didn't exist. He was the only thing tied to them that he knew of.

His mind swirled in a flurry of questions and conspiracies. Beneath it all was the fear of all the unknowns. He stared at the darkness, his hands on the dagger beneath his pillow. The sound of his breathing was all he could hear as the stones of the chapel prevented all sound from reaching him: celebration, nature, even damnation. He waited for sleep to come.

THE SOUND of the lock clicking and door opening woke Allek from his light sleep. The gentle voice of the priest projected from the light coming from the partially opened door.

"I apologize for waking you, but I have to go to the village and didn't think you wanted to be locked in this room all morning."

Allek propped himself up on one shoulder, the cool morning air washing across his bare chest. "Thank you, I'll be up."

The priest entered the windowless room and lit the candle on the nightstand. The first day it felt slightly suffocating to one so used to the open road. Now, fueled by his paranoia, it felt vastly more secure.

"I hope you're feeling better. We'll talk more as soon as I'm finished with my morning business."

"Thank you," Allek replied.

He was left alone in the silence once more. Father Marcus also left a basin of water and a clean cloth, so he washed and dressed. Then, he decided to take the dagger from under his pillow and strap it around his waist, under his clothes, to take with him for the rest of the day and night.

Visiting the village was tempting. Fresh air and a walk under a blue sky might be good for him, but he couldn't bring himself to leave the chapel. Seeing those things so close chained his courage, broke something in him that he couldn't fix.

All morning, he sat in the stone confines of the chapel of Auchmeer. There were hymnal books and religious texts to read, which made for boring company. At one point, he even dared to crack open the other door in the building to peek inside the priest's room. It was remarkably similar to the one he'd been loaned, albeit more lived and worked in as it apparently doubled as Father Marcus' office.

Just a simple priest, indeed, Allek thought to himself.

Father Marcus eventually returned and found Allek sitting at the table where they'd first talked, just inside the front doors. Allek was reading about Auchmeer's teachings of hospitality in great detail. It made more sense to him why the village was so welcoming if this is what they believed so wholeheartedly and heard at every sermon. The idea of welcoming others into your community like family also gave rise to calling Auchmeer's priests 'father' and the priestesses 'mother'.

"Have you been here all day?" the priest asked, surprised.

"I haven't felt like going anywhere," he responded.

Father Marcus pulled out a seat for himself. After sitting down, he clasped his hands together and looked at Allek sympathetically.

"I've asked around town about the things you've seen," he began. Allek looked up at him with tired eyes, not expecting any good news.

"No one has even heard of such creatures. None of those who've visited us in the past ever mentioned any such thing to the villagers, either."

Allek stared for a moment, his mind churning. Finally, he asked, "Could it have something to do with the old village?"

"How do you mean?"

"Could the runes be weakening? Could the revenants be getting out?" Allek asked flatly.

Father Marcus shook his head. "No. I check the stones daily. Make sure the runes aren't wearing away. My ancestor left notes for how to replace them if one looks ready to break or is too far worn."

Allek ran his hands through his hair. There was little that made sense in this world, but finding yourself stalked by horned shadows was a nightmare come to life.

"Have you ever heard of anything like this in your own travels?" the priest asked.

"I've heard a lot in my travels. Any story that started like this was never good. How can I stay in a town where these things haunt me? And yet I'm too afraid to leave."

"This world is a strange and dark place. Tonight is the last night of the festival. I'll stay with you and we'll solve this together."

Sighing deeply, Allek felt a wave of relief and thankfulness wash over him. "Thank you, Father."

The two of them spent the rest of the day on Father Marcus' rounds. Allek was privy to every aspect of the priest's daily life. Some of his preconceived notions were proven correct, but others were pleasantly defied. Father Marcus seemed a man who truly loved his village family.

The sun grew low as the day wore on. Instead of the streets emptying as people returned home, the crowds began to grow in anticipation of the final night of the festival. Most villagers were gathering near the festival grounds. Father Marcus took Allek around to a few homes to check on stragglers to see if they would be attending. The side streets were practically deserted, as nearly the entire village would be in attendance.

The festivities started earlier than usual, before the sun had set. Everyone was eager to begin the celebration, knowing this was the last night until the following year. As the sun disappeared and the candles replaced it as best they could, the music and laughter seemed to grow even louder.

Allek and Father Marcus enjoyed a drink and a pastry, sitting near a table of elderly farmers reminiscing about celebrations past. A young woman approached them, her eyes glistening with unspent tears.

"Father Marcus, may I speak with you?" she said, her voice shaking.

"Of course; what is it, young lady?" he replied with genuine sympathy.

Her eyes flicked to Allek before she added, "Could we possibly speak in private?"

"Yes, of course. Allek, excuse me for just a moment."

Allek nodded, happy to sit in the middle of the revelry and

wait for him to return. No one else bothered him, not even Sten, and he drank and ate in peace.

Then, something tugged at the back of his mind. He felt eyes on him. Walking alone for years tended to make one wary of being watched. He looked around and saw nothing unusual at the festival. He stood slowly and looked toward the edges of the crowd; still nothing unusual. When his eyes went beyond, to the darkness of the streets, that's where he saw it.

Hidden within the confines of a narrow alley, only visible because he would recognize that shape anywhere, was the horned head of one of them. For just a moment, Allek thought that he only imagined it, that there was no possible way one of them would wander into the village, but then the head moved. It slid gently to the side, exposing one narrow arm and shoulder. It raised its arm and pointed at him. Allek looked around to see if anyone had noticed, but every other villager continued to drink and laugh and eat and dance. The arm never moved; it continued pointing in his direction.

"Marcus!" Allek shouted and began turning around, looking everywhere for the priest. He couldn't spot him in the crowd. He then tried imploring those nearby so that anyone could look at the figure that continued pointing at him. Everyone was either too drunk or too distracted to pay him any attention. After trying time and again to get another witness, Allek looked over to the shadowed alley and saw nothing was there.

At that point, he began frantically asking if anyone had seen the priest. No satisfactory answers were given. Allek searched and couldn't find him, either. He slid his hand under his shirt and touched the dagger that was sheathed there. It calmed him somewhat. He decided to make a run for the chapel.

This time, he hadn't drunk enough to inhibit his wits. He ran as fast as his legs would carry him up the chapel's path. He slammed into the doors upon reaching them and pushed them open. They creaked loudly, and he was greeted with terrifying, unfamiliar darkness; all the candles inside had been snuffed out. In the cold light and sharp shadows cast from the night through the wide-open chapel doors, several sinister figures waited near the dais. They stood facing in his direction, standing there as they always did.

Allek stared back, panic rooting his feet in place. The figures didn't move. They didn't even appear to breathe.

"What are you?" Allek shouted at them. "What do you want with me?"

His voice echoed against the stone. He thought he heard one of the things laugh or possibly growl. He couldn't be sure. He turned to run back to the village, but another one came from the side of the hill, opposite the copse of trees.

Allek turned sharply, just in time to not be grabbed by a fiendish hand. He stumbled and fell, rolling down the hill in the grass and wildflowers. He saw them not far behind, in a crouched run, their hands clawing at the grass. They made horrible grunt-like snarls as they drew near.

He picked himself up and ran, urging his feet to move faster. One of them leaped from off to one side of him. Two muscular arms wrapped around his waist. Allek grunted as he fell onto the ground, grabbing at the creature's saggy flesh. He couldn't reach his knife, so he began pummeling the creature in the side.

He got away and continued running. Trees passed him as he ran. He looked around and saw the shapes darting in and out among the trunks of the woods. He was disoriented again and knew if he was lost in a forest, there was little he could do to get away from these creatures. However, it wasn't long before he was in an open field again.

No sooner did he see the stars in the sky; however, than another one of them tackled him from behind. The others had caught up. One reached out and pulled at his shirt. He screamed and wrenched away, the cloth tearing off in the thing's grip. He fell back and rolled again, this time hearing a splash and feeling soaking wet. When he stood, he began to feel the cold seep in. His mind had become a blur once again, a mad panic of survival instinct.

He reached for the knife, but one of the creatures came at him again. He grabbed at its arm and let its weight carry it off to the side of him. The thing was fast, however, and turned to grapple with him again. They tussled—the world spinning and splashing until he felt his feet catch on something and he fell like a toppled tree. The creature came with him and they both crashed to the ground in a tangle.

Laughter came from nearby. Allek's foot ached, as did the back of his head where he landed. His chest heaved, and he heard the sound of the creature next to him standing on its feet.

"Fucking hell!" came a man's voice, followed by more laughter. "You got him good, Sten!"

Allek's gut grew cold. His heart continued pounding. Allek flinched when he saw, standing over him, a human-shaped figure wearing dirty clothes that hung off their body like loose skin. A hideous horned mask made of papier-mâché covered their head. He scrambled to his feet and backed away from them.

"You fucking prick," came a familiar but muffled voice under the mask. "You ripped my shirt. I save this one for the fields. Asshole."

Allek looked behind the figure to see three others, all dressed similarly with masks of their own, standing in the tall grass. A young man and woman were running out from the trees to join them. Allek recognized the woman as the one who came to Father Marcus in tears.

A couple of the figures removed their masks. They were all the youth that were a part of Sten's little clique. Allek looked over to the figure next to him as they removed their mask. An angry Sten was glaring back at him, a half-smile on his face.

"Has he shit himself yet?" one of the women asked, calling from the other side of the river.

"What the hell is this, Sten? Why..." Allek began, his voice filled with anger.

"We have a good thing here, and don't need others bringing shit in from the outside," Sten interrupted, practically growling the words. "Every new body in this village comes from out there and who knows what they'll bring with them."

The angry youth put his hands on his hips and turned around to look behind him. He cursed to himself softly before turning back to Allek.

"I know Father Marcus will make my life hell if he finds out about this." Sten gave Allek a look that said the games were over. "You say a word, and we'll both suffer for this, we clear?"

Sten looked over to his waiting friends. They all returned glares that made their point to Allek clear.

"Just so we know where we stand," he finished, before turning to go back across the river.

"The river..." Allek whispered to himself. His rage at the pranksters making his life a living hell the last three days burned within him, but something colder was beginning to take its place. He looked down where he fell and saw that what he tripped over was a melon-sized stone. It was partially buried, sturdy in its position, and didn't roll out of place.

"We're in the old village," Allek whispered, a different kind of fear entering his voice.

Sten turned and gave him a disgusted look. "You believe all that shit? Get back to the festival before we get caught."

"You've come here before?" Allek asked in a low voice, thinking he heard something down one of the crumbling streets.

"No," Sten scoffed. "That's an offense punishable by banishment. No excuses. So keep this to yourself, too, for fuck's sake."

Sten turned his back on Allek and walked away. He went all the way to the stone ring and stopped.

"Come on, Sten. We have to get back," called one of his friends.

"Ok, I'm coming," he replied. Allek noticed his voice had changed drastically. It had trembled.

More unsettling noises came from the empty buildings and dark windows. A scraping and crackling noise, difficult to place what it was.

"Stop fucking around; let's go!" another voice called.

Allek saw something moving from the darkness. He blocked it out, tasted bile, and willed himself to turn around. He started to walk quickly back across the rune-written stones, but stopped next to Sten.

What's happening, Allek thought in a panic. *Why can't I move any further? I need to get past the stones...I have to get past the stones!*

"Sten, what's going on?" one of the women shouted, her voice beginning to shake, as well.

Allek looked over; Sten's eyes were wide and his face pale. "I can't move," he said flatly. "I can't move. Help me!" he shouted to his friends. One of the young men began to walk forward when he stopped, as well. Several of their mouths opened and they made the worst kind of scream: the silent kind. The color drained from their faces and one of them fell back into the grass, catching themselves by the elbows.

Hoarse, dry cries came from behind Sten and Allek. The scraping and crackling sounds increased until they sounded like a storm. Dozens of skeletal bodies, draped in rotting clothes and strips of mummified flesh, threw themselves against the invisible barrier of the stones. They clawed and wailed at the people gathered across the river. They screamed, a sound like fire whipped about in a fierce wind, as they impotently longed to be free of their confines.

When the revenants saw they were still prisoners in the village, they stopped. The sudden silence rang horribly in Allek's ears. Next to him, Sten's jaw clenched, and veins pushed through sweating skin, likely attempting to fight the magic of the stones just as he was.

With hideous swiftness, skeletal fingers wrapped around Sten's face. More gripped his arms and legs. He was pulled back as the hideous sounds of gurgled screams and fiendish ripping caused tears to fall from Allek's eyes. Some of the gathered young folk screamed now, and they all fled back into the trees, back toward the village.

Allek looked up at the chapel, rising above the stretch of trees. No lights shone from the windows of the main room. Father Marcus had yet to return from the festival. Likely, he was looking for Allek. He kicked at the stones, but from this side, they refused to move at all.

Pulling the dagger from under his shirt, he turned around to face the damnation behind him. Many of the skeletal revenants were soaked in red. What was left of Sten was unrecognizable. The poor man was reduced to red, exposed bones with a few strips of flesh hanging from them. The rest of him was scattered in bits and pieces. He had been hollowed out, made ready to hold the flickering light of the dark goddess.

A dark fire flickered in the sockets of the revenants' skulls. Where their joints met and moved, pale sparks accompanied a crackling, grinding sound. They were held together by the hatred and wickedness of the Night Flame. Driven by Her desire to murder and snuff out the light of the living.

At least, that's what the books in the chapel described. He'd find out soon enough. The dagger clattered to the ground. It would do no good here. He could run and fight the horned creatures all he wanted; they were just men and women with selfish motives. There was no running from the damned nor the magic that contained them.

The revenants did nothing quietly. A hundred crackling joints sparked at once. Dozens of rustling screams filled his ears. He closed his eyes and hoped it would be over quickly. As hard fingers broke his flesh and centuries-old teeth drew his blood, it certainly wasn't quick enough.

FATHER MARCUS RAN to the back of the chapel. When he couldn't find Allek, he returned to the chapel to see if he had better luck there. Finding the doors open and candles snuffed, he knew something was amiss. He'd called for Allek but received no reply.

Looking down at the bottom of the hill, he saw a group of people fleeing for the copse of trees near the village. He couldn't tell who they were from this distance, but he would go find out immediately. Everyone knew to avoid the river and the trees that grew next to it, and all had agreed; every villager born agreed from the moment they could walk and talk. He assumed it was Sten and his lot. They were always rebellious, but there were usually six of them. Those running from the trees counted only five.

His eyes scanned over to the old village and found the source of their flight. The revenants revealed themselves this year. The young people must have gotten quite close. As he continued to look among the evil hauntings of former Edgewick, something caught his eye and made his heart sink. Dark stains covered the ground and the stones, glistening black in the moonlight.

The number of revenants had always numbered thirty-seven. It took him several years and many attempts to count them all, but he arrived at that number every time they appeared. They always tested the stones' durability, but Father Marcus' ancestor must have woven magic into the stones to bind them in place against the creatures.

Now, however, as he finished another count and hoped that he arrived at the same number, one of his worst fears was realized. There were now thirty-nine. Two more dark candles had been lit for Subiri. He didn't need to guess who they were. Those who fled, having disappeared into the copse of trees, will have to explain themselves tomorrow. They will likely all be banished, and they will count themselves lucky they aren't held accountable for murder, for they took part in nothing less.

All that was left of the night, the final few hours of the Festival of Candles, would be spent in mourning. At least for him. He would let the rest of the village celebrate. They would have plenty of time to dwell on the horrid fate of Allek and Sten for many years to come. May it be a stark reminder to them of their foundations, of what happens when darkness prevails.

THE RITUAL

THE DARK LANDMASS ON THE HORIZON YEARNED TO TOUCH THE deep purple of night above it, but try as it might, stretching from one end of the world to the other, a line of deep magenta cut the two like a slithering flatworm, forbidding them to embrace. It would linger there until the black of night took hold and the stars shone, refusing to reveal the secrets between them.

Kael breathed deep the sharp air of twilight. The time had finally come. Years of research and sacrifice, both metaphorical and literal, led to this moment. He would finally get to do his own research; gain access to the oldest and most sacred of the Dread Praises, study the most consecrated and profane incantations of the Fourth Sect. His induction as a full member of the Black Gnarl would take place tomorrow evening when that holy band sat once more on the horizon. Tonight, a lucky few would undertake the ritual first.

One more mundane clerical task was handed to him. After tomorrow, he would be doling out such trivial matters to others. Perhaps he'd receive an acolyte of his own to pander to his simpler needs whilst he was busy furthering the greater purpose of the order.

He briskly walked across the worn stones of the castle's main bailey. Old, tattered banners hung from the keep and main corner towers. The smaller turrets had pennants of similar disheveled quality whipping in the wind. The Black Gnarl currently had bigger plans than holding castles and territory, so they left the old heraldry of the once-glorious Promise Hold where it was. The security and ample rooms provided by the location were its real value to the order.

Other black-robed members of the Gnarl were scattered about various parts of the grounds, like wraiths haunting old ruins. A few individuals didn't wear the robes. There were very, very few of these types. All were speaking in inaudible tones with their contacts within the order. They served some purpose or another, but their time here was always brief and they were never left alone. None ever made it past the main bailey, let alone the gatehouse to the inner corridors of the hold.

Not even Kael was allowed to venture beyond the basement level. He sighed, wondering what awaited below; he'd find out after his final initiation rites. The deeper parts of Promise Hold were the topics of rumor and myth among the Gnarl's acolytes. To the order's guests and collaborators, they were the subject of fearful conjecture. Such power was a valuable commodity.

Many nights were spent around simple dinners with his fellows discussing things they'd heard and the slightest glimpses of what awaited those who passed their ritual initiation. The followers of the Many-Faced Worm were secretive even among other denominations of the Black Gnarl. Their own acolytes knew that knowledge of their god and the powers it so closely withheld and cautiously relinquished in jealous trickles to its followers, was only meted out to those who were worthy. Those that were not, were never seen nor spoken of ever again. You entered the gatehouse an acolyte—nameless and ignorant—and emerged a brother or sister of the order. Or not at all. You remained nameless and were forgotten. Who knew what else became of you.

He arrived at the outbuilding to which he had been summoned. The plain, square structure was attached to the western inner wall. The diamond symbol of the Black Gnarl was painted on the door but was embellished further with a worm-like serpent with several screaming faces circling it. This was the symbol of his denomination. Kael knocked and waited patiently.

"Enter," came a loud and firm reply.

The old door creaked open. Inside, the room smelled of paper, ink, and wax. Books, both old and new, were stacked in piles of many sizes. Lit candles created orbs of dancing yellow light in seemingly random places. A cluster sat, melting, on top of an old but well-maintained desk. A black blob of a man sat at the desk, writing. His robes stretched over his large, meaty shoulders, his quill scratching endlessly on a page before him. Many different pages lay scattered and piled atop one another on the desk. How he knew which one to write on was a mystery to Kael.

One of the pages contained a sketch of their denominations' patron god. It was crude and undefined, as most depictions were. The words of one of the order's masters echoed in his memory. "To see the great worm is to see death, to taste madness, to hear unfiltered despair." It was taught to all acolytes that this was meant to be a trial. To receive the blessings of their god, they must be able to bask in his presence. More would be revealed as they passed one initiation and onto the next, those who were strong and worthy passing into higher echelons of their god's favor.

The hooded head looked up and a soft-featured, many-chinned face was exposed by the candlelight. Small but intelligent eyes peered back at Kael.

"You summoned me, Master Bolthus?" Kael asked.

The round, baby-faced historian and record keeper squinted at the acolyte as though he didn't recognize him. After a moment's hesitation, he nodded, causing his jowls to shake.

"Yes, acolyte," Brother Bolthus said in a bored tone. Kael wasn't even worthy of having his name mentioned as an acolyte. "I need you to deliver this to Master Dunscale."

He reached under the haphazard pile of papers and pulled out a folded letter sealed with wax. The seal bore the order's diamond symbol without the embellishment of his denomination. This letter was from some other chapter of the Black Gnarl elsewhere in the world. Kael saw the dark, curling tattoos on Bolthus' hand, denoting him as a full initiate. The same tattoos that would be written on Kael's own hands soon.

Master Dunscale was among the inner circle, the lead "diplomat" of Kael's denomination who assisted in turning any remaining cities and leaders to the order's agenda and dealing with other branches of the Black Gnarl. He was often away, and even when present at the hold, would rarely interact with the acolytes. Why Kael was summoned to deliver a message to him was puzzling, but he wouldn't dare decline.

"You'll need this." Bolthus grabbed something off the other side of the table. It was a tarnished silver disc roughly the size of Kael's palm. His order's symbol was, however, on this disc. It would allow him passage into the deeper halls. In the case of a silver pass, he could go as far as the second subfloor.

Kael took both the letter and the pass, placing them in a pocket within his robes. He felt the weight of the disc pulling the cloth against his shoulders and sash. He felt a tiny thrill at the anticipation that he would see past the first floor.

The record keeper squinted his puffy eyes at Kael. Kael realized he was smiling. Repressing the grin on his own face and apologizing for delaying, Kael left Bolthus to his work. Returning to the bailey, he saw the time of day drew closer to tonight's initiation. If he hurried, he might even catch a glimpse of the new full-fledged brothers and sisters or even hear some of the ceremony.

The gatehouse, set in a secondary, smaller wall surrounding the keep, opened for him as soon as he stepped within ten feet of it. Kael looked up and saw the black, yawning windows where the gatekeepers saw him arrive. The courtyard that led to the first floor was nearly empty. Only a few shrouded figures meandered about the weed-clotted area.

As he made his way inside the large, imposing stone heart of Promise Hold, the light of a dozen torches greeted him. The castle was old even before the Rupture, so few windows were present and many torches, candelabras, and chandeliers were required to keep it lit. The greeting hall, at least that used to be its purpose, now served as a checkpoint for all who entered. A few guards were positioned here, the rare members who wore belts with sheathed swords on their hips. These were mostly for show, as their magic would be their first line of defense against any intruders. The swords were a badge of office, of sorts.

They ignored Kael, immediately recognizing him. After entering one of the open, arched doorways and arriving at a door that led to the first subfloor, however, one of the guards stopped him. He revealed the silver disc from within his robes and was allowed through.

Kael took a deep breath. Even before his initiation rites, he would be graced with sights forbidden to him for years prior. He smiled again, anxious to see and hear what awaited.

The door led directly to a hall, much like the rest of those in the castle. At the far end, however, A staircase trailed down into darkness. The stone used in its construction was different from those of the hall floors and walls. It was newer and less worn. This had been added after the Black Gnarl acquired the structure. The stairway was fairly short and stopped at an open doorway. The room beyond was built of the same stone as the stairway. Kael assumed from here on, he would see all new rooms constructed strictly for the order's use.

A pair of guards swiftly approached him but stepped aside after being shown the silver disc. Kael looked around and saw multiple large arched doorways in each direction. He realized he was so excited to see the lower levels he never asked exactly where Brother Dunscale was or what floor.

He hazarded a guess and went to the left. Multiple doors passed him by, all closed. They were heavy set and he couldn't hear anything through them. The acolytes were only told that the first floor consisted of a library, dormitory halls for new full initiates, and study rooms. It occurred to him that Brother Dunscale would have little reason to be here.

He returned to the central room and decided to ask the guards where he might find the Black Gnarl diplomat. They instructed him to make for the third subfloor, the last the disc would allow him access to, and make for the center passageway. Brother Dunscale's study would be on the left.

Thanking them, Kael went to the center arch, past the guards, and down the staircase. It wound back on itself, showing that at least the central rooms were directly atop one another. Kael repeated the same process as before, passing the guards with the disc and skipping the second floor altogether. Acolytes weren't told what this floor held, but it appeared much the same. So far, the trip into the underground levels of the Promise Hold, the soul of his order's operations, was quite mundane.

He felt deflated. He'd always held grand visions of what awaited beyond initiation. Stories of what the Black Gnarl had achieved in centuries past made them more than what they appeared to be. He'd hoped the drudgery of an acolyte's duties eventually led to something more glorious, more rapturous or euphoric. Perhaps the Black Gnarl was little more than an old religion that reached its prime during Alda's darkest hours.

The world reached a new era, a dark and unenviable one for many, but his order had profited and grown as a result, just like many religions from before. The idea curdled his ambitions and excitement. The Black Gnarl offered the best prospects that Kael had seen, but he had truly hoped for more than waiting out these awful days in a dark, repurposed monastery.

When he passed through the threshold into the third floor's central room, however, everything changed. This floor was different. There was only one hallway here—directly in front of him. On the right was a large lift attached to a pulley system. Currently, the lift was in use, and a gaping black hole waited with ropes leading down into the darkness. On the left, a large alcove contained the effigy of his denomination: A scaled, powerful worm-beast with countless faces protruding from its body. It was impossible to tell where it began and where it ended.

Kael's breath caught. He'd seen crude drawings of the being and read multiple descriptions, but never before had he seen something so life-like and of such scale. It looked like it was about to crawl, writhing and horrifying, out of the alcove and come claim him at that very moment. It seemed to move before his eyes, and sounds escaped every mouth on every face. Faces within faces and mouths within mouths. Eyes peered from every angle, covering the squirming shape like a pox.

Kael swallowed, his throat dry and aching. He barely noticed the lone guard, a towering specter, approach him with ethereal grace. This one had a sword sheathed on their belt and held a staff in their hand. Around their neck was a gold pendant, large and circular, bearing the embellished symbol belonging to that twilight worm.

He showed the silver disc once more, but the guard

remained, the face below the dark hood fully cloaked in shadow, unlike the others, whose faces were at least mostly revealed and could be confirmed as human. This towering being only left such conclusions as a wild guess. It moved so unnaturally, made no sound other than the shuffling of its flaccid robes, and loomed over Kael by a head and shoulder. As slow as the crawl of death, it turned to the side and backed toward the alcove. It didn't even answer when he asked where he could find Master Dunscale. The guard may as well have been another statue in the room.

He looked back at the pitch-black pit and stared for several moments. Subtle sounds drifted on stale air that wafted from the opening. They sounded unpleasant but were so faint and muffled that it could have been his imagination working in tandem with the frightening aura pulsing from the sculpture. He could feel eyes boring into him from the hidden face of the sinister guard, as well. A sense of urgency pricked his chest, and he decided against any further questions.

He left through the only door available; in actuality, a set of double doors of iron-reinforced wood. Pushing one open on its moaning hinges, he entered a hallway that split into a dozen different directions. Some were wider and more well-lit than others. The intimidating guard probably thought that if he was down this far in the subfloors, he knew where he was going. However, Kael was little more than a messenger with no clear direction to Master Dunscale. A slight oversight, it seemed.

He then entered the large center-most hallway and found it contained no other entrances. Slight ruts were worn into the stones. They led to the end of the hall where another deep, black pit awaited. This one was a more natural shape than the previous pit. There was no pulley-operated lift system here, only a dark, unblinking eye in the depths below Promise Hold. It had the look of a subterranean tunnel that had been here for a very long time. Circular holes cut into the natural stone of the pit's walls alongside shallow, knife-straight striations. Something had cut and dug along here, but the holes—they looked as though they had been chewed into the rock.

The hairs on his neck prickled and his skin broke into goose-flesh. The darkness in the pit was sourced from more than a lack of light. A visceral evil came from its gullet. He felt himself being watched as he peered over the edge. Not watched by the guard in the previous room but from something very deep down below. In his soul, Kael knew that something down there waited, watched, and wanted him. He felt his stomach lurch and he backed up, a sharp fear of falling, grabbing his bowels and squeezing.

Solid ground felt wonderful. He nearly tripped over his robes, backing away from the pit. Turning away and refusing to look back, Kael tried another hallway. Each door had some variation of the embellished Black Gnarl symbol, but each worm-like portion of the symbol was slightly different. At the end of the hall, a closed door awaited that had the worm-symbol embellishment colored in red. This was a stark contrast from every other he'd seen. This had to be the office of a master.

The door was locked, so Kael knocked gently. No one answered, so he tried again, rapping his knuckles firmly on the door. After moments of silence, he backed away and noticed a round impression in the iron bracings of the door. It was roughly the size of his hand. He removed the disc from the pocket in his robes and placed it inside the impression. Not only a perfect fit, but something clicked as the disc settled into place. He turned it to the left and it didn't move, so he tried the right. It spun effortlessly, and soon a louder click resonated from deeper within whatever locking mechanism this was. He gave a gentle push and the door creaked open.

A unique smell came from the room: rank and cloying, along

with a sickly-sweet perfume odor. Weak torchlight flickered but cast its tortured light on nothing living or human within; only things that scarred the mind and were better left undescribed. Kael closed the door and rested his head against it. He breathed slowly, forcing panic out of his mind. When his hands stopped shaking, he spun the lock back into place and removed the disc, resolving himself to not open any further doors unless someone called from behind them.

In that regard, he tried other doors in other hallways, all without an answer to his attempts at knocking and, at times, when he thought he heard sounds or voices on the other side, he called out. More than once, the noise stopped at his interruption but never started again by the time he moved on. One door after another, each hallway the same result. He feared he would have to return to Brother Bolthus and ask for clarification. After all this time wandering the subfloors, such an action would earn Kael a stern rebuke, possibly resulting in a delay of his time in the ritual. Though, after all he'd seen here, the shine had very much been taken off of that jewel. Fear and doubt crept into him, tarnishing his hopes and anticipations. Finally, he arrived at a door with muffled but audible voices on the inside. A man and woman were arguing in a manner suggesting they were both of the upper echelons and quite immovable in their opinions.

"Your little holdout here has been uncooperative for long enough," the woman said. Her voice was flat and stern.

"Uncooperative? We merely have our own particular interests to pursue, in league with the higher purposes of the order, of course. Ours simply requires a little more privacy and devotion than, say, the grand plans of the sons and daughters of Bac'thule." The man's reply was now calmer than the agitated tone throughout Kael's approach.

The woman's reply dripped with sarcasm. "Privacy and devotion? Your methods are questionable and unseemly at best. At worst? Perverse and grotesque. The time's come to attract followers. Supplicants. Even soldiers. What you're doing here could prove contradictory to those efforts, Dunscale."

Master Dunscale. Kael had finally found him. He thought to knock but hesitated to interrupt the master and whomever his guest was.

"No disrespect meant, my lady, but who is any member of the Black Gnarl to debate the tenets of any of the Inheritors? The Many-Faced Worm has its doctrine, its preferences. We—"

"Don't lecture me, Dunscale," the woman interrupted, her voice barely carrying through the door. It was sharp as a sacrificial blade and coated with venom.

"Look at me," she continued. Silence accompanied her demand. "Look at me, acolyte," she repeated harshly. A cold feeling crept out of the door and crawled over Kael. He knew to whom Master Dunscale was speaking. The order would never have gotten far, especially holding to such secrecy over millennia, without hierarchy or discipline. There was only one within the order titled the Crown of Night. He'd never met her, as few had. He didn't know *who* she was, but he knew *what* she was. At this moment, he realized he was happy with such ignorance.

"Who am I?" she asked. Though the question seemed rhetorical, it was clear she wanted an answer. It took a few moments for Master Dunscale to answer.

"The Crown of Night," he replied. He sounded sufficiently cowed.

"And what are you?"

"An acolyte in service to the Great Others. Inheritors of the Obscured Throne."

When she answered, her voice sounded pleased, like a mother who had received a proper answer from a scolded child.

"Very good. We are all acolytes to them. Nameless. Meaningless. *Obedient.*" She placed noticeable emphasis on the final word. "You are blessed by your patron god. And I?"

She stopped talking, and eventually it must have dawned on Master Dunscale that she wanted him to answer. He must have been seething in anger at the verbal lashing he was receiving.

"Am blessed by them all," he said flatly, using all the begrudging respect he could muster.

"As much a pitiful speck to them as you, but I have earned a multitude of their gifts. Even survived yours, vulgar as it was."

"You flirt with blasphemy," Dunscale rebuked, although he did so softly.

The Crown of Night scoffed. "There is no blasphemy when They care not for our existence, nor even notice it. We deign to touch their unspeakable divinity and hope a sliver of a shard of their power graces us. Then we hope they notice when they claim everything as their own and allow us to carry on as insects in the dirt beneath their ruin as they walk our world. You would do well to remember that, *Master* Dunscale, amidst your zealotry."

"My zealotry," Dunscale said in a low voice. "You mock my efforts, yet how fairs your probe of the northern city?"

The Crown of Night's voice replied with a stern calmness that bespoke her refusal to give in to his baited argument. "I continue to seek an appropriate route into Kalthav. The defenses born of the Fifth Magic there are unprecedented. Our own agents consistently fail to report back after venturing there. And my own efforts..."

Kael felt a prickle in the back of his neck. The muffled discussions beyond went silent. He raised his hand to knock when the Crown of Night spoke again.

"We have a visitor."

His heart stopped for a moment. Fear of reprisal, of the Crown of Night's retribution, sapped the will to make his body move. He wanted to knock on the door and make their suspicion subside, but he only felt sweat beginning to bead on his forehead.

"Enter," Master Dunscale barked.

The irritation in his master's voice broke the stiffness in Kael's joints. He grasped the door handle and pushed, grunting when the hinges didn't move as easily as he expected.

Inside, Master Dunscale sat at a large desk made of near-black mahogany. Candles burned in tarnished holders, while books were stacked neatly atop each other on the sides. It was much more organized than the workspace of Brother Bolthus.

Next to the desk stood the lady herself. Her robes looked to be made of soft velvet, dark as wine. Her cowl was down, and her hair fell against her shoulders like thick veins of gold running through fresh blood. She wore a gold chain around her neck with a symbol only vaguely familiar to him. It belonged to another of the Inheritors, but not one Kael was overly knowledgeable of.

"Why are you here, acolyte?" Dunscale asked pointedly.

The words refused to materialize from his dry throat. Dunscale's bitter stare, coupled with the unexpected beauty and fearsome presence of the Crown of Night, was overpowering. He reached into his robes and removed the letter. Feeling the paper in his fingers reminded him of his purpose, and he found some measure of strength there.

"Brother Bolthus said this came for you," Kael replied hoarsely. He cleared his throat and held out the letter.

A sneer curled Dunscale's cracked lips. "Of course, that overfed toad couldn't be bothered to bring it to me himself."

The lady smirked. "Be nice. I like Brother Bolthus. He's harmless and dutiful. Perfect for his position."

She stepped towards him, her face returning to an unreadable mask. "I'll take that," she said. The sleeves of her robe pulled away from her pale hand, which bore the tattoo of his denomination. A strange smell hung around her. It was cloying but sweet. He'd heard the blessed of the Sanguine Garden bear such an odor wherever they go. It was her eyes that were the worst. They hurt to look at and were a color Kael could not describe. She truly possessed the favor of each of the ancient ones. Each one that the order knew of that is. Possibly some they didn't.

She pulled the letter open, the wax seal lifting from the page. As she unfolded the halves, Master Dunscale looked on with his eyes squinted in irritation. His liver-spotted, balding head turned a little redder. The wax seal with the symbol of the Many-Faced Worm was obviously meant for his eyes. The Crown of Night always trumped a mere master, however.

Her piercing eyes scanned the page. No sign of it being good or bad news crossed her face. Then, she smirked and folded the letter back up, handing it over to Dunscale. "You were to read it and inform me immediately upon my arrival."

Dunscale took the letter with practiced obedience, but his eyes spoke of other, more volatile emotions. He read the letter more fully, taking his time. It felt to Kael as though they had forgotten his presence; however, he didn't dare speak up. He was only a nameless apprentice, after all.

"The masters have chosen to return to the island," Dunscale said, still looking at the letter.

The lady subtly nodded, appearing disinterested. "They were instructed to inform me of their decision. So be it. We'll coordinate with the other holds. We have quite the task ahead of us."

"Are we sure it's time?" Dunscale asked, his scowl returning to his more normal sneer. "We've made this mistake before."

It was the lady's turn for her placid face to curdle. "Gideon was an overzealous fool. Years of his efforts were destroyed because he became impatient and greedy. Years of *our* efforts destroyed. Nel Aldyri was a test run, we'll say. We were too lenient with the greater populace, but this time we'll maintain tighter control. Our numbers have grown since then while the world continues to shrivel and decay. Make no mistake, Master Dunscale, that place is the locus of the Inheritors' power. The Obscured Throne's window into our world and Its beacon to find it. Have Bolthus prepare letters for all the masters. We'll convene at my hold to discuss how to move forward. Two weeks' time."

Dunscale bowed his head stiffly. "I'll have him start immediately."

His head turned and a pair of cold brown eyes rested on Kael. "You're still here?" he grumbled, his voice as hollow as the fiendish pit down the other hall. Kael opened his mouth but struggled to speak. His chin bobbed, making him look like a suffocating fish.

"Leave him be, old man," the Crown of Night said with a hint of mirth in her voice. Kael's eyes darted over to see her approaching him. "This man is the future of our organization. You may also call me 'my lady,'" she cooed. Her hand reached up and cupped his chin and her eyes met his. Both her gaze and her touch hurt. Her look stung deep into his mind while her touch burned like a hot iron on his flesh. He whimpered. His hands trembled, and he began to sweat again, but he did everything he could to not move or insult the Crown of Night.

The compulsion to look in her eyes overwhelmed him as though she had some passive charm incantation constantly drifting about her. He couldn't resist. His eyes darted up, met hers, and he gritted his teeth against the pain. It was a sensation he lacked the poetic aptitude to describe. He felt naked in front of her, physically and spiritually. A moment of panic gripped him, knowing that any secrets he held, even those forgotten, were laid before her as his memories were stripped bare. A name whispered behind the barbed gauze that was being stuffed into his mind, the owner of the fingers that lovingly put it there: *Janesca.*

She finally turned away, the greatest mercy he'd ever been granted. His eyes watered with hot tears. Blinking them away was even more painful. A thousand razor-legged insects crawled over his mind. His jaw hurt from being clenched so tightly, fueled by the agony.

"Best of luck with your initiation tomorrow evening, Kael," she said, patting his cheek. "You're going to need it."

"Yes, my lady," he barely managed to say aloud.

He never mentioned his name. No acolyte would. What else had she seen when she looked at him, no, through him?

She smirked, a slight chuckle coming from her throat. The Crown of Night, the grand leader of the Black Gnarl, both beautiful and horrible, pulled her cowl over her head and left the room. After the door clicked shut, an emotional sigh escaped the room itself. Master Dunscale ran a wrinkled hand over his mouth and chin. Kael felt near to soiling himself. Both remained quiet.

Finally, Dunscale cleared his throat. "Our divine lady. Janesca. Crown of Night. She is not without her charms," he said, his old voice hoarse.

"Yes, master," Kael replied emotionlessly, his words forced through his teeth.

"Hmph," Dunscale grumbled. His quill scratched over a piece of paper for several moments. He sealed the letter and summoned Kael to his desk.

Forcing his feet to move, Kael walked stiffly to the master's desk. He dared a glimpse at the organized papers on the top. Some appeared to be letters, while others showed diagrams and depictions of the human body in various states of duress. He swallowed, his mouth dry and throat hurting. The images contained notes and arrows and such of what Kael could only describe as medical and detailed in nature. He caught various words that, when coupled with the images, made it clear they involved the rituals of the Many-Faced Worm. Kael felt his knees grow weak.

Just when he thought he would need to lean on the master's desk to stay on his feet, his head swimming and the room suddenly feeling stifling beyond measure, Dunscale reached out with the letter and, in a gravelly voice and disinterested tone, ordered Kael to deliver it to Brother Bolthus straight away. The librarian was to draft copies for every master and send them out immediately.

Kael bowed quickly and curtly, then immediately took his leave. The air in the subterranean hallways was somewhat cooler than the master's office. He realized that it was likely due to the cold drafts coming from the gaping mouth down the central corridor.

He made his way back to the main room, where the stairway led back to the above floor. The fiendish guard remained in the same position. The statue in the alcove remained as menacing as ever. His eyes made their way over to the lift opposite the alcove. It called to him. Faint sounds gliding in on the cold drafts wafting from down below. Like the eyes of the Crown of Night, he became entranced. A rhythm began to build in him. There was no music that he could hear. No rumbles or beats flowed through the ground or the walls. This came from deep within him. It was nauseating but euphoric. He wanted to dance and vomit, strip his clothes from his body and flesh from his muscles, leaving the nerves exposed to feel the cold of the ancient subterranean air, light his screaming flesh on fire with the torches on the wall, climb on the scaled statue in the alcove and allow it to pierce him over and over...

And vomit he did. The contents of his stomach emptied onto the floor and Kael fell back against the wall next to the stairway's door. He expected to feel the wrath of the guard, but when he looked over, the tall shrouded thing was wavering side to side slightly in tandem with the unheard rhythm—a sight so silently hideous it made him want to be sick again.

On nights that the holy twilight revealed itself, when initiations took place, and new brothers and sisters of the Many-Faced Worm were added to their ranks, there was always a slight sense of vertigo felt among those in Promise Hold. The acolytes were always told it was the presence of the holy twilight itself and their understanding of it that made them more connected with their patron Inheritor and therefore feeling his presence. What Kael was feeling now was different. Leaning back against the wall, he felt the waves of vertigo he remembered, but the obscene waking nightmare he'd just experienced left him trembling and unable to move.

He waited there for the sensation to subside. The grotesque urges continued to call to him, but he placed his open palms on the stone wall and let himself remain grounded. He tried to lift his hand once and just turn and open the door, but the moment his palm left the cool stone surface, his feet nearly carried him to the lift, where he had the thought to throw himself into it.

Everything returned to normal, but he wasn't sure how long it had been. The tall guard became still once more. Kael felt in control of his own limbs. He prepared himself to open the door and run, not stopping until he reached the librarian's office.

A creaking noise stopped him. The mechanical sounds of the lift echoed in the chamber, accompanied by the groans of taut, winding ropes.

Kael waited. He didn't know why, but he had to. Something was coming up the lift, and he had the sudden realization that the night's ritual was over. He needed to see what came up that lift.

The ropes continued their ceaseless complaints for over a minute. Three shrouded heads were the first thing to peek over the edge of the floor. As the lift rose, a flat, low cart appeared when the figures were at waist height. Multiple bodies were piled on top as though they were simply thrown there haphazardly. One of the Black Gnarl members held a crossbar handle in both hands and began to push, the cart trailing behind them, the moment the lift stopped. None of them paid Kael any heed.

The grisly procession went past him slowly. Men and women both were heaped, naked, upon the simple wooden cart. Their limbs intertwined with many at seemingly odd angles. The more he looked, the more repulsive things he discovered. Some of the bodies were lacerated, but no blood flowed from the wounds. Some were missing limbs altogether. Others were bruised so badly that barely an inch of unspoiled flesh could be seen. The faces, of course, were the worst. Kael stifled a cry when he saw them.

The words of their revered text rang in his ears. The first thing they memorized as acolytes; it came flooding into his mind, forcefully and with a context never before realized.

They will feel the force of countless breaths upon their faces, and bask in the haze lest their skin reject the blessing, and melt in rapturous agony like pleasant wax.

They will see with a thousand eyes, and be bestowed with eons of forbidden revelations, lest their minds break from the truths and drain from their very resting place.

They will sing with the billions-strong voices, the symphony of painful promises, that resonates in the stars, lest their songs prove weak so that their jaws break with effort and throats tear with strain.

They will writhe in ecstasy, like hellish snakes in their mating ball, as one flesh, lest their bodies prove feeble and their bones crack and limbs contort in shame.

What lay before him was the result of words he once thought held spiritual and metaphorical meaning. The unspeakable tangle of suffering in front of him was quite literal.

Every body on the cart was twisted and desecrated in a uniquely revolting way. Faces melted like candle wax. Eyes of all sizes sprouting from cheeks, foreheads, and ears. Throats splayed and empty like burned-out tree trunks. Some of them died smiling, often with multiple mouths. There were other wounds that Kael simply refused to reflect on. He saw them once, felt his skin prickle, and let it alone.

The two other Gnarl members followed the cart to the large door opposite Kael. They opened both doors to allow it passage into the main corridor. Once the cart was through, they released the doors, and Kael watched as all three made their way down the hall toward the pit. The doors shut and all was eerily silent.

He pushed the images of the mutilated corpses out of his mind. The lift began operating once more and started lowering to whatever waited beneath the darkness. With what strength he could muster, Kael pushed the door open and left the subfloor behind.

The path up the stairs seemed to take longer. He opened the door to the outside air of the hold and breathed deeply. No one else was outside. The sky had few stars out, making even the outside dark and smothering. The gatehouse was still manned and they let him through. Two torches flickered by the outbuilding where Kael would deliver the sealed reply in his robes. The symbol of the Many-Faced Worm on the door taunted him. He waited for it to call to him, much like on the lower floors of Promise Hold.

Kael walked swiftly to the librarian's office. He knocked and waited. The door creaked open and Brother Bolthus, obviously having dragged himself out of the bed in the corner of the room, waved him inside. The large man plopped in his seat and rubbed his eyes, waiting wordlessly for Kael to say his piece and leave.

"Master Dunscale wants a copy of this letter sent to every master straight away," Kael said in a dull monotone. He tossed the letter on the desk and left without giving Brother Bolthus an opportunity to reply.

The night was still and quiet. A slight breeze blew and kissed his face and hands that were left exposed from his robes. Kael went to one of the stairways leading to the upper walls. He looked toward the countryside, but nothing could be seen. The darkness was too deep. The black of the pits below Promise Hold creeped out to devour the lands around it.

Kael slumped against one of the parapets and wept. He would have to go back the following night. The lift would take him down to what awaited beneath this former castle, glorious in the old days. Something awaited him down there, he and his fellow acolytes, during the holy twilight that will make them full members of the Black Gnarl, devoted to the Many-Faced Worm; or it will devour their bodies, minds, and souls in a thousand unimaginable ways.

"I'm sorry," Kael said quietly, gripping his robes in his fists. He apologized to his fellow acolytes whom he studied and bonded with over the years they spent here.

He stood and peered out over the night-shrouded landscape before him; the things it held in its shadows were unknown, and too many to count. He stared at a future of uncertainty beyond these stone walls. He looked behind him and saw the torchlights of Promise Hold flickering like demonic eyes. He looked back at the soul-flaying truths that had been revealed to him. A future defined by horrors that numbed the mind.

Kael tightened his grip on the worn rock of the wall. Drops

fell silent and softly against his bare hands. He looked up and saw that clouds had partially covered the moon, casting silver strands across the sky. The rain increased, pattering against the stone as the wind began to pick up. After a few minutes, a full downpour began. Kael glanced back over his shoulder and saw everyone in the courtyard making for the nearest door. The torches hissed against the rain and would soon release their last sigh for the night.

He closed his eyes and pulled his hood back, letting the rain course over his face and soak through his hair. "I'm sorry," he repeated.

THE RAIN HAD CEASED by the following afternoon. Another ritual was scheduled for that evening. The order needed all the nameless acolytes in the hold fully initiated and working to further their cause as soon as possible. When one of the nameless couldn't be located, a few of the newest initiates were sent to find him. They looked in the storerooms and dormitories, in every dark corner they could find. They pitied him already. Not only would he be denied initiation at this point, but also severely punished—and the deep pit from which the cries and moans wafted up on rank winds immediately came to mind.

The final place the initiates checked were the walls. They figured they should have seen him, but perhaps they missed him tucked away against one of the towers. The parapets were narrow, forcing them to walk one in front of the other. The initiate in the lead stopped, so suddenly the one in the rear bumped into them.

"What is it?" the rear initiate asked, annoyed.

The lead grabbed the side of the wall, still cold and wet from the rain, and looked over the edge. Their head was pointed further out, looking into the muddy field at first, then slowly angled down to the very bottom of the wall.

At the base of the wall, a puddle had formed in a thin line all along the perimeter. Directly below the initiate was a bundle of robes: crumpled, empty, and soaked through. A trail of footprints in the mud-slick ground led away from the abandoned robes all the way to the nearby trees, where they disappeared into the forest.

THE LORDS OF FELKIRK

THE MORNING FOG FINALLY BURNED AWAY, WITH THE SUN PUSHING skyward in the east. The burning eye rose and revealed all beneath the heavy fog of the marine layer that blanketed the village. Between hills that bordered dry grasslands, themselves wedged between the opposite coast and the Oakengast Forest on the southern border of the Brindlecrag, Rainward had endured. Besieged by hard times and weighed down by bad harvests, the people grew harder. Fishermen strayed further, farmers tried different crops traded with merchants, and hunters grew less particular about the types of animals worth hunting. The people may not be thriving, but they were not starving or freezing.

None of these silver linings on the dark clouds of life helped Lyra with her grievance. She handed over a small gray package, tied with string, to a burly, mustachioed man on the docks. His large, callused fingers, used to working and repairing nets, undid the simple knot holding the crisp parchment together. He lifted the revealed herbs to his nose and inhaled.

"Ah, yes. Those will do nicely. Thank you, Lyra," he said, his voice as coarse as dry sand.

In return, he passed over a string of fish. Smaller fish like anchovies and sardines clustered together at the top like strange flowers. A few sea-trout hung along the middle. At the bottom, a small tuna nearly dragged on the ground. It was this generous specimen that made her hold the rope with two hands.

She looked at the fisherman in his sea-green eyes, nestled behind layers of sun-kissed wrinkles, and he could tell she was dubious about the gift. The herbs would cover the rest, but not the tuna.

"I can't afford the blue one, Halbert," she said and looked at him with irritation.

He sighed. "I know you don't like handouts, girl, but think of your old man. He needs it. He can pay me back when he's able to work again."

If he's able to work again, she thought to herself. Forcing a smile, she thanked him and noted quite adamantly that she would hold him to it.

"Best get home now, girl," he said as he turned his head to look toward the Stone Sea, its cold, deep waters restless with churning whitecaps. Gray clouds formed on the horizon, thick and lofty as a cliff wall. Such features gave the town its name. It also gave some peace of mind to those who sailed on it as it was more benign a thought than going out on the Wailing Ocean that waited beyond the horizon. "Looks like another torrent is coming."

She nodded and thanked him again. Hurrying home, the stiff winds promised to make good on Halbert's assessment. The shadows of the clouds loomed overhead, harrying her on the trip home. The wind stalked her, and tiny droplets teased at her neck. No sooner had Lyra reached her family's house down a rough cobblestone street than the rain started.

Slamming the door behind her, a warm fire from the hearth welcomed her inside. Her mother shuttered the last of the windows. Her father coughed softly from their bed in the other room. She hung the rope full of fish on the wall, where she and her mother would prepare them later.

"Oh, he did it again, didn't he?" her mother said, a knowing tone in her voice.

Lyra shook her head, but a slight smile graced her lips over the kind fisherman's gesture. "He insisted. And you know Halbert. He'll give Dad hell about it when he's better, and eventually, Dad will make it up to him. But the old sturgeon's not going to take any form of payment until then."

"Yes, when he's better," her mother said softly.

"Is that Lyra?" her father called from the other room. "Marna, is Lyra home?"

"I'm here, Dad!" Lyra called back. She rinsed the fish off her hands in a bowl of water, dried them on a towel, and went to greet her father.

He was still in bed, where he had been for over a week, and looked thinner and paler every day. She kept his face shaved and washed his bedsheets constantly, trying to keep him comfortable and healing. A book sat untouched on the nightstand next to him. When the downpours came, he preferred to sit and listen to the wind howling outside and the rain assaulting the walls and roof.

"How did things go today?" he asked, smiling weakly. His voice was raspy and hollow. It broke her heart to hear it.

"Ok," she replied. Sitting next to the bed on a small stool, she took his frail, bony hand in hers. "I found plenty of herbs to trade and helped a few of the bakers. The rains came in before I could finish getting everything done, but I have plenty of fish for us."

"That's good."

She squeezed his hand. It felt cold and clammy. His eyes looked sunken and wet, like one of the many tidepools on the outskirts of town. Yet, his lips were dry and cracked, speckled with blood from his coughing fits.

"You look better today."

She smiled as she lied, forcing back the tears and letting the sobs languish in her throat to appear strong for him. Any glimpse of hope she could manage to give him wasn't wasted. It was all she could offer for now.

MARNA AND LYRA sat quietly at a table, sipping hot tea they made for sharing with her father. The fire in the hearth crackled and spit as the smell of the tuna stuffed with herbs from the garden grew stronger as it cooked. The rain and wind continued their onslaught outside, as if making the town of Rainward continue to earn its name.

"Tilling will be here tomorrow," Marna said. Both her hands cupped her mug to keep them warm.

Lyra stared into hers, watching fragments of the leaves that settled in the bottom of the sepia-colored drink. "We can't afford his services anymore, either."

"We'll figure that out when your father's better. For now, him getting well is all that matters."

They continued to sit quietly, listening to the storm beat on the small seaside town. Lyra seethed at the world, wishing she could cast her wrath on it like the storm was doing against Rainward. No medicine was helping. Tilling couldn't figure out what disease her father even had. She blamed the world, the Rupture, and the ancient things whispered about that ravaged the world and all the people in it.

They carved up the tuna, Marna taking a healthy portion to her husband. Lyra poked at the food, taking small bites here and there. She decided to check on her father and saw that he'd eaten nothing; his food had turned cold. He was asleep; weak, wheezing breaths escaped his parted lips. Lyra returned with the still-full plate and told her mother. They both continued to sit at the table quietly, having refilled their cups.

Marna rose slowly from her seat. "I'm going to make a bed next to your father. You should get some rest, too, dear. The storm may last through the night."

"I will, Mother," she said, smiling softly as her mother kissed her on the top of the head.

The door to their room closed. Weak coughs could still be heard. With the fire to warm her, the torrent to perpetuate her mood, and her anger and sorrow as company, Lyra remained awake for some time. Her thoughts were many and troubled. Each one fed into another, like tortured beasts feeding each other in a bloody food chain until the worst, most horrifying one among them was left alone, screaming in the dark.

The majority of her tea remained cold and untouched. She gave in to her melancholy and went to her bed in the small remaining room of their house. She put on a nightgown to help fight off the cold from the storm and slipped under her simple sheets. Sleep didn't come easily, her mind too frenzied.

Sleep did sneak up on her, however, and she didn't notice until her eyes opened to a foggy morning. Early morning risers walked the street outside her bedroom window. A dull haze of fog trapped by the marine layer of the Stone Sea settled on the town and made itself at home.

Marna made porridge for breakfast, mostly to see if her husband could attempt to swallow some of the warm substance for nourishment. Lyra took him the bowl but saw he was still asleep. She returned and put the bowl on the table. She added some berries and attempted to eat. Her appetite was slightly stronger, having skipped most of dinner the night before. It was her mother's turn to stir her food absent-mindedly.

"Please try and eat, Mom," she said gently. "I don't need two people to take care of."

Marna reached out and gently grasped Lyra's hand, then squeezed. A sniffle escaped from Marna, and she rubbed one eye with the back of her other hand. They sat quietly, taking small bites of their breakfast until a knock came from the door.

Lyra opened the door no more than a few inches. Outside, the humidity from the fog and the previous night's storm rolled into the room. An old man waited right in front of the door. His wrinkled face greeted her with a half-smile. A bald, spotted head rimmed with long white hair running to his shoulders framed bony cheeks and a once-strong jaw. His brown eyes were gentle and spoke of a caring nature that she'd come to know her whole life.

"Good morning, Mr. Tilling," she said, opening the door for him. "Would you like some tea in this cold?"

"That would be nice, Lyra, thank you," he replied in his old, hoarse voice.

Lyra went to the pot of hot water and poured him some of the herbal tea that the apothecary recommended for her father. Steam rose from the small cups, the smell of chamomile and ginger coming from the hot liquid. She offered it to him and he thanked her softly. He sat the cup on the table to let the tea cool. He'd become more sensitive to such hot drinks in his old age. The herbs still smelled nice and soothed his nerves, though.

"How has he been? Is he awake now?" Mr. Tilling asked.

"He is, Hermaias," Marna replied, bringing him a few bites of sweetened bread to have with his tea. The recipe was a simple one, passed down from her mother, and required readily available ingredients instead of expensive sugar. "But..." she paused, swallowing as fresh tears threatened to flow. "He's no better than he was when you last visited."

. . .

TILLING SHOOK HIS HEAD. Robern, Marna's husband, was sick with something he'd been so far unable to diagnose. It was driving the former crab catcher's family mad. The home was still in order, but the weight of despair was heavy here. Weak smiles, fake and feigned, were the only ones the two women offered anymore. Lyra also burned with something else. Her helplessness was turning to anger. Who knew where it would go after that. She'd turned such feelings on the old apothecary more than once. He couldn't blame her. What she had said wasn't entirely misplaced; he did feel useless in this scenario.

A wasting sickness had come through Rainward before, taking dozens of people with it. When Robern first started showing symptoms, Tilling was afraid the disease had returned. However, that didn't appear to be the case. Robern was just very, very ill—and Hermaias Tilling, the only skilled healer in the town, could offer no respite. He took a sip of the tea, letting its soothing warmth calm his dreary thoughts. After a few more sips, he rose to see his patient.

"I'll go tend to him. I truly hope to return with good news."

Marna nodded while Lyra sat quietly with her face staring at the ground. Tilling took his cracked leather bag filled with medical utensils, ingredients, and medicines. The silence and stale smell of sickness greeted him when he entered Robern's room. It gave him the grisly impression of entering a tomb. The man in the bed, decades younger than Hermaias, looked almost as haggard and frail as the old apothecary. It took only minutes for him to perform the evaluation.

Outside, Lyra and her mother waited quietly. Their tea and bread remained untouched. Hermaias saw the expectant sorrow on their faces but also the faintest glimmer of hope in their eyes. He wiped his forehead with a towel and stuffed it back into his bag. It hurt him to deliver the news, much as it had every time before.

"It's as you say, I'm afraid. Nothing I've done or continue to do is aiding him. He's just...slowly slipping away." He removed the small, round spectacles from his face and wiped them with another, smaller towel from within his coat pocket. It helped to avoid the devastating looks of the wife and daughter of the slowly dying man in the room behind him.

Tilling looked at the hems of his white apothecary's coat. They had been stained pink from blood for years. As the only practitioner of his trade in Rainward, he'd seen more than enough death and blood for several lifetimes. Not all of it washed out, either psychologically or literally.

"I'm very sorry," he said in a low voice. "I can come back in another week to see if he's improved. Other than that, we can do nothing more than let time and his body decide."

Lyra swept her cup off the table, the tea splattering across the wall. "No, I won't accept that!" she yelled.

Tilling's eyes went wide, the outburst leaving him speechless. His mind searched for a reply, digging through every rote apology and empty encouraging statement he could think of. As one statement after another rolled against his lips then ducked cowardly back into his throat, he imagined it left him looking like a gasping fish.

With little to say herself, Marna took her daughter in her arms and held her tightly. "I don't want to, either," she whispered, her voice breaking. "But we don't have a choice."

"There has to be something else," Lyra said as she sobbed into her mother's faded dress. She then pulled away, held her mother's tired, cold hands for a moment, then turned to Mr. Tilling. Her eyes, fierce and blue as a calm sea, met Tilling's, which were wet and sunken as though he had always just stopped crying.

"What would you need to help him?"

"Excuse me?" he replied reflexively.

"You're a good apothecary, Mr. Tilling, even in our small town. I won't for a second believe you've just given up."

His face hardened, not in anger or offense, but in acceptance. She was right. He was damn good and would do whatever he needed for his patient. She was also correct in that his resources in this oceanside burg were limited. The only other options were too terrible to consider.

"You're correct. I've done all I can with what I have. Other options are limited, no longer viable, or far too dangerous."

Lyra crossed her arms. She squinted, her face becoming a stone mask. "What are the limited options?"

"I could try something more potent, more aggressive, but it's basically more of the same treatment. With no reaction to the standard doses, I doubt increasing them would do any better," he replied, pushing up his glasses.

"And those 'no longer viable'?" she asked, her tone dubious.

He pursed his lips, causing his mustache to bristle. "Another apothecary, someone with a different perspective, maybe. However, the nearest town even possible to have such a person is a week's ride from here. One way. I doubt your father has that much time left. The other option would be healing magic. Unfortunately, there aren't many around here that have magical talent of any kind that I know of, let alone of the kind that was already going extinct by the time of the Rupture."

LYRA SHOOK HER HEAD. She also knew of a local with some magical talent. Nothing extravagant, but enough to make him memorable. Her mother tried to introduce them once. He was handsome, intelligent, and had all the personality of a sun-bleached rag. She'd never heard of healing magic before, but the Rupture was a distant, haunting memory. That thread may be too thin and frayed to even pull.

"Ok. What about the dangerous ones?"

Hermaias took a deep breath, then let out a long sigh. "Other places may have more history on rare medical diseases and treatment. Most likely cities with large libraries and hospitals."

"Like Felkirk," Lyra interjected, her inflection revealing her intentions. Hermaias raised a bony hand, his head shaking sharply against the plan already fermenting in the young woman's mind. He opened his mouth to protest, and protest vigorously, but Lyra was already approaching him with firm, determined steps.

"Don't give me any excuses, Mr. Tilling—"

"Young lady, I said this was a *dangerous* option," he interrupted, but before he could continue, she, in turn, interrupted him.

"I don't care how—"

"Now you listen," he barked. He didn't raise his voice so much as speak with such conviction and sharpness that gave Lyra pause. He stared at her sternly before continuing. "Felkirk is abandoned. A large place full of death and horrible, horrible things of...gods-know-what. There's never been any reason to forbid anyone from going there because no one has been so damn *stupid* as to want to go there. Any travelers from the north take a full day to go around it on their way south, leaving it a good, wide berth. No living thing approaches the place; not even bandits, cults, or any other sort of ne'er-do-wells. How old are you?"

Lyra looked at him quizzically, lowering her head slightly while keeping her eyes on his as she answered, "Twenty-three."

Hermaias sniffed and nodded. "I'm Sixty-eight. That's forty-five more years of experience, of stories and legends and tales of what has happened to those who last tried getting anything out of Felkirk. No one goes there. Ever. And neither are you."

Lyra looked at her mother, whose face clearly showed she

agreed with the old apothecary. Lyra turned back to him so sharply her brown hair whipped in her face.

"Stories. Legends. *Tales*. Do you have any evidence of anything? Anyone who left from here and never came back? Anyone who approached the city and saw something so awful they couldn't go any further?" Her pitch rose as she spoke, gaining intensity as her plea for reasoning continued.

"Not in several years. Decades, even. No one has been so...so *foolish*."

"Then call me a fool. A hopeless one, even. I've watched my father waste away for weeks. *Weeks*, Hermaias!"

Tears began flowing freely down her face. Her mouth contorted into a thin, heartbreaking line that wanted to hold back the painful bellows pushing against the inside of her throat. Hermaias winced, wanting to hug her and tell her that her father would be okay, that he had much more than a few days at most. But he couldn't—wouldn't—lie to her. His next words came out barely above a whisper, "You cannot go there, Lyra. You won't come back."

"You don't know that," she pleaded. "If there's just a chance I can find something to bring back and help you heal him, it's worth it."

"Robern isn't going to make it!" Marna shouted, grief flowing from every word.

The sudden but truthful outburst shocked the room into silence. Lyra turned to her mother, fresh tears flowing from both of them. "You know this, Lyra; we're just biding time, hoping something's going to change, but we know it won't."

Every word was agony to Lyra; she could tell this was true for her mother as well, who appeared ready to collapse. As Lyra approached her, prepared to embrace her mother so they could share in their grief, Marna's knees buckled. She stumbled, catching herself on the back of a chair and then plopping down into the seat. She broke into loud sobs, resting her head in her hands.

Lyra stopped mid step, letting her foot fall to the floor as she nearly stumbled backward. She turned to Mr. Tilling, her eyes red and puffy, her mouth partly open, and mucus beginning to slip from her nose. She sniffed loudly, then looked to the apothecary with hard but sad eyes.

"What if it was Denna?" she asked, her voice flat.

Hermaias' eyes widened. His wife had passed last year but of wholly natural causes. Her death was peaceful; heartrending but peaceful. She left the world with a soft sigh, holding his hand.

"What if it was Denna wasting away slowly as you watched, helpless to do anything?"

The room was quiet save for Marna's sobs. A muffled cough came from the next room, punctuating the question. Hermaias' face aged another ten years in that moment. His face grew long, his eyes grew moist. He had no response to the question. Lyra went to stand by her mother and wrapped her arms around Marna's shoulders. After several long, painfully silent moments, he had something to say. A final desperate attempt to stop the young woman from traveling to her doom.

"Do you want your mother to lose you, too? Her whole family? Robern to his illness and you to...what? We may never know. All Marna will be left with is questions and pain."

Lyra approached him and knelt down, taking his hands in hers. She looked at him with both determination and sympathy. "And I'll be left with the worst question of all: *what if*? What If I could've done something to save my father but didn't because of legends and scary stories?"

The old man removed his glasses, slowly placed them on the table, and rubbed his eyes. Marna's crying had quieted, but she still sat in the chair, head in her hands, and tears pooling beneath her. Lyra continued standing, staring at him with a determination bordering on obsession. She no longer cried; her eyes red from the memory of tears but now sparkling with a fire that frightened him.

"Even if I said no, you would still go. I couldn't live with myself if I didn't do anything I could to see you back here safely."

The words rang somewhat hollow. He felt a sadness grip him, a feeling forecasting the grief he knew was to come when she never came back. He asked her to step outside with him. She nodded and followed Hermaias out to the humid morning air, where the fog was slowly burning away, and the glow of sunlight promised a clearer afternoon.

"It's a four-day walk to the capital. Two, if you can find someone to lend you a horse. Felkirk is a large city, but with nothing living there to keep you from looking wherever you want, you should need about two days to scour the libraries, hospitals, and temples for something to bring back to me. Look for texts on medicines, treatments, even healing magic if you can. It was called the Fifth Sect, so any mention of it could be helpful. Let me know before you depart if someone lends you a horse. I'll be counting the days. Four there, two to search, and four back. Ten days on foot, six by horse. If you're not back by then, I'll...I'll have no choice but to tell Marna that she's lost her daughter as well. Do you understand? Do not make me do that. If you see, hear, or smell *anything* that gives you pause, you turn and you *run*. Understood?"

The adamant, forceful way he asked reminded Lyra of when her father was upset. It almost forced a smile out of her. Instead, she nodded firmly. "I don't know anyone who would lend a horse these days, so I'll walk. Run if I have to."

Hermaias stood from his seat and went to stand next to Marna. He put his hands gently on her shoulders. One hand reached up and placed itself gently over his. Lyra's mother looked at her with pitiful eyes; red, swollen, and utterly defeated.

"And I *will* return. I promise." She felt the urge to assure both of them, but her mother most of all. "I'll come back with something. I don't care if I have to learn magic myself while I'm there. I'm coming back with something to help Dad."

Hermaias placed his other hand on top of Marna's, patting it gently. He didn't dare hope. He looked to Lyra, allowing no emotion to show on his face. Within his soul, he knew he was looking at this girl for the last time. He started preparing himself for when he had to break the news to her mother. The lines of regret and sympathy already forming in his head.

"Then let's get you prepared," he said.

Lyra looked back. Rainward was already lost to her sight, tucked behind the hills that wound up from the ocean's shores. Mr. Tilling had packed a traveling bag for her that should last her the duration of her trip. Food that wouldn't spoil, water enough to last her until she made her way inland and could refill her canteen in a fresh stream. A flask of liquor for the hard nights. A blanket to sleep with. A list of things to look for that could be helpful with her father's recovery. A few other things to round out her supplies for a ten-day trip that she knew Mr. Tilling did not expect her to return from.

She saw it in the way he packed the bag and the tone of voice he used when speaking with her. All his advice and warnings were edged with sorrow, though he tried to hide it behind a veneer of thoughtfulness and intellectualism. She had hugged him goodbye and the strength with which he held her spoke volumes.

The road leading to Felkirk, the capital of the region and

largest remaining city for a hundred miles, was once well-traveled. Passersby were common, with mounted men-at-arms patrolling the stretches and protecting merchants and commonfolk against threats. Milestones jutted from the ground to let people know the length they had yet to go before reaching their destination. The road cut through the green countryside, bordered by thick forests on the west and open plains to the east that ran straight to the wide beaches and open ocean.

Now the road was overgrown. A few ruts were the only sign of the light travel that graced it. The milestones were held to the ground by vines that crawled over them, partially obscured by the tall grasses and weeds that grew at their bases. The things patrolling the path were memories, all but forgotten, and the occasional wild beast looking for a meal.

Lyra favored the side of the road near the plains as instructed. Mr. Tilling was unyielding in his instructions to avoid the forest, despite her thoughts of shelter and hiding places. Forests, he'd said, were nearly as dangerous as the cities. She was to never approach anyone or anything she saw while on the road. If she did spot someone or something, she was to find the nearest hill or thicket or patch of high grass and hide, completely silent, until whatever it was had gone.

Strangely, she hadn't seen anything so far. The road was empty, the countryside quiet. One day was bright with sunshine, and a few birds sang from thickets or as they flew overhead. The next was cloudy and dark, making her fear that she'd be caught in the open during a storm. But none ever came, just a chill wind accompanying the bleak overcast sky.

A few hamlets sprouted from the fields like gray and brown thickets of their own. Mr. Tilling said these were to be approached with the utmost caution. She ignored the first few, and they appeared to be abandoned anyway. But, on the third day, she wanted to sleep under a roof rather than the open sky.

After several days of utter loneliness on the road, with nothing but a few birds as signs of life, she'd hoped that maybe some folk were making a self-sustaining living in one of the run-down burgs. Unfortunately, this turned out to not be the case. A handful of crumbling hovels, shaped in a circle, faced a central area paved with stone. The focal point of the village was a community firepit that was long cold and becoming reclaimed by nature.

Lyra sighed and checked each of the small houses, choosing one made of stone that was still standing. It must have belonged to the head of the village. It appeared the most well-made, and the inside was more spacious than the others she'd examined. There was a small fireplace that she filled with fallen, dried timber and then lit. She covered the windows with old, tattered blankets to keep the light from being seen. The blanket she wrapped herself in kept her quite warm. The bed of tattered remains she'd made herself was more comfortable than the grass she'd used for the prior days.

It was cozy, truth be told, but still lonely. She never realized how much her own small town teemed with life compared to the abandoned places of the world. As the thought lingered, it began to take on a different shape. Perhaps it was the stillness of the night; crickets chirped faintly in the distance and the heavy clouds returned that evening, leaving a starless, deep night. The thought of being alone and several days from home began to churn in her stomach, the hope of helping her father and the determination that drove her began to sour and turn to fear.

Her eyes went from the fire, flickering hot, bright, and welcoming, to the small sword in its sheath, strapped to the pack that now lay against the remains of a cabinet. The firelight flashed against the smooth steel and reflected in her eyes. It was the final thing Mr. Tilling had given her. He had no martial training and made that clear, but had a town guard show her a few basic swings so as not to hurt herself with the weapon. It could protect her against mundane threats, Tilling said, such as wild animals and robbers, but it would do nothing against the evils that came with the Rupture. Those, he'd clarified, could only be fled from and hope against hope that they deem you not worth their effort.

Staring at the blade brought her mind a small measure of peace, but then her thoughts threatened to stray to darker places, to darker possibilities. She shut them out as best she could, focusing on the bright reflections of the fire on the sharp edges. She focused on her efforts to save her father. The anger that she felt against the helplessness. Eventually, those thoughts and the warmth of the fire smothered the fear that clutched at her mind like a beggar's thin fingers grasping at a wealthy man's robe. Lost in those thoughts of possibility, sleep soon came for her.

LEAVING the nameless hamlet the following morning left a pang of sadness in her stomach. Lyra realized that she'd not even seen any corpses, bones, or other evidence of the people that once lived there. The place was wholly abandoned and appeared to have been so for many years, if not decades or even centuries. The stories of those who dwelt here would never be known. This was one of several that she'd passed. She shook off the melancholy that dampened her spirits and set forth on the final leg of her trip to the city.

As she approached the outskirts of the once great Felkirk, the overwhelming silence suddenly gripped her. She stopped midstride and listened to the wind blow in rhythmic gusts across the barren farmlands outside the looming city wall. The western edge of the forests reached out here, nearly touching the city. Despite the robust white clouds rolling in the sky, the green hills in the distance, and the highest peaks of the mountains just visible on the horizon to the north, the large city of Felkirk languished like a black and brown scab on the countryside. The walls of the city held no pride as they slouched in their watch over the districts within. Sunlight peeked through the holes of towers, some so large that the support beams within were revealed, stretched like ancient tendons holding the rotting corpse of the once-magnificent city together. She imagined carrion birds circling the decaying structures, but no life presented itself this close to the city. That prospect alone was unnerving.

The closer Lyra approached the gate, the more an ill presence pressed on her. Not a warning that her experienced mind gave of an incoming storm or of bad news involving her father when she returned home. This felt more acute. More embedded in her mind and body. Her hair stood on end, tickling the back of her neck. Her mind warned her of things that she didn't understand, like someone standing on a rock outcropping shouting and waving their hands but unable to be heard. And, much like she would likely react to such a warning, she mentally shrugged it off and carried on. Though, she realized her hand was reaching back to touch the blade lashed to her bag.

The walls looked much more morose and defeated from a distance. Now that they were before her, they still gave the impression of a last, desperate stand against those who would enter the city. Their imposing nature lent more of an impression of a once-fearsome warrior now slumped against his dead horse, staring fiercely at his enemy despite the light having gone out of his eyes.

Thick, splintered wood barely held together by rusting iron frames made up the remains of the main gate. Lyra feared to touch them, thinking that the whole structure would collapse and bury her under rotting wood and heavy metal. The main gate was large enough for opulent carriages and palanquins of the rich and powerful of the pre-Rupture world to enter undeterred with room to spare. A smaller wicket door allowed individuals entry, but it refused to budge.

Heeding the warning against making too much noise, she pushed down on the door's handle, hoping to feel it give. The iron handle jostled uselessly. She placed her hands against the door, felt the cold iron and splintered wood against her hands, and pushed. Other than a few annoyed creaks, the door offered nothing in return. She pressed sharply a few more times as though trying to pump life into the old hinges. Still, nothing.

Lyra gave up on the main gate for the time being. Following the stone walls left her impressed at the scope of the old cities and deeply saddened at their current state. The walls were built to last, apparently; despite their age and disrepair, they stood strong. Portions of the ramparts had fallen to the ground where grass and weeds poked out around them, and some of the collapsed sections were quite large, enough for her to see the roofs of the buildings within.

She looked up at one of the wedge-shaped holes that plunged further down than others. She could try to scale it, but it would still be quite a climb. Getting a firm grip on one of the rough, protruding stones, she pulled herself onto the wall. She moved up slowly, finding pieces of the wall that looked secure and stuck out enough to give her a good hold. When she felt a stone wobble, she went to the next. The hole grew closer at a painfully slow pace. A few more handholds and she would be there. She managed to make the entire climb so far without looking down. The temptation became overwhelming, but when she came close to craning her head back, she buried her eyes into her shoulder and breathed. Just a few more handholds.

She gripped a jagged piece of stone that looked snug

between some other pieces. She gave it a slight wiggle to make sure it wasn't going anywhere. Feeling nothing move, she pulled up, her arm feeling the strain of the climb, and felt the stone disintegrate. Her other hand held on for a moment, but her fingers slipped from the cold surface, and she felt the wind rush around her as she fell.

Bracing for death, Lyra felt a few tears slip from the corner of her eyes. "I'm sorry, Mom," she whispered, and moments later she felt the ground meet her back, and everything went black. It was quick as a blink, and when her eyes opened she felt an unbelievable pressure on her chest. She grasped at her clothes in a panic, thinking some of the wall's larger stones had come down with her and were crushing her, but nothing was there. Her lungs refused to receive air even as she gasped and wheezed in large, fruitless gulps. She rolled on her side and found nothing had improved. She forced herself to stand, approached the wall and leaned against it with one arm, the other rubbing her burning chest.

The cool mercy of air finally reached her lungs. Each breath came a little easier until she no longer thought she was dying. She fell to her knees and wrapped her arms around herself, crying and breathing and grateful that she'd only had the wind knocked out of her. Lyra turned to look at where she'd landed. A stone, with grass growing around it rather crushed, telling her that it did not come down from the wall with her, was next to where her head hit the ground. She had been inches away from having her head cracked open like an egg.

Tears continued to flow, but so did the air in her body. She sniffed, rubbed her nose with the back of her sleeve, and stood. She looked up and saw the gaping V in the wall, seeming even more distant, staring back at her mockingly.

Fuck, she thought to herself angrily. *That was close.*

The idea of scaling the wall was no longer an option; that

much was clear. She considered returning to the gate but wanted to walk further along the outside for a while to see what other options may present themselves. It was nothing but the same crumbled bits of stone for the longest time. Just as she'd prepared herself to return and try the gate again, she saw a copse of trees ahead of her. Stuck against the wall like a tuft of fur, the clutch of trees was thick and shadowed, obscuring everything within.

Lyra felt energized at the simple change of scenery and jogged to the trees. She stopped suddenly when she remembered Mr. Tilling's words of caution: trust nothing and no one. Every tree, every creature, every shadow and stone is dangerous. She winced when recalling that last one.

Plenty of stories were shared about the mundane made strange and horrifying; she'd grown up with them and it was a part of everyday life for those in Alda. Rainward was fairly sheltered, however, and she'd never been fully exposed to the horrors the world had to offer so freely to others. These thoughts made the shadows in the copse grow denser, the silence more menacing. Where the trees once called to her as a sign of hope, it now felt more like whispers from a strange shape in the dark.

For the first time since starting her journey, she drew the blade from its sheath on her bag. It didn't feel as clumsy as it first had when she began less than a day's worth of training with it, though it still felt unfamiliar. It made her anxious to hold it, mostly out of fear that she may have to use it.

She approached the shadowed thicket, sword in hand, and gritted her teeth. Her breathing intensified, but she forced herself to focus her breaths through her nose—a calming technique suggested by Mr. Tilling. She walked forward in the ready stance she was shown. Her feet felt heavier and moved clumsier than normal. She was afraid. This small cluster of trees and shadow and brush became a villain all its own. Crossing the threshold, her eyes adjusted quickly to the low light. No bugs chirped in the cool undergrowth. No birds sang in the shaded branches. No squirrels or rabbits took shelter in the dappled light. Despite being a perfect haven for small creatures, this copse was as abandoned as the hamlets she'd passed. Other than the strange lack of any animals, there was nothing else sinister here.

In fact, after returning the sword to its sheath and taking time to look around, Lyra saw something that caused her to stop and stare. A small entrance, large enough for a single person to walk through, opened into the wall. Shrouded by the trees, the dark postern gate almost escaped her notice. She walked up to see it lead into the ground below, but at a shallow angle that let her see where a hallway began a few feet under the ground. Her attention was drawn to some carvings on a few of the stones composing the frame. They were carved on the right and left sides of the doorway, fairly small but very ornate. The stones were carved from common rock but within the runes were soft veins of what looked to perhaps be quartz. The white, glistening striations didn't seem to fit within the plain rock. A slight wave of calm washed over her upon viewing them. She enjoyed the brief respite and took it as a sign to continue through the postern.

She took the steps down and felt the air grow colder from the stone and shade. A breeze cut through and led her eyes to the broken remains of a door about halfway through the tunnel under the wall. It grew fairly dark, and she had to take slow, cautious steps, but the tunnel seemed to last just as long as the wall was wide. A bright square of light awaited her at the other end.

Traversing the short hall of the postern gate gave her the sensation of passing into another world. The chill of the wind turned and twisted in her gut as she emerged through the other side. Wide, paved avenues were flanked on either side by buildings of varying stories but similar designs. Felled signposts lay on the ground amid broken barrels, tattered clothes, ruined wagons and carriages, and other various debris and refuse. Something felt off about the smashed remains. Lyra circled the various carts, some designed to be pulled by a human, others by horses. The carriages ranged from very plain to incredibly ornate. Some of their doors were open, but nothing was inside, and that's when she realized what was wrong.

There was no evidence of any remains—human or animal. Even the largest of the carts and carriages that would require a team of horses had no decayed remains of the animals, not even bones. She did find bloodstains in various sizes, though. Some small and smattered along walls. Others belonged to what were once large, dark pools that had long dried and stained the stones. It made her ill to think about, but the lack of any remains from whence the blood should have come disturbed her in a completely different way.

Also, she noticed that the shattered remains of the traffic all led one way. Lyra followed the endless trail of the panicked flight back around to the main gate. The broken wreckage piled up so thick that she was forced to begin walking on top of it, stepping from cart to carriage. It was almost as perilous as attempting to climb the outer wall. The wood cracked and moaned under her feet, sometimes splitting and only held together by the rusting metal framework. Once, her footing slipped and she tumbled through the frayed top of a maroon carriage, the fabric dull, faded, and bereft of almost all color, and landed inside an interior more opulent than anything she'd seen in her life. Again, no evidence of any living creature could be seen.

All the belongings and transportation bottlenecked at a

point near the gate before stopping abruptly. The area around the large, closed doors was empty for several dozen feet all around. Her jaw clenched and her stomach tightened when she saw the courtyard was stained red, from wall to wall and from the gate to the edge of the streets filled with debris. Like elsewhere, the stones were stained a deep crimson with not a spot free of dried blood. Some of it had long clotted and left a grotesque texture in places. She covered her mouth, but her nausea overwhelmed her. She turned her head and vomited onto the street. Her heart raced and her mind flooded with horrid possibilities of what could have done this. Mr. Tilling warned her about coming to the city, and the first pangs of regret began to gnaw at her.

She refused to let fear send her retreating. This was a massacre, a full, relentless, merciless genocide of all the people of Felkirk, but even human hands could commit this atrocity. If she used the term "human" loosely, that is. Only a soulless husk of a person could be involved in such brutality. Her purpose here was not to mourn the decades-old destruction of the city but to find a way to help her father. That was what should drive her.

This grotesque state would be here forever; she didn't have to be. She turned and left, forcing her eyes away from the carnage and her mind away from the morbid thoughts that fought to intrude on her. Walking over the mass of derelict coaches was tiring, so she found the nearest clear point and started there. She imagined Felkirk would be laid out much like Rainward, certain districts for their given purposes. She imagined they'd just be far larger. No one in Rainward had a map of the city, and none had visited it before. As Mr. Tilling said, the place was strictly avoided. It had been generations since the last visitor from Rainward made it to Felkirk, and that person had long since passed, having not shared any of their experience.

Away from the stomach-curling sight at the main gate, the streets Lyra found herself in were not of any particularly frightening sort; however, they were eerily empty. Some open doors and windows stared back at her, dark and lifeless. A faint breeze blew refuse along the cobblestones and occasionally whipped into small, circular flurries. This was also the only sound. Her footsteps didn't even appear to echo. This began to make her recant her earlier thoughts on how frightening the dead city appeared to be.

She tried to read the signs posted above certain buildings and find out what sort of district she may be in. Most of the buildings appeared to be townhouses or offices, but most of the signs had either fallen and rotted away or had become so faded she could no longer discern what they said. Looking inside the buildings provided little else in terms of information. Some appeared to be houses, and others contained furnishing of a sort that could belong to homes or offices. After leaving one particularly empty building, she sighed heavily and wrapped her coat around herself tighter. The chill had grown noticeably, though the sky hadn't changed. No heavy, gray clouds worked their way overhead and the sun hadn't yet begun to go down.

She tightened the belt of her coat and took a small pull from the flask Mr. Tilling provided. Coughing, she returned it to its pouch. She'd never cared for brandy, preferring the smoky sting of whiskey, but Mr. Tilling only had the sweeter drink available. She thought it was the liquor hitting her partially empty stomach that caused a tingling sensation in her gut. However, she knew this not to be the case. This tingling was the instinctual reflex of her body telling her someone was watching her.

If there was one person here, she had to assume there were others. She calmly looked around, trying to appear as though she were deciding on where to go next. Meanwhile, her eyes scanned every alley, window, open door, and corner her eyes landed on. She saw no one and began to think her mind was trying to let fear overcome her again. She was momentarily agitated, in part at having made no real progress since entering the city, but then something fluttered in her peripheral vision. She blinked and looked in the direction of where it came from. She expected nothing, but her heart sank when she discovered she was wrong. Ice filled her stomach, and panic poked at the back of her.

Beyond the end of the street, over the crumbling tiled rooftops, the wall of the city rose like a black background against the sky. The clouds rolled behind the evenly-spaced towers, providing a stark white backdrop. In between two of the towers, standing perfectly still, was the stark silhouette of someone watching her. The hooded figure's ragged clothes whipped in the wind, tattered strands curling and flicking like a reptilian tongue. She stared back, squinting to make out any details she could. The only defining feature of the figure was its complete esotericism. They seemed formed of darkness itself, standing in defiance of the daylight surrounding it. Lyra felt pressure on her chest again and thought for a moment she would relive the panic of having the wind knocked from her.

"Hello?" she called out. Her voice broke, but not enough that it shouldn't have carried on the wind all the way to the figure on the wall.

They didn't reply and continued to stand so still that Lyra thought for a moment that she wasn't looking at a person at all but rather some torn and tattered flag or banner that wrapped itself around a tall, thin pole. Then, the figure shifted on its feet slightly and cocked its hooded head somewhat. This subtle gesture, even from a figure so far away, caused her heart to skip, and a frightened chirp escaped her.

"What do you want?" she asked, yelling at the figure but not making herself sound threatening. "I don't have any food or valuables. I'm looking for a library or, maybe, a temple?"

Still, no reply. She felt for the blade on her bag but didn't draw it. If this person was alone, they might only be cautious; she couldn't blame them for that. But she wanted them to see that she was armed in the event they had cohorts lurking about or had ill intentions themselves.

She began to walk in their direction. Slowly, her hollow, unechoing steps brought her nearer to the dark figure. They were so far away, though, that she couldn't discern any further details about them. After a few steps, she stopped and grabbed the hilt of her blade. She couldn't explain the feeling; it washed over her as quick as a cloudburst. The feeling was as sharp as stepping barefoot on a scorpion's sting: a wave of malevolence so fierce and hateful that it took her breath away. Her feet refused to move, as though her body denied her the choice to flee some danger she was unaware of.

Her eyes couldn't move away from the figure on the wall. She was enraptured by it. The hooded head cocked in the other direction, then Lyra felt a weight come off her shoulders. It felt safe to move again, or so her body told her. Her arms felt like they weighed a dozen pounds each. Her knees threatened to buckle. She breathed in and out steadily, trying to calm herself. The streets around her were still empty. No other people came out of the shadows. Her fear of being ambushed abated. Looking back to where the figure should have been, she saw no one. They had gone. Her eyes hadn't left the wall for more than a moment; she would have seen the figure run off or even fall if that was the case. No, they had simply disappeared.

The warnings about the city once again echoed in her ears. Memories of her father—pale, weak, and frail as an autumn leaf— stoked her courage and burned away the bad feeling in her gut. She pressed on, searching dwelling after dwelling in hopes of finding something that would lead her to a more useful district. Each place provided more of the same; no information to help her quest and no food to refill her supplies. So she searched some more, unaware of that figure that continued to watch from a different vantage point, high atop the pointed spire of a watchtower. Its unknowable gaze followed her, eternally patient, as the tattered, stained rags it wore flapped in the wind like a fiendish flag.

THE FIRST DISTRICT must have housed merchants and craftsmen. Even had Lyra found any texts, they'd likely be for smithing, food preparation, or some other trade. If the social pecking order of Rainward was anything like Felkirk, the alchemists and apothecaries would be held in slightly higher standing, though not quite to the level of any aristocracy or nobility; not that there was such a thing as nobility in Rainward. Not even the mayor and his council.

If this district was such merchant housing, then the market must be nearby. When she needed more supplies, she would have to remember this, but finding the area used by the medical experts was her higher priority. A library would be closer to them.

She followed the main thoroughfare, expecting it to guide her from one main area to the next. To her delight, it seemed she was proven correct. She found another wall, this one with another wide and tall gate closed before her. This appeared to be more of a partition than the large outer walls, however, and had a large plaque hung next to the grayish wooden doors: "Glass District, Under the Purview and Protection of Lord Dimetrius Faulan."

Strange, Lyra thought. Did all the old cities section them-selves off like this?

She groaned inwardly, wondering if most of her time was going to be spent finding a way through walls. She tried pulling on the large handle and felt the door give, her worries easing. The opening wouldn't relinquish any further, but it wasn't locked. It felt as though someone was holding it from the other side.

"What the hell?" she grunted. "Is someone there?"

No one answered. She continued to pull, yelling as the opposing force on the other side made her efforts useless. She gave a final, baleful shout before letting go. She screamed again, her frustration overflowing. The anger and carelessness with which she ripped her sword from its sheath nearly tore the whole thing from her bag. She struck blow after frustrated blow against the door, chipping away at the wood, dulling the blade, and getting nowhere in her efforts. It made her feel better, though.

Her labored breaths came heavy and rhythmic. She leaned against the door with her forehead, let the blade fall from her hand, and heard it clang against the cobblestone at her feet. She didn't want to cry again. The thought of crying only made her angrier. This stupid city, with its blood-stained cobblestones and magically locked gates. She was getting nowhere, and her first day was wasting away as she made her way at a snail's pace through Felkirk.

Lyra grabbed her chest. Her breath caught and she felt the overpowering malevolence from earlier. It gave her the impres-sion that someone was trying to grab her and haul her away to some horrible fate. It became hard to breathe again, and she dropped to a knee to grab the sword.

Let go of me, she thought. *Let. Go. Of. Me,* she repeated in her head, louder. She squeezed the handle of the sword.

Different

She heard the word in her head, but it wasn't her voice.

"Who said that?" she asked out loud. Her hand still gripped her chest, where panic pulled at her from some foreign source.

You are...different

"Who is that?" she shouted. "Where *are* you?"

Here

The way the voice revealed itself, the fact it said it was "here," shocked her out of her paralyzed state. She gripped the sword with both hands and held it in front of her, turning around to look for the source of the voice. How could she find a voice in her head?

The street in front of her was empty. The door behind her was still closed. She searched the walls of Felkirk that peeked above the faded rooftops. The wind was picking up as the daylight dimmed and the afternoon grew late, and there was no shadowed figure with ragged clothing whipping in the gusts. No voice came from an alley or one of the empty houses.

I am here. In city. I...am...city. I am Felkirk

The voice buzzed in her head. It reminded her of the time when she was young and saw a tarantula quivering strangely in a field. The large spider was enough to terrify her, but its odd movements made her wonder what was wrong. When a swarm of tiny wasps broke free and crawled over the poor spider, she screamed so loud her father came running from town. The tiny, shimmering, blue-green wasps crawled over the poor creature and began devouring it. By the time her father had arrived, thousands of small bites from thousands of small mandibles had rendered the tarantula to a near husk.

That memory came back in a horrifying, droning rush. Her brain and ears must feel like that tarantula once did, with the voice rising in prickling tones before stinging her ears and registering as words. She clenched her head in her hands.

You do not belong

The pain dulled as the voice continued speaking, as though her mind had become accustomed to the wrongness of its origin. Her body still shuddered every time it spoke.

Why are you

"Why am I?" she replied aloud. "That makes no sense."

Why are you

The voice repeated itself, though there was a deeper level of malice to the question. Lyra continued to look around for it, turning slowly in place. The voice said it was the city, Felkirk. Such a statement would have made sense coming from an egomaniacal lord or noble. She'd once heard a captain say the same thing about his ship. All his sailors disagreed, though they did come to the unanimous decision that he was an insufferable asshole. She gritted her teeth as the memory of the pain from the voice's introduction still rang in her ears. She was inclined to come to the same conclusion about its owner were she not so afraid.

This voice didn't come from a narcissistic sea captain. It came from within her, like her own thoughts turned against her. She had no choice, it seemed, but to answer.

"I need to find a library or a hospital. Or a temple. I'm trying to save my father."

Father. The voice echoed the word, but the strange inflection left her wondering if it was questioning her or the meaning behind the word itself.

"Yes, he's very sick."

What sickness

Her eyes grew warm with tears once again. The strangeness of the city and the fear induced by the malevolent voice melted away for a moment as her heart ached for more familiar reasons.

"We don't know," she answered with a crack in her voice before clearing her throat. "That's why I'm here."

There was silence. It dragged on until Lyra felt the source of the voice had left, faded away to leave her once more alone in the bizarre streets of Felkirk. She soon found herself not quite so lucky.

Did his body...grow. Does it feed the Garden

If this truly were the voice of the Felkirk itself, it appeared to only speak in riddles. Even its questions didn't quite sound right. The inflections were all wrong.

"What do you mean?"

Does he look...changed. Is his...skin pale. Is there growth. On him. In him. Blooms and gristle. Upon the flesh.

The words alone made her soul shrivel. The way the voice said them compounded it further. She wanted to physically curl herself up and shrink away so the voice couldn't find her. The description, asked so respectfully, almost reverently, that it left her hands shaking.

"N-no," she stammered, hoping that answering would make this thing go away. "Nothing like that. He's weak and frail and... not getting any better."

A sigh—at least she assumed it was a sigh—rolled through her mind like a foul breath. It seemed to stir up the winds in the streets, as well, as swirling breezes kicked up refuse and carried it down the vacant avenues. Dirt stung her eyes, and she reflexively clenched them shut. Her hair whipped about as the air funneled through a nearby alley and billowed around her. She covered her face and held her hair down, waiting for the wind to dissipate.

She opened her eyes to a scene different than the one moments before. The buildings were still in place, and the cobblestone streets still ran in the same paths, but they appeared aged by centuries. A brown film covered whole patches of the city, all the way to the outer wall. The roofs appeared rotted and had several holes, revealing the beams of wood underneath. The towers, which already had the look of collapsing, were decayed further still. Some leaned over, on the verge of falling into the city. Others stood by the grace of a few stones and luck. Felkirk looked like a decomposing animal's corpse lying in the sun. Bits of refuse, silhouetted against the sky and carried by the wind, drifted around like buzzing flies.

In spite of this sudden transformation, one thing stood out above all. Lyra had heard many words associated with the city of Felkirk: vile, evil, despicable, wretched, dangerous. These all defined that fel shape, the black banner of Felkirk now perched atop one of the leaning, half-collapsed towers like a crow watching a corpse. The surroundings felt more appropriate with whoever, or whatever, that figure was. It was more than just some aesthetic fancy; Lyra realized that upon seeing the city in this state, her mind felt less strained looking at it despite its more horrific state.

"Please," she said loudly but without begging, "whoever you are, let me through this gate."

Lyra had a very strong feeling that this person had sealed the gate somehow. Too many strange occurrences were tied to them; the depth of their power was both unknown and frightening to her. She knew nothing about magic and could only assume the worst about its capabilities.

She was quickly proven right, however, as she turned to give the gate another pull and found it already open. It was unsettling that she hadn't heard the large door and its old hinges when it opened, but she took advantage of the opportunity.

Cautiously, she walked through the gate and under the small, ornate arch looping across the threshold. The buildings were different here. They had stone foundations reaching nearly halfway up the structure and what were once much finer designs than the previous district. It was still as decrepit and dismal as what she'd seen before.

The windows here were larger and gaped like dead, black holes of dozens of skulls lining the street. The doors were all open, too, and this made her swallow nervously. There wasn't any natural disarray like in the previous district: some doors were open, some closed, some falling on their hinges and others broken to pieces. All the doors here opened outward, swung out fully on their hinges in some strange, grand showcase.

Her footsteps echoed as she passed the houses, too afraid of the yawning darkness behind each doorframe to go inside. She resigned herself to looking for more specific buildings before daring to go in. She stopped at a crossroads to look in each direction, hoping to see something helpful to guide her way. A building on the corner was built to face the crossroads itself, the door opening in Lyra's direction. Now that she'd stopped, she could hear something coming from inside the building.

It sounded like a gasp. A weak, short gasp, but another soon followed. Was someone in the building? Her heartbeat sped up, thumping loudly in the silence.

"Hello?" she called out; no one answered.

She heard more gasping, this time coming from another building to her left. She spun on her heel, seeing only darkness inside. There should have been shadows or weak light from the windows visible within the buildings from where she was standing, but it was only a deep blackness. The gasping came from behind that ink-dark wall between the frames.

This isn't right, she thought. *I need to get out of here.*

Nothing was right about this city, but she felt a different sort of urgency. The gasping sounds took on a different form after hearing them over and over again. Some were gasps, some poor souls trying to suck in air so sharply it sounded painful; others were more of a moan.

She felt pressure on her ankle. When trying to pull her foot away failed, she looked down and saw a hand grasping her.

Screaming, she pulled and kicked at the thing holding her. It looked like an arm, but it emerged from the cobblestones—no, it was a part of the cobblestones. The shimmering, wet-looking appendage reminded Lyra of a drowned man who once washed up on the shore near the docks. The gray-green skin looked about to disintegrate into a disgusting mush at any moment, yet it held her firmly. The skeletal fingers dug into her ankle painfully.

Her eyes widened with terror and her screams died in her throat. From the infinite blackness of the doorways, something slithered onto the street. A bubbling mass of molten flesh slunk from the doorway and fell onto the street like a mass of sloughed skin. Her eyes refused to believe what they saw, thinking that such horror was impossible.

The bubble shapes were each separate heads, with faces melting into the rest of the mass. Their eyes were either dark, empty sockets or contained the barest visage of eyes; white, wet orbs that alternated between squinting in pain and widening in fear.

The moaning and gasping came from multiple gatherings of the fleshy masses. The hellish growths crawled slowly across the street towards her. The head-like boils burbled and writhed, disappearing and reappearing within the combined wax-like glob of flesh. Sometimes the masses converged, merging into a larger form, all moving together towards Lyra.

More of the arms, the color of grave moss, reached from the cobblestones in all parts of the street. She screamed again, her throat nearly raw, as some of the slime-slick arms pulled themselves up, producing a torso from the ground. They moved with the slowness of one buried for ages, rising at the sign of life. A drooping head emerged attached to each set of shoulders that managed to make their way out of the cobblestones. The spines of the bodies were protruding, attempting to push through the stretched skin.

As with the arms, the corpses emerged from the stone itself, blending into the worn rock where they made contact. The faces of these pitiful, wicked things were nearly worse than the demonic tumors. Cold, gray eyes burned in the sockets like white fire; teeth gnashed and clacked. Something hung off them, either skin or old clothing, but the wet, gray-green color made the whole figure appear coated in slime and impossible to discern much else other than the general shape.

She unsheathed her sword again, gripping it so tightly her knuckles were white. She gritted her teeth, bestial grunts spurred by her horror-stricken will to survive escaping her throat. She looked down at the hand holding her, its opposite now trying to pull up the body to which it belonged.

Fuck you! she screamed in her head, over and over again. She swiped at the arm, trying as hard as she could within her panicked thoughts to not cut off her own leg. The sword connected with the arm and, with a sickening squelch, severed it at the wrist. A thin black fluid poured from the wound, pooling on the ground. Her foot freed, Lyra ran from the crossroad, not looking back. She continued to squeeze the hilt of the sword until her hand hurt. The black fluid ran in rivulets from the blade, splattering onto the cobblestones and her pants. Choking sobs came from her aching throat, burning from the screams.

When she finally stopped, it was to stagger against the wall of a building. There, she let the blade fall again as her panicked flight left her spent. She fell to her knees and let the crying consume her for a moment. Her mind went numb, lost in anguish and confusion, then began to race with questions and possibilities. *What happened in Felkirk? Who was that ragged figure? Were they responsible? Was that the work of magic that damned those people to such a fate?*

As her breathing slowed, she picked up the sword and stared at the foul substance coating the blade. It turned thick and sticky like black honey. She tried wiping it on her pants and the substance only clung to the blade, pulling the cloth along with it.

Disgusting, she thought, feeling a lump in her throat that may have been from crying or an attempt to vomit. Or, honestly, both.

She didn't want to risk putting the blade back in its sheath in this condition, so she held on to it as she stepped out into the open, looking for any sign of the shrouded figure or the horrible abominations. She found neither but saw something much better. An official-looking building stood on a small hill that sloped up from the surrounding buildings.

She walked towards it quickly, making a beeline for the door. Without knocking, she pushed it open and stepped into an interior that looked unmolested. No discolored stains, remnants of blood, bodies, or any refuse could be seen. Desks were lined up properly and each had an inkwell sitting on top of it. The contents had long since dried. Paper and quills, both brittle and faded, were all she found in the drawers. But as she continued looking, she came upon a number of shelves containing books. She smiled, tempted to cry tears of joy, but resisted. Mr. Tilling needed specific kinds of books, and she didn't yet know what these were.

Most of the pages were filled with ledgers and histories. Some of them were even in languages she didn't know. As volume after volume turned out to be useless, she began to lose heart. Finally, in one of the second-story rooms, she found the former workspace of someone adept at using potions and chemicals, complete with an array of equipment, most of which consisted of various glass vials and bottles. Of course, there were also scrolls and books. She didn't know many of the terms and words used, but there were a few things that looked like it would be very helpful. She carefully placed these in her bag and made her way out of the workspace and down the stairs.

Her heart and burdens finally much lighter, she left the building and wondered if this would be enough to help her father. The risk was great; if she left Felkirk now, she knew she could never make it back. If she continued, she could happen upon some other form of malevolent magic—the only explanation she could think of for the events at the crossroads—or the strange figure. She sat on a bench outside the building, surrounded by dead trees and yellowed, barely-living grass. This was a tough choice. She pulled the flask out of her bag and took a swig of the brandy, then tried pouring some onto the blade to see if it would help clean off the foul gunk. To her surprise, it worked. When she tried rubbing the blade against her pant leg again, the alcohol had managed to work away some of the grime. However, she noticed the spots where some of it had landed on her pants during her escape when it was fresh from the wound. Where the foul blood had landed, her pants had faded, almost wearing through the fabric. It didn't burn like anything acidic, but the cloth was certainly faded and thinned away.

She sheathed the blade and focused back on her decision. The brandy had warmed her stomach and stoked her courage. Finding something useful for Mr. Tilling gave her a spark of inspiration.

"One more place," she said to herself, just to hear a normal voice. "One more, and I'll leave this cursed, horrible place behind forever."

She stood from the bench and looked down the small hill. She saw where another thin wall noted the transition into the city's next district. She sighed, hoping this time it would be easier to cross over. She located the small arch that signified the location of the gate and mentally marked out a path by seeing what streets and turns would take her there the quickest. As soon as her first step was finished, her eyes flicked momentarily back to the arch; there, she saw it waiting.

The figure stood on top of the arch; this time, no wind tore at its robes. The long strips of the night-black cloth hung flaccidly over the rusted arch. The faceless hole within the large cowl leered in her direction, the shoulders slightly rising and falling a single time, like some sort of shrug or stretch rather than any indication of a breath. Regardless, it seemed an exasperated gesture.

You live

The words were again strangely inflected, so she couldn't tell if the figure was asking a question or stating a fact, angry or uncaring.

"Yes, I do," she replied flatly. "What were those creatures at the crossroads? Were those your doing?"

She asked the question carefully, guarding her emotions. If this was some powerful mage, she didn't want to anger them, especially now that she had something to return to Mr. Tilling with.

Yes

The frank honesty and brevity of the answer took Lyra by surprise. She pursed her lips as her gut curdled and knotted. Her next words lodged in her throat, causing her to stutter as she tried to get them out.

"Are you...are you trying to kill me?"

The cowl dipped slightly. A brief gust of wind rustled the robes. The clouds moved slow and lazy as though buying time so they could see what would happen. The figure didn't answer right away, and the moment seemed to last for years.

No

"You hesitated—you're lying."

She fought to keep her voice even. The more this figure looked at her, the less it seemed to be human; and a subtle sense of dread crept into her bones like cold, persistent rain.

Not lying. Wrong word

What did he mean? Wrong word?

"I don't understand you; what do you mean 'wrong word'? Who *are* you?"

The frustration in her voice was starting to slip. The living nightmare of Felkirk and the constant stalking of this strange person—if it indeed was a person—pecked away at her resolve and patience. The persistent magic being used to invade her thoughts and summon unthinkable atrocities in some attempt to frighten her away, since this entity insisted it wasn't trying to kill her, gnawed at her sanity. Powerful mage or not, she knew there was something here that could help her father, and no mysterious, riddle-posing magic-user was going to hinder her.

She glared back at the figure as it watched her, refusing to answer her question. She grimaced, eyes flaring, and wrapped her fingers around the handle of the blade. She didn't draw it, only let her hand hold it in a gesture of her own defiance.

That weapon. Useless

The overwhelming, evil pressure struck her again. It rang in her ears and made her head swim. She closed her eyes and shook it away. A grunt of pain escaped her as a sharp pang rattled in her skull. When her focus returned, the strange mage was once again gone. She sighed in frustration and began her descent down the hill and toward the arch. She drew the blade once she reached the streets, just to be safe.

No further interruptions arose on her walk to the gate. As she drew closer, a flicker of light caught on the face of another large plaque. This one read: "Pearl District, Under the Purview and Protection of Lord Dautrus Kaul." The plaque must have been beautiful once, its entire surface made of silver and framed in an ornate golden frame. Now, everything was tarnished and smattered with more bloody stains. The gate under the arch was identical to the one entering the Glass District.

She grabbed the textured iron handle and pulled, expecting the same resistance as the previous gate. To her surprise, the wheels and hinges squealed as it slid to the side, unhindered. The iron support on the bottom made a harsh grinding sound to complement the screeching hinges. She grunted as she pulled the gate aside. It was difficult, but not due to any magic; just an old gate wishing to stay locked in place for all time.

Once she had enough room to get proper ballast by placing one hand against the gate and the other against the wall, she gritted her teeth and pushed outward, making enough room for her to walk through. She smiled, pleased with herself, and then looked into the next district. Her blood turned cold. She reflexively stepped back as a thousand featureless faces turned to her at once, their naked bodies standing shoulder to shoulder, crowding the streets and houses beyond.

THE TERROR she'd experienced thus far began to harden her senses, though not by much. She'd recovered from the shock quicker than before and practically leaped at the gate, grabbing the handle and trying to pull it shut. Now, it refused to move. She pulled until her muscles hurt, then dug her feet into the crevices between cobblestones and tried to gain any extra leverage she could. Nothing worked; the gate held firm, and it was likely the work of that damned mage.

Breathing heavily from the exertion and fear, sweat dripping from her face, she waited for the appalling horde to rush her. Surprisingly, they merely stood there. Their bodies, in disturbing unison, turned toward her to align with their—literally—blank faces.

Lyra's mouth hung open, once more aghast at the sight before her. To get through any of them, she'd have to push them aside. There was no clear path.

Fuck that, she thought. *And fuck this city.*

She turned to backtrack through the Glass District; certainly, there was another gate into the Pearl District somewhere along the partition wall. When she spun around, though, she found her way blocked by more of the faceless atrocities. Now, they crowded the streets behind her, all the way up the hill to the building she'd departed only minutes ago. They were everywhere.

How'd they get around me? She thought, panic starting to grip her.

None of them made any noise. The large crowd and the complete silence grated on her nerves. Her heartbeat became audible, pounding in her chest and threatening to burst forth from it. She drew the blade, black stains streaking along its once-shining sides. She stepped forward slowly, waiting for one of them to make a move. There were men, women, and even children among them. All of them were pale-skinned and of all body types. Fat, thin, tall, and short; muscular and gaunt, young and old.

When she came within a few steps from where the horde started, they began rapidly clenching and unclenching their fists. She stopped and placed her other hand on the sword's grip, ready to strike at any of them. The strange clenching made the sound of ten thousand whispers echoing through the streets. It was worse than any moaning or gasping.

"Back away," she threatened, her voice a comfort in the midst of the awful shuffling sound of their hands. No one answered. They had no mouths to answer with, but she hoped that at least the blade would frighten them off.

She suddenly felt very foolish. *They don't have eyes.*

Her own eyes darted among them. They had ears, though, and despite all the other missing features, their hair and other body organs, exposed by their nakedness, were fully intact. All combined to make them as soul-shuddering a sight as possible.

"I have a sword," she said as authoritatively as possible. Nothing changed.

She was an arm's length away now; all their heads followed her movements, hands clenching and unclenching and clenching and unclenching; damnable whispers of the other-wise mute and expressionless. She placed the flat edge of the sword against the muscled physique of the faceless man in front of her, if he was still even human at all. The blade had to be cold against his bare skin, but he didn't react in the slightest.

"Please," she said, a knot building in her throat, "move away."

The humanoid thing continued clenching its hands. She realized, being this close, that they weren't looking *at* her; they were looking through her, as though they were ordered to look in her general direction.

She pressed the tip of the blade against its stomach, but not enough to draw blood. She closed her eyes, preparing herself to run this man-thing through if they refused to move. Maybe it was for the best. She might be relieving their suffering, whatever they were.

A slight sob escaped. She couldn't do it. This thing still appeared human, cursed though it may be. She lowered her arms, the tip of the sword dropping away and passing by the constantly moving hands. Lyra kept the sword ready but lowered it to her side. Steeling herself against the fear and dread mounting inside, she began walking forward.

Heads turned, followed by bodies, and always was the whis-pering sound of the hands. She shouldered past one after the other. None of them attacked or approached; all stood still other than to turn in her direction. This continued for a few dozen steps, all of them agonizingly slow. She walked unmolested and then heard a muffled, echoing cry. It was brief, like someone shouting and having their mouth abruptly covered. It broke her from the haunted focus she'd maintained to get through the fiendish throng. Her eyes darted around first. Seeing nothing, she continued pressing forward until she heard it again.

Her shoulders brushed passed one of the bodies as the sound came from somewhere close. The next even closer. She dared to look around now at the hundreds of featureless, hair-framed faces. One of them flickered; no, not a flicker, rather something changed momentarily on their face.

She heard one of the strange cries, and one of the faces stretched, an open mouth running diagonally the length of their chin to their forehead. Lyra gasped and forced herself to keep moving. Another face, this one directly in front of her, made the same noise as a large set of teeth briefly tried chewing through the face's flesh, chomping and gnashing from behind it.

The shouts became more frequent, punctuating the whispering noise of the hands. No words ever formed, just echoing, stifled cries one after another. Lyra continued to press through them, her steps picking up faster and faster until she was jogging, shoving the pale, nude bodies away with force enough to knock them down. She didn't even know where she was going. She just wanted to run.

The bodies fell to the side, one after another, as she continued pushing her way through in a directionless flight. She once tripped and fell against one of them when she came to a street corner and lost her footing. They both crashed against the wall of a building, and she felt the lukewarm temperature of the rubbery flesh against her hands. The grotesque face filled her vision, and she screamed when one of the cries echoed in her ears and an open mouth, distorted in pain, pressed from the other side of the figure's facial skin. She swung her blade, not aiming anywhere in particular, and cut the head from the body. It fell to the ground, hands still making the same horrible gesture, while the bloodless, exposed neck stared back at her.

She continued running, cutting them down now that she knew they couldn't be human. Each body fell to the ground, hands whispering and whispering, no blood escaping what should have been gushing wounds. The shouts chased her until she finally fell against another partition wall. She never thought she'd be so happy to see one again. She followed it, keeping one hand against the rough stones so she wouldn't get separated from it, using her other hand, still holding her sword, to push and hack away at the humanoid things that never ceased appearing.

An arch came into view, and she thanked any gods that were listening. The sight gave her a renewed burst of energy. A half-sane cackle escaped her lips as she pushed even harder to get to the gate. Every swing of her arm removed a limb or a head, or opened a dry gash in a stomach or side. The heinous whispering noise was broken by staccato cries, interspersed with the thud of dismembered parts and falling bodies, all blending together into a cacophony of insane music.

She didn't realize she'd made it to the gate until her sword dug into wood and stuck there, shaking her out of the panicked fugue. The final didn't even land against one of the hideous, inhuman things. It cut through air. Her head cleared and her eyes beheld empty streets once again. They were all gone. The hideous whispering sound and muffled screams both ceased. The only blank faces around belonged to the sides of buildings.

Lyra didn't stop to look at anything. She grabbed the handle to the gate and pulled with a strength born of desperation. This gate opened fairly easily, but her mind was too frenzied to notice. She went through and slammed the gate behind her. A plaque fell from where it had hung perilously on weakened supports, but Lyra didn't hear it. It landed on the ground and cracked in half, its tarnished silver face marred with deep scratches. The only visible words were "Papyrus District;" the name of the lord or lady in charge being unreadable, but Lyra didn't see it. She only wanted to be through, away from the faceless horrors.

"What fresh hell waits for me here?" she asked aloud to herself. There seemed to be very few homes here. Most of the buildings looked bland and official. The streets were paved differently, with a reddish stone cut into shapes more akin to bricks than cobblestone.

She wandered for a while, waiting for any sign of some unthinkable monster to chase her or some undead children to try and eat her. Perhaps the shrouded figure would show itself again. Every anxious step was met with silence and emptiness. Lyra decided it was probably best to focus her efforts on her search and push her other thoughts and fears aside.

The sun grew lower in the sky. It seemed like it should be later, but with all that had occurred, her concept of time was likely greatly skewed. She didn't even feel hungry, and it must have been hours since she'd last eaten. She pulled the flask from her bag and took a drink, followed by several swigs from her waterskin.

Nothing useful presented itself, not even another wall partition. She did find a plaza, complete with a decorative but dry water fountain. She sat on the edge and took a moment to think. The buildings here were mostly single-story, with a few two-story structures popping up here and there. The red-bricked streets fanned out from this plaza, so she must have been in a central location for this district. That could prove helpful.

This sane, technical line of thinking calmed her. Formulating a plan grounded her in reality, and she began to think more clearly. It wasn't meant to last. She felt something pulling at her brain, like two sharp claws pulling at the membrane of her mind. Lyra turned her head to see the familiar black tatters of the cruel mage atop the outer wall again. He refused to ever get close, always waiting and watching in the distance.

"Are you afraid of me?" She called out, turning away to not give him the satisfaction of too much attention.

No. No fear

"Then why do you always pop up on a wall far away like some kind of annoying squirrel?" she mocked, tired of his or her or its games.

I see from everywhere. I talk from everywhere. Distance is meaningless

"So, you've been watching this whole time." It was a statement, not a question.

Yes

"Those things—the faceless people—you did that, didn't you?"

After a few moments, the figure answered, *Yes*

Lyra stood, nearly jumping from her seat at the fountain. "Why? What did you do to this place?"

She shouted at the figure, who continued to stand unmoving while its robes rustled in the wind atop the wall.

Consumed. This city is, was mine

Consumed? The thought horrified her, but she didn't quite understand what the figure could mean.

"I thought you said you were the city; that you were Felkirk?"

I am. That and more. Consume its people, take its meaning. Continue my purpose

"You aren't making any sense! What are you? Are you human? Elf-kind? Something else?"

Beyond those. Tried to understand your language. Only one of mine to try. Curious. Wanted to know

"There are others like you?" Her heart sank. "Is your kind a religion? A people? Are you from another country?"

No country. No people. Religion...strange word

"You studied my language. It sounds wrong. Maybe you should've studied it more before you 'consumed' Felkirk; whatever the hell you mean by that."

Language. You are human. Human, cattle, insect. This is order of life. Do you talk with cattle

Her face scrunched. What was he getting at? "No, I don't."

Insects

"Of course not; what are you—"

The voice in her head cut her off.

Cattle speak. Insects speak. They must. All things speak. You are not capable of speaking with cattle. Cattle do not speak to insects. Language is different. More simple, but impossible for you to replicate. I seek to speak with humans, elf-kind, dwarves. Like insects. I cannot replicate such simple thought. Language too simple

Cattle and insects speaking? She wondered if he meant 'communicate.' If that's the case, then he must be saying their language, that of the people of Alda, is too simple for him, like her trying to buzz at a bee and make sense. That would mean that, whatever this figure is, it wasn't human, dwarf, or elf-kind. It wasn't even from Alda. Other realizations began to creep in, and her mind tried desperately to hold those truths at bay.

"You're not from here, from Alda; where are you from?" she asked breathlessly, but feared the answer.

The Throne

The phrase held something within, as though the words themselves beget some kind of power. Her soul shuddered, and she felt a fear she never knew existed. It was quick in passing, like a sword opening her bare back before the pain suddenly ripped away. She didn't realize she was shaking.

"What throne? Are you a king? Did you lay claim on the city and name yourself the King of Felkirk?"

No. Throne is...wrong. Wrong word. Cannot be said. Cannot be spoken. Language is too simple to describe. You will see. Wait first, then see. Lords of Felkirk wanted offer. I am king...they live

She didn't understand the first part: a throne that couldn't be explained in her language. However, the second part did make sense. The lords of Felkirk tried to bargain with whatever this figure was.

"The lords of the city wanted to make a deal with you. Were they that afraid of you?"

Fear. No. Terror. Yes. They see my efforts and want to be spared

"Your...efforts?" she repeated hesitantly.

Hunger must be sated. I need to continue. Persist. Felkirk provided

Dear gods, she thought, her head aching as the unspeakable picture began to fall into place. "You didn't want to rule. You wanted to...feed?" she could barely get the last word out. The thought made her want to vomit.

I cannot rule. Refuse. Not made to rule. Throne rules. I feed. Wait. No bargain to make

"I thought you said that 'throne' was the wrong word?"

It is. Only one to use with limitations

"So all these things I've been running into; the puddles of heads, the melting bodies, the faceless people..."

They are what remains

Lyra fell to her knees, catching herself with her hands before she fell into a curled ball on the floor. All the horrible things she'd seen were what remained of the people of Felkirk. But what exactly did this dark, evil thing mean by remains?

"Are they still alive? Can they still feel?"

The words came out so quietly no one could have heard her, but the black figure of Felkirk did. And it answered.

Perhaps. Unsure and does not matter. Purpose served. Except for the lords

Her face grew hot and her stomach felt hollow. She leaned up, then fell back against the fountain, still unable to find the will to stand.

"The lords got away? You did strike a deal with them!"

No bargain. Offer insulted. Angered. Why rule insects. Meaningless anthill. Insult to Throne. I do not rule. I feed. I wait. Lords still...

Her anger abated, but more terror quickly filled the hole left by it. The figure hadn't yet elaborated on what happened to the lords.

"What happened to them?"

Seek explanation. Word evades me

"What could be worse than what you've done to the people? These, what, remnants?"

Take the fuel from their essence as needed. What remains is left for me. Curiosity piqued. I grow bored

"You toy with what's left of their souls?"

Soul? Interesting word. Nothing better to describe. Their...energy. Soul. I take nutrients. The rest is dross. Detritus. Chaff

Warm tears flowed down her face; she was overwhelmed by the revelations. This was no mage. No human. No being from this world or possibly even this reality. It was a monstrosity that couldn't be defined.

"The lords. What happened to the lords?"

A malignance bubbled in her chest. Her stomach felt sick, and her mind stung like her brain had been turned into a hornet's nest, a thousand hemorrhaging pinholes threatening to drown her sanity in blood. It was akin to the feeling that had assailed her during her time in Felkirk but much worse. Had she not already been sitting on the ground, she would have collapsed. Her mouth opened to gasp, but nothing came out.

She saw visions of suffering, each unique in a way that only one who'd lived an eon in the embrace of cruelty could fashion. Images of pain not meant for humans, elf-kind, or dwarfs to know or understand. Experiences built by one who created brutality itself. In those brief flashes, she witnessed agonies that were immediately forgotten. She only knew she'd seen them because of hollow recollections that stained her subconscious like pigments of castigation—knowing and not knowing, remembering but refusing to recall. Within those fractured recollections, each lord continued to exist all these years later at the whims of the vile scourge of Felkirk.

Digesting

The word brushed against her mind as she sobbed uncontrollably, her body wracked with sorrow and desperation.

They will not be absorbed. They will not be vomited out. They shall...experience...devouring. Eternal. Always

Her sobs turned to cries of anguish. She wished with every fiber of her being that the tears would wash away the things in her mind that clanged against the walls of the now-forbidden memories. Even the trace of such witnessed torments drove her to scratch at the ground as her wails echoed among the streets.

When her breathing finally slowed, she looked up and saw the figure still on the wall. Its robes had changed somewhat. They were still dark tatters curled in the wind, with a drooping cowl hiding whatever unspeakable visage lay beneath. But the tattered rags didn't look dark and filthy any longer. They were black as a moonless night. The space within the cowl was no longer hidden in shadow but empty as the space between stars; in the deepest, starless night imaginable.

She looked away, unable to gaze upon the timeless being any longer. In averting her eyes, however, they fell on a building made of light-colored marble. Columns in the front guarded a large, open doorway. Inside, she could see rows of books. Some of the shelves were partially empty, their contents strewn across the floor.

Go. Search

Lyra stood mindlessly, her body feeling numb. The assault against her sanity and senses overpowered her. She stumbled toward the open door and the books beyond. Something in there might help her father. That was what she needed to focus on—her father. Help him. Find something in this hellish place to make everything worthwhile. She could deal with the nightmares later.

The steps were shallow and should have been easy to climb, but her heavy legs stumbled up them with difficulty. Each one felt like a mountain she had to scale. When she reached the top, she looked back and saw the entity—wise enough to no longer call it a human or mage—watching her.

Once inside, she managed to shake off some of the demonic fog that clouded her thought processes. She could focus again, but only slightly. Her hands gripped weakly at the spines of books before her. She pulled them off the shelf and read their titles, her eyes lazily glossing over them. She let them fall from her hands onto the floor with many of their fellows if they sounded useless. She absent-mindedly kicked books out of the way, tread over scrolls, and heard them crunch under her feet. She combed through row after row until she realized she'd stuffed a few volumes into her bag. She didn't even remember doing it.

"Oh," she mumbled when one she found on medicinal herbs wouldn't fit. She let that one fall to the ground, as well.

"Wait," she said to herself when she saw a staircase before her leading down to the library's first floor. "When did I get upstairs?"

She shrugged off the lack of memory and made her way down the staircase with leaden feet. Her hands gripped the railing tightly, feeling inebriated. The bricks attached to the bottom of her legs slammed into each other and fell upon each step with a heavy thud. They implanted themselves on impact and refused to move except with a deliberate sluggishness. She was drunk on trauma, disbelief, and looming insanity.

The door back outside to the cursed city of Felkirk, the capital of the damned and the forgotten, shined with a sick yellow glow. She stumbled out onto the front stoop. The columns holding up the large portico cast long, deep shadows, splitting the ill light like a prison cell. The outside was different, enough even for her shattered mind to recognize.

The red-brick streets and official-looking buildings were in a state of dereliction before but now appeared utterly decayed. The gossamer lining before her eyes had been removed, and everything seemed much as it had in the Glass District, with the natural decay of centuries of abandonment coupled with other-worldly putrefaction that returned the city's image to that of a sun-rotten corpse. The refuse once again drifted on a lazy breeze, heavier than before; the image of buzzing flies swelled to a virulent cloud. The outer wall was nearby, only a street over. The towers reached into the sky like fractured arms with the bones exposed.

Once she'd passed the columns, it felt like she'd stepped into another world. The sun's light was no longer bright; a heavy, tawny hue deepened the shadows everywhere. The clouds took on a slightly lighter shade of yellow, appearing more like an acrid miasma. The air was thick and, even with the breeze, bore a weight that felt wrong.

On top of a nearby temple, where the statue of some forgotten god belonging to better days had split at the waist, perched that bleak crow with its feathers flexing in the wind. It was closer than it had ever been before. Lyra never realized how thin and tall the figure was until she saw it only a few hundred feet away. This amplified the haunting aura surrounding it and increased its menace by a hundredfold.

She stared at it; stared at the night-black thing that had caused her and thousands of others so much misery and torment. Lyra never knew the lords of Felkirk. If they tried to bargain with this otherworldly thing, it might have been to save their city or possibly just to save their own lives. She couldn't imagine they still deserved whatever fate befell them. Her mind couldn't recall the unspeakable agonies the entity allowed her to glimpse. Still, the ripple of their memories was enough for her to know that no one deserved what they continued to suffer and would suffer for eternity.

The immeasurable malice once more pressed against her; wave after wave of ill and evil washed against her. When she was a child, the ocean would crash upon her, pull against her body and her legs as it tried to drag her to its depths. This was similar, though it was felt with every sense of her body. The tides of malevolence pulled and pulled, threatening to wrench her soul from her body. She fought against it, feeling the wicked longing for her life essence wrap around her like brittle, clawed fingers, scratching at the door of her consciousness as she barred the entry with everything she had.

Lyra fell to her knees. She thought to draw the sword but cast the idea aside almost instantly; the weapon would do no good. She couldn't move, couldn't flee. Her arms dropped to her sides, her eyes closed tight, tears building and then streaking down her face. She cried out, screaming against the struggle, the pain, the shadows of repressed and tormented thoughts, and the vile entity itself. She screamed until the reason for screaming turned from pain and sorrow to anger and then back again. The claws kept scratching. The wicked fingers curled into fists and banged on the gateway to her inner being. It was angry, too. Frustrated. She didn't know why and she didn't care. This fucking monster could claw at her mind and soul until she died of exposure on the steps of this library. She would continue to scream back at it until she could no longer.

~

A VOICE CUT through the raging battle. Even through her screams, she heard a profoundly normal, physical voice. It seemed so long since she last heard one that it was unmistakable; a green island in a vast ocean. She went silent, falling over and catching herself with one hand. Gulps of air filled her lungs and raked against her raw throat. As she stared at the ground, listening, dark drops pattered on the hard surface before her. Something blurred her vision, and she had to blink several times before it cleared. She tapped at the drops with her fingers and lifted them close to look at them due to her hazy vision. It was blood; she was crying blood. She wiped frantically at her face, seeing the crimson streaks left behind on her hands.

"Remember me?" a voice called out. It was distant, barely audible.

Her vision was clearer, and she saw the feather-like ragged cloak of the entity droop into flaccid strips, no longer billowing in the wind. The dipped cowl rose sharply; whoever it was certainly had the entity's full attention.

Cockroach. Buzzing, droning insolence

"There's another one of us in there, isn't there?" the voice said, shouting at the scourge of Felkirk. In an instant, the figure melted into the breeze like oil swept away in water. It reappeared on the outer wall, facing away from Lyra.

You will be consumed

"No, I won't. And neither will the other person in there. You can't claim them, can you? All your cosmic power, and you can't claim the morsel so precious to you."

The voice was male, young, and spoke with derision.

"If you can hear me, I'll get you out. I promise!" He shouted even louder, knowing someone waited inside.

Mine

The entity's voice growled.

Leave

A rumbling shook the ground and worked in Lyra's chest.

Leave

Lyra thought she heard a scream come from the other side of the wall. The cowled thing looked as it always did, with no outward displays giving away its disposition. The way it seethed as it told whoever was on the other side of the wall to leave spoke plenty to its anger, though.

She realized her legs and body were free to move again. It took great effort to stand; her extremities were all numb, but she managed. Wherever the figure was focused, that's where the other person was. They said they wanted to help get her out, so she moved for the outer wall as fast as her legs would allow; no more than an awkward stumble yet again. The rumbling continued, throwing her off to the side to fall heavily against the walls of buildings.

"Oh gods," she moaned. She'd caught herself against a wall, and the force spun her back around to face behind herself. The rumbling was such that she couldn't hear the thousands of hands once again working in unison to create the horrible whispering, nor the staccato stifled screams of the tumorous figures that filled the streets behind her.

The slimy-skinned corpses from the crossroads began crawling from the stones once more, this time by the hundreds. The burbling, malignant masses of flesh and heads slid from windows and doors, plopping on the ground and merging and splitting into various sizes. Then, something new and uniquely horrifying emerged from between some of the buildings.

Giant, misshapen humanoid forms lurched out from alleys too narrow to have possibly contained them. Their bodies molded and twisted to fit through. They were merely echoes of human shape; their arms and legs were too long or too short, and none of them were of the same size on any of their respective bodies. The skin sagged from various places and was drawn too tight over others. Bones cracked and tendons creaked as they moved like marionettes with broken strings.

Worst of all, they walked through the hordes of other nightmarish things with complete disregard for any of them. As they stomped over the pale, faceless ones and slipped on the oily corpses and gasping, sucking growths, all were absorbed into the giants. The various parts of flesh melded into the large, ungainly monstrosities with sockets devoid of eyes and mouths missing teeth and gums, only a smeared black substance rimming the vacant orifices. Either none of the creatures felt pain, or their agony was such that it all combined into one cruel sensation of endless pain.

Lyra turned, forcing her legs to turn and keep going for the outer wall. None of the inhuman things behind her followed, seeming focused on their master high on the outer wall and the person who was the current focus of its wrath.

She heard the sound of stone breaking and falling apart. Beneath the angry entity, a hole opened at the base of the outer wall. Individual stones fell as though the mortar holding them together disintegrated or disappeared altogether. The effect spread until an entire section of the wall had collapsed, ground to ramparts. Clouds of dust settled around piles of rubble. The entity hovered in midair as though nothing had changed. The ragged strands of its nocturnal cloak continued to billow and curl around itself. At this close distance, Lyra saw how unnaturally the 'cloak' moved. She also saw no legs or feet belonging to a body to which the shreds of night were attached. Though, she couldn't be sure if the strange attire was simply hiding these, as well.

Something else collapsed along with the wall. The sluggishness in her body began to slip away. Her troubled steps became more controlled. She broke into a run for the hole in Felkirk's wall. The nightmarish creatures also worked their way toward it, but they could only shamble and crawl. Lyra grabbed onto the shoulder straps of her bag and bounded up the piles of rubble, a gazelle freed from the hunter's snare.

She stopped momentarily at the top, looking through the breach to the world outside. This wasn't intended for her to take in the view, though the fields outside had never looked more beautiful; she needed to get a look at where she could run. The wall fell in myriad piles all around the inside and outside of the city. The figure remained where they were, floating directly overhead. A new silhouette waited for her beyond the wall: a very human one.

The man was shrouded in dust, her vision of him obscured further by the sun's harsh rays reflecting off the obstructing cloud. She tried to cover her eyes against the billowing debris and harsh brightness. It became clear it wasn't the sun but a bright sphere of flickering white light above him. He stood there, casually, with one arm held high in the air as the orb flashed and pulsed in his hand. Silvery strands curled and whipped from the source, visibly pushing and churning the air and dust around it. When the brilliant phenomena reached her, it passed over Lyra and continued spreading. She felt a burst of resolve and continued her desperate escape.

"Stay in your rotting hovel!" she heard him shout. "You didn't take me, and you won't take her."

She loped deftly through the rubble while keeping a safe distance between her and this potential ally. Once her feet left the last of Felkirk's rubble, and she was solidly on green grass once more, she quickly looked over her shoulder to see if the city's abhorrent denizens followed. To her great relief, there was nothing there. They'd all disappeared, recalled by their master that remained hovering over the felled wall, unreadable and unknowable.

THE BLACK BANNER of unspeakable nightmares, the scourge of Felkirk, watched the two humans below. The wind blew through the breach into the city, a breach never to be repaired. No one cared for the once-great city of the Eight Lords, the lords of Felkirk, who doomed all under their watch. Though, they had little choice in the matter of their fate or anyone else's.

Time is nothing. Insects live. Insects die. Light on the wind. Glimmer then gone. Forgotten. Meaningless. Life in world, in Alda... inconsequential. Life...inconsequential. Only the Throne. You will know. And you will regret.

The words rolled through Lyra's mind much like the entity itself had described: as a glimmer on the wind. She breathed the fresh air of the field, closed her eyes and felt a cool, untainted wind brush her skin and tousle her hair. When she opened her eyes, the figure was gone. The shadows beyond looked like a whole different world, one she would never visit again, though she'd never be able to forget.

The sound of footsteps sounded next to her. She turned immediately and backed away, drawing the sword from its sheathe. With her free hand, she pointed to the man before her and spoke as directly and commanding as possible: "Don't come near me."

The man put both hands in the air. Some of his fingertips were bloody, and a thin, dark line trickled down his palm. He slowly moved his hands to the faded gray hood that shadowed most of his face. His hands slowly gripped it and pulled it back, revealing a handsome but travel-worn face. He could be fairly young, but the wrinkles under his gray eyes spoke of hard years. A layer of brown stubble framed his thin face and sharpened his features even more than they already were.

She looked him over for any weapons, but his cloak hid much of his body. From what she could see, he carried little on his person. No pommel poked against the cloth, and neither was the tip of any sheath peeking from the edge of his frayed cloak. However, she'd learned much of hidden and unexpected dangers. He'd somehow taken down an entire section of a city wall with his bare hands. That smacked of powerful magic.

"You're a mage, aren't you?" she asked curtly.

He smirked. "How'd you guess?"

"The lack of a sword and the weak chin," she quipped. "Oh, and the way you collapsed an entire fucking city wall. Explain yourself before I cut you down and run. I've had enough of magic for the rest of my life."

His face softened. The look in his eyes almost seemed to be filled with pity. That elevated her from cautious and impatient to angry.

"How about we get away from this evil place first?"

She continued to glare at him, sword tip aimed at his throat. "That *thing* is gone, and I'm outside the walls. I'm ready to get out of here, too, but not before I know who's in my immediate vicinity."

He nodded his head in understanding. "An introduction; then, can we please leave the home of an eldritch god-like extension before anything else happens?"

"A what?" she replied, the sword dipping slightly as her concentration cracked.

"My name is Victor. I'm a mage. And I have much to tell you. I'd rather do it somewhere over there, though," he said, gesturing towards the empty fields where the wind blew the grass along in rolling waves.

NIGHT CAME SWIFTLY. Lyra was so disoriented after emerging from the city and confronting Victor that she didn't realize how late in the day it already was. Had she really only spent a single day in that damnable place?

Victor stoked the fire with a thin sword he'd taken from a scabbard attached to his horse. He'd placed a pot from his saddlebags on the fire and filled it with water, vegetables, and some game. The smell caused Lyra's mouth to water. She caught herself staring at the small pot throughout their conversation.

"I'm sure the owner of this blade would be pissed if he knew I was using it this way," Victor said as he wiped off the thin sword and sat it across his legs. "But, I never use it, anyway."

They'd had little time to talk since leaving Felkirk. No sooner had they made a safe distance than they realized they'd have to make a fire before night set in. The mage heard Lyra's stomach rumble and insisted on getting food ready. She kept her sword drawn and watched him carefully. He didn't seem to have any harmful intent, but now was no time to let her guard down.

She sat down by the fire and laid her sword across her legs, as well. The thin black streaks were still visible. She debated placing the sword in the fire to burn them off. They only served as a reminder of her experience in the city.

The horse nickered, and Victor rubbed its flank with gentle, broad strokes. He unbuckled the remaining packs and set them down for the evening. They would have to camp here.

"How did you know I was in the city? Or was that just some kind of miraculous circumstance?"

"I had a dream," he answered simply, as though such a thing were a common occurrence.

"A dream? You risked coming to Felkirk for a dream?"

Victor stared into the fire, the light reflecting off his eyes. "People like us, our dreams are different. Several people claim that dreams speak to us of things to come or that could be. We can take comfort in knowing that it's true in certain cases if we pay attention."

Lyra shook her head, trying to absorb all his esoteric speech. "People like us? Humans?"

"No, people with a certain magical skillset. I told you I was a mage. I was raised for most of my life in a sanctum; do you know what that is?"

She shrugged. "I've heard stories; that it's where mages used to live. I've been told there aren't many left, at least trained ones."

"Close," he said, his tone indicating he looked forward to explaining more. "Mages fled there not long before the Rupture to escape persecution. There aren't any left that I can find, at least where I've traveled so far. Do you know much about magic?"

Lyra thought back on her years in Rainward. A few individuals had unique but meager skills that were attributed to magic, but no one knew how to train any of those people or how to work with their potential. It was a simple and benign oddity. Only fearsome tales of witches and necromancers skulking in the woods gave any credence to the idea of powerful magic still existing and, of course, the rumors that surrounded Felkirk, which she was all too familiar with now. She told Victor all this as the fire continued to crackle and the smell of food continued to waft around them.

"Magic very much still exists," Victor continued, stirring the contents of the pot. "Like fire or a blade, it's not evil except in how it's used. With two exceptions."

His tone grew serious; even his timbre seemed to drop as he explained: "The first three types of magic, called sects, involve things like fire, water, and other elements, the potions and enchantments, other such things. The Fourth and Fifth Sects have been the focus of my studies for the last few years. The Fourth is, well, many felt it abhorrent enough when they thought it was merely necromancy practices and other dark arts, dubbed 'the magic of death.' They had no idea how paltry that understanding was; you witnessed some of its real potential in Felkirk, no doubt."

He removed the ladle and tapped it on the side of the pot. "The Fifth Sect," he continued, his voice rising and the shadow draining from his eyes, "is something that could save us. It was rare even before the Rupture and is practically non-existent now. It was another misunderstood branch of magic. Practiced by healers and the like, many thought it was the 'magic of life.' This was also a great understatement. The Fifth Sect is tied to Alda itself; a direct antithesis to the Fourth Sect."

"Anti-what?" Lyra wasn't ignorant. Her parents made sure, through Mr. Tilling's teachings long before her father became ill, that she learned to read and write. They couldn't do so themselves and felt that such skills could give their daughter a better chance at a decent life later on. Victor spoke in a manner that made Mr. Tilling seem uneducated, though.

"When you were in Felkirk, you felt something was 'wrong,' no?"

"Yes," she replied. "The entire city was just awful. Evil."

"It's stained by the worst and darkest aspects of the Fourth Sect. Magic leaves behind a resonance, depending on how extensive and how powerful the use was."

"The power of whoever that entity was must have been immense," she commented, speaking in part to herself.

"That entity was..." Victor paused, looking for the words. "It was no mage. It wasn't human or elf-kind, not even of flesh and blood."

Lyra wrapped her arms around herself, shivering, and it wasn't due to the incoming chill of the night. "I could tell."

There was silence between them for a few moments, the mere thought of that otherworldly thing breaking their conversation.

"What was it?" Lyra finally asked.

"Something...outside of Alda. I don't even know if it comes from our reality. Or any reality at all. Even time gets muddled around them. Such explanations are what I've been searching for. It's an extension of a greater being. I visited Felkirk once before, though I never made it through the first district. So, kudos to you on that."

She smiled and relaxed somewhat. The compliment did little to ease the haunting memories of what dwelt in that city's partitioned districts, though. She sheathed her sword and set it on the ground. Victor offered her a small blanket, which she happily accepted. It warded off both the cold and the darkness of her thoughts.

"When I came into Felkirk, I knew something about the city was terribly wrong. I felt it as soon as the city came into sight, actually. Gilfoyle," he said, looking towards his horse, "refused to go any nearer once he saw it, too. This," Victor gestured around him, "is as close as I got last time."

The horse whickered as though it understood.

"But inside, that was a different story. The first time I saw it, I knew exactly what it was. We 'spoke' briefly, and I left, despite Erysikthion's best efforts to keep me there."

The way Victor mentioned that they spoke told her that the

figure communicated with him in much the same strange way. He'd also mentioned a name.

"Is that the thing's name? Erysikthion?"

"That's what it calls itself. It has trouble reproducing our language, but I did get the thing's name."

"Erysikthion," she repeated softly. The name rolled in her mouth like oily, spoiled meat. It made her nauseous. She put her hand over her mouth as the urge to vomit came on her so suddenly.

"Yeah, you don't want to repeat it too often. That's why I just call it by the names other cultures have given it over time: The Black Hunger, The Cowled Feast, That Which Consumes."

"It looked more like an evil, black banner to me; or the scourge of Felkirk."

"The Black Bannered Scourge of Felkirk; it's long, but I like it. Maybe we'll add that to its history."

They both shared a chuckle. Brief and dry but a moment of alleviation, nonetheless.

"It killed everyone," Lyra said, returning to a more morose topic. "Not just killed them, but ate them or consumed them. It showed me things..."

"The Scourge is more than just hunger," Victor interjected gently. "I think it's the very nature of consumption. Forever reasons unknown, it chose Felkirk and devoured everyone and everything there. Did you see the decay that consumed the city?"

"It looked like a rotting corpse, even the buildings." Lyra's eyes stared through the flames dancing within the campfire. The sharp yellow of the fire was a sharp contrast to the dull ochre of the sky surrounding the city once the gossamer lie was pulled from her eyes and the cowled Scourge revealed the city for what it truly was.

"That's all they do. The Inheritors; they torment and rend

apart everything around them. All in uniquely horrible ways." Victor's voice was low, severe, but what he said next held a note of defiance, even hope. "Except for us."

Lyra looked over at him, an eyebrow raised. "What do you mean 'us?' I just met you, strange mage. What do I have to do with any of this?"

"My dream. We got a little off-topic, didn't we?"

"There's...a lot to understand," she said hesitantly.

"And we're just getting started. In my dream, I saw a corpse. Fetid, decaying in the sun, surrounded by a yellow miasma and buzzing flies, pecked at by a crow black as night."

"That's not entirely subtle," Lyra observed sarcastically.

"Only in retrospect. I had to think about the dream for a while. The crow pecked at the corpse over and over, but it wasn't eating. It was trying to get to something. A small jewel that sparkled with light despite being buried in old viscera."

"Disgusting," she interjected.

"Focus," he returned sharply with a slight shake of his hand.

"I was in the Brindlecrag Mountains again and remembered I was near Felkirk. The corpse and crow reference made sense at that point. When I understood the crow was That Which Consumes—"

"The Scourge," she interrupted on purpose. 'That Which Consumes' just sounded pretentious to her.

"When I understood the crow was the Scourge," he repeated, sighing, "I then knew what the jewel was for certain. And I had to move quickly. I knew that the jewel was a person, and a person instilled with Fifth Magic."

When Lyra looked over at him, his eyes had grown more intense. His face was a veneer of sincerity, the fire casting deep shadows under his eyes that betrayed the self-doubt beneath the prophetic explanations.

"Me?" she replied incredulously. She scoffed. "If I had magical talent, someone would have certainly known by now."

He shook his head gently. "Not necessarily. The Fifth Sect was hard to come by even hundreds of years ago. Now? No one would even know what to look for, especially if there were none trained in magic in your town. You make it sound like the only magic anyone knew about was that which could be used innately, reflexively; like a kid swinging a stick."

"That's about right."

"Then I assure you no one could know. That's why the Scourge was so frustrated. At least, I assume. It certainly was frustrated with me."

Lyra's forehead scrunched in thought. "It did seem annoyed. Especially after bouts of these strange, no, awful feelings I'd get."

"Like you were under some sort of psychological or even magical attack? It felt like the core of evil itself was trying to pull you in and tear you apart?"

Her heart fluttered in fear, both at the memory of the events and Victor's startlingly accurate description. "Yes. I didn't know what it was; I just fought back any way I knew how."

"That was the Fifth Sect," he said, almost sighing in relief. "As I said, it's the antithesis of the Scourge, his master—if that's what you can call the Throne—and all They are. It wraps around you like a cloak, a shield, or a net. Sometimes all of them, I think. The magic of the Fourth Sect and the insidious effects of the Inheritors are much weaker against us, often unable to touch us at all."

Lyra winced as she recalled the horrid sensations in Felkirk. If that was a restrained amount, she shuddered to think what this Fourth Magic and Inheritors could do to everyone else.

She pulled her pack closer and started to open it, trying to put the awful thoughts out of her mind. She wanted to ask

Victor questions about the books and scrolls she found to see if anything could help her father; he seemed very knowledgeable.

Her heart pounded when she felt pages so brittle they fell apart in her hands. She pulled one of the books out and saw a cover so rotten it was illegible, the pages falling from the binding. Some of the yellowed paper crumbled apart as it fell to the ground, some of the pages turning to ash before her. She reached back in and grabbed a scroll, only for it to crumble in her hands within the bag.

"No," she whispered, the realization beginning to settle in and claw at her heart. "No! *No!*" she began to scream as the claws opened bleeding wounds in her.

Victor stood, shocked by her sudden outburst. He raised his hands and begged her to quiet down lest someone or something hear them. He walked over slowly to see what had caused her to start crying uncontrollably.

"Are these books? From Felkirk?"

"They were," she managed to say through the sobs. "Everything I came here for. They were perfectly fine when I put them in my bag." She dropped her head and let the sobs continue as though they would reverse the damage done.

Victor shook his head and sat down beside her. He picked up the faded, rotten cover Lyra had dropped on the ground. He'd wandered Alda the last few years, seeking answers in old, forgotten libraries and temples. Pages turned brittle, and words faded, but not like this. This was a level of decomposition beyond normal boundaries.

"It's because of him," Victor said, putting the remains of the book down. "The Scourge. The city, the people, and all within it have been consumed by it; the remains no different than the waste our own bodies leave behind, useless and toxic. That's probably the only thing about us that it can somewhat understand. I wouldn't doubt that just having those pages around are causing residual issues, like bathing in a sewer. You need to rid yourself of all of it."

Lyra turned her bag over and watched the contents tumble out: ashes, random scraps of paper, tattered book covers, and a metal flask.

"Nothing...all for nothing," she whispered.

"What were you looking for?" Victor asked, his voice sympathetic.

"My father is sick." Lyra stopped for a moment, the memory of the frail and dying man threatening to bring fresh tears.

"Our apothecary can't figure out what's wrong. He mentioned something may be found in Felkirk that could help. Texts of medicines or procedures that could show him something he missed or didn't even know to begin with."

Victor's brows curled, and he grimaced. "He sent you to Felkirk? Alone?"

"No. He was quite adamant that I not go but knew he couldn't discourage me. He gave me ten days to return before assuming I wouldn't be returning. Six by horse. I thought these books might help, now I'm returning with nothing. My father is dead."

Lyra choked the words out. The last one struck her like an iron hammer to the gut. She'd have to say it to herself many more times on the walk home and hope that it would soften the blow of the inevitable. Right now, it threatened to tear her apart. She already felt herself emptying, becoming a shell. Perhaps it would have been best to let Erysikthion consume her.

"That *thing* put a glamour on me," she continued, clenching her fist. "Letting me think I was finding what I wanted. These books were nothing but dry and crumbled, useless the whole time."

She seethed. Her face reddened and the muscles in her jaw

clenched. She watched Victor begin to dig a small hole to bury the pieces of the books.

"The taint of the Fourth Magic reeks," Victor said as though he'd just smelt a dead animal. "It's was so strong it threatens to seep into everything the ashes and ruined covers touch."

Victor sighed and shook his head before continuing. "It was stringing you along. Testing you, trying to see why it couldn't claim your soul or life essence. A crow pecking at a jewel, right? When I showed up, It was reminded why. It knew that you, too, held the power of the Fifth Magic in you."

"To the hells with all of it," she said as she used her boot to kick all the rotted remains of the books and scrolls into the pit. "Fourth Magic, Fifth Magic, crows and corpses...damn all of it."

"Best to put the bag in, too. And the flask. It all needs to be burnt."

He spoke softly, seeing the hurt and hopelessness that filled her eyes. Lyra tossed the bag and flask into the pit, using the last of the brandy to wash her hands of any of this taint that Victor was concerned about. When she'd finished, the mage reached a hand out to the pit and crossed his fingers, flicked them apart, and fire sprang to life on the contents within. The spilled alcohol fed the flames, and soon a second fire was burning, this one with blue flames, courtesy of the brandy.

They watched this new fire in silence for a while. Victor wanted to be respectful of Lyra's struggles. As the blue flames lowered, he buried everything again before returning to his seat by the original campfire.

"It wasn't all for nothing," he said, stirring the food that was just about ready.

"What do you mean? The books are gone. Mr. Tilling has no other methods to help."

"I'll go with you. We can both fit on Gilfoyle and return much faster than on foot."

"How does this change anything?" she replied, her voice devoid of any emotion. "I'll be returning a day early with nothing to show for it."

"We're both touched by the Fifth Magic, but I've been practicing it for a few years. Trying the healing properties on any settlements I've come across that needed it. I'm self-taught; no formal training like I've had in other sects of magic. But I can try. And it's magical healing, very different from what your Mr. Tilling has been trying, no doubt."

He saw a light spark in Lyra's eyes. A bit of color returned to her face. He smiled slightly; he wasn't a skilled healer like the great clerics and priests of days gone, but he'd learned a few spells and incantations that he was confident of.

The pot's contents bubbled, and fragrant steam carried in the air. Victor pulled two small cups from his travel bags—the only two he had—and served up the thin stew for them both. Lyra blew on the contents in her cup, holding it with both hands. She smelled the savory combination and sighed.

"Gods, that's the best thing I've smelled in a week. Thank you so much."

"Sometimes it's the simple things, no?" he said, smirking. He took a careful sip.

They enjoyed their meal together, not forcing any conversation and enjoying the peace of a warm fire, warm food, and a starry night away from the evils of Felkirk.

THE RETURN TRIP to Rainward was much swifter and easier on horseback. Gilfoyle was a well-traveled and stout horse. He carried both Victor and Lyra without complaint and kept a solid pace. At times, Victor kicked him into a canter to make up time.

Victor was nearly as eager as Lyra to return and see if his healing powers could help her father.

Heavy gray clouds greeted them as Rainward came into view; the afternoon would see, at the least, light rains. This hurried them along more so. The townsfolk were about their usual business, but they seemed to stop and stare as the cloaked mage and his passenger made their way through the streets.

"Do you often get greeted this way?" Lyra asked, leaning in to whisper the question to Victor.

He turned his head slightly, his eyes peeking through the shadow of his cowl. His response sounded equally as confused. "They're looking at you."

She paid more attention to each leering gaze as Gilfoyle trotted past. Indeed, each man and woman they encountered stared at Lyra as though a ghost were riding through their town. She didn't know of them personally but recognized some of the faces. At least some of them should have recognized hers.

They came to a stop at her house. She dismounted first, followed by Victor, who hitched Gilfoyle to a post while she approached the door. Lyra overheard a few whispers and low voices from a group of women nearby.

"Poor girl."

"Someone should fetch Hermaias."

"Who's that with her?"

She found the incessant whispering annoying and rude. It also rekindled her memory of the sound of a thousand clenching and unclenching hands.

The door squeaked slightly as she opened it. The familiar smell of her home filled her with a bittersweet wave of emotion. However, something wasn't quite right. There was no smell of the medicinal tea, nor of any food, flowers, or herbs, common things that were always present in her home even before her father was sick.

"Mom?" she called out. No one answered.

Her heart quickened. She saw the door to her parents' room closed, as usual, but she had an awful feeling coagulate in her gut. She ran over and threw the door open, not wanting to frighten her sick father but giving in to the building fear. Her hand remained tight on the door's handle, and her heart felt as though it dropped in her stomach when she looked upon the room.

It was empty.

The bed was made, the floors and table cleaned, and the windows open to let in the low light of the cloudy afternoon. Her father wasn't there; neither was her mother.

"Mom!" she screamed. "Mom!"

Over and over again until Victor came rushing into the house. He went to grab her as she crashed into him in a grief-stricken flight. Lyra pushed him away and made for the front door.

"I have to find them," she said, her voice hoarse and determined, cracking from the tightly restrained tears.

She ran into the white robes of Mr. Tilling, who stepped into the doorway just as she was about to exit. Lyra gripped him and pulled him into a hug without thinking. The old apothecary gasped in both surprise at the gesture and the force of her running into him.

"Mr. Tilling," she said, the sobs finally breaking through. "Where is he? Where's my father? My mother? Where are they?"

Hermaias made a slight gasping sound at each question, not knowing how to answer any of them. Rather, he knew the answer but not how to deliver it—nor wanting to.

"Where have *you* been, girl?" he replied, though without irritation. He was simply shocked to still see her alive.

She looked him in the eye, her face crinkling in confusion.

"You know where I've been; I'm back and early at that. This man returned with me on horseback. He may be able to help Dad!"

The old, mottle-headed apothecary looked at her with wet eyes. He didn't need to say anything. The sorrow and hurt on his face said all she needed to know. Lyra pulled away from him. "No," she said, almost too low to hear but repeated it over and over again, each time louder than before.

"He's still alive. Tell me he's alive," she begged, her eyes on fire with disbelief and desperation.

"You've been gone nearly three weeks, Lyra. Your father passed two weeks after you left," Hermaias said with as much sympathy as he could muster, coupled with a fair amount of confusion.

"Three weeks?" Lyra said, the words falling from her mouth and making her sick to her stomach. "It's...it's only been seven days. One week." She turned to look at Victor, whose lips pursed and eyes squinted with sympathy. "Right, Victor? It only took two days to get back and I was only in Felkirk for one; how could—"

Her question caught in her throat as she recalled her conversation with Victor: *Even time gets muddled around them.*

Her eyes went wide, and she stared blankly at the floor, holding herself up against the wall next to the open door. She felt the room begin to spin. When she spoke, Hermaias had to lean in to hear her question and ask her to repeat it.

"Where's my mother?"

Hermaias' mouth once more opened and closed like a landed fish. Finally, he sighed as he found his courage and resigned himself to simply telling her the truth. He put a hand on her shoulder.

"You need to sit down, Lyra," he said, calmly but with conviction.

Lyra's head snapped around to face him. Her breaths came heavy and shallow. "No, where is she?"

"Lyra..."

"Where *is* she, Hermaias?"

LYRA ALWAYS CALLED him Mr. Tilling. Ever since she was a little girl. Never in all her twenty years had she ever referred to him as 'Hermaias.' Hearing his name from her lips in such a manner felt as though she'd drawn the sword that she'd borrowed back on himself. He removed his hand from her shoulder and took a deep breath. He let it out slowly before speaking.

"When you didn't return after ten days, I went to go see her. Robern was in the worst state I've ever seen. He was unresponsive to any stimuli, wouldn't take food or water. I told her he only had a few more days at most. She asked when I expected you back."

He paused and looked at her. Did she remember his promise? He would tell her mother that Lyra wasn't coming back if she hadn't returned after ten days to spare her the hope of ever seeing her daughter again after Lyra insisted on going to Felkirk. He warned her. Hermaias warned the pig-headed child that if she insisted on going to that cursed city, he wouldn't let Marna waste away thinking her daughter was going to return because *no one* ever did. Faced with the fact that he was wrong this time would haunt him forever.

"I told her, 'soon.' After losing your father four days later, she fell into a grief that I feared she wouldn't come out of. She stopped eating. She asked when you were coming home and I kept telling her, 'Soon.' Soon! I *knew* you weren't coming home from that damn city, but I couldn't tell your mother that!"

The old man was reduced to a sobbing wreck. He ran his spotted old hands over his eyes and sniffed incessantly. Victor approached him and offered to help him sit. The apothecary followed him almost mechanically, shaking the whole way.

"I came over a few days ago to check on her. She..."

Hermaias swallowed. His throat was dry and hurt. His lips cracked and he struggled to breathe through the sobs and images of the past several weeks.

"What happened, Mr. Tilling?" Lyra asked, her eyes still on the floor.

"She...she...killed herself. Next to your father's bed."

His hands shook uncontrollably. He lifted one to his head to hold his face as the tears pulled up the memory of finding Marna's body, thinking he'd witnessed the death of an entire family all from different sources but for the same reason: an illness that he couldn't fix.

Lyra screamed. Once more, the sounds of her anguish filled her ears. The tears she'd grown sick of came back again. Her legs gave way beneath her and she fell to her knees, wallowing in the mire of grief that threatened to pull her down and consume her. She fought off the evils of Felkirk, an entity outside of explanation that digested the physical and spiritual. But this grief sunk its desperate fingers in and she had nothing to fight back with.

VICTOR WALKED to Lyra and knelt by her, slowly. He placed a gentle hand on her back. The grief-stricken cries wracked her body. His own heart ached for hers, the Fifth Magic amplifying his empathy. He placed his other hand on her forehead, feeling the intensity of her anguish in her brow and the sweat forming there. The words flowed through him, relaxing prose intended to calm the mind and drain the heartache like surging water released through a causeway. Her breathing was still heavy and strained, but came slower now. Victor felt the heat of her despair wane and give way to the dull pangs of sadness. Her shocked mind could now try to come to terms with all the revelations. She turned her face into his arms and cried. These were the tears that cleansed, not those that choked and strangled.

Hermaias looked on in amazement. He saw the effects of Victor's words and recognized a spell when he saw and heard one. The anger had bled from the room like pus from an infected wound. Whatever spell this was must have some sort of secondary properties because the old apothecary felt it, too. He still grieved for Robern, Marna, and Lyra, but the pain had subsided somewhat.

"What did you do?" the old man asked, his hand no longer shaking.

Victor looked at him with heavy eyes and a slight smile. "There is good magic left. Not much, but I'll find more."

Hermaias could only shake his head and force himself to rise slowly from the chair. He fetched water for everyone. When he laid a cup down next to Lyra, he saw her hands holding tightly to Victor's cloak. This relieved him somewhat. Perhaps she might have someone else to be there for her if this man wanted to stay. It seemed many were looking for a home anymore; perhaps he was, too.

After the last sobs left her, Lyra let go of Victor and apologized. He waved it away, only hoping that she felt better and offering his condolences. The mage honestly had no idea what she was going to do after this. They all three sat together at the table. Hermaias had opened a bottle of wine to help remove the sting of the day's events in a more mundane but still effective manner. Lyra readily accepted.

"That was some amazing magic, young man," Hermaias said. "I've never seen such before, let alone of the healing kind."

Victor nodded after taking a sip of the deep red liquid in his cup. "I have a long way to go."

"I want to go with you."

Lyra's statement landed heavily among the three. She looked into her cup before downing half of it in one go. She set it back down and refilled it from the dark glass bottle. Victor raised an eyebrow.

"You only met me a few days ago. And who's to say I'll take you with me?"

Hermaias' head looked back and forth between them like a dog following a bouncing ball, unable to think of anything to say himself.

"I don't want to stay here," she replied, looking around the house. Her lips quivered. "Stay in this place where my father and mother died? I have no family left. I mean no offense, Mr. Tilling; you've been wonderful to my family."

"N—no offense taken, dear," Hermaias stammered. He cared for and treated the young woman and her family since they were all children; but they were not *his* family. She was also an adult and could make her own decisions. He only hoped they no longer involved Felkirk.

Victor took another sip. "What do you hope to find out there? Alda is not a kind place. It's not even simply uncaring; I'd say it's actively malicious. You know this now, surely."

She traced the top of her cup with her finger. The light glimmered off the dark liquid and the sounds of rain began to lightly patter outside.

"Whatever magic you used to calm me, you said I had it, too. I want to learn. And I can use a sword, a little anyway." She looked up at Victor, her eyes meeting his. Despite his analytical and dispassionate questions, she saw in his eyes what she felt in his words and his magic. "You're a good person. I can tell. You're after something, yourself, and I want to help. Especially if it's saving people from things like that creature in Felkirk. Inheritors?"

Victor shifted in his seat. Hermaias eyed him strangely. "Yes, that's part of it. But I never know where I may go next. The journey I'm on is dangerous and that's a grave understatement. I'm searching for answers that, honestly, I don't even know if I can find."

"Sounds like you could use some help."

Victor smirked. He took a long drink from his cup and refilled it. Bringing the cup up slightly and towards Lyra, he said, "Here's to finding answers."

"To moving on," Lyra said softly.

The cups clinked and they drank slowly together.

"See here, I helped watch over this girl for twenty years; I won't be left out of seeing her off," Hermaias chimed in grouchily. He raised his cup towards them and glared at them both.

The three cups clinked together and they all drank once more, Hermaias taking a deep, messy pull of the wine. He had to wipe his mouth and beard with his sleeve, adding fresh red stains to the clothing.

"We can stay here for a day or two; or for as long as it takes for the rain to stop, whichever you prefer," Lyra said. She looked over at the door to her parents' room which had since been closed. Wincing and forcing herself not to cry again, she turned back and looked at Mr. Tilling. "When we leave, Mr. Tilling, give the house to a family that needs it. I won't be coming back here."

Victor went to take another drink, but first spoke into the glass, "I never thought I'd return to Felkirk, either. Nothing is certain."

Lyra shrugged. "I'll never come back here for any length of time."

Hermaias nodded and made her a promise. His chest was heavy at the thought of never seeing the spirited and headstrong woman again. But, he'd lived long enough to know that very few things were permanent in Alda, especially the good things.

They finished off another bottle of wine, the last available in the house. Mr. Tilling made his way home on shaky legs, refusing aid from either Victor or Lyra. She hugged him one last time before he left, thanking him for all he'd done.

She also thanked Victor; for his help in Felkirk, for guiding her and helping her that first night, and for just giving her a ride home—despite the terrible news waiting for her. She also thanked him for using his magic to put her heart at ease. She hoped to make it up to him and more on their journey together.

Victor, ever the kind soul, told her there was nothing to make up. The world was getting darker and more malevolent every day. Any act of kindness that can be spared will only help. That's all he could ask of her: to aid him in seeking answers to the terrors that plagued the peoples of Alda.

They both slept in beds that night. Lyra in her own and Victor in her parents; Lyra had insisted. If she was going to move on, she couldn't place attachments on things she'd soon be leaving behind forever. And Victor agreed with her that this may be the last time they would sleep in a real bed for some time. Their night passed in peace. The wine played its part, but so did the lingering essence of the Fifth Magic used to aid a broken heart. It wouldn't last long, but a few hours were all they needed.

The next morning was still heavily overcast; Rainward did earn its name, after all. The skies were dry, however, and they rode off together. Lyra looked back on the town one last time as they made their way south away from the tormented city and on to other, stranger horizons.

THE GODS' LOST CHILDREN

Lyra came to learn that Victor, while not necessarily a man of few words, was a man of random questions. They rode Gilfoyle together for the first leg of their journey. She assumed he remained quiet to let her grieve the loss of her parents. Though it was appreciated, the entire point of traveling with someone was to enjoy the company, conversation, and safety. He'd asked if Rainward had been a town before the Rupture. Was it always along a body of water, or was that only once the Wailing Ocean was created? What did she do before her fateful journey to Felkirk—trade, skills, friends? How much training did she have with the sword? All acceptable questions, but they were spread out over the course of days and at odd intervals.

When she pointed this out, Victor stated he'd never had someone to travel with before. His last long-term contact with any person was the deceased former arch-mage of his sanctum. Gilfoyle had been his only companion for years. The horse obviously didn't mind him asking random questions; but it made it feel like Victor wasn't talking to himself. He apologized, but Lyra smiled and assured him it was ok. In fact, it was time she asked some questions of her own.

She recalled that Victor said he had been to Felkirk once before; she wanted to know why. What had originally brought this mage to the heart of evil as she knew it? He'd called out and taunted the Scourge of Felkirk, something that seemed unthinkable now that she knew more about it, and they'd both managed to walk away.

Victor explained that he'd left a small town being used as a recruiting center for a vile cult. It was during his early days after leaving his empty sanctum behind. His first real test as a mage occurred in that village, and it was by no small amount of luck that he walked away alive. It was also where he acquired Gilfoyle.

His travels south resulted in more encounters, but they were both benign and fruitless. He heard tales from the people that the city of Felkirk was once the capital of this region long ago and may have what he seeks. However, they warned him of the same things Lyra had heard; those that traveled there never returned, and the city was drenched in a curse, a living vapor that turned the city itself into a corpse.

"Don't remind me," Lyra muttered.

When he found the city, he saw it for what it truly was. No fake veneer had been cast over his mind. He went in blind and foolish, relying on what he'd been told about the Fifth and trusting it to protect him. His magic was potent but still greatly unpolished. When the Scourge first appeared to him, it attacked him outright, much like it had Lyra. However, it found a tougher foe in him. Victor understood, at least to the extent the human mind can understand anything about the Inheritors or the Obscured Throne, what he was facing and recognized the connection to the Fourth Sect in the efforts put forth against his body and sanity.

"Our conversation beforehand was very brief, but I left and never looked back. I could feel the malice behind me, seething at its impotence against the Fifth that dwelt within me and wrote Felkirk off as lost."

It seemed in this instance that Lyra knew more than he. She explained her experience and what she'd seen and heard, and what the black-bannered Scourge revealed to her. She couldn't remember all of it, her mind locking out parts of it of its own accord, but what she did have to share, curdled Victor's insides. She felt his muscles tense as she rode behind him.

Victor continued, explaining that he left Felkirk and headed west. A fishing village had a boat departing for the north to trade with the elf-kind south of Athyl'glin. Lyra was greatly interested in this topic, having heard about the mysterious people and their forest realms. Victor's voice turned melancholy as he explained they suffered hardships all their own. Their forest kingdoms were treated much like the human city-states and bore the worst of the atrocities.

A tavern in the elven port town of Lit'th was where Victor caught up on much of the plight of elf-kind. An old fisher-elf, eighty years old and still looked Victor's age, he pointed out, told him they couldn't return to the deeper parts of the northern forests lest they rejoin their ancestors in the worst ways. Wicked revenants consisting of the twisted souls of slaughtered elf-kind roamed the woods, seeking to add more to their number. Some sort of creature made of 'the black coils of night with a thousand eyes like cold stars' controlled the heart of the kingdom.

"It sounded like another Inheritor," Victor said, "but I, or anyone, will likely never know."

The elf-kind explained much to Victor. They were connected more closely to magic than other peoples and learned to make more of the time they lived as those years grew shorter and shorter with each generation. Victor's understanding of the Principle Triad reached new levels. Each elf-kind in the town referred to him to another and then another. They feverishly attempted to perpetuate the magics of the world, to keep them alive. When some of the elf-kind learned that he had some talent in the Fifth, their entire demeanor changed. As connected as they were to magic, that rarest of sects ran thin in their blood, too. They helped him in every way they could, however, and his skills with the Fifth went from non-existent to at least somewhat tangible.

"Those are the skills I used in the other towns and villages I came across. The spell I used to help calm you and ward against the Scourge."

"What made you come back here?" Lyra asked.

Victor replied that he had recently returned to the eastern shores of Alda to trek into the Brindlecrag Mountains in search of the dwarves there. He'd come into some information that might lead him to another bearer of the Fifth magic. Unfortunately, the doors to the underground halls of the dwarves were sealed. None would answer his pleas, so he returned to the base of the mountains, where he had the dream that sent him to Lyra and Felkirk.

The two companions traveled east. Over the next month, they boated the Leen River and its port towns; worked their way inland to the Peaks of Deor and the dwarf kingdom of Meibion Tan. The great doors to the under-mountain kingdom were also closed. The brass-and-gold likenesses of multiple dwarven kings and queens carved into the twenty-foot gate stared back at them, cold and uncaring. The thought of what happened to the dwarvish people, what they were enduring, sometimes tugged at Victor's mind. He wanted to hope that they survived, maybe even prospered, but that would go against all historical patterns as he'd experienced them.

Victor and Lyra came down the opposite side of the mountains. From their vantage point, the rest of the continent spread before them. In the distance, the sea glistened like liquid crystal. The waters ran up to a stretch of a dark-stoned shoreline to their right, rolling up in gentle whitecaps until they started crashing into the cliffs that jutted from the land directly in front of them. Roads as narrow as spiderwebs curved away, ending suddenly at broken hills or rambling off into nowhere. Chunks of stone shot up sharply from the ground, creating crystal-like monuments to the chaos caused by the Rupture's reshaping of the world. The sad remains of villages and a small town speckled the country-side like liver spots. Victor pointed out that the ones still inhab-ited were only sparsely so. This was mostly due to the settlement curled up against the flat, highest side of the cliff to the west: Giranta, the Broken City.

The outer wall of this fallen capital circled the dull stones of many structures that once glistened in the sunlight. The cres-cent shape that remained was once a full circle, a white moon of splendor near a large forest unclaimed by elf-kind. Wisps of long, thin white clouds enclosed it all, settling around the jutting stones, broken hills, and patches of trees.

Victor imparted the tale to Lyra as she took in the dichotomy of the scene of haunting, tragic beauty before her. When the world fell, Giranta fell with it. The countryside collapsed into the earth, the Wailing Ocean rose to replace it, and the city was literally cut in half. The forest that mostly surrounded the city nearly disappeared. Only those stretches on the northern and eastern portions survived. Even then, it was in sparse, broken patches that clung to the shattered country like tufts of fur on a mangy animal.

"Does some Inheritor torture that city, as well?" Lyra asked as they made their way cautiously down the steep mountainside path.

"Honestly, I can't be sure," Victor replied. Lyra frowned, not at his answer but at his body's response. He was trembling. "I asked the townsfolk and villagers about the city before daring to head there myself. They all said it was abandoned, and no one goes there."

"Same as every other city, it seems," she interjected flippantly.

"Yes. So, I scouted the area around the city and found nothing too off-putting. A strange feeling, yes, but nothing overtly malicious. So, I went inside. There was space to enter near where the walls met the cliff. The town was utterly abandoned. Not a single living thing there. It wasn't like Felkirk; there were no bodies or remains, no undead or half-consumed souls lurking on the streets. There was absolutely nothing there. The city was just...empty. It was almost peaceful. I thought for a moment that there was actually a city-state that the Inheritors ignored or perhaps overlooked. I heard the sound of the distant ocean, the waves crashing against the cliffs. The salt air carried on a breeze through the streets. It was quite nice. Then, I...I got curious. I walked up the main thoroughfare to where it met the cliffside, where the rest of the city had collapsed into the ocean. I thought I'd see if any of the city's remains were still down there. I don't know if I saw any of the city, but under the waves...there was something."

Victor's voice halted for a moment. He stuttered uncharacteristically and the trembling intensified.

"Victor, are you ok?" she asked, her voice low. He didn't answer but continued speaking as though he were trying to finish the tale as soon as possible.

"I saw something, something so large I couldn't imagine that it would go unnoticed. It...it waited there, under the water's surface. Unmoving, save for some strange and subtle pulsation. I don't know if it was breathing or...it called to me."

Lyra clenched her jaw. The way Victor stated that chilled her.

"It called to me to come into the ocean. To join it. If it wasn't for the Fifth Sect protecting me, I would have—"

Victor breathed deep and steady. The action of one trying to remain calm against the promise of panic.

"I fought back. Stared over the edge of that broken street to rocks and remains below. They were all there...all of them. All their voices joined with the other. The voice of that pulsing thing just below the water's surface, stretching out so far I lost sight of it. I don't know if I screamed or not. I remember suddenly being back outside the city. I used magic to carve a warning into the walls for any others who find it to not enter under any circumstances. I can only hope it worked."

Lyra laid her head against his back. Victor's breaths rattled within him. He may have been sobbing; possibly, his body was simply reeling from the memory. She understood completely.

"I understand. You know I do," she said, hoping to help soothe him.

They traveled the remainder of that leg of their journey in silence. The villages and the small town were emptier than before. Victor wanted to ask questions and see if anything had changed since his last time here— strange occurrences or visitors and the like. The land remained quiet and dismal. History books told how life during the golden age before the Rupture was hard for peasants and commonfolk. Despite now being out from under the heel of tyrants, royalty, and nobles, the crushing fist of unspeakable nightmares took their place. Everyone longed for the older days.

There was nothing left for them here, and Victor said it was time they travel north across the Howling Straight that would land them in the region of the former city-state of Ligothi. Victor was headed in that very direction from Carnelia, further in the north, when he'd come across the aforementioned tidings that brought him down to the Brindlecrag.

They crossed the strait, discovering its well-earned name via the harsh winds that constantly swept across the turbulent waters. The ship and its crew gave them plenty of leeway; Victor wished it was due to their respect for one versed in magic, but he and Lyra both knew it was out of fear and, in some cases, repulsion. The old prejudices still ran deeply.

More wind greeted them as they docked at a small port town to the southwest of a large range of ragged cliffs. Their clothes beat about them as the captain rushed them off the ship and pointed them toward the town. Victor and Lyra managed to barter for another horse, a smaller, lither breed than Gilfoyle. Lyra stroked its muzzle as it whickered in delight. She smiled and, for a moment, her cares trickled away. The bright, intelligent eyes calmed her and held a promise of companionship and loyalty.

"What will you name her?" Victor asked.

Lyra cocked her head. "I don't know. I've never had a pet and certainly never thought I'd own a horse."

Victor shrugged. "Gil came to me already named. No idea who named him or why."

After the saddle and bags were all strapped to their new companion, Lyra climbed onto her back and petted her mane. "Tula," she said confidently. "Her name is Tula."

Victor smiled and looked over at Lyra sitting atop the beautiful brown and white mare. She leaned forward and rubbed the horse's brown muzzle, then stroked its cream-colored mane. The beast flicked its tail, also a lovely cream color. Light brown splotches spattered Tula's white flanks. She was a perfect fit for Lyra—a fair-skinned, brown-freckled woman with a kind heart and fierce spirit. The horse's name was fitting, too.

"The goddess of hope," Victor said. "That's quite optimistic. I didn't think the knowledge of the old gods still existed. Was there a temple in Rainward?"

"A few, but they were rarely attended. One didn't even have a priest."

She was quiet for a moment, her thoughts jostling between concentrating on avoiding people in the street with Tula and remembering her years growing up in the town covered in clouds and fog.

"I remember going to Tula's temple when I had hard days. I'd sit there in the quiet, listen to the rain beat off the old marble that the one priestess barely managed to keep maintained on her own. But there were always torches and fireplaces lit to ward off the cold. Fresh water from the streams and apples from the fields. The priestess picked them herself, I believe. Anything she could do to bring a spark of hope to others, even if it was just some quiet, warmth, and an apple."

"Sounds like she was doing her goddess' work."

Lyra nodded and patted Tula's neck as they reached the edge of the port town. "She did. She passed a few years ago. She was old but not elderly. She was probably my parents' age but didn't have the wear of hard labor on her. Mr. Tilling said it was a fever that took her."

Victor shook his head. "Something the Fifth could have handled, I imagine. Think of all the lives spared when such magic was more accessible, more of us who could channel it and had proper training. It must have been incredible."

Lyra remained quiet. She didn't want to dwell on the past and possibilities that could never be. She wanted to move forward to whatever the future held. It was murky and unsure, but at least there were possibilities that *could* be. The past was set, written, unmovable. For her, its foundation was one of misery and terror.

The two rode side-by-side, their horses' hooves clopping at a slow and steady rhythm. Like the past, the town faded into the horizon behind them. It was slow and the sounds and smells of the town and ocean lingered for a long while, but eventually both dissipated into a vague memory. They never even learned the town's name.

SOME WEEKS LATER, once they'd made their way past Ligothi—and given it a wide berth—they found themselves beneath a rocky outcropping once known as Sleeper's Rock. The smooth stone formation appeared like a humanoid form lying down on its side, half-buried in the earth, with an arm reaching up to rest its sleeping head. It used to be the site of festivals and gatherings. The Rupture shook the dreamer awake and crushed it where it had slept. The arm upon which the head had rested had been pulled out, creating a tiny ravine. Victor had heard the place referred to now as Cadaver Rock, used by others as a traveling landmark more than anything else.

Victor and Lyra made camp for the night in the small box valley at the end of the ravine; "the corpse's armpit," Lyra had jokingly remarked.

The fire was protected from the wind and resulted in a pocket of warmth and shelter. They ate dinner in silence, the journey to the site long and arduous due to their avoiding Ligothi, swinging around in a bow-shaped arc just to get where they needed to go without risking any encounter near the infamous city. The horses nibbled on the grass and tossed their manes.

Lyra stood and went to Tula, retrieving her bedroll. As she laid out her spot to sleep, her eyes caught the firelight dancing off some strange shapes on the wall. Her instincts didn't prickle at any danger, only her curiosity. She approached them slowly and discovered her initial assumptions were correct. They were carvings. Not of any magical or sinister nature, but a simple message made by a sharp stone:

Nel and Deetrik
Made Camp Here
Remember Us

SHE SMILED at the humble gesture. Travel, she'd learned, bore a heavy weight on the body and mind. Who knew what these two were doing on their journey? Did they get to where they were going? She wanted to hope so. "I hope you made it, Nel and Deetrik," she whispered. She wanted to say their names out loud so that this simple wish could be granted.

She then noticed other etchings made around theirs. All of various hands and legibility. They appeared to have inspired a trend within the arm of the stony corpse.

Valary Thomas Doria Dale
Friends

Amakia Family

Pernias Dell
Born Here, Date Unknown

Ben Dromas Fel'il Sera Iris Cale Denor
To Mark Passage
Here We Part Ways

THERE WERE MANY OTHERS; the carvings stretched beyond the firelight, high and low along the rock's face. So many people, so many names. All with stories of their own. Lyra couldn't help but wonder at what triumph or tragedy befell each of them. She stared at their names for a long time. Her fingers traced many of them, some beginning to show signs of wearing away. She ran her hands along the wall and walked up to the very edge of the firelight, taking in the grandiosity of the willpower of these unknown people, united by a common gesture here at a place with such a grisly name.

"Good night, Lyra," she heard Victor call from over by the fire. She turned and wished him goodnight as well. He sounded exhausted and was soon snoring softly. She'd been quite tired herself, but an idea reinvigorated her. She found a sharp-edged stone on the ground and began to work away at the stone. She didn't know how long it took, but by the time she was finished, she felt a new level of exhaustion begin to drag her down. This task had to be finished before she slept, though. She crawled into her bedroll at some unknown hour of the night and was near-instantly within the folds of deep sleep.

Her rest was untroubled and unbroken. Lyra didn't wake once to get comfortable or start at some noise. Though tired from the late hour at which she retired, she woke with a slightly better sense of peace. The result of last night's endeavors cast away some of her burdens. After they had packed all their things to return to the road once more, she showed Victor the tribute-filled wall. He was equally impressed as she had been.

"I'll certainly never forget this," he complimented.

"One more thing," Lyra said, her voice happy with a hint of pride. "Look here."

She pointed out a once-empty space on the wall. A fresh set of etchings were there:

Victor and Lyra
Off To Parts Unknown

VICTOR CHUCKLED. He knelt down and ran his fingers over the message, feeling the rough edges yet to be worn by time. He looked at the others along the wall and sighed. He thought of all these people and the purposes they set out with. Some of the carvings invoked blessings; those short-lived mortals who appealed to the gods of centuries past to protect them and return to save their children in this world. This was stone etched in passing, so there were little more than sigils of the old pantheon, but the purpose and reasoning could be easily surmised.

"I did the same thing," Lyra commented, seeing Victor staring wistfully along the long rows of engravings.

"Enduring spirits, all of them," Victor said.

"You think any of them are still alive?" Lyra asked. "Think they got where they were going?"

"One can hope," Victor replied somberly. "We're nothing, really, without hope."

Lyra offered Victor a hand to help him stand. He grunted, rose to his feet with her help, and dusted himself off. The fire had been doused and their equipment packed. Their horses protested slightly as they were mounted, jostled from their grazing. The two returned to the road, the hills of the Carnelian region ahead of them. Their journey was far from over.

SERPENTS OF GODSCROWN

A SEA OF BANNERS WHIPPED AND CURLED ABOVE ROWS OF armored troops, shimmering like whitecaps as the clouds passed beneath the sun. The proud golden griffin on a green field, symbol of the Gallancrest city-state, dominated one-half of the battlefield. Among the golden griffins were banners bearing black shields overlayed by white anvils: their allies from Monte Virl. Banners of red circles with white roses signified the presence of armies from the great house of Dansford with their multitude of heavy cavalry.

Across from this gathering of powerful western forces was the great city-state of the east, Weldenbern. A massive banner the size of a horse curled in the wind; it bore a black field with a golden shield encircled by a red crown. This symbol towered above all others, with many more heraldic symbols of more varieties than could be counted. Weldenbern's allies were many but consisted mostly of noble houses and warrior's guilds, united under their liege, the 'Shield and Crown.'

The tension built in the gathered thousands. Beneath the griffin's banner, a young scout rode up and brought his horse to such an abrupt halt that its hooves threw dirt into the air. It pinged off the spotless armor of a glowering man with his helmet's visor raised. Cold blue eyes flicked down to the scout, who ran up to the man, breathless, to report the news the scout wished someone else could deliver.

"Lord Verdaun," the scout began but had to stop and catch his breath. He leaned over, drew in a few deep breaths, then forced himself to stand straight in the presence of the general. "Lord Verdaun, we received word from Thayn. They can't send troops. We're not to expect any assistance from them."

The man next to the general, rail-thin with a styled mustache and impeccably clean mail armor that had yet to see battle, scoffed. His horse whickered as he cursed and spat into the dirt.

"Fucking countess," Verdaun swore. His voice sounded like someone dropped gravel into his helmet. "Can't send troops. *Won't* send them. She's switched sides again."

"Countess Nyall is a knife-eared bitch who'd rather bed both capitals than commit to one," the thin man added.

The scout winced. The weasel-faced lieutenant's voice grated one's nerves with its nasal sharpness that reeked of aristocratic privilege and combat ineptitude. Lord Verdaun noticed the scout's momentary reflex and smirked. The scout's face turned red, regardless. He was still well below the rankings of the jumped-up lieutenant.

"He's not wrong," Verdaun commented, looking out at the battlefield before them.

The cavalry would excel here. The two armies were planted on top of hills opposite one another, but below them were open fields spotted by thickets of trees. The Iris River was over a mile to the south, the Gullstern River two-and-a-half miles north. No creeks or other tributaries crossed the battlefield, no bridges to hold or break their charges. This was good for Gallancrest; however, Weldenbern boasted superior archers both in skill and number. Thayn's aid would have evened the playing field in that regard.

Verdaun looked down at the scout. Still a young man, he'd likely not survive if it came to him seeing combat this day. He must have ridden non-stop for as long as his horse could manage to deliver this news at such a time. The general looked back at the gathered army on the other hillside. His eyes followed them up, beyond the waving banners to the incredible mountains behind them. The peaks were close, and near the top, beyond where any other trees could grow, the white flowers of an aldyr orchard blossomed so fully it could be seen from here, like a tiny cloud nestled on the mountainside. It was one of the largest groves of the trees known to exist.

The general leaned over, his sour face softening somewhat. "What's your name, boy?"

"Private Richaud Ingvold, sir."

"Private Ingvold, return to Gullstern and inform the Griffin's Council that Thayn has betrayed us and we will fight the battle without them; when we return victorious, it will be without the countess' aid and they should prepare to act accordingly."

The scout nodded and replied with a sharp, "Yes, sir."

Verdaun beckoned the young man closer. He leaned over, as close as his armor would allow, to give an additional order— more a personal request—to the quick scout.

"Find my wife, Lady Martess Verdaun, and tell her that the aldyrs bloom more lovely than ever. Mention this to no one but her," he finished sternly. He looked the scout in the eyes and saw Private Ingvold's courage tremble. "Ever," he added.

As any good soldier would, he'd also send back words of anticipated victory; and they would fight like the forces of all the hells were at their backs. However, should they lose, which any pragmatic man knew was a possibility, he wanted his wife to know about the aldyrs. She loved them. They always parted with words they knew could be their last; however, he wanted to send her one more surprise. If he could retrieve one of those snow-white blossoms himself, he would. The hoofbeats of Private Ingvold's horse faded so quickly that it left the general, a veteran of many battles, impressed.

Godspeed, Ingvold. May you become a legend in your own time.

"An odd thing to send a scout away on," the nasal-voiced lieutenant said. "We could have simply informed the council of high lords upon our return. That's one more sword we could have used."

Verdaun's lip curled. "This from a man who no doubt expects a retreat if things were to go south, to save your own powdered ass, Desille?"

Lieutenant Desille's horse whickered and tossed its mane, mirroring its rider's scowl. The sharp-featured, thin-faced man's lips—narrow, pale slits covering small, unnerving teeth—spread across his face until they practically disappeared. He looked about slowly, seeing if any of the nearby soldiers, retainers, or heralds heard or, worse, reacted.

"That's unbecoming of a general, Lord Verdaun. I'd hate to—"

"Tattle on me to your auntie?" Verdaun interrupted, not looking at the lieutenant. "I'm simply making sure your expectations for your first battle are well within reason. There will be pain. There will be blood and screaming and men shitting themselves as their guts spill out. Those that walk away won't be thinking of glory. They'll be thinking of their friends whose blood they're wearing as a tincture on their armor. *Is that right, men?*" he shouted. The soldiers within earshot, be they infantry, cavalry, knights, or archers, returned a wordless, bellowed cry.

Verdaun looked over at Desille. This was a wretched man whose only purpose was to follow the storied general into battle and return alive so his family could feed on the influence bought from members experienced in combat victories. It was a vicious and reprehensible manner of political currency which was not unlike good marriages, good holdings, or secrets. He was a liability, and if Verdaun returned without him, it would blemish his own family's name and, therefore, the name and prosperity of his wife and children. So, Verdaun would let this petulant tick ride in his shadow and do everything he could to keep him alive. Unfortunately, 'ride' in this sense would mean a manner of leadership Verdaun found unpleasant; he would command from the rear. Although a temporary measure conducted in this battle only, it was no less regrettable.

"You stay on my horse's flank; no matter where I go, understand?" Verdaun commanded the lieutenant. "We'll stay in the back ranks, commanding our soldiers. You do nothing without my say. Is that clear?"

Desille's rat-like features crinkled at the old man's tone, though he was pleased at the idea of not being involved in direct combat.

"Look at that mountain," Verdaun said, pointing to the peaks behind the enemy forces. "You see that white patch near the top? Drink in the sight of those aldyrs, lieutenant. They're the last beautiful thing you're going to see today."

Verdaun turned away from Desille's sneering face. He looked at the enormous grove of trees himself. Now, it was time to prepare for combat; there would be nothing snow-white or romantic about it. He gripped the visor of his helmet in his gloved fingers and slammed it down.

～

"GENERAL THOMYS ALEXANDER. Warrior. Poet...and a damned fool."

"Talking about yourself again?" Theobold asked, chuckling. The well-dressed steward to the general rattled the sword at his side in its scabbard. His lightly filigreed breastplate itched him horribly where it rubbed against the black, red, and gold gambeson, but he couldn't reach the spot to scratch it. So, he took it out on his sword.

"Just stating the truth out loud," the general replied. He held the reins to his horse and gazed across the wide green field with its yellow patches of wildflowers. His bare head, shaved to hide his middle-aged baldness, beaded with sweat thanks to his heavy armor. He always held off on donning his helmet until the last minute, when he knew the fight was about to begin, when he'd lead the charge of their meager cavalry, but not until their archers had diminished the enemy numbers.

"No doubt Gallancrest is aware their 'allies' from Thayn will not be arriving," the general continued. "It still doesn't cover the houses that denied His Grace. Seven hundred soldiers from Thayn against fifteen hundred from Barkanest, Dublyn, and Holcourt. Even more from smaller houses. Gods-damned cowards. And I told His Grace this is a battle we could win. *My* insistence. *My* honor."

Theobold sniffed and sighed. "We've told King Alyxander for years that the Council of Lords are stronger because they rule in tandem, tied with each other's interests; not old vows granted to a monarch who only shares shards of his power. This is what you get. If he retaliates against those houses, they could easily unite into a revolution that would cause, well, no small amount of trouble. Battles like this," he emphasized with a nod to the banners waving on the other side of the field, "will be occurring all over his lands."

"Civil war," Thomys growled. "While Gallancrest strikes at our doors."

"A war our good king started, my lord," Theobold whispered loud enough for only the general to hear.

"Watch your tongue, Theobold," the general warned. His steward was as loyal as they came and honest to a fault. He'd hate to lose such an advisor to poorly timed words. The king had been in a very unforgiving mood as of late.

General Thomys stared at the line of cavalry on the opposite hill. They would be problematic. Their horses were armored, the midday sun glinting off the barding like an insult. His archers would be useless against them. There was no time to prepare anything beforehand at this battlefield. The two armies met here as a matter of honor between city-states so no trenches could be dug, no hay bales could be rolled into the field and pikes dug into them to create walls to break those charges. Perhaps he could send pikemen out with the infantry and create mobile pike walls to discourage charges? If he kept his infantry within a certain distance, his archers could fire on the enemy as they approached, whittling them down. There were options, just not many good ones.

A damned fool.

He summoned his captains and relayed some corrected orders. He then ordered a brief council of the many knight bannerets—fancy men with fancy titles whose only real use was their own subordinate troops they brought with them—and gave them additional orders, as well. Truly, the lands of Weldenbern were becoming more fractured as each noble demanded their favors be paid in more land and titles.

"At least the bridge is still secured. The new Countess of Thayn certainly won some royal favor today. She'll need it," Theobold said. "That tiny Thaynian arm along the Gullstern is about to become a highly valuable property. Even more than it already is if our more superstitious lords and ladies can be reasoned with."

Countess Nyall withdrawing her support from Gallancrest served as more than a blow to their force's numbers. The small region had a thin arm stretching off from the main body of its territory, earned in some marriage arrangement in generations past, most likely. It served as a border between Gallancrest's lands and Weldenbern's. Of important note is that it ran along the Gullstern river, most notably a bridge connecting the Gallancrest region of Monte Virl to Thayn, the northernmost part of Weldenbern. The newest countess, Janesca Lisbeth'Nyall, took control of Thayn from her lands at Gray Manor after her sister's people revolted and sealed her in her tower before abandoning their lands further east in the region. At least, that's what common sense dictated. There were more sinister rumors swirling about the insurrection involving black magic and a necromancer; Thomys was among those who thought this was all rubbish.

The new countess struck a serious blow to Gallancrest in a battle fought in perfumed rooms with glasses of wine and sharp words. It did little to help them here, on this field, where the only smell will be death, the scarlet color of blood instead of wine, and the sharp edge of blades and bodkins.

"Tell me, Theobold, do you know that mountain behind us?"

The steward didn't need to glance behind him. He knew the peak his lord spoke of. "Godscrown, my lord? What about it?"

The general turned to look at the sharp, steep landmark. Jutting like a broad, gray-blue spearhead against the sky, the mountain appeared to have a band of snow beneath its peak. City-states from Carnelia to Felkirk knew that this mountain rarely had snowcaps. Instead, it was crowned by the aldyrs of legend.

"My grandfather attended the peace talks there during his day," General Thomys observed. "Last time any great leaders met there was when I was a child. Beautiful place. Breathtaking, really. That it lies within our borders should be a sign for us today, seeing them bloom so brightly."

"I'm not a believer in signs, I'm afraid, my lord," Theobold replied, his eyes remaining on the other army. The crescendo to battle was building. He had no time to look at mountains, even close or beautiful ones. "Maybe we'll see more peace talks there soon."

A damned fool, the general thought to himself again. This time it wasn't directed at himself, though.

General Thomys donned his helmet, a black bucket of stout and masterful make, with a plume of gold and red signifying him on the field. He liked to ride with his men and feel the bones of his enemies break beneath his mace. He'd heard plenty about General Verdaun, as well, a fellow commander who preferred to join in the chaos of battle and get his hands bloody. He had that to look forward to, at least.

He looked one last time behind him at the mountain peak, crowned in white. It was a small mountain, to be sure, but among the most majestic of all. The gathered men of a hundred houses joined right at Godscrown's base in the foothills that rolled low like supplicants in worship. It would bear witness to this battle, fought over whose land it would remain on. In the shadow of that sharp, jutting peak, it felt like the mountain itself would choose the victor here; they were all merely pieces in a game.

"I hope you favor us," General Thomys muttered in a soft prayer, the sound echoing in his helmet.

He then nodded to Theobold, his faithful steward, who bowed slightly before grabbing his own helmet. Before placing it over his head, he shouted into the air for all to hear, "Trumpeters, sound the first call! We go to battle!"

∾

METAL RANG AGAINST METAL. Hammers, maces, axes, swords, and lances crashed against shields, armor, and flesh. The cries of men were cut short as arrows pierced them or blades opened them up. Bones crunched against the blows of weapons and hooves. Horses screamed as pikes brought them to the ground, crushing their riders beneath them. Blood soaked the ground, creating a slurry of viscera and mud. Shield lines pushed and grunted as they tried to hold back the enemy. Trumpets called, signaling forces from one side or another to rally or retreat. The thunder of cavalry was pierced by the crack of weapons landing their blows, sending its horrendous dirge to the top of Godscrown itself. The glory of war sang its dreadful song, its long chorus of lament.

Lieutenant Desille did as instructed. He followed closely to the flanks of Verdaun's horse. The great beast of war was far less shaken than the sallow-hearted noble and his fidgeting stallion. Neither had seen battle, only heard the sanitized words of poets and attendants who brought word of glorious victories.

At first, he doubted if he should stay with the general. He briefly fancied the idea of riding out and claiming a kill of his own, some nameless bastard infantry who'd be no match for a noble-born son trained on the castle grounds at Velise, his home. He'd prove the general wrong, make him kowtow, and apologize for his insolent assumptions. When the first wave of soldiers crashed against each other, and the arrows rained like whispering death, sending clusters of men to their knees with bloody gurgles, what little he knew of courage snuffed out like a candle in a gust of wind. He snapped his horse's reins and sidled up to the general; this was not what Lieutenant Desille was expecting.

"Had enough of glory, yet?" General Verdaun asked, his stone-throated voice rattling and reverberating even more within the confines of his helmet.

"I am...here to learn of battle," Desille said, choking back his pride and anger at the general's veiled insult.

"You're going to learn plenty and real fast," Verdaun replied before raising his hand, turning his head, and bellowing at the top of his voice: "Tuluse Cavalry! Ride to the south flank and reinforce them!"

Verdaun dropped his arm and watched the young herald assigned to Tuluse's forces race off, carrying his banner in both hands. The heraldry of the Tuluse region was a complex one with its quartered shield, each with a different set of symbols and colors all its own. They prided themselves on their number of landed knights and long, complex noble lineage. It was time to see if the sons of Tuluse earned such gallantry here.

Verdaun drew his sword. A small band of skirmishers had broken past the main line of engagement and were approaching his direction. He smirked at the thought of Desille having to fight. Unfortunately, a few light cavalry held in reserve, to protect him and the lieutenant, intercepted the would-be assailants and cut them to pieces.

The general grumbled. This fight was stalled, each side refusing to give way. He needed to be out there with his soldiers, driving them forward, but he was stuck here with a powdered whelp. This loss would be no fault of Desille's. He refused to make any excuse for the outcome of his battles. However, Verdaun believed that the tide of war strongly favored a man who waded into its depths with his own men. It stirred a fire in his gut when he saw the plumed helmet of Weldenbern's general among their opponent's cavalry, cutting down the men of Gallancrest. He longed to face him in combat, see what mettle the opposing general was made of.

A tremor rattled Verdaun's armor. His horse, accustomed to battle and all its horrors, whickered and stamped in discomfort for the first time. He thought for a brief, panicked moment that a cavalry charge was headed there, that a surprise force had flanked them. He looked around and saw no such impending attack. He also noticed that no one else seemed to be concerned about this, not even Desille. The men on the battlefield continued their bloody stalemate.

"Did you feel that?" the general asked the lieutenant.

"Feel what, general?" Desille responded in disinterest.

Verdaun grumbled under his breath. He returned to surveying the carnage. He needed to find some way to change this battle's course. Men and horses were dying, with no progress being made. This was turning into a battle of attrition. The Tulusian cavalry had met in battle with the Gallancrest infantry there, and it appeared they'd pushed the Weldenbern forces towards a gathering of trees. The retreating infantry was favorable, at least, but once they reached the trees, the Tulusians would be at a disadvantage. Their commander may not even continue to engage, depending on the thickness of the trees there.

He looked over at the two commanders nearest him. One headed the contingent of Gallancrest's archers while the other led the cavalry units that stayed to defend Verdaun. The slit of his visor concealed his face, but his voice spoke with the irritation and impatience that boiled within him.

"You!" he barked, pointing to the cavalry commander, "You see that red and gold plume out there? Atop that fucker in the black armor?" His arm swung out to the main line of battle ahead of them. The commander's eyes followed, and after a few seconds of scanning the field, he replied, "Yes, sir?"

"See the opposite side of the battle from him? Where those Weldenbern shit-heels aren't fighting quite as brash out of the sight of their precious fucking general?"

"Yes, sir!" the commander replied, his own blood stirring at the fierce words of his own general.

"Ride out to that flank, take a trumpeter…no, take two! When you get within arm's length of those pricks, I want those trumpets to sound like the gods themselves are returning. Break their resolve and send them back to Godscrown! Then, hold our troops back, on my orders!"

Verdaun's helmeted head turned to the archery commander. "When those bastards start running, I want our archers shooting at will and picking off every one of them we can—every single one!"

"Yes, sir!" the archery commander returned.

Verdaun addressed both commanders simultaneously but spoke loud and clear so that every archer and horseman within earshot would hear and know of his fervor and intent.

"If I can't be out there with them, with you, I want you fighting like I'm breathing down your fucking necks. You hear me?"

"Yes, sir!" came the rallied cries of nearly a hundred men.

"You send those milquetoast Weldenbernians screaming to their gods or running back to their whore wives in shame, you understand?" General Verdaun was nearly frothing at the mouth as he bellowed at his men. "The time for pussy-footing around with these pricks is over! Go get our victory!"

The men shouted a collective, indiscernible rejoinder. The cavalry commander cried, "To me! Ride!" as he spurred his horse on. The rest of his unit followed with swords in the air and trumpeters in tow. The archery commander returned to his own lines, shouted "Nock!" and heralds raised flags to relay the order down the lines to men who couldn't hear. The sounds of a hundred bowstrings stretching promised to rain death on their enemy after the blades of the cavalry broke their spirits. Desille's brows raised, and his lips curled in a mouth shrug, fighting not to show that he was slightly impressed.

Verdaun's tension showed in his body language. His horse

stamped impatiently. The cavalry trailed in a loose oblong shape at first before maneuvering into a wedge shape. They closed in on the clashing soldiers, drawing nearer and nearer as neither side noticed their advance.

"Now. *Now*." Verdaun said through gritted teeth.

Both trumpeters sounded their horns, a reverie familiar to Gallancrest ears. No sooner had the last echoes of the horns vanished than the riders slammed into the Weldenbern line to the side of the cavalry's allies. Muffled cheers came from the Gallancrest men as bodies began to fall, limbs went flying, and heads started rolling. It was a gamble, a shock attack that hopefully would see Verdaun's men able to advance and begin to surround the enemy forces.

It worked. Opposing infantry began to break on that particular flank, retreating from the main line. Verdaun watched as the cavalry commander and some of the other riders began shouting at the infantry to hold back and press further into the main line. Unfortunately, a number of Gallancrest troops either didn't hear or didn't obey the commander's orders. Some of them, in their fury and bloodlust, gave chase to the retreating forces. The other soldiers followed the commands given and pressed into the main line, curling around to begin surrounding them.

"Damn it," Verdaun cursed under his breath. The joy of his gamble paying off was tainted by what was to come next. He turned his head to the archery commander. The man's arm was raised, ready to order his men to loose, but the look in his eyes reflected Verdaun's own concern. Their own men would now be among the casualties.

"Damn it!" he shouted. "Commander, loose! If we don't, we'll lose more men; we have to take this opportunity!"

The commander's arm dropped, and he shouted, "Loose!" and the flags went up again. The sound of the arrows was like a demon's whisper promising blood and pain. As the first wave dropped, many hit their marks. Men of Weldenbern dropped, and sprays of blood shot across the green field. So, too, did a number of Gallancrest soldiers. After a stunned moment, they turned and fled back to the main line. The Weldenbernians continued to flee back to Godscrown's foothills.

"At will!" the commander cried. The harsh whisper of the demon became a staccato cackle as archers fired volley after volley. Verdaun felt the ground tremble again, but so, too, did those around him. Desille's face scrunched as he looked around. The archery commander's eyes fell to the ground. Verdaun was not alone in his concerns this time.

"Keep firing!" Verdaun shouted, keeping his troops focused despite the tremor. They were finally witnessing the battle turn in their favor. If this kept up, soon they may just see the enemy retreat, and their superior cavalry numbers would ride them down, giving Gallancrest the day.

THE GREAT GENERAL of Weldenbern rode abreast with his men. Blood soaked the ground and flew behind their horses in grotesque clumps as they slammed into and through cluster after cluster of enemy forces. Heads flew as swords separated them from their bodies. Bones broke against the armored beasts and were trampled under their hooves. Thomys' blood burned with battle and he felt victory was imminent.

Then, the first sounds of a dying horse reached his ears. He looked in the direction of the horrible sound and saw one of his men flailing their arms as their mount fell to one side, the horse's legs kicking as it did so. The knight was trapped under the beast. The general saw a pack of men in green gambesons and blood-stained helmets descend on him like wild animals, stabbing into the joints of his armor as blood began pooling beneath him.

"Cowards!" he shouted, and spurred his horse to charge them. They barely managed to stand upright before he was on them, hacking at them and sending two of them to the ground. The other reared back to strike at Thomys' shield side as the general lifted the shielded arm and showed the wretch his city-state's crest. A long blade protruded from the soldier's chest and blood poured from beneath his helmet. A pikeman from the knightly house of Ashmouth pulled his weapon out of the enemy and turned to continue the fight.

Through the sweltering, closed-in space of his helmet, the general took in the fight for a moment, seeing where he would be best needed. The fight had stalled, with no side gaining ground or losing more men than the other. He needed to rally his cavalry again, but they were in the thick of the fight now. It would be a wasted effort.

Where was the Gallancrest General, Verdaun? Thomys' eyes scanned the chaos before him but found no sign of the other leader. He then glanced up the hill beyond the bedlam and saw Verdaun there with some of his own cavalry, archers, and a subordinate.

He scoffed and cursed. This didn't align with what he'd been told about this general. Verdaun was supposed to be a man akin to himself; one who led from the field, who bled beside his men. Not this man in shiny armor and nursemaids watching his men die. Thomy's blood burned again, this time in fury. Would that he could charge Verdaun directly, but that would be suicide. He cursed once more and continued to fight. Once the battle shifted and his men brought the others to their knees, he'd show General Verdaun all the respect he deserved.

General Thomys didn't know how much time had passed when he heard the call of trumpets nearby. He pulled his blade out of some poor bastard's throat and looked to the noise, finding it across the battlefield on the opposite side. A whole line of fresh cavalry was running through his men while shouts of renewed vigor came from the Gallancrest soldiers.

Damn it! Damn it all!

He looked to see Verdaun still at the crest of the hill, now without his escort.

Perhaps not as much of a coward as I thought, Thomys said to himself.

He saw the lines of his own men breaking and retreating. Then, he heard the sound of the wings of death. Volleys of arrows took down those retreating, but also some of the Gallancrest troops who followed. A bold move, almost cruel.

Fucking brilliant.

This would prove devastating for the forces of Weldenbern. General Thomys knew he had to think quickly. It may be worth pulling his own cavalry back now or at least rallying some of them for a push of their own. He didn't have time to consider many options. A shudder made its way through the ground below him. He felt it, his horse cried out, and his men, as well as the enemy, stopped in their tracks. Some men fell as the tremor shook them and their steel-shod feet slipped in the mire at their feet.

ANOTHER TREMOR HIT, this one the largest of all. It shook the battlefield itself and scores of troops from both sides stopped their slaughter of one another to stare, dumbstruck, and focus on maintaining their footing. The sudden silence after the roaring clash of steel, men shouting, and screams of the dying left the field eerily silent. The remains of the clamorous noise echoed and faded, leaving a tense apprehension over the men on both sides. Thousands of heads turned in confusion, many looking to the ground below them. Confusion and fear mingled as they all felt something wasn't right. Men who, moments before, were killing each other in the most gruesome and callous ways now looked to one another, hoping that someone had an answer.

Verdaun's horse neighed and stomped the ground, its barding jingling and clanking. Hundreds of feet away, Thomys' did the same. Their horses were nervous, the animals' instincts reeling at some unknown danger. Many more horses, all belonging to the various cavalry, knights, and lancers followed suit. The sound of hundreds of nervous horses began to unsettle even the most stalwart soldiers on the field.

The two generals looked at each other, their eyes hidden behind the shadows of their respective visors, but the intensity of their gaze was not lessened for it. Decades of instinct honed through many battles told both of them that something more dangerous than their own men was at work.

A wretched sound tore the ranks of bloodied and tired men. It sounded like a scream within the soul, the groan of a dying god as its head lolled to the side, like so many deaths they'd seen and heard before. The sky became bruised, and a black tear opened like a ghastly wound.

The forces of Gallancrest and Weldenbern all looked to the sky and witnessed what lay beyond that horrifying rend. Dead worlds and black stars hovered in even deeper darkness. Beyond those forlorn celestial bodies were things that defied explaining. They were not like any creatures the generals had ever seen or heard of—and they had fought much more than just men.

This indescribable event, a rupture that tore the sky open and revealed places not meant for mortal eyes to see, took what remained of the men's courage. Weapons fell from limp hands and frightened cries began to build. A few broke for their side of the field. That's when a full quake brought many to their knees.

It was a sudden and acute eruption. The sound came from deep within the world. Another terrible sound, deafening but far more tangible, caused armored plates to clank together and teeth to rattle in skulls. The soldiers of Gallancrest looked ahead while those of Weldenbern turned to stare behind them. The core of the great tremor was coming from the mountain, a moan deep within the heartstone of the grand peak that sounded like a massive, godly hand gripped and twisted until the mountain cracked.

Godscrown shook as clouds of dust broke out across it like a destructive web. Massive landslides began to roll down the steep slopes. Weldenbern's forces stood in awe as the mountain crumbled. Some of them came to their senses and shouted for their fellows to run. Those who remained on the hillside began fleeing into the battlefield. The terrible event stopped the battle altogether, as soldiers under every banner fled together in fear of their lives. No longer were they the shining soldiers of mighty nations, fighting bravely for noble and just causes, but insects fleeing the boot-heel of a deity's wrath.

As Godscrown crumbled before them, the gathered soldiers continued their retreat. They fled until their generals ordered them to cease. Both Verdaun and Thomys, despite not speaking to one another directly, knew that this should be safe enough of a distance to ride out the sundering quake. They were more concerned with the strange phenomenon overhead. Their men saw the monumental landslides cease as clouds of dust rolled over them.

When it cleared, all was strangely silent again. Some dared to hope the catastrophe was over. Confused glances and muttered questions flittered among the thousands of former enemies. There was little time to contemplate. Something stirred in the black gash above them. Arms raised with pointing fingers while a shadow beyond the sky coiled and stirred in the cosmic graveyard. For the briefest of moments, it passed over all that were present. Verdaun shivered and Thomys gripped his horse's reins to control his shaking hands.

The ground shook once more and the field before them, now covered in scattered rivers of rock, began to swell in places like great roots were trying to burst through the ground. As the soil and grass pulled away and trees fell to the side, pure darkness was revealed beneath. Massive cords pulled from the ground and reared like midnight serpents before slamming back down. They appeared in various thicknesses and lengths, but they were singular in purpose. The twisting, sinuous strands curled in and out of the field and hills, constricting and rending the terrain as whole chunks were turned asunder. Underground rivers were exposed, creating waterfalls in the craters.

Theobold felt his heart thumping against his armor. He looked to General Thomys and desperately willed him to give an order. The general was one of the most decisive and observant men he knew; only he could give the orders that would save their lives.

Thomys saw many things, and all of them threatened to unnerve him. Their route of retreat was cut off by the landslide. If they followed Verdaun, they would be giving themselves, an entire army, over to the enemy; this, of course, was if they survived whatever monstrosity they faced. He feared this creature had yet to show its true self. The multitude of black serpentine shapes all led back to Godscrown. Were they the extensions of a single, blasphemous thing or an ophidian mass working together? Regardless, they or it were waging war on the world of Alda itself, rending it to pieces like wolves on a deer carcass. There was still a stretch of the field left leading back to the mountain. His army had a new enemy. They only needed the will to face it.

"Let these Gallancrest pigs run back to their lands, men. Our home lies that way!" he shouted, pointing his sword toward the creatures surging in the field below them.

"We can't fight whatever those are, my lord; there's too many!" Theobold protested. Several men, including the knights, nodded in agreement. "We should retreat with Gallancrest, part in a treaty to be discussed by our lords."

The general's plumed helmet turned to the steward and the weight of his displeasure was palpable. "Stories are never told about dragonslayers who run, steward. Do you want that to make its way to Weldenbern?" he gestured to the things still wrapping themselves around the mountain and hills, ducking in and out of the ground like worms in a frenzied, gluttonous feeding.

"Draw your swords, men! Kill the beasts!"

General Thomys led one more charge down the hill. His men shouted and followed, though some did so with hesitation. Verdaun grimaced and looked at Desille. The man had gone pale, with sweat beading all along his forehead exposed through his open visor. The battle had changed. No longer were they fighting men from nearby countries with differences imposed on them by their liege-lords. Rather, they were now in a fight to survive against creatures from an unknown and unthinkable sky.

The ground wavered beneath them, and some of his men screamed. Verdaun turned to see some of the archers in the back lines lifted from the ground and whipped about by some of the creatures. They were flung to their deaths with supernatural strength or crushed against trees and the ground in the grips of the dark things. Soldiers began fleeing from the terrifying sight, but there was only one direction to go. Verdaun raised his sword and barked at his men: "We ride with Weldenbern! Kill these fucking things!"

Verdaun cast a quick glance at Desille, who sat there with his mouth agape.

"You're fighting today, lieutenant. Draw!"

With more shouts, the forces of Gallancrest joined in the fray with those of Weldenbern, former enemies now riding and fighting together against something they could not explain or understand. To their great horror, they discovered they were at an impossible disadvantage. They saw, with their own eyes, the serpents tearing up the ground effortlessly. However, pikes and spears pierced the creatures to no avail. Swords cut gashes that didn't bleed and removed chunks that dissolved into gelatinous piles. Whole infantry lines were swept aside with blows powerful enough to liquefy their insides. Horse and rider were grabbed mid-charge and wrapped in a ferocious coil that turned bones to powder and squelched as organs and blood were expelled with unnatural force. All the while, the strange black serpents continued to tear the land apart. The armies of men were depleted in moments.

Verdaun found Thomys on the field. They rode next to each other and removed their helmets. Each man was drenched with sweat, confounded looks of looming defeat in their eyes.

"Where's your steward?" Thomys asked, too casually for the event unfolding around them.

"My lieutenant. Dead. One of those things smashed his face in."

"I lost my steward somewhere in this chaos. I'm sure he's dead, too."

The old warriors spoke evenly, their tactical minds spent. There was nothing they could do against such creatures beneath such a sky.

"What are these damned things? Snakes? Dragons?"

Verdaun asked, watching as the last of his men were smashed against the scattered remains of the mountains.

"I've a feeling it's neither. Look," Thomys replied, pointing to what was left of Godscrown. "it's like they're all attached to something beneath the mountain. Or in it."

"Gods..." Verdaun saw it. The 'serpents' were all originating from somewhere within Godscrown.

"What can men do against this?" Thomys asked aloud. He looked up and saw that the once-sharp peak had collapsed on itself. The crown of aldyrs was gone.

Verdaun had no time to answer. The black, sinister strands seemed to find purchase on the land after it had dealt with the gnats biting at it. The serpentine tentacles spread like a black web around the center of Alda. Had Verdaun and Thomys been able to see the full extent of the destruction, their minds, though experienced in horrific sights, would not have been strong enough. Verdaun didn't see the destruction wrought in his home city-state, where his wife lay motionless under a pile of rubble with the night-hued serpents running along the cracks and crevices of mortared stone. Thomys didn't see the great castle at the heart of Weldenbern reduced to a pile of rocks similar to what remained of Godscrown.

The world was still for a moment, then the web flickered, flexed, and brought the world of Alda crashing down. The city-states of men, ancient forest kingdoms of elf-kind, and the deep halls of the dwarves were shattered from Carnelia to Thayn, Felkirk to the Blackwood. Whole pieces of the continent were disintegrated as new cliffs were formed and the oceans and seas poured into the new ruinous space created by the world-spanning catastrophe. Mountains were drowned, and kingdoms were obliterated in an instant. The wave of devastation was so acute and potent that the generals, the last of the gathered thousands for a battle destined never to be concluded, were reduced to red smears in their armor.

For a lucky few, the birth of the Wailing Ocean was experienced as an earthquake and nothing more. For millions of others, their worlds were disintegrated in an instant. Stunned individuals looked on as the ground collapsed at their feet and the unholy sound of a new ocean flooding over the ruins created a breathtakingly terrifying new horizon.

None, however, could see the center of that ocean where the heart of the world's newest and worst evils took root. Godscrown was the site of the Wailing Ocean's creation. However, it was spared the fate of the surrounding regions. Godscrown was braced by those black, serpent-like extensions belonging to a terrible entity. The remains of the great mountain jutted above the sea; in place of the beautiful crown of aldyrs it once bore stood a single aldyr tree larger than any that had ever existed.

GHOSTS OF ALDA

Part I

THE CURRENTS AND TIDES THAT WOVE THE WATERS OF ALDA WERE fickle and unpredictable, much like the wilds and cities. The new ocean and seas created by the great catastrophe of the Rupture sunk entire continents, caused others to rise from the depths of the old oceans and reworked the boundaries of the lands that once touched them. Sailors could manage those haunted, troubled waters after years of experience. For the uninitiated, to dare those waters was to beckon a slow and terrible death into your open arms.

Annica had heard many stories from the sailors in her old village. The types of ghost stories that chilled even grown men. Men who stared at those waters every day and pulled fish from its depths. Men who should have been accustomed to its waves, its noises, its weather; respecting its power but not terrified of it. Instead, the stories were told with reverent fear as though they were history passed down verbally through the generations rather than something meant to entertain.

Annica was curled up in the small boat that carried her from the cursed island city of Nel Aldyri. A blanket covered her and a layer of gray and white ash covered the blanket. Her hands twitched and she whimpered. Her eyes shut tight as sleep held her in its grip.

She knew she was asleep but was unable to affect her surroundings. She was adrift on an ocean of souls; the waves were their flailing arms and cries of torment. They washed over a beach of powdered bones, pulverized by centuries of the wailing damned washing over them. Beneath the surface of those spectral waters, an ocean floor of tangled skeletons stretched out below, somehow visible even from the water's surface.

The screaming voices called out a name, but Annica couldn't make it out. She looked to the distance, where the echoes seemed to carry, and saw the silhouette of a tower in the distance. It was old and broken, but the ramparts surrounding it were a sharp, spiked crown. Large rocks surrounded it and the ocean of the damned threw themselves against it, breaking apart only to be replaced by others fated to do the same. Cold snow fell as the secluded stronghold grew closer.

It reminded her of something. The shape of the tower, its cruel outline dark and featureless against the bleak clouds. Its bulk covered the majority of the island it called home, almost like a tree burned down to its trunk; a grotesquely large tree. The snow landed on her fingers and she pinched it, watching it smear like ash.

Annica's eyes opened. She wasn't sweating, but her heart pounded against her ribs. It slowly ebbed and returned to normal, but the fearful grip of her nightmare wouldn't fade. Already, its details began to slip. She only remembered vague flashes of images and the terror tied to the shadows in her mind.

Her body trembled. She was curled into a fetal position and reached down to wrap her arms around her knees. The shaking wouldn't stop. She smelled something, like a campfire, and tasted blood in her mouth. When the ethereal effects of her nightmare finally faded, the trembling waned into a shiver. She was cold. Physical sensations began to return to her. She was lying on something hard and cold; the wood of a small boat. Her eyes stung and her body ached.

She took a deep breath but choked as something filled her lungs. It tasted like a campfire, just like the smell surrounding her. She pushed herself up and coughed until her throat hurt. She remembered there was water on the boat. Her vision was blurry, so she wiped her eyes and thought for a moment that hadn't helped, that the world around her was still fuzzy and gray. She realized, after several long moments of no improvement, that nothing was wrong with her vision. The inside of the boat was covered in ash, and it was still falling.

No, that wasn't ash; it was lighter. White flecks dappled the gray film covering the inside of the boat that had been her only respite for...how long was it now? She steadied herself on the cold wooden floor and prepared for the familiar rocking sensation of standing while the boat rocked in the ocean once more. Her dreamlike state had almost completely dissipated, leaving an equally bleak reality before her. Standing, however, came very easily. She saw the ocean behind her, waves rolling in as snow fell all around. The boat rocked, but very gently rather than in large rolling swells.

Annica turned around and expected to see more ocean, stretching out for untold miles to the horizon. Instead, the dark stones of an unfamiliar shore greeted her. Confusion gave way to panic; had she returned to that malevolent island and its forsaken city of Nel Aldyri? Had her friend, Edrik, died for nothing? And worse yet, were the black-robed followers of Bac'thule lurking nearby?

Tears burned in her already irritated eyes. She stepped out of the boat, shakily setting foot on the ground. The terrain of this island looked different from Nel Aldyri. The beach here was cold and consisted of dark, smooth rocks, made darker by the waters splashing over them; the shores of Nel Aldyri that she remembered were sandy, green, and warm. Just beyond the rocky beach waited a thick forest of large spruces and conifers, dark evergreens that she never saw on the cursed island. The flames that ravaged that sorrowful land when she departed had engulfed it wholly, from one side to the other. No trees could have survived.

She was certain that she was somewhere else. It made the panic fade for a moment, but then it swelled back with a new and different purpose. Annica didn't know where she was. It never got this cold in her village. She tried putting pieces together to get some kind of idea of her location. The Wailing Ocean connected to all parts of the interior of Alda's continents. She'd learned this from Sisironi. A pang of heartache pulsed in her chest at the thought of the swaggering, strong, and beautiful captain that she would have called friend; however, the forces conspiring against Annica on that fell island had different plans, and Sisironi was another that had been taken from her.

Forcing her mind to return to the task before her and shake off the reins of sadness, Annica took in her surroundings. The trees were, indeed, solely composed of evergreens. Only those species that could withstand the cold survived here. They grew thick and close together, the shadows within them cloistering deep and dark; stolid sentinels that promised mystery. The sharp-needled forest loomed before her, rising with the stony shore as it angled steeply up until the line of trees, all dark gray boles, began like a beckoning wall. They grew so tall she couldn't see the horizon beyond.

She turned and looked behind her. An arrowhead-shaped inlet stretched out with other dark shores, obscured by white strands of mist crawling over the black stones like pale snakes, bordering each side. The Wailing waters pushed in, rolling over one another like the dead in her dreams. Annica could almost see the hands of the countless drowned souls grasping and stretching out from the foaming crests.

A biting cold. Dark cedars and falling snow. A cold inlet of water. Annica still only had a guess, but she'd seen maps in the library of Nel Aldyri during her time there and assumed the currents had brought her north judging by her surroundings.

"I must be near Kalthav, or what's left of it," she said aloud. Her voice disappeared in the chill wind and rustling branches.

In between her studies on magic, Annica managed to scour a few other books before the horrible events set her to sailing alone on the ocean. Some of those books taught her of the world before the Rupture and what the Children of the First Son had learned of Alda's remains since. The former city-states were all destroyed, their capitals claimed by various Inheritors of the Obscured Throne; in some cases, like Carnelia, the minions of Inheritors who let them make the land and its people their play-things. Annica shuddered at the memory of learning such things.

Kalthav was the northernmost city-state. Its former glory was no more. The large ships and heavily armored warriors that adorned the paintings and murals brought back to Nel Aldyri were only memories of what was left of the proud and stalwart people. Or so Annica had been told. It appeared time to find out for herself what remained of the grim north.

She returned to her boat, her home for seemingly endless days by the count of the tally marks she'd scratched into the interior hull. Her arrival at the cold shores was most timely, she thought as she drank the last bit of water she had left. Her dry provisions had run out a day or two before, and Annica would have been in a situation most dire.

Annica shook off the thick wool blanket that had been tucked inside the boat. Ash and snow flew into the air in a burst of white-gray cloud. She stepped from the boat, pulled the blanket tightly around her, and took her first steps toward the unknown land ahead of her, beyond the dark evergreens.

Within the sheltering, woven boughs of green needles, the wind blew far weaker and the snow consisted only of the luckiest of flakes that made it through the gauntlet overhead. The insulated forest felt warmer and, dare she say, safer. Annica's breaths still materialized in front of her in long, steady puffs. Snow, pinecones, and shed bark crunched beneath her feet. It boomed and echoed like drums in the stillness around her. The time of day eluded her. Was it late or early? With the thick gray clouds overhead, it could be midday and she wouldn't know any different. Those long days and nights on that boat, alone, were best spent sleeping as much as possible. She never wanted to close her eyes again. And yet, she was still so exhausted.

Her stomach grumbled, which she had grown accustomed to, but now sharp pangs began to join them, a harmony of misery and hunger. She'd seen no berries or fruits of any kind, at least none that were safe to eat. She had no tools, no weapons. But she did have her magic. A fire would be nice, so long as she didn't burn the forest down. At least that might get someone's attention, she thought.

Her only real talent was in the Second and Fifth Sects. Arcane manipulation wouldn't help her here, anyway. Though, nature magic might have proven useful. Annica found a clearing, gathered some stones, branches, and bark, and built what she thought was a passable site for a campfire.

But first, food, she thought to herself, placing a hand over her aching stomach.

She sat down and leaned up against a tree. She focused on the Fifth Magic around her, the essence of life and the world of Alda. There weren't any larger animals nearby, but the sense of smaller creatures drew into her; birds, rabbits, squirrels. The rapid pace of their tiny heartbeats thumped in her head, reminding her of her fingers drumming in boredom on the boat. The rustle of the trees' needles was a low, ambient drone in the harmony of existence. Annica slowed her breathing. She let her own essence tangle with that of the trees. In essence, she had become invisible to those creatures of instinct. Even her scent was disguised by the scent of spruce and wet bark. She knew this because, as the blanket of existence wrapped around her, she willed it to be so.

Time slipped away. It may have been five minutes or five days; she didn't know. The rapid pattering of a small heart drew very near and roused her from the flow of life's energies. She slowly opened her eyes and saw a brown smudge in her blurred vision. As her sight returned, the smudge materialized into a round, brown-and-white feathered bird a few feet away. A grouse.

Slowly, she pinched a fallen pine needle in her fingers. Annica pointed the needle at the bird, much like she'd seen other magi use wands. The intent was to use this small thing to focus her magic. Her lack of control was still a nagging issue. She focused on the tiny needle and the temperatures around her. The timing was critical, as the grouse wouldn't linger for long. Thankfully, no incantations were needed for Second Sect magic, so her voice wouldn't be an issue in scaring off the animal. However, the lack of heat around her was proving difficult to conjure the fire she so desperately required. The energies in flux around her were cold and chaotic, swirling with elements that were of no use at this moment. The grouse meandered about silently, once looking in Annica's direction.

A desperate idea came to her. The best source of heat was her. Annica felt warmth drain from her arms like she'd stuck them in cold water. Finally, the coalesced energies she needed began to build at her fingertips. A tiny pinprick of light glowed and grew warm. She fixated on it, intensified it, magnified it, then let it loose along the guiding edge of a pine needle.

A shard of flame shot forth and struck the grouse, piercing its body. The small creature collapsed on the ground, a small wisp of smoke rising from where the spell struck. Annica's heart beat faster and her frozen forearms began to feel warmth spread back through them. The pine needle was no more than a brittle, black stick after the spell had finished. She dropped it, stood and shook the snow from her, then walked with a clumsy combination of speed and caution to where her meal fell. A pang of sadness for killing the bird thrummed in her, but when her stomach growled painfully again, it went away.

Before she could pluck and prepare the grouse for cooking, she needed to make a fire. The flames would have chased away any potential game, but now that was no longer an issue. Gathering dry wood was difficult, if not outright impossible. The snow had been falling too steadily for too long. Annica managed to find enough kindling and larger branches to build a decent fire. Some rough stones, not smoothed away by the ocean's waters this far away from the shore, formed the protective barrier around her meager firepit.

Once again, the lack of natural heat prevented her from easily conjuring her fire magic.

"Come on," she said out loud, "just enough for a fire; I don't need to burn the forest down."

She spread her hands over the bark and twigs that composed the kindling. Any amount of warm essence would do. But the ground was hard and cold, the wind stiff and chill. The snow continued to fall, slowly blanketing everything around it.

The elements always exist, everywhere, the arch-priestess, Helen, once told her. The warmth of summer waters, the wind winding through stony ravines, rivers coursing through mountains, and rains bringing relief to sweltering summer seasons. A particular element may feel smothered or distant, but they are always there.

Annica closed her eyes. Fire was her gift. Water, wind, and stone were areas she found her skills lacking, but the snow and wind stood out here even to her. However, above the hushed sounds of the evergreens and the dark gray clouds of the northern sky, a warm heart radiated. The light itself bore traces of the sun's energy. Now, as she focused, she could feel it where before her mind had ignored it. Or, rather, simply looked past it for more obvious sources.

A slight cooling touched her as though a cloud shrouded the sun. She imagined her small clearing must have dimmed slightly as she drew on the heat of the sun's light that punctured the branches and clouds above. She spread her hands just above the kindling, letting the concentrated magic flow from her hands. She heard the *wuff* and crackle of a successful fire.

"Oh, thank you," she said, opening her hands and feeling her fingers, stiff and aching from the cold, warm and loosen before the burgeoning flame.

When she could feel her hands once more, she retrieved the grouse, still resting from where it fell and began to rip the feathers from its body. A small knife was all she had available from the boat, but it was enough to let her cut open and remove the entrails from the bird and prep it for cooking. She sharpened a stick and speared the meat, then held it over the fire. She turned it slowly, listening to the fire pop and smelling the smoke of the damp wood. The thought of creating a proper spit came to her, but spinning the food on her own gave her something to do and kept her moving and warm.

Her mind wandered as the small game bird cooked and browned over the fire. The flames licking the raw flesh brought back memories, sharp and sudden, of panicked final hours on the dread island of Nel Aldyri. She imagined the fiendish, massive aldyr as a large black husk, now; ash perpetually falling from its swollen, burnt trunk. The thought of that wicked man, Gideon, dead and buried in that tomb of suffering and sacrifice he and his vile cult constructed, brought her a measure of peace. Then, however, the images of the city itself, of so many innocent people who didn't escape the fires of her untamed magic caused her to shrivel inside.

Finally, the last glimpses she had of Edrik fighting to the death to buy her time to escape filled her mind's eye. She saw the blade of the cultist that killed him drive into his body, somewhere near his heart. She blinked and let the tears fall down her cheeks, forcing that picture away. A memory of him smiling at her, of their time on the *Dawn Rose* before any of the nightmares had even begun, and other, happier, memories took the place of fire and grief. It did little to slow the tears or quell the anguish.

The smell of the food, once so tantalizing and overpowering, shriveled beneath the shadows of loneliness and heartache. Even Helen, in those final moments before she'd fled back into the city, appeared heartbroken at the thought of Annica betraying her and not embracing the tenets of their faith. Other faces flashed behind Annica's tightly closed eyes; their names forgotten, their kindness and humanity swept up and blown away with the rest of the ashes.

And Mya. The girl who suffered so much and tried to warn Annica of what Nel Aldyri truly was, what festered below its gleaming surface. She was dead, too, and what a long, horrible death it was. Her emotions swung back and forth like a heavy pendulum. Her sadness and depression of all the lost people and those she cared about would swell until thoughts of Mya, the giant aldyr, that vile hooded bastard, the sacrificial chamber, and other dark things caused anger and hatred to pull those more gentle and unhappy waters back into darker depths.

Annica sighed, opened her eyes, and wiped the tears away.

The food looked ready to eat and despite losing her appetite, she knew she needed the energy. She stood and wiped the accumulated snow off the blanket wrapped around her.

Just as her hand reached out for the branch skewering her meal, she paused. Her eyes stared at the flames, hearing them crackle softly. Another sound. Just louder than the crackling. Snow being crushed underfoot came from somewhere in the woods.

She dropped quickly to one knee. The tongues of fire flickered unnaturally as she prepared it for further summoning. The crunching of snow grew louder. The steps came slowly and there seemed to be multiple sets of them. They echoed among the trees and Annica couldn't determine where they came from.

"My, that smells pretty good," a gruff voice called out.

Annica's head whipped over to where it had come from and saw a large figure shadowed beneath the boughs of the pines.

Part II

"Tell me who you are, or I'll cook you where you stand," Annica said sharply.

The man raised both of his hands in the air and slowly stepped into the opening of her camp. His clothes were thick and lined with furs; they looked incredibly warm. A salt-and-pepper beard shaped his face into a round, grandfatherly shape, though his eyes looked young and vibrant.

"I don't think I would smell as good as that bird if you did," he said matter-of-factly.

Annica saw one of his raised hands, balled in a fist, gripping a rope. She followed it to where it was tied to a harness on a donkey shadowed under the trees. Packs and bags of various sizes hung from the beast who stood there wholly disinterested.

"Where am I?" she asked, still letting the fire dance dangerously.

The bearded man squinted. His youthful eyes became suddenly buried under many folds of wrinkles and crow's feet. "Don't get a lot of lost people around here. Not living ones, anyway. Just cold bodies under the snow."

The more she heard him speak, the more a nasal accent stood out.

"I assume I'm near Kalthav. I don't know exactly where."

He nodded his head. "My arms are getting tired. Might I put them down?"

"Where are your weapons?" Annica asked, her tone still stern.

"Got an axe on Hilna over there. Mostly for wolves and the like." He nodded towards the donkey. "Look me over. Nothing on my person."

Annica took a few steps forward and looked him up and down. Other than warm clothes over a husky frame and a long belt that wrapped around his large belly, she saw nothing that made her think he was dangerous. Though, she would make sure to keep near the fire just in case. She nodded for him to lower his hands.

He made a clicking sound with his mouth and the donkey began walking towards him. Annica went back up to where she stood before, near the tree, and put the fire between them.

"Don't be so frightened. Hilna's more dangerous than I am. Stomped several chickens to death a few days ago. More than I've killed in my life. Do I look like a warrior to you?"

"I've seen worse from more surprising sources," she mumbled.

The man grabbed a dead log and pulled it over to the fire. He plopped down on it with a grunt, removed his gloves, and put his open palms toward the fire.

"So, you don't know where you are," he said, rubbing his hands together. "The Cold Stones. It's a wretched little wedge-shaped inlet just beyond that tree line."

"I know that much. I just came from there."

He grunted. "You swim? Did you walk here from out by Carnelia? Or did you come from the east? Don't know what's the worst prospect out of any of those, honestly."

Annica sat by the fire, sitting cross-legged on the ground. "By ship. A small one."

She grabbed the stick skewering the bird by one side, lifting it away from the fire. She held on to it for a moment, letting it cool. Her stomach rumbled as she stared at the browned skin.

"I've got some bread rations if you'd like to split that bird. Some fruit, too," the man offered. He stood and went to the donkey. Opening one of the packs, he removed a package and a small sack. Annica watched him closely. She still couldn't see the axe he'd mentioned earlier.

The man approached her slowly, keeping one item in each hand to show her he meant no harm. He sat next to her slowly and unwrapped the package. Inside were chunks of bread, roughly square-shaped and light tan in color. The small pouch was closed with a strap. He pulled on the two strands and opened it, revealing deep purple berries inside.

"Give me a little of that bird and I'll trade some bread and snowberries, here. Make that meal a little more interesting. I've got whiskey, too." He grunted, standing suddenly like he'd forgotten about the liquor. He went back to the mule and pulled a flask from the same pack the food came from. He also removed a large canteen and carried them both over to Annica.

"Water and liquor. I recommend both."

Annica blinked. Her eyes darted to the bread and berries, then to the two containers with the drinks sitting in the snow. She tore a chunk of the cooked bird off with one hand and gave it to the man, who took it in his hands and nodded his head deeply in thanks.

Annica began eating her portion of the game. "You're quite friendly to someone whose name you don't even know, that you met in the woods near a 'wretched little shore'."

The bearded man licked his fingers and grunted in what sounded like a positive tone. "I travel out in these parts on a regular basis. Family tombstones that I come to visit in a village long rotted away. I meet people sometimes. You get to know the ones to be careful around, those to approach, and those to avoid entirely."

"And I give off the impression of someone approachable?" she scoffed.

"You give off the impression of one in dire straits," he clarified. "Improperly dressed, a shabby blanket, and a small game bird cooking on a sad little fire."

Annica finished chewing her mouthful and swallowed. She sat quietly for a moment and then sighed.

The man chuckled. "As for my name? Pyotr. The donkey's Hilna."

She looked over to see him eyeing her expectantly. He slowly placed a bit of cooked bird in his mouth while he waited.

"Annica," she said reluctantly.

"Hmm," Pyotr grumbled as he swallowed. He picked up the flask and took a swig, shaking his head afterward. The liquid burned as it went down. "A southern name. Someone from warmer climates."

"Much warmer," Annica commented.

"And what are you doing up here?" he asked, tossing back a handful of the berries.

Annica grabbed one of the pieces of bread. It was slightly stiff, obviously meant for travel, but not stale. "It's a long story," she said in a low voice. She bit off a piece of the bread and winced. It was bitter and had the hint of some sort of herb.

"Something wrong?" Pyotr asked. He picked up and offered Annica the water canteen. She accepted it and drank meagerly at first, but once the water hit her stomach she realized how thirsty she was. She continued to drink and drink until she realized what she was doing.

"I'm sorry," she said, gasping for air as she handed the canteen back to Pyotr.

He capped the canteen and gave her a sympathetic look. "How long have you been out there on the Wailing, or in these woods for that matter?"

She stared into the fire and took another bite of the bread. It went down easier this time. "I don't know. I slept as much as I could. My supplies ran low just before I landed here. I only just ran ashore a few hours ago."

"Lucky," Pyotr commented. "I found you before anything got worse."

"Things can get worse?" she said miserably, the memories causing the pain in her chest to return.

Pyotr took another swig from the flask. "Where exactly did you plan to go from here?"

Annica remained silent, unsure how to answer.

"Let's say you chose west. Do you know what's west?"

"Carnelia, you said."

"Sure, but about a mile that way and there's a fort on top of a hill; brigands there can see the treeline clearly as well as miles around. They'd notice you right away. I don't think I need to explain what a bunch of wretches like that would do to a pretty girl like you."

Annica pursed her lips.

"East then? You'll head straight into the Withered Groves, called the Blackwood long ago. Place so haunted it's forbidden for any Kalthavian to travel there. You can risk it if you like, but nothing good ever came of that place. South just takes you back to your little boat, the Cold Stones, and the Wailing Ocean. That leaves north, straight to Kalthav. The only option you have, but a safe one."

"I read that all the major city-states have been destroyed or cursed, or both," she commented. "Are you from Kalthav?"

"I am," he replied assuredly. "Maybe it was our remoteness. Maybe it was just too damn cold for the monsters. But, despite being cut off from the rest of the world, or maybe because of it, we're making do with our isolation."

Annica finished off the bitter-tasting bread and drank a little more water. She was quiet for a while, listening to the wind blow, the fire crackle, and Pyotr continuing to eat and drink. She was lost, not just in these frigid northern woods, but in spirit and purpose. There was no direction in her life. She'd learned a unique and amazing skill with no purpose to use it. No one to further train her. The horrific secrets revealed to her left a scar on her soul that smothered any hope she had for the future. Perhaps in Kalthav, if the city remained intact, she could find purpose. Answers. A life.

"I'll come with you to Kalthav," she said firmly but quietly.

Pyotr slapped his knee. "Excellent! We'll be returning after I visit my family's graves. It's not far from here."

They finished their meal and doused the fire. Pyotr dug up a spare jacket and cloak for Annica to fight off the cold. He also pulled out some thicker boots for her feet, which had become numb due to the cold. They were all comically oversized, making her look like a small child accompanying her uncle, but they kept her exponentially warmer. It seemed Hilna was used exclusively as a pack animal. Pyotr never rode her, and Annica noticed there was nothing resembling a saddle on her back—only more satchels and packs.

The gray-furred mule was nothing but obedient. The rope attached to her harness never pulled taught. She seemed to follow her master at a given pace, never getting too close or too far behind. Annica listened as Pyotr made casual small talk, not with her, but with Hilna. Annica found it very amusing. It was as though he were used to the company of the mule but not another person.

"Almost there, Hilna, and you can rest some more," he said, facing forward.

The snow continued to fall slowly and steadily. Their feet crunched the wet, white layer and the carpet of dead pine needles, sticks, and pebbles below it. It was very serene once Annica had gotten over how it reminded her of the rain of ash that followed her for days on the ocean.

Annica approached the snow-covered stones ahead. None of the buildings looked intact and the same could be said for the walls. The bridge that crossed a narrow creek looked ancient and treacherous but Pyotr and Hilna walked over it without hesitation. Annica stopped and peered ahead at the holes and loose stones comprising a large portion of the crossing.

Man and mule stopped. The thick mat of hair, flecked with the gray of age and white of snow, turned to look back at her. He gave a wry smile and beckoned her forward.

"Come on, young lady. No ghosts here. None that mean you any harm, anyway."

"That's not funny," she called out in a monotone. Her voice was muffled by the trees and snow, landing flatly on the surroundings.

She still walked hesitantly across the bridge as though expecting it to collapse at any moment. When her feet were once again planted firmly on the opposite bank, she noticed the old village in full. No building remained complete. Crumbling walls, half-standing arches, and the skeletal remains of shattered wood beams spread out before her, laced by overgrown dirt roads scattered with more stones and broken carts, crates, and barrels. Scraps of cloth, large and small, grayed and fraying from years of weathering, waved like flags of surrender from random perches all around the village.

Pyotr and Hilna walked past it all, not sparing a single glance in the direction of the dereliction and decay. Although, as she drew closer, Annica noticed a hint of sadness on his face that even his rotund beard couldn't hide. He kept his eyes forward and she followed them to their destination: a cemetery at the end of the sad, littered road.

A dark iron fence, rusting in places, surrounded a small field of crumbling headstones covered in an overgrowth of grass, weeds, and ivy. A few of the gravestones had the weeds and vines cleared out and showed signs of being cleaned. A stone arch, half-fallen, rose above the gate they entered through. Trees surrounded the graveyard, nuzzled around it like a dark green wreath.

Annica followed quietly until Pyotr came to a stop by a section of cleared, cleaned headstones. He removed the dead and dried flowers on top of each one. He tossed them over the fence and went to Hilna, reaching into one of the packs and pulling out four small bundles of flowers. They looked like lilac sprigs tied into tiny bouquets with colored twine.

He placed one bundle atop each of four gravestones. They all looked the same, except they had a different name roughly carved into each. Pyotr took his time, placing the lilacs and then putting his hand gently atop the stone. He bowed his head and said a few words for each one. Annica couldn't hear, but some of the statements were longer than others, so he must have been saying something different for each person.

As he walked back to where Annica waited next to the mule, his sorrowful expression brightened slightly. He showed a smile, somewhat forced, it seemed, and stepped more heavily and purposely as the overgrowth crunched under his booted feet.

"So, you ready to see Kalthav?" he said, his eyes somewhat reddened and his smile thin.

Annica had the cloak wrapped around her, held there with her hands. She fidgeted with the cloth as she answered uncomfortably, "Yes, of course."

The walk back out of the village and into the forest was quiet at first. The snow continued to fall quietly and speckled Annica's black hair like stars on a clear night. She kept the cloak wrapped tightly around her, stumbling slightly here and there due to the oversized boots.

"Those graves...they belong to my family," Pyotr said, his head forward but calling out so he could be heard clearly. His voice was a little huskier than before. "I'm sorry you have to see me like this. I'm sure it's uncomfortable. But, it's never easy even after so many years."

Annica took a deep breath. She understood heartache and loss as much as anyone. She'd lost people she'd consider dear to her, but these were family Pyotr must have known for so much longer.

"I couldn't possibly blame you," she began, her words coming hesitantly. "There were four headstones; you lost so many..."

"My parents and brother. The fourth was...my wife."

Annica grimaced. Her heart flinched and she recalled the fourth gravestone that he'd lingered at the longest.

"What was her name?" she asked.

He was quiet for a moment. A soft, sad smile lifted his mustache. "Anya," he replied. "Not too different from yours, no?"

Annica chuckled. Then, she frowned at the thought of her next question but had to ask.

"What happened to them? And to the village?"

She dreaded the answer. One never knew the kind of fate any place or person met during these times.

Pyotr grumbled and looked to the west. Nothing could be seen through the trees and rocks, but he seemed to be staring at something very specific.

"Those bandits that took up in that fort I told you about? They began raiding when they started running out of supplies, or so we imagine. A few villages were still clinging to life. Trade with Kalthav and amongst each other was somewhat sustainable, so we managed. Then they showed up. One village was ransacked and everyone hoped it was just a singular tragedy. We all feared otherwise. Kalthav couldn't spare soldiers for every village; they barely had enough to protect themselves. Weeks went by, another village was burned to the ground. Ours was the only one left. Kalthav spared a few soldiers for our lone village, but..."

Pyotr went quiet. He swallowed hard, a knot building in his throat. Hilna continued to walk as though nothing had changed, the animal seeming as much like an automaton as anything else. Pyotr sniffed and rubbed his nose between his fingers.

"The soldiers weren't prepared for their savagery. The look in those bandits' eyes; something had a hold on them. I saw one of 'em get an arm lopped clean off by a Kalthavar soldier and the beast just kept coming. The soldier was so stunned the bandit ripped his throat out with his teeth, then used his other arm to hack the body up until it was nothing but red chunks."

Annica covered her mouth. She tasted bile.

"I tried to get my family out, sneak through the cemetery, but they were everywhere. We were making our way into the trees around the cemetery, I thought my wife was right behind. I *swore* she was right behind me," Pyotr rubbed his eyes as his voice broke. "I turned when I heard her screams. They...they were taking her, right there on the cemetery ground, stabbing her over and over again as they..."

He stopped and fell to his knees, breathing heavily. "My brother and I ran to fight, but an arrow caught him in the forehead the moment we took our first steps. Spears ran my mother and father through. I ran before I was surrounded."

Pyotr's voice had become flat and hollow. "I returned several days later to bury them. Myself and a few others who escaped."

The other gravestones that looked like they'd been cared for, Annica thought.

She quickly went up to him and placed both her hands on his shoulders. His grief swelled within her, channeled reflexively by the Fifth Magic. Her eyes grew warm.

"You didn't have to tell me all of that, Pyotr, to open those wounds to a stranger."

"It's not as bad as all that," he said, his voice growing stronger. "I hold all this in, not talking 'bout it much. I don't know why, but...maybe I just want to forget until I come out here.. People in Kalthav are civil and kind enough but suspicious and slow to trust. It's been years and I've yet to make any true friends. Even those who fled the village are scattered about the city and we find spending time around one another too painful. They just want to try to forget—except for their visits to respect the dead."

"Have those marauders attempted to attack Kalthav? Do they have that many among their numbers?"

Pyotr shook his head. "Not enough to take the city, by any means. But, they do harass the outlying farms and occasionally the walls. They don't seem to care for their own survival, only to cause pain and make life miserable for those they can."

Long stretches of silence were punctuated by the occasional comment. Mostly regarding mundane subjects. Annica noticed the trees becoming less dense as they walked. She imagined the city would come into view soon, another city full of people seemingly surviving amidst the chaos of what appeared to be the slow end of the world.

"Has Kalthav not attempted to destroy the marauders? Wipe out their fort?"

Pyotr ran his hand over his face, heaving a deep sigh. He took a drink from his flask and finally answered. "They tried twice, I think. At most. The first time some soldiers were sent to check out the fort and its strength. They were confident that with enough numbers they could destroy the marauders to a man and raze the fort to the ground. A hundred Kalthavar soldiers marched on the fort last year."

"None of them returned, did they?" Annica assumed.

"One did," he replied.

Her stomach grew cold. She had an idea of what was coming in the story.

"It was kept quiet as much as possible, but word can travel quickly in a lone city shut off from most of the world. As the rumors go, the guards saw one of their own approaching the main gate. The survivor had a strange gait like his legs and back were injured. They were prepared to go to him immediately and bring him inside for treatment until he came closer. His armor consisted only of metal plate. The jerkin, pants, everything else was gone and, it's said, the metal glowed where it touched his body like it had been placed in a forge. The skin was black and cracked, bleeding from wherever armor touched his flesh. His hands and face were covered in soot. His eyes glowed like fire, as did his mouth behind blackened teeth.

He called out to them, but in some strange language they'd never heard before. His voice sounded like a crackling stove and coals being stoked. After finishing whatever it was he was saying, he raised both hands in the air as if expecting something from them, then...exploded. One of the plates supposedly embedded itself in the walk next to a tower guard's head, barely missing him. A pair of guards went to see what happened and found blood and ash smeared around where the survivor stood. Finally, they also say that it looked like a symbol was left there, crafted in the congealed blood."

He took another drink from the flask. "Who knows how much is true, though, and not just a bunch of twisted conjecture."

I have no doubt that most of it is true, Annica thought to herself.

"A few scouts were sent to the fort again, hoping to find prisoners of the previous force. Rumors, again, are all that I've heard. They found the bodies of the soldiers staked, dismembered, put on display. There was also talk that the same kind of symbol left by the front gate was drawn in blood all over the fort, likely from the soldiers."

He shrugged. "A few farm boys went missing for a few days and came back saying they wanted to check the fort out themselves and said something similar, so it seems those thugs are truly capable of such things."

Annica thought back to her lessons, all that she'd learned of magic. More importantly, she dwelt on what she'd learned of dark rituals and the things working in the shadows of the world. She'd survived Nel Aldyri, nearly dying on the ocean, and now fell into the lap of another city haunted by strange occurrences.

Pyotr, as if reading her thoughts, turned to her and gave a genuine smile. "Don't let all this scare you, Annica. Other than that, we've had no problems with the marauders. We live quietly and get along with the occasional traveler making their way here."

Well, I suppose that's some sort of relief. She thought. "You still have travelers arrive? Any merchants ever among them?"

A world with merchants and travelers, people moving about

the world like blood through a living being, was a sign that Alda still had a chance. Ashwater didn't see many of their like. It was quite isolated, lonely, and self-sufficient. Despite the atrocities that the Black Gnarl committed in Nel Aldyri, the town itself was thriving due to the ships bringing in new blood to the island. Annica also learned in her time there that not all of the ships were strictly looking for new citizens and—a shudder rolled through her at this thought—unknowing sacrifices, but some actually went out to trade and scavenge. Nel Aldyri, as a city, thrived; as a society, it was poisoned.

Pyotr rubbed Hilna's muzzle as he answered. "Yes. They grow fewer every year and a few wish to remain in the city, but we only have room for so many. Growth is limited by our borders. The winters grow colder and longer every year, but we survive. We never get any travelers from the east, though. No one ever comes from the Withered Groves anymore, or beyond it."

Annica remembered the maps she studied in the library at the temple. The Withered Groves often drew sneers and grimaces when discussed. Beyond that ill-spoken forest were the Belgallant Mountains, a few pockets of human settlements, then the elf-kind kingdom of Athyl'glen. Elf-kind had been struck particularly hard by the Rupture, from her understanding. They were dying out and from the number she saw in Nel Aldyri compared to other races, it was probably true.

After the long and cold trek through the rocky, pine-covered countryside of the north, the trees suddenly gave way to an open vista of the rocky cliffs of the northernmost coastline of the world. Annica wasn't sure if it was the sudden gust of cold air or the view of the city of Kalthav and its surroundings, but her breath caught in her lungs.

The terrain cut at a sharp angle downward, becoming less and less rocky. Arable land was covered in a gray-blue grain of some kind that grew in ordered, checkered patches. Fences, a mix of wood and stone, sectioned off areas where sheep and goats grazed or slept in clusters within small sheds to keep warm. Farmhouses and other outbuildings peppered the land until the cold, gray stone of the coast took over once again.

Kalthav was separated into a citadel behind the farmlands, where the stone walls protected the inner portions leading up to the coast. A massive bridge, a feat of engineering lost to time, spanned the cliffside citadel to a walled castle crowning a round set of sheer cliffs that dropped straight into the ocean. The pillar of dark stone rose from the churning, freezing waters like a scepter, the heart of Kalthav its cold jewel.

"This is..." Annica began but found herself lacking words. The scope of the city before her, combined with the biting wind and cold, took her words away.

"Kalthav is old and struggling but still quite a handsome sight, no? That first wall there, behind the farmlands, that's called the Cliff's Pillar, where most of Kalthav's people live. That bridge is the Drottinsvegur; it's old Kalthavian for 'The Lord's Road.' Because it leads right to that pretty little castle there, on the Lord's Pillar," Pyotr pointed to each location, directing Annica's gaze. He and Hilna continued to move ahead. The path before them wound down the hillside, the rocks and stone growing smaller and scarcer like the scales of a beast giving way to its soft belly.

Annica began walking at a faster pace to catch up. She watched her breath come out in large, white puffs. They walked through well-worn paths cutting through the gray-blue grain and fields of animals. Workers bundled in warm furs and animal skins worked the fields and paid them no mind. It was a stark difference from her arrival in the warm climate of Nel Aldyri.

They entered a small clutch of wooden buildings, most of them houses, with smoke slowly drifting from some of the stone chimneys. The air smelled of smoke from the fires within the homes and hay from nearby barns.

Pyotr led Hilna to one such barn and removed some of the packs and satchels. He hitched her to an empty stall. The animal entered and stood there with the same disinterested demeanor it had the entire time Annica had been with them. As Pyotr left the barn, Annica smirked and walked over to Hilna, rubbing her snout.

"You must be a really good girl," she commented softly.

Annica caught up to Pyotr as he was reaching the front door of the house nearest the small barn where Hilna now grazed on a small pile of white-colored hay. She assumed it to be the result of the gray-blue grain drying out and losing some, or most, of its color. The mule seemed to be enjoying it, though, munching slowly and purposefully on its simple meal.

"Is this your home?" she asked, but then Pyotr knocked on the door.

"No, it belongs to Hilna's owner."

That caught her by surprise. The way Pyotr and Hilna behaved and the manner in which he spoke of the animal gave no indication that he wasn't her owner.

The door creaked open and a tall, thin man stood inside the doorframe. His pale blond hair was tied back in a ponytail and several days' worth of pale stubble grew on his chin. His small mouth curled into a smile when he saw Pyotr, who was a full head shorter than the blond man.

"Karl!" Pyotr said cheerfully and put out his hand.

Karl gripped Pyotr's offered hand tightly and pulled him in for a hug. "You were gone a lot longer this time."

The tall man's voice was thickly accented and Annica had to pay close attention to understand him.

"Yes. I doubt these trips will be worth the time after much longer."

"Hilna will be disappointed."

Pyotr chuckled. "How can you tell? That mule has all the personality of a wet stone."

Annica listened to the two men talk casually for a few minutes. She learned that Pyotr borrowed Hilna when he went off to visit his family's graves and scavenge for anything in the surrounding villages and towns. He'd been gone nearly two weeks this time, which apparently was much longer than usual. As payment for using the mule, Pyotr handed a small sack to Karl, who thanked him heartily. From what she could hear, it contained some herbs that only grew in the Wilted Groves. The tall man then switched immediately from gratitude to consternation. He didn't specifically request these herbs, and to know that Pyotr went to such a forbidden place irritated him.

"You've always let me take Hilna, no questions asked, day or night. I thought I'd bring you back something special," Pyotr explained.

Karl's bony face and thick lips scrunched in a grimace. "Won't do anyone any good if you both go missing in those woods, friend. They're forbidden for a reason."

Pyotr waved a hand and gave a throaty *bah*. Karl lowered his head and shook it slowly. They shook hands and parted, the door closing and shutting with a soft thud.

Annica waited as Pyotr returned. He motioned her to follow, then went to pet Hilna farewell.

"See you soon," he said with a smile.

"Do you only barter here in Kalthav, or do you still use currency?" Annica asked, remembering how surprised she was when she saw Nel Aldyri printed their own coins for use. If Kalthav had survived the Rupture, she wouldn't be surprised if they still had minted coins of some kind.

"We tend to prefer bartering, but," Pyotr answered as he tucked his hand in a pouch on his belt and then brought out and opened his hand, revealing some tarnished silver and copper coins. "We do use old Kalthavian currency, too. The nobles prefer it, of course, because they have plenty more. But these days, they're more open to bartering, as well. The copper ones are a single ora. Ten ora make a silver krona, and a hundred krona make a gold kol."

"Interesting," Annica replied. Hearing about an old-world currency system felt somewhat calming, like the roots of normalcy were still in place here to some degree.

"Is this your first time seeing money? I know it's worthless outside our walls anymore, but we're a stubborn people."

"No," Annica replied softly. In a way, she wished she'd had a few of the Nel Aldyri coins to show him, but in the end, she decided she'd rather never look at them again. "I've seen and used currency once before."

"Oh," Pyotr replied in surprise. "Well, you're one of the first I've met who have. A trader tried to buy from me with some old Carnelian florins. I had to refuse. We only use our own currency with trade basically down to bartering with anyone else who's come through. I did offer him a few trinkets for some of the florins as a keepsake, though."

As they approached the larger path that cut through the fields and buildings, Pyotr led Annica in the direction of the walled, cliff-side citadel. The distant sound of thunder coming from below told of the perilous ocean nearby. They reached an area consisting of more houses than fields, with small personal gardens sprouting crops and herbs of all kinds. Pyotr returned waves from friends and acquaintances as they made their way through the citadel's outskirts.

"Do you live near the wall?" Annica asked, curious how much further they had to go.

"No," he said casually. "I live inside it."

She looked away from him to the large, light gray wall

looming over the town of wooden buildings and gray-blue fields. Two large, circular towers rose at the very edge of the cliffs, opposite each other, with curtain walls forming a half-circle, echaugettes jutting from the top at regular intervals, and meeting at a large gatehouse, which is where Annica and Pyotr now stood. This seemed like a place for soldiers and nobles, but Pyotr said he lived within with many other citizens.

As they approached the gatehouse, Annica stopped so suddenly her feet skidded on the ground. Her heart began thumping quickly and she felt a wave of cold followed by her body flushing to the point of sweat beading on her forehead. Something echoed in her mind, but she couldn't understand it. She breathed, trying to calm herself, as Pyotr turned and his brows furrowed over his soft, fatherly gaze.

"Are you ok?"

Annica clenched her fists as the moment passed. She looked around and thought for a moment she could see the source of the strange, terrible feeling. Perhaps a black-hooded figure hiding in the shadows or lurking among the people. She half-expected to see a giant tree with serpentine branches in the distance. But there was nothing. Her breath caught when she suddenly remembered Pyotr's story about the last survivor from the marauder attack. This is where he describes the soldier uttering his last words before his grim fate. Was this the residuals of dark magic? Specifically, the Fourth Sect?

She marched past Pyotr, desperate to get away from this spot as quickly as possible. She drew in the presence of magic around her, particularly that of the Fifth. She drew it in as one would take in a breath, then locked it away inside her, wrapped in a blanket of concentration and paranoia.

"I'm ok, just eager to see Kalthav beyond this massive wall."

Pyotr grunted and shrugged, then quickly caught up to her.

Part III

After Pyotr showed some papers to a guard, the gate opened and both of them walked through. Inside, all the buildings were composed mostly of stone. Each structure had a lot, separated by the streets, with tough, ruddy grasses and the occasional pine or fir tree growing in the open spaces. It wasn't as lively as Nel Aldyri; the cold made sure to keep those who had no business on the streets indoors, but there was a buzz of activity, nonetheless. The smell of chimneys and stones, wet from melted snow, overpowered her. There were large main avenues with small alleyways and side streets branching off in different directions.

This was not a citadel but rather a section of Kalthav separated from the castle proper, an area more like a massive barbican. The roar of the ocean was nearly lost to the sounds of the city. The carriages and carts that passed beside and in front of her were of a simpler, less opulent design than what she'd seen before and the horses large, hairy-hoofed beasts rather than lean, elegant stallions.

"My home is just down this street," Pyotr said, turning onto one of the smaller side streets.

They walked halfway toward another main avenue when he stopped at a narrow two-story building that looked much like the others, but a wooden sign engraved with a combined ring-and-brooch emblem hung above the door. He took out a key from one of his pockets and unlocked the front door, motioning her inside. She hesitated for a moment and realized he'd had ample opportunity to cause her harm before now. Slowly, she stepped inside.

He left the door open, the interior being dark and difficult to see in, and lit some candles before closing the door again. He opened the shuttered windows, letting in even more light, and Annica saw a rather typical-looking workshop.

"Is this where you work?" she asked.

"And sleep," he returned cheerfully. "Upstairs is my bedroom and a living space. Along with a spare room for guests," he added pointedly.

He removed his thick coat and revealed he was also wearing a scarf underneath. He placed both on a standing coat hanger and took Annica's borrowed clothing, and hung them, as well. He then immediately went to a stone-mantled fireplace, cold from weeks of not being used, and started a fresh fire that quickly turned warm and roaring.

Without his heavy layers, Pyotr was only wearing a plain white shirt underneath that clung to a slight potbelly, though his arms bulged with thick muscle. He had the physique of a well-fed but hard-working man.

Annica looked around. She didn't recognize any of the tools or machinery. She did see several tiny necklace chains, rings, and brooches with empty settings and other half-made jewelry set in piles or laid out among the tables.

"You're a jeweler?"

Pyotr chuckled. "I am. Only one in Kalthav at the moment. Still not busy despite that, but enough to keep me well fed, obviously." He patted his belly and chuckled again.

"I understand journeying back to your old village to pay respects to your family, but what exactly are you scavenging for with Hilna? There couldn't possibly be anything left in the old towns by now."

Pyotr nodded. She must have overheard his and Karl's conversation. "You'd be surprised. Not many are concerned with gems and finery anymore. Life is more about survival in every village, hamlet, and haphazard gathering of people I've come across. I don't even try to sell to them. In fact, they often have such things to trade with me and are surprised I'm willing to barter food and medicine for 'useless' extravagances."

Annica looked at some of the rings, silver and gold with no jewels to make them stand out, and wondered if these were items he'd made and was searching for something to fill them or pulled the stones from to add to others.

"And I don't suppose any dwarves come through here with any stones," she said, more of a statement than a question.

Pyotr shook his head. "A few live here in Kalthav, but they haven't heard from their kin in decades. I haven't met any in my travels and none have come through this way in just as long."

"So, that's why you're risking the Wilted Groves."

Pyotr was quiet, not answering at first. He went to a cabinet and pulled out two small, squat glasses and a dark bottle. He beckoned her to sit at an empty table, apparently meant for sitting with visitors, and filled both glasses with some of the bottle's golden yellow contents. He pushed the glass over to her. She sniffed it and smelled a sweet, alcoholic aroma.

"Ice wine," he said before taking a sip. She followed suit and found it to be quite pleasant, almost syrupy in its sweetness and texture.

After another few moments of silence, Pyotr took a long drink from his glass, drained it, and poured himself some more. He poured a little more into Annica's glass without asking, then let out a deep breath.

"What do you know about the Wilting Groves, anyway?" he grumbled. "You were lost when I found you so what could she possibly understand about our region or its troubles?"

Annica gently swirled her drink. She looked off vacantly to one side into a shadowed corner where a small bookshelf sat with its shelves partially full. Memories of her own small shelf in her dormitory returned, along with all the time she'd spent poring over them in between lessons and before bedtime.

"The place where I learned to use my magic," she started, hesitantly, and found she couldn't bring herself to name the temple out loud, "they had plenty of books on other subjects. I also talked with a few other apprentices who came from different places around Alda. Most of what I know is probably rumors since no actual books have been written or distributed since the Rupture, but the forest wasn't always called the Wilted Groves."

Pyotr nodded. "My folks still called it the Blackwood even after all this time."

"Apparently, an Inh—" Annica caught herself; she didn't want to reveal too much about what she learned back on that island and its vile cult. She still didn't know much about this city which seemed to be maintaining itself just fine during the world's death throes, not to the extent of Nel Aldyri, but enough to make her cautious. "Some type of creature, a very powerful one, took over the forest after the Rupture. It's been considered haunted ever since. Some say the whole forest has been abandoned and is home to strange beasts and stranger sounds."

Pyotr took another sip of his wine. "That's about it."

The way he said it was deeply unsatisfying and struck Annica with a pang of suspicion.

"There must be more than that," she insisted. "You've lived here for generations. There's nothing more that anyone has learned about one of Alda's largest forests, unclaimed by elf-kind, other than it being abandoned and haunted?"

"Karl was unhappy with me, as I bet you saw," he said with a smirk, glancing her way. "We have rumors. Ghost stories. Old wives' tales."

"I find that hard to believe."

Pyotr chuckled. "You're an insistent one. As hard-headed as any Kalthavian, that's for sure. Now I know why you lasted out there on those waves."

He poured more wine into both their glasses, Annica's getting closer and closer to the top. She took a long drink out of the glass, wanting to start feeling its soothing effects. She began to feel like he was hiding something; she began to feel like this city, too, was hiding something. She didn't mention some other important information she'd learned about the world. Information that came from first-hand accounts written and handed down, then brought to Nel Aldyri by those on the ships. The cities, especially those seats of power for the city-states, were the most corrupted and hardest hit by the Rupture and those things that came with it. Nel Aldyri was the only newly-built city Annica knew of from her lessons and readings, but Kalthav was one of the original city-states—now, the only one she knew of that had survived the Rupture in some livable state.

"Well, it's true we don't know much ourselves," Pyotr continued. "Fear is the rule of life, now. Too many things we don't understand anymore and are far too afraid to question. Those that have, met unknown ends, at best."

Pyotr took another long drink from his glass. He told Annica more, but his words were gruff and distant. He didn't want to admit what he felt when he had seen those trees lined up so neatly, a perfect border between the known and unknown. The trees had seemed separate from everything else, like seeing a life-like painting of trees next to real ones. He'd only made it a few hundred paces into the border of the Wilted Groves. The herbs were easy to find, the forest going undisturbed for so long, he told Annica.

However, he would swear he had seen something moving in the distance. Something watching him. He'd traveled the smaller patches of woodland surrounding the shores of Kalthav and never once felt such soul-shriveling terror. The forest was utterly silent. No birds or insects called. The wind stopped as soon as he set foot beneath the first of those cursed boughs.

Pyotr explained how every instinct had screamed for him to flee. He should have known when Hilna refused to enter the woods. Despite all the stories, he wrote it off as her refusing to enter an unfamiliar area, even though that had never happened before. He blinded himself to so many things in order to enter those woods because he'd nearly exhausted every other area. At that moment, he regretted his ignorance.

Something *had* been watching him. He was sure of it. For the longest time, he couldn't see anything other than dark trees and underbrush. Then, within the dappled shadows deeper within the woods, a figure stood silhouetted beside a large beast. He felt as though his heart had stopped. It took several long moments before he realized the shape of the figure was unusual and its head nearly brushed the bottom branches of the trees. That meant whatever shaggy-haired creature stood next to it was the size of a small horse.

It never approached him, only stood unmoving. The beast trembled slightly, and the figure appeared to stroke it gently; that's when he ran. He didn't know if the raucous sounds were his running alone or that of the beast giving chase, but when he made it past the border of the woods he felt the cold fear in him ease noticeably, though it didn't entirely fade away. He'd stumbled, fallen, and turned to look back, expecting some horrible demon to come rushing from beneath the shadows to devour him or drag him back into the woods. Instead, he saw only the strange borderline of the trees.

ANNICA LET the story simmer in her mind, mingling with other stories and information she'd gathered. By the time his story was finished, his glass was empty. He emptied what was left of the bottle into the glass and drank it down in one go. He took a deep breath and a heavy silence followed. It sounded, for all intents and purposes, like Pyotr had survived an encounter with the Inheritor of the Wilted Groves, much like she'd survived her encounter with Bac'thule.

"That sounds awful, but I actually know how you feel."

Pyotr chuckled. "I found you washed up on a frigid beach; I'm sure you have plenty of stories to tell."

Annica smiled. *You're not wrong*, she thought.

"Where are you from, Annica?" Pyotr asked. "All I ever found out is that you come from somewhere south. That's a pretty big batch of territory," he added humorously.

"That's a bit complicated," she said after a moment's hesitation.

"It's too bad we're in such a hurry," Pyotr replied with a sardonic smile.

Annica chuckled. "I'm from a fishing village on the River Leen. After that..." she paused, unsure of how to answer. Did she need to explain everything? Be vague as possible? "After that, I went with a ship captain to another town. Things didn't end well there."

Pyotr's forehead crinkled. "A raid? War with another town? It'd be the first I've heard of a conflict between settlements in a long time."

"More like within the town itself. I fled when some very bad people came out of the woodwork, so to speak."

"Hmm," Pyotr grunted. He didn't sound like he was happy with her answer.

"I lost a good friend. He's the only reason I'm still alive," she said in a voice heavy with pain. Her finger absent-mindedly traced the top of her glass. She took a long, slow drink, feeling the sweet, syrupy alcohol fill her stomach. Eventually, the last of it slipped down her throat and she put the glass down softly.

"I'm sorry, Annica. Truly, I am." Pyotr said, his voice husky. She realized he would understand completely how such a loss would feel.

She felt her eyes growing warm and threatening tears. She sniffed and turned away, embarrassed at the sudden display of emotion.

"Well," Pyotr said, slapping his legs. "I don't know about you, but the wine is doing its job. I need to go sleep this off. Just head up the stairs and there's a room on the right for you. Take your time; there's no rush."

His face flushed red from the wine. Pyotr stood and groggily made his way up the stairs. Annica listened as his footsteps fell clumsily on the floor above and then a door groaned and thumped shut. She sat in the silence for a while, listening to the fire. Her wine was gone, too, and she found herself wanting more. Sleep had not been kind to her for many months. While on the open ocean, she began practicing using the Fifth Magic to lace her mind in its peaceful auras, like a soft silk hammock wrapping around her mind. It helped, but dark things pushed and prodded at the wrapping and made for fitful bouts of sleep.

She couldn't use that defense now. Her Fifth Sect powers now sat in a warm pocket deep within her. After experiencing the harsh residuals of dark magic outside of the walls, she wasn't taking any chances of her magic being discovered like it was at Nel Aldyri.

She began drifting off to sleep in the chair, her head nodding and time slowing as it does when one is dipping their mind in and out of that semi-sleep state. She stood and balanced herself on the table. Her lips tingled from the effects of the wine and she wanted desperately to feel a bed beneath her.

Quietly, or as quietly as she could, she made her way up the stairs and entered the guest room that Pyotr had described. It was much more quaint and homely than her old dormitory. Just at first glance, the moonlight cast soft light through a window where a bed waited. A few other furnishings decorated the room and made her feel somewhat at ease. It was normal in every way.

She practically fell onto the bed, not even taking time to remove her robes. She pulled the thick blanket over her and let her head sink into the pillow. Pyotr's work as a jeweler must pay fairly well. He didn't live in luxury, but he certainly wasn't going without. The fear of what awaited in her dreams was momentarily washed away by sweet wine and a comfortable bed.

SUNLIGHT FELL across Annica's face, waking her. The warmth splashed across her cheek and one of her eyes, telling her there was a soft chill in the room, waiting for when she removed the blanket. She lazily pulled the sheets further up and bundled herself in the bed. She felt a level of relaxation that she hadn't felt in ages, if ever. As she lay there in comfort and quiet, she had a realization. No strange or disturbing dreams woke her in the night or lingered on the edges of her waking mind like wolves on the prowl.

In fact, she hadn't dreamt at all.

This caused a rush of adrenaline that roused her from her lazy state. Her mind began to fumble over the many meanings and possibilities behind this. She also considered not thinking about it all and just enjoying the fact she had a good night's rest.

She got out of bed and fixed her robes as best she could. They still smelled of smoke and were hopelessly wrinkled. They were also the green robes of a temple magi that she no longer desired to wear but were all she owned. They were her only possessions, period.

After making the bed, she walked quietly out of the room in case Pyotr was still asleep, but smelled the wonderful aroma of food coming from downstairs. Her stomach growled and her mouth watered. With a good night's sleep clearing her head, her body's physical needs were crying out more desperately.

She walked downstairs and found Pyotr setting plates and silverware on the table they were sitting at last night. A bowl of fruit was already on the table, along with a carafe of red-colored juice—it was too clear to be wine—and a jug of water. He walked out of sight towards the fire; apparently, he didn't notice her. She did hear him humming to himself.

When she reached the bottom of the staircase, he was returning from the fire and pouring some kind of porridge into the two bowls. After turning around, he finally saw her and smiled. He offered a bright "good morning" without breaking his stride. Pyotr instructed her to have a seat as he went back to the fireplace.

Annica sat down quietly, taking in the aroma of the porridge and something else that was yet to be discovered. Pyotr returned, holding an iron skillet, and scooped a large slab of sizzling ham onto her plate along with potatoes and onions.

"My gods..." she said. Her eyes widened and her mouth hung open.

"Have to eat well to keep out the cold!" he beamed.

He poured her a cup of the red juice. "Grape juice," he said, "watered down a little. I can't have mine too strong."

Then, he poured her some water and began taking care of his own portions.

"Eat!" he said. "There's more if you want it."

Annica took a moment to bask in the sight of the feast before her. The meals in Nel Aldyri were good, but this was different. She began with some of the porridge and moved on to the ham. Each mouthful was exquisite. Simple but filling and flavorful. She ate everything he'd put in front of her but couldn't stomach any more, even though Pyotr offered multiple times.

While he was finishing his second portion, Pyotr asked, "What would you like to do today, Annica?"

A look of shock mingled with disbelief crossed her face. She had no idea how to answer. Not once had anyone asked anything like that in her life, even in Nel Aldyri when she interacted with more people. She didn't know the first thing about the city or what she wanted to do there. She rubbed her forearm, trying to think, when she felt a catch in the robes. A hole had worn through the long sleeve.

"I wouldn't mind getting some different clothes. These robes aren't warm enough here, but they're the only thing I have to my name."

Hearing the defeat in her voice, Pyotr grunted in a way that gave the impression of, *That won't do.*

"Then let's go get you some proper Kalthavian clothing. I haven't had the opportunity to buy anything for a lady in...well, quite some time," he said with a sad smile.

Annica smiled back and replied, "That's nice of you, but I don't want to be indebted to anyone. I'm sure as a mage, I can find paying work somewhere."

"And I'm sure you will, but in Kalthav, we won't force hospitality on anyone. If you want to pay me back, I certainly have work around here that you can help with for the time being."

He gathered up the dishes and placed them in a pile next to an empty wash bin. There were no leftovers to worry about. Between a starving Annica and the robust Pyotr, all the food had been taken care of. He then grabbed his coat, handed her the cloak and boots, and insisted they depart for the shops immediately.

Being a jeweler, Pyotr lived very near the market district of Kalthav. Annica noticed mostly foodstuffs for sale here. Pyotr explained that most of the trade took place in this first partition of the city, so the market district was quartered off into produce, manufactured goods like clothing, shops for more specialized work such as cobblers, herbalists, and himself, and then a generalized area for anything else. Pyotr walked her around and let her see some of the city before they went to the portion selling clothing and the like.

As the morning grew late, the city became more bustling. Individual conversations being held around them were lost in the noise of a general murmur of activity. It was cold, but massive fires burned in stone wells along the walls and in massive pits in circular plazas. The intermittent warmth kept the temperatures much more bearable.

Late afternoon came and Pyotr gave a deep squawk, sounding like a surprised seal, when he realized the hour. He insisted they head right for the clothing shops before it grew much later. Annica chuckled. She was only following him, after all.

They reached a shop with a sign above the door bearing the symbol of a bird holding a threaded needle in its beak. Pyotr had a wide smile on his face as they approached the door. Annica wondered if he really was as happy to be buying her something as he appeared.

When they entered, a small bell hanging above the door chimed, announcing them.

"One moment," a female voice called out. It sounded like it belonged to an older woman.

A kind-faced woman, large-hipped with a graceful swagger, came from a back room. She turned her head to look at her customers and her thickly-braided ponytail of gray-streaked red hair swung like a rope along her back. She gasped when her eyes fell on Pyotr.

"Pyotr—oh, it's been ages!" she said, her voice a cheerful, Kalthavian-accented contralto.

"Lorna," Pyotr said tenderly, opening his arms for a hug.

She nearly ran to him and took him in a long, heavy embrace. Once they released each other, she slapped him on the side of the arm.

"It's been years, you foolish man. Years!"

Pyotr hung his head and nodded sheepishly. He mumbled a string of indecipherable clumps of words, but Annica couldn't make them out.

Lorna's face softened. "Have you gone to see them recently?"

"Just got back," he replied in a low, gruff voice. Then, his tone shifted. "Speaking of which—"

Lorna's eyes flicked over to Annica and her whole face widened with her smile. "Who is *this*?" she asked, as though Annica were a new puppy that had just been handed off to her.

"This is Annica. I found her stranded by the Cold Stones on the last leg of my trip. She was lucky."

"Oh, that she was. Look at you, Annica; your robes are barely holding onto you. And you're bone thin. Have you not fed this girl?" Lorna asked Pyotr accusingly.

"No," Annica interrupted with a nervous chuckle. "He's fed me very well. It's my first day here in Kalthav. He's given me a room and food and no reason to be concerned." She made sure to be as supportive of Pyotr as possible. The matronly aura given off by this woman was powerful, and her caring nature seemed to be as smothering as it was genuine.

"Well, that's good to hear. Now, let's get you into something more fitting and *warm*." Lorna said before turning and leaving to the same back room she had come from.

Annica looked around her shop and noticed there was very little actual clothing to see. Some finished pieces hung over long round poles stretching across the length of the shop, but it was mostly a variety of rolls of cloth, textiles, and patterns on display.

She must take orders from customers first, Annica assumed.

I will never be able to pay Pyotr back for this, she thought with a pang of guilt.

Lorna returned with two items draped over both her forearms. She went to an empty table and laid them out for both Pyotr and Annica to see. Annica's mouth opened slightly, her hand running along the sapphire-blue dress on the table. It felt like it was made of material both thick and soft but also tightly knit and not easily torn. It buttoned up the front, starting just below the waistline, and had a soft collar around the neck. Annica felt a lump in her throat. She had been grateful for the robes provided by the temple, but this was the first time she'd ever laid her hands on something so beautiful.

"Of course, that alone won't keep you warm on Kalthav's harsher days," Lorna chimed in as she laid a long coat over the dress. It was made of leather to keep out the rain and was a light gray to pair with the stunning blue of the dress. The collar and cuffs were lined with the thick fur of some brown-haired animal that was as soft as down. Inside, a thick layer of cotton cloth lined the coat to make it comfortable and warm.

"I can't accept this..." Annica said breathlessly.

"Oh, yes, you can," Lorna rebutted, then looked to Pyotr, "I still owe you for my daughter's wedding ring, you old ghost. Even with these, I don't feel comfortable saying we're even."

Annica struggled for words as a knot built in her throat. "I don't see how I can ever pay you back for this, Pyotr."

A thick-fingered, meaty hand gripped her shoulder gently. "We've already discussed that," he said quietly. His tone suggested the subject was over.

A tear ran down her face, followed by another. She turned away so they wouldn't fall on the new clothes.

"Oh...Oh, my dear..." Lorna said as she wrapped her arms around Annica. "What in the gods' names have you been through? It's ok now; Pyotr is a good man, he'll take care of you. And so will I. You don't have anything else to fear, sweetling."

Lorna stroked Annica's hair, knotted and tangled as it was, and Annica let her. Annica just breathed. Lorna had a daughter. If she perhaps had other children and possibly countless grandchildren, it would not surprise Annica. Her embrace was something you could melt into.

"My word, this hair," Lorna said in a manner both soft and stern. "Before you put on any new clothes, we're going to get you a bath where there are proper things for a lady to get clean with. I'll get some water warmed up."

Lorna's grip on Annica tightened just enough to say the matter was settled and then looked to Pyotr with a serious gaze he was all too used to. "Go to Mikkel's around the corner and get her a proper pair of shoes; not these oversized, beastly things you have her clomping around in. Tell him I'll cover it, and that'll cover my debt to you. Knock at the back door when you're done."

Pyotr blinked, processing all the information he'd just been given. "Yes, ma'am," he grunted as he turned to leave.

Lorna led Annica back through the door the motherly woman had been coming in and out of. The back area was actually a hallway with a few doors on each side. Annica peeked through one of the open doors she passed and saw what looked like living quarters. Lorna must also live and work in the same building. Annica wondered if this was the case for most of those who lived in this part of Kalthav. When they reached the last set of doors, they turned through the one on the right and entered a room that smelled of lavender and some other, spicier scent. A wooden trough was filled with steaming water. Annica saw bundles of lavender and some sort of orange berries filling a bowl on a table with a hairbrush, hairpins, soap, and other toiletries.

"I'll give you some privacy," Lorna said, patting one of Annica's hands. "That red bottle on the counter can be used on your hair; it'll feel smooth as new snow. Just leave these old robes by the door and I'll take care of them. Wash up; I'll have you and Pyotr stay for dinner."

She left and closed the door behind her. Annica was amazed by what she could think to call Lorna's 'aggressive kindness.' It was nice, though. She'd never been treated this well. Lorna's forwardness took some of the guilt off of Annica's conscience, but it still simmered behind all the joy she felt from the pleasant treatment.

She removed the old robes, realizing how threadbare they were after seeing and feeling the new dress. She was incredibly grateful that Lorna didn't choose anything green, thinking it was possibly her favorite color. Annica never wanted to wear anything in green ever again. Or visit another temple of any god whatsoever.

Annica breathed in the steam and lavender, letting the unpleasant thoughts and memories slip away. She still didn't want to rely on any Fifth Magic to help her, so she let the natural remedies in her immediate vicinity do the work.

She slipped a foot into the bath, flinching from the sudden heat, then let her leg sink into the water. She finished climbing in and let out a sigh that came from the depths of her exhausted soul. She sank up to her neck, smelling some of the lavender in the bath.

Did Lorna put bath oils in here? Bless this woman.

Annica had never even heard of bath oils until Nel Aldyri. She saw them for sale in the town shops but never bought any, though she had been intensely curious about them.

She drew her head back and soaked her hair in the water, then ran her fingers through the tangled strands. She managed to get out some of the larger knots, but reached over to the table and grabbed the brush to fight the rest. Several painful minutes later, she freed her hair from the snarled mess it had become. Her eyes caught glimpses of the ash and dirt floating in the once-clean bath water.

Grimacing, she returned the brush and grabbed the red bottle. She removed the cork with a soft *pop* and placed her nose just over the opening. It smelled like flowers. Annica closed her eyes and breathed softly for a few moments. She finally poured some of the bottle's contents, a thin oil, into her hands. She massaged it into her hair. She then exchanged the bottle for the soap and washed her face and body. Dunking her head in the water, she rubbed her face clean. Finally, she leaned her head back and soaked her hair again, washing the excess flowery oil from it.

A soft knock came from the door. Annica's head whipped around, expecting someone to come in.

"Annica?" A voice came from outside. It was Lorna. "Annica, I'm leaving your clothes outside the door, dear. Come out whenever you're ready; no need to rush."

Annica sighed. Standing from the bath caused a sudden chill to prickle her flesh. She stepped out of the water and grabbed the soft cotton towel and wrapped it around herself. Leaning over the bath, she wrung the excess water out of her hair and grabbed the brush. After brushing her hair, she slowly opened the door just enough to see the neatly folded dress sitting next to some sleek, black boots. Pyotr must have returned.

She picked them both up with one hand, holding the towel around herself with the other, and then closed the door. After drying herself off, she tried on the dress. It fit her almost perfectly; Lorna definitely knew her trade. The boots looked both stylish and utilitarian, like they would do well in the snow but still look nice with the dress.

What am I doing? she thought. It wasn't so much guilt over the lavish, at least to her, gifts and treatment as much as a feeling of alienation. Did she belong here? Was she going to stay? Were Lorna and Pyotr going to be her mama and papa now? She shook away the thoughts that quickly began spiraling into the negative and obnoxious. The shoes fit her well, too, and she wondered how Pyotr managed to get a size so close to hers.

A long mirror stood in one corner of the room. Annica felt a twinge of nervousness before stepping in front of it. When she did, the woman staring back at her was a complete stranger. She'd lost weight from her time on the Wailing Ocean, but still hadn't become gaunt. Her cheekbones stood out a little more, but her skin was still smooth and healthy. The dress made her look more feminine than she'd ever felt before. The robes were made for a purpose and fit both men and women equally. Her clothes from back at Ashwater were exactly what one would expect of a fishing village barely clinging to life. She placed a hand over her mouth and forced herself to maintain her composure.

Lorna and Pyotr waited for her out in the shop. She heard them talking, their voices echoing slightly down the hall as she approached. A strong and savory smell wafted from one of the other rooms. That must be dinner. Her footsteps clacked against the wooden floor from her new boots as she walked down the hall. When she came into view, Lorna gasped and Pyotr's eyes went wide.

"My, you are the prettiest young woman. Pyotr, who does she remind you of?"

Annica felt her face flush. Pyotr's did, too, after a few mumbled comments betraying his confusion at Lorna's question.

"My cousin, Revna; don't you remember her?"

"Ah, yes. Oh, she does!" Pyotr replied, showing genuine surprise at the revelation.

"If she were still alive, we'd go meet her immediately. You are just stunning, dear." Lorna said, her face beaming. "Her name meant 'raven' in the old Kalthavian. It would suit you, too."

"Aren't ravens omens of bad luck?" Annica said, fidgeting with her dress.

"Not here," Pyotr clarified. "In Kalthav, ravens are symbols of strength and intelligence."

Annica smiled. "Well, that's good."

She felt awkward. The clothes were nice, but she'd never worn anything that fit this snugly before. She eyed the long coat still sitting on the table, wishing she could put it on.

Lorna squeezed Pyotr's arm and walked towards Annica.

"Dinner should be ready, let's go eat and I can learn all about this lovely young lady," Lorna said with a smile as she gently took Annica's hand and led her back into the hallway.

They entered the back room on the left this time, opposite the bathroom where the smell of lavender and flowers mixed with the savory smell from the other room—creating a strange amalgam of aromas. Inside, a round table with a vase of wildflowers was set for three diners. A square, stone firepit had a pot on a spit with some sort of contents steaming within. Skewers of vegetables sat cooking separately over the burning coals.

Lorna sat both of her guests down and poured them glasses of wine. This was a stout red wine, quite different from the sweet ice wine Pyotr had provided. It wasn't quite to Annica's taste, but she sipped at it gingerly so as not to offend Lorna. More importantly, to not invite more of her assertive kindness in some way.

Their hostess then sat mugs in front of them and poured them full of water. Then, humming the entire time, Lorna brought a loaf of bread to the table and began tearing chunks off for each of them. Pyotr smiled and gestured for Annica to begin eating. He whispered, "Don't be shy," and began munching on the bread and drinking his wine.

Annica followed suit, but at a much slower pace. The bread tasted similar to the trail bread Pyotr had back in the forest but a little less bitter and grainy. It was softer and combined with some kind of herbs that made it much more palatable.

Lorna served up dinner for them all, large portions that Annica knew immediately she would be unable to finish, and they sat for an evening of food and conversation. Pyotr and Lorna caught up after all their time apart. It seemed the mention of her cousin, Revna, wasn't out of the ordinary. Lorna spoke much about her, growing teary-eyed at one point. Pyotr put his hand over hers and they steered the conversation to happier topics.

Eventually, the topic became Annica. They both asked questions about her past, her training as a mage, her home village, and the like. Some of the questions Pyotr had already asked when they met, so she was comfortable discussing these or dodging them, whichever was more convenient for her. Others she had a harder time with. Discussing her magic was bittersweet, as she took pride in what skill she had but didn't want to delve too deeply into other branches of that topic. She made sure to omit any mention of the Fifth Sect altogether. Anything asked about her time in Ashwater was met with a wistful smile, although she admitted that Kalthav had been exponentially more pleasant. Thankfully, Pyotr and Lorna didn't press her on any topics that obviously made her uncomfortable or squirm in her seat.

Much to her relief, Pyotr began asking Lorna about other happenings in the time he'd been gone. The last leg of their conversation involved the two of them discussing local events while Annica nibbled on leftovers and sipped on what remained of the tart wine.

At some point, Annica felt her eyes grow heavy. The food and wine combined efforts to assault her senses with drowsiness. She felt her head nod and subtly pinched herself in the side to try and stay awake. It wasn't long before Lorna took notice.

"Pyotr, why don't you get this young lady home? She looks exhausted. We can continue catching up later."

Lorna smiled at Annica and rose from her seat. She began grabbing the dirty dishes. Annica stood and began to help when Lorna firmly shooed her away. Annica began to insist when Pyotr put a gentle hand on her shoulder.

"Might as well come along, Annica. She won't back down," he said with a smile and wink to the round, friendly woman.

Annica thanked Lorna for everything: the clothes, the bath, the food, and, even though she didn't mention this specifically, even the big, motherly embrace. This was truly a day she would never forget, and she wanted Lorna to know it. The kindly woman blushed ferociously at Annica's comments and insisted it was nothing any other Kalthavian wouldn't do. Pyotr rolled his eyes.

They left the clothing shop after dark, and the cold of night had set in. The new overcoat proved its worth immediately. Though the frosty night air bit at her cheeks and lips, her body was quite warm and insulated. Annica did make a mental note that, when she had earned some money or trade of her own, she would buy a pair of gloves.

The streets began emptying as light from windows and firepits provided a clear path on their way back to Pyotr's home workshop. Raucous sounds from a few buildings gave the impression that taverns dotted this part of Kalthav. Annica had no desire to eat or drink any further, only to return to a warm bed.

Inside Pyotr's workshop, a fire was already lit. Annica wondered if he stopped by on the way from Mikkel the shoe-maker's to have it ready for their return. She sighed at the feeling of the warm interior and removed the jacket, hanging it on the coat rack. She also removed her boots and set them neatly off to the side.

"I'm sorry, Pyotr, I'd love to stay up and chat with you, but Lorna's meal has me so tired."

She yawned as she finished the apology, showing her sincerity. The infectious action spread to Pyotr, who returned a bear-like yawn himself.

"I couldn't agree more. Let's turn in, and tomorrow we'll talk more. By the way, while I was out, I picked you up something to sleep in. You definitely can't sleep in your dress and, well, no one should sleep nude in this climate," he said, blushing slightly.

Annica walked up to him and wrapped her arms around his wide chest. She squeezed him tightly and said, "Thank you, Pyotr. Thank you for everything. I don't know what I would've done...where I could've gone..."

The older man grinned and put one arm on top of her head, looking like a father with his long-lost daughter. "It's ok, dear," he said gruffly. "We've all had our share of tragedy. You're in an old, safe city now with an old, safe man. And Lorna," he added as they both chuckled. "Go on to bed. No doubt you'll sleep like a newborn pup tonight."

Annica smiled, told him goodnight, and walked up to her room. Locking the door behind her, an old habit that would likely never go away, she removed the dress. After folding it neatly, she placed it in the small dresser in the room. A plain, white nightgown was folded and waiting for her on top of that same dresser. It was thick and comfortable, a perfect thing for sleep and to stave off the chill.

She climbed into the bed and pulled the covers fully up to her chin. She rolled over and faced the window, looking out at the night sky. Clouds, darkened by the covered moon, hid much of the sky. Her eyes began to close of their own accord.

Like a newborn pup...she thought. That would be nice.

She slipped once more into the impossible: a deep, dreamless sleep.

THE NEXT FEW days were both interesting and, in the best way, mundane. Pyotr provided another set of clothes for her, suitable for work, so that her dress wouldn't get dirty or torn. He made sure to point out to Annica that these were just cheap, simple wool pants and a shirt, along with some work boots that Mikkel, was throwing out. There'd be no need for her to fret over this adding to her self-imposed debt. She learned many new things from Pyotr, like polishing rings and brooches, repairing delicate chains for necklaces, and the differences in gemstone qualities. It was simple, honest work compared to studying magic. However, she was curious if she could help Pyotr by infusing some of his work with magic. That would bring in much more money for him but also draw attention. It would also require skill in the Third Sect, in which she had very little training or talent.

Annica chose to let it be. The idea of a simple life in this city with Pyotr and Lorna grew on her more every day. The kind older woman visited the two of them and they shared dinner together one night, at the jeweler's shop this time. Another day they met for lunch while Pyotr and Annica made deliveries. The more time Annica spent with Lorna, the more she noticed how the kind tailor looked at her. There was a sadness in her eyes sometimes that a wide smile and nice words had trouble hiding.

"Pyotr," Annica asked one night while they ate dinner alone, "if I may ask: what happened to Lorna's cousin? Revna?"

Pyotr's brow furrowed. "Why do you ask? Has Lorna mentioned anything?"

Annica gently shook her head. "No, but I can see the way she looks at me sometimes. She said I reminded her of her cousin, and they must have been close if my resemblance sometimes makes her sad."

The bearded head nodded stiffly. His eyes scrunched in thought and gathering memories.

"They were very close. Revna passed some time ago here in Kalthav. It was unfortunate. She was a nice young lady, much like you. Very assertive but ever so gracious."

Annica was silent for a moment, the question she wanted to ask on the tip of her tongue. She wasn't sure if it was appropriate, but to her, information was the most valuable asset in this world.

"How...how did she die?" Her tone made it clear that she wasn't comfortable asking, sounding like she was apologizing at the same time.

Pyotr's lips pursed, drawing his mustache and beard together. He blinked a few hard times, then patted the table with his hand. "There's no need to end the night on such talk. Let's get some sleep and we'll discuss more tomorrow."

He offered a weak smile as he stood and stretched, his old joints cracking and creaking. The dishes would wait until morning for now, or so he mentioned as his footsteps thumped up the staircase. It was the first time he'd headed to bed in such a way. Annica hoped she hadn't upset him. She took the dishes and cleaned them, anyway, feeling guilty for bringing up such a topic. She'd still only known him for a short while, even though he and Lorna had treated her better than anyone she'd ever known—with the exception of Edrik.

With her own heart growing heavier, she retired to bed as well. Annica stared out at the night sky from her bed again, trying to make her mind clear of the intrusive and depressing memories that threatened to worm their way in. The view outside her window was doused in heavy clouds. The light of the moon barely traced the edges of a large, black, storm-bearing front. Her curiosity over Revna took the place of the memories she shoved down, and she found these thoughts just as grim. Perhaps it was best if she just focused on trying to sleep. Her mind kept roiling, though, like the clouds outside.

Annica wasn't sure if it was just guilt from the personal questions she had asked or maybe her instincts developed from a history of horrible experiences, but the feeling in her chest was unmistakable. It unnerved her, and she felt a pang of fear at the normalcy she had finally found being threatened. Something loomed on the horizon, more than just a northern storm. Some weight settled into her. Something was wrong.

Part IV

The next morning, Annica woke to the sound of rain against the window. The sky was heavy with dark gray clouds that made it impossible to tell what time it was. The rain was a lazy drizzle of heavy drops that smacked in an irregular rhythm against the glass panes.

She got out of bed and put on her work clothes. They were comfortable and made thick enough to remain fairly warm so long as she was indoors. Then, she pulled her hair back in a rough ponytail to allow her room to work. She'd made up her mind not to bring up the topic of Revna again.

By the time she'd gotten downstairs, Pyotr was already working. He'd pointed out a bowl of porridge for her on the table, still warm, and insisted she eat before helping him.

"What miserable weather this morning, eh?" he said, fitting a pendant onto a necklace chain. "When this lazy rain comes in, it tends to last the rest of the day. Mark my words."

Annica smiled. "Well, for what it's worth then, good morning?"

Pyotr chuckled.

Annica had barely begun eating when a harsh series of knocks came at the door. Pyotr stood and immediately made his way over when a second set of impatient knocking followed.

"I'm coming, I'm coming!" he grunted.

He opened the door and stood aside, calling out Lorna's name and waving her in at the same time. The woman was drenched, probably having stood in the rain for some time. Her eyes were frantic, and when they landed on Annica, she grimaced. She grabbed Pyotr by the shoulder and pulled him over by the fire. Despite her best attempts, even her whispering was loud and harsh enough for Annica to make out every word.

"Pyotr, gods, the Courier is back. It can't be; they were only here a few weeks ago."

"While I was gone?"

"Yes!" she hissed. "Why are they back so soon?"

Pyotr risked a glance over at Annica, whose eyes had gone wide and jaw clenched. His face scrunched and he turned back to Lorna. "Your guess is as good as mine. Damn it all."

A voice, small and questioning but stern, caused both their heads to turn.

"Who is 'the courier'?" Annica asked, her face an impassive mask.

Pyotr and Lorna both looked at one another with the same question in their eyes. *Should we tell her?*

"We need to head outside, anyway," Lorna said in a soft tone. "If she wants to stay in Kalthav, she needs to know."

Needs to know what? Annica thought frantically. What the hells is it now? It was safe here!

Frustration, fear, denial; these began to give way to anger, panic, and desperation as Annica felt the world giving way beneath her. She stood from her seat so quickly it nearly knocked the chair backward. She stormed over to the coat rack and grabbed her jacket, wrapping it tightly around her. She then wheeled around on the two by the fireplace.

"Show me," she demanded.

Pyotr grabbed his own coat and Lorna followed the two out of the workshop. The rain continued to fall in slow, heavy drops. Peals of thunder echoed far off in the distance. Annica imagined the raging ocean at the base of the cliffs was making a similar noise as the waters were tossed haplessly against the stones.

People lined the streets but said nothing. Everyone watched and waited. The silence among the crowd was eerie and unsettling, chilling the soul more than the rain chilled the bones. Annica followed the grim faces to where they all looked: a figure shrouded in dark blue robes trimmed in red walked slowly down the street. A rune-covered hood covered their face, and leather gloves, deep red and giving the appearance of blood while they were wet, hid their hands. The hooded head turned from side to side slowly, painfully slowly. Sometimes it would stop and stare in one direction or another. Other times it seemed to stare at nothing.

The robes were clean and well-made. Most importantly, they weren't black. None of the runes remotely resembled the awful barbed, dotted diamond of the Black Gnarl. It still couldn't be ascertained if this 'courier' was human or not. It did look and move like a human, or humanoid, but its robes were too heavy and its face was utterly covered in shadow. Even as it passed right by Annica, Pyotr, and Lorna, it barely made a sound.

Seeing the slow, steady white puffs around her, Annica realized she was holding her breath. Something else struck her, as well. She still held her powers of the Fifth cloistered inside her, masked by other magics. Still, some of the innate tendencies of the sect always seemed to be active. In this case, she felt no hostility from the courier. It carried no lingering stain of the dark magic she'd expected. This drew her curiosity even more.

Then, the courier stopped and didn't move for several moments, longer than in any previous instance. The thing turned and ever so slowly raised an open palm to one side of the street. Annica leaned forward to get a better look. Her breath caught again when she realized the courier was offering its hand to someone. A few in the crowd in front of it stirred, a few inaudible whispers escaped, then a young man stepped forward.

"Jacob," Lorna whispered sadly.

The man, Jacob, didn't look back into the crowd. If he had family or friends there, he didn't acknowledge them. He simply stepped forward and took the red-gloved hand. A flash of light and a loud crash of thunder caused several in the crowd to cry out and most to cover their ears, Annica included. When she could see again, the courier and Jacob were gone.

"Poor Jacob," a voice said from somewhere behind Annica.

"Nothing to be done about it," came another.

The crowd dispersed, ready to get out of the rain. No tears were being shed, no cries of mourning or shouts of defiance. The people of Kalthav simply broke up as though they had been shooed away from a bar fight.

PYOTR SAW Annica look at him and Lorna with wide, questioning eyes. Her brows furrowed and her mouth curled. They recognized the look of betrayal. Both of them were silent, sometimes opening their mouths as though to say something but ultimately remaining silent. Finally, Pyotr spoke up.

"Let's all go back to the workshop."

Annica left without responding, her quick, heavy footsteps splashing water from the puddles built up on the street. Lorna and Pyotr looked at each other and simply shook their heads as they followed. Annica quickly made her way out of their line of sight, turning the corner to where Pyotr's shop was located. He breathed a little easier knowing she at least wasn't running away.

When Pyotr and Lorna reached his workshop, they slowly opened the front door, dreading the conversation to come. The door felt a little heavier this time. When they entered, Annica was standing in front of the fireplace, her arms crossed, staring into the flames.

There was a tense silence as the elders removed their coats. Pyotr took a seat while Lorna approached Annica, moving to put her hands on the young lady's shoulders. Lorna grimaced when she felt Annica tense under her gentle hands.

"What was that?" Annica asked tersely. "What awful secrets does *this* place have?"

"Annica..." Lorna began before she was cut off.

"I want to know *everything*," Annica said in a harsh, quiet voice. "No half-truths, no beating around the bush, no excuses or rosy-eyed bullshit—*everything*," she barked, her anger unmasked.

"We were hoping there would be more time for you to get acquainted with the city before we had to lay such hard realities on you," Pyotr's voice came low and husky from the table.

"It's not what it looks like, Annica," Lorna added, almost pleadingly.

Annica shrugged off the woman's grip and turned on her slowly. "I have seen so many horrors committed in such a short time; what good could there possibly be in that thing taking people away? Where was he taken to?"

Pyotr shook his head and Lorna hung hers low, staring at the fire behind Annica.

"We don't know, but we do know it's for our good and the one carried away," Pyotr answered, his words slow and heavy.

"Bullshit," Annica muttered.

"We've seen what happens to those who stay," Lorna said, going to sit next to Pyotr.

Lorna explained to an impatient and surly Annica that the silent courier had spoken only once, long ago when the Rupture occurred. The history passed down in Kalthav to its people and their sole city's salvation from the fate of the others began the very night the sky opened and bled.

Their forebears spent a day in terror as the great wound stretched across the sky. Everyone waited in fear as the king, Haakonsen IV, closed off the gates to the Lord's Pillar and Drottinsvegur. The sky turned dark and a storm moved in unlike any that had ever been seen before. The sickly light from the Rupture shone through even the blackest stormclouds, as unnatural and unwholesome as a bleeding ghost wandering the night. Eventually, all returned to normal, for the most part. People came from various parts of the world bearing tales of horrors too terrible to describe, but Kalthav continued on. As the merchant caravans slowed, patrols were sent to investigate. Not all of them returned. Those that did confirmed the accounts; the other cities had fallen. The world's landscape itself had changed. Alda had been broken. Over time, the travelers, merchants, and even refugees trickled in slower and slower until not a single soul was seen for months on end. Kalthav, however, remained. The people nurtured their crops to survive harsher temperatures, especially the gray-blue wheat variant that had become a staple of their diet.

After many years, another storm similar to the one on that awful day returned. The sky turned black with clouds so low they threatened to touch the towers of the castle on the Lord's Pillar. At some hour, as none could tell if it was day or night, a voice echoed among every home, shop, and farm.

A hollow sound, reverberating like thunder following lightning, demanded that the people of Kalthav heed it. People came from their homes and gathered in the streets. The roads and alleys of the Cliff's Pillar and the Lord's Pillar were filled shoulder to shoulder. At the peak of the Drottinsvegur, a hooded figure stood, the air crackling around them. Some thought it was a powerful mage and demanded to know if they were responsible for the horrible phenomenon in the sky that broke the world. This caused angered shouts to begin breaking out, but the voice repeated: *Heed me.*

The sound trembled their hearts. It carried an ancient, powerful weight. The figure warned them that the darkest of times was upon them. It would return when needed to gather those that pose a danger to Kalthav. It would not force obeisance but woe to those who denied its hand.

The figure had made its way up the great bridge to the gate of the Lord's Pillar. The gate remained closed, but the figure walked through the iron bars as though they weren't there, crackling and sparking as though the figure were made of lightning itself. It approached a man, remembered only as a wealthy banker whose name is lost and meaningless anymore; the only importance being that he denied the figure, which came to be known as the Courier.

After that, a flash of light and a ferocious peal of thunder preceded its disappearance. None saw it again for many months. Stories began to spread of the banker in the following days. His behavior had changed. He was found trespassing in the castle and asking odd questions. He was slain after he tried to make his way into the castle by force.

The Courier returned and was denied again. The woman who had done so was from the farmlands. She hanged herself after only a few days. Rumors spread of black-robed figures lingering in the woods, asking questions of the loggers and hunters. Soon, they grew brave enough to venture into the farmlands. The same day they did so, the Courier came for someone else. This time, the chosen individual went back with the figure. The black-robed individuals that had disturbed the city's peace disappeared the next day.

The decades carried on, and the Courier's visits continued sporadically but were often limited to once or twice a year. The last individual who denied its hand was, however, the most notable. A nobleman's son refused to go, and within a few days he began behaving strangely. Lingering in the library when he was never an academic to begin with. Asking the guard to allow him to use a ship as his father didn't own one. His answer was deemed unsuitable and he was denied. At a banquet held by the current king in honor of his daughter's wedding, the nobleman's son was found by himself, standing on the grand balcony behind the castle, staring out at the ocean. He only kept repeating, "I must get there." That night, he was seen throwing himself from the balustrade edge before anyone could stop him.

"But, this is the second time the Courier has shown itself in as many weeks. That's never happened before," Pyotr interjected.

"Where was he trying to go? He said he 'needed to get there'?"

Another moment of quiet as the two seemed to be contemplating their response.

"The third pillar. Another castle that's been a part of Kalthav's history since its earliest days. More a fort than a castle, supposed to be there for the royal family and castle guests if invaders made it to the Lord's Pillar. There's a dock accessible somehow, but only within the castle. You can see it if you get close enough to the cliffs outside the farmlands. Ever since the Rupture, though, I don't believe anyone has ever gone there."

"How do you know that?" Annica asked skeptically.

Pyotr stiffened his lip, causing his mustache hairs to bristle, and nodded firmly as he answered. "You hear a lot when making deliveries as the city's only jeweler. The only other one near the castle died years ago; the one that taught me. I heard a lot then, too."

"Is there anything...going on at the other pillar?" Annica asked, unsure of how to phrase her question but knowing what happenings she had in mind.

"That, no one knows," Lorna answered this time.

Annica's mind immediately began concocting multiple possibilities.

"The Courier, it takes nobles and peasants alike?" she asked.

Both of them nodded. "There have been times we've seen a flash, thinking lightning was close by, but then we hear the loud thunder we know is from the Courier departing and it comes from the Lord's Pillar. Word tends to spread quickly within the day of what happened," Lorna clarified.

Annica still thought it strange that no dark magic radiated from the Courier, even as its haunting presence passed her by. It didn't discern between social classes, so it would be unlikely that anyone on the Lord's Pillar was up to something by using the working folk. This Courier also, unlike the Black Gnarl, worked very openly. The Temple of the First Son was visited by everyone, but their true purposes were still a closely guarded secret. The nature of the Courier's visits was still unknown, too, but at least there was evidence that those who refused it truly did meet terrible fates.

"Does this have anything to do with the marauders? You told me that they were notably more violent than others, not to mention that strange occurrence at the gate," she asked, her question directed at Pyotr. She didn't mention the lingering essence of the Fourth Sect she felt at the spot where the surviving soldier died.

Pyotr shook his head firmly. "Unrelated entirely. They only

recently showed a few years ago. Since that day at the gate, they've never moved against Kalthav again."

Annica's mind twisted around the events; turned over every stone of possibility. She simply didn't know enough about the city. She'd been so comfortable and happy with the life Pyotr and Lorna had provided her that she had let her guard down.

"I want to see this cliff where the noble's son committed suicide," she said, her mind set.

Pyotr stumbled over his reply. "I...I don't know if that's possible, Annica. You can only get to the cliff from the castle itself and you can't just walk in there."

"So, the Lord's Pillar is off-limits to anyone who doesn't live there?"

"I didn't say that," Pyotr said, raising his hands defensively. "The Lord's Pillar can be visited by any citizen of the city, but none of us have any reason to ever go there. The goods tend to be more than we can afford to trade or barter for. The castle, of course, is for the king's family and retainers only."

Annica nodded. That was understandable but didn't change her course of action. "I need to go to the Lord's Pillar, then."

Pyotr sighed and Lorna squeezed his hand. He was quiet for a moment. Annica turned back to the fireplace and watched the flames dance on red-hot coals that remained of the logs. If any citizen could walk over the bridge to the next pillar, she would do so on her own if need be.

"At least wait until tomorrow; hopefully, the rain will stop. The guards will be on edge after the Courier visited so soon after the last time." Pyotr asked in a tone that said he knew Annica would do so, regardless. He'd have to be with her since she'd need his citizen's papers and no doubt would try to persuade the guards or sneak in otherwise.

"Ok, Pyotr," she said quietly, then turned to face him. Annica went up to the old man whose face had drooped in a way she hadn't seen since they'd met. She felt terrible for her suspicions, but they weren't without merit. She took his other hand in hers. His was cold from the rain, while hers was warm from being near the fire. She squeezed his hand, feeling the warmth seep into his thick, tired fingers. "Thank you."

He smiled a small but genuine smile. Annica then did the same for Lorna, taking one of the older woman's chilled hands in both of her own. "You, too, Lorna. I'm sorry for my behavior, but please trust me when I say I have my reasons."

Lorna smiled and shook her head. "We kept this from you for a reason, too, dear. Maybe we shouldn't have, but this world is no longer what it used to be. We're grateful things have remained relatively the same here. Whatever the Courier is protecting us from, it appears to be serious so we deal with the occasional heartache. From what we've heard, it's much less than what others have had to endure."

Annica couldn't argue with that. She gave Lorna's hand another squeeze and only gave a gentle smile in return. Moments of silence hung in the air. The fire crackled and grew weaker. The cold from the storm seeped into the building. Pyotr finally stood and added fuel to the fire and then offered to make everyone something to eat.

No work was completed that day. Lorna returned to her shop, and Pyotr and Annica remained inside, making small talk for a time before retiring to their rooms for the rest of the day. Annica found a book to read in her room, a collection of Kalthavian heroic stories. Pyotr brought some mulled wine at one point and checked on her. She thanked him for the drink and returned to her reading; every once in a while, looking outside to see the clouds remaining as thick and dark as they were in the morning. Eventually, she fell asleep. The book slipped from her hands and slid into her lap. Another night of dreamless slumber.

THE FOLLOWING day spared them the rain but brought instead a heavy chill. Annica found herself yet again immensely thankful for the dress and coat that kept much of the cold out. She felt further pangs of regret over the way she had reacted towards Lorna and Pyotr yesterday. This world truly left none unscathed, and so to find that Kalthav had its own struggles with something otherworldly should have come as no surprise. However, Annica still felt the reflexive defensiveness well up in her even as she thought about it. She decided it was perhaps better to be cautious of the city but kinder to her hosts. They were far more genial than even the nicest people on Nel Aldyri, after all.

The guard at the gate to the bridge, known as Drottinsvegur, gave the same bored reaction as the one in front of the gate-house to the Cliff's Pillar. Pyotr showed him his papers indicating he was a citizen of Kalthav and could enter the walled vicinity of the Lord's Pillar freely.

"We should visit the city official's office and see about getting you papers of your own," Pyotr remarked as they walked over the large, arching bridge. It was several dozen feet wide, as large as the main thoroughfare, and still maintained in good condition. In its prime, it must have seen traffic during all hours of the day moving back and forth between the two sections. A handful of people still traversed the old structure, some even walking alongside oxen pulling carts, showing Annica that the people of Kalthav did indeed have open travel between their greatly partitioned districts.

The opposite gate opened for them immediately. They stepped through and Annica saw the upper-class districts of Kalthav in all their splendor. She thought this to herself somewhat sarcastically as the streets and architecture looked much the same, only better maintained and larger. Some had more opulent embellishments and the people were dressed in the manner one would expect of bankers, aristocrats, and officials. There were also more trees and statuary.

No one cast them strange glances or awkward stares. This was life as normal in the cold region of Kalthav. Although, a few young men did smirk in Annica's direction. She ignored this, though, as there was only one place and purpose on her mind.

The castle itself was surrounded by a twenty-foot tall iron fence, spiked on the top to prevent being scaled, and manned by a guard every ten feet. The main gate the cobblestone road led to was reinforced with stone pillars topped with regal-looking elk statues on each. A guard stood by each pillar, behind each of them a polished shield bearing a royal crest.

"That's the Haakonsen family crest," Pyotr leaned over to whisper into Annica's ear. He explained that the Haakonsen family had ruled since the Rupture. Without wars due to the collapse of the other city-states and the desperate times causing noble squabbles of succession to quickly die out, the Haakonsens ruled peacefully for the most part. Annica's mood darkened when she saw the colors on the crest: dark red and blue.

The guards thumped their halberds as the two approached. "State your business," one of them ordered brusquely.

"We request access to the castle. Specifically, the grand balcony behind it. This young lady would like to see the ocean view from there."

"A strange request," one of the guards said flatly. "But, the king is not accepting visitors or requests today. You'll have to return at some other time."

Pyotr gave Annica a frown and whispered, "That's that, then. We'll try again tomorrow."

Annica peered through the gate and saw nothing other than lush gardens on each side, cut through by a paved stone path lined on each side by three statues, making six in total. No one loitered in the area that could be seen. The castle was like those Annica had always read about: large, beautiful, with round towers jutting in patterns both regular and irregular. Windows were all around the structure, providing what must have been stunning views. If she had the chance, she'd like to look inside the castle itself, as well, just for a few minutes.

They made their way back through the gate of the Lord's Pillar leading to the bridge. Annica's thoughts churned like the thunderous waves hundreds of feet below. It always sounded like a storm was on the horizon. Perhaps that's what leant its namesake to the Storm's Pillar a man had killed himself trying to reach. It was the most likely place the Courier may have come from, especially if it had been abandoned for so long. It also wouldn't surprise her if that was either the local's suspicion, as well, or if they outright knew it but let it be, as their lives were overall stable and comfortable. The color of the Courier's clothes matching those of the ruling family's crest, however, troubled her deeply.

"Pyotr, the Haakonsen's family crest—the elk on the red and blue background—is that unique to that particular family?" She asked, trying to sound casual.

"Well," Pyotr began, grunting in thought before continuing, "The elk is, as is the checkered pattern of the blue and red, but those colors are the chosen of Kalthav. All royal families before the Haakonsens bore those colors on their heraldry in some form."

"I see."

Annica became lost in thought once more. The Courier, then, wore robes in the Kalthavian colors, not just a particular family. Her thoughts went on and on, like the heavy white clouds stretching to both ends of the horizon above them. They also came to no conclusions. Annica and Pyotr were almost near the end of the bridge when she asked him her other burning question.

"When we were talking to the guards, I looked past the gate into the castle's courtyard. There were some statues lining the path leading up the castle's stairway. Each of them was a different person; they looked like royalty. Are they anyone in particular?"

A smile cracked the older man's face. He chuckled, a growly sound from his throat, and began what sounded like a history lesson.

"The kings of old. Not just from Kalthav's past...there have been too many to count. Those statues are of some of the first of Kalthav's founding and greatest rulers. The one in the front on the right was Kalthav's first king, Baldyn the Stormchaser. He founded the first parts of the city, including the Cliff's Pillar."

Annica remembered that statue. Not only was it one of the closest, but the figure was dressed in near barbaric clothing with a fur-lined cloak and massive sword planted tip first in the ground before him, his hands resting on the top of the pommel.

"The one across from him was King Tholm Sturlsen. Sturlsen," Pyotr continued, assuming Annica was unfamiliar with Kalthavian naming conventions, "means 'Son of Sturl.' Sturl is the god of construction, ingenuity, and cities. Well, at least that was what was believed before the Rupture turned the faith of many sour." His tone grew forlorn before picking up again. "Can you guess who built this bridge and constructed a new castle on the Lord's Pillar?"

Annica chuckled as she answered. "I can imagine. There was a woman next to that one, Sturlsen. Who was she?"

The gate back to the simpler streets of the Cliff's Pillar clanked open. Pyotr clapped his hands together as they walked through. "Ah! Livda the War Queen. A few centuries after Sturlsen's time was a dark era for Kalthav. A few other cities wanted to secede and become their own sovereign city-states. This would've severely weakened all of them in the long run, but we're a stubborn folk. The king at that time, I can't recall his name or his family's, was killed in battle and his queen threw herself from the balcony behind the castle in grief."

"That seems to be a popular spot for such a thing," Annica said in a low voice, a dark jest that neither laughed at.

"So it seems. Her son and daughter did the same thing when the pressures against them continued to grow and Kalthav withered under civil war. An entire family lost to grief, strife, and war. The land was left without a united ruler, until a stout-hearted woman rose up in the southern stretches, at least what was called the southern stretches before the Wailing Ocean rose."

"Livda?" Annica asked.

"Indeed," Pyotr continued. "Livda gathered quite a following. She reunited two of the three warring factions, her own city and Kalthav itself, and cowed the third in a few decisive battles. She became queen after that, earning her moniker and taking a husband. But that her husband's name was always overshadowed by her own. So, she became one of the six Storm Kings; those forever captured in those statues you saw."

"Has there not been any others?" Annica asked, her curiosity genuinely piqued.

Pyotr shook his head firmly. "The last to be given that title in our history was the last statue on the left: Hafjor Silford. About a hundred years before the Rupture, he negotiated a historical treaty and trade agreement with the Belgallant dwarves. Kalthav entered a golden age after that, which lasted almost up until the sky ripped open. Some say it was that prosperity that has helped us endure all these centuries since."

Annica listened intently. She wished Pyotr would have continued, but they were nearing home.

Home. Annica thought, smiling slightly. *Is that what this has become?*

"I'd love to learn more about Kalthav. Your history sounds so interesting."

Pyotr put a gentle hand on her shoulder as they stopped in front of the workshop's door.

"You know, I haven't mentioned this the whole time you've been here, but you're quite intelligent for a girl who washed up on some cold rocks covered in ash with nothing but a ragged robe to her name. They must've taught you well on that island."

Annica grimaced at the thought of Nel Aldyri. She'd much rather discuss the old and fascinating history of Kalthav than that of a small island city that sought to forge a new dark legacy of its own.

"I actually learned to read back in my old home, Ashwater. I thought it set me apart from the others there; everyone seemed so miserable, trying to eke out a living. Thinking about it, I think I thought myself better than them. Or, maybe I wanted to be. I feel...really bad about it now. The more I think on it, the worse a person I realize I was."

Pyotr jutted his jaw and nodded his head in thought. "Well, I don't know what you were like then, but you certainly don't seem like that person now."

"I hope not," Annica said and gave him a smile.

They went inside to get warm and eat. A few chores had to be handled and then they had dinner and called it a night. Annica looked forward to returning to the castle. Her goal was still in the front of her mind, but now she wanted to see the statues again, knowing some of their history. Until then, she planned on enjoying another night of dreamless sleep.

. . .

THE NEXT SEVERAL weeks saw the Courier return twice more. Once was in the farmlands and Annica rushed and pushed her way through the crowd to get as near to it as possible. The same feelings as the first visit returned. This thing was old, still undiscernible as being human or otherwise, and cast no detectable aura of evil or dark magic.

The second visit came from the Lord's Pillar. Like Pyotr had said, one could only tell due to a flash like lightning, the crowd gathering, and then a monstrous peal of thunder. Annica wasn't able to make her way through that crowd as the bridge became choked with shoulder-to-shoulder onlookers. Annica also had the disturbing inclination that the Kalthavians gathered as though it were their duty to wait and see if they were chosen.

Unfortunately, this all meant that the castle gates remained sealed. Annica was unable to get inside, and it appeared like it would stay that way for some time. The royal family seemed to become quite on edge whenever the Courier visited. The unprecedented frequency with which the Courier was coming had the entire city on edge.

Pyotr went out on another foraging expedition after the second visit from the Courier. He promised her he wouldn't stray into the Withered Groves and estimated he'd return in a few days. She declined to accompany him as she had some business of her own to attend to. She promised to keep the shop clean and take any orders that would wait for his return.

While he was gone, Annica went out to the farmlands and to the cliff where Pyotr mentioned the docks below the castle could be seen. He was right; there, at the base of the Lord's Pillar, a single pier stretched just into the line of sight from the rounded edge of the rocks. It looked like each post and board was crafted from a whole tree to hold against the powerful, crashing waves.

She looked out further to where the morning fog and evening mists tended to shroud the horizon from one's eyes. It was late morning, and heavy clouds, a mix of both white and dark gray that seemed to contrast each other and make their colors stand out all the more, stretched out to the horizon on the ocean. To the northwest of the Lord's Pillar, nestled in thick strands of white mist that crawled over that part of the ocean like sea serpents, the third pillar rested among the distant waves. Pyotr had said it was called the Storm's Pillar. That seemed both dramatic and unnecessary, but it was named by the king who'd had it constructed, and he was one who was obsessed with Kalthav's war gods that wielded lightning, thunder, and the sea.

True to Pyotr's description, the castle that sat atop the tall column of rock was built more like a fortress. Annica couldn't even see a way to get to it from her viewpoint. There was no visible dock, stairway, or shore to make it to the structure above.

Several of these tall stone landmarks jutted from the waters along the steep cliff shorelines. They were all manner of heights and widths, hauntingly beautiful natural formations that felt appropriate to Kalthav's stout people. The largest, of course, had both been used as the Lord's and Storm's Pillars.

Though it was some distance away, the fortress' windows could just be made out on the keep peeking above the walls. None of them seemed to be lit from within. Such a fortress would be wasted if no one was using it. It appeared the safest place to be in the world if it had food and clean water stored away. She was also painfully suspicious of the whole thing.

Throughout her time in Kalthav, she had kept the Fifth Magic shrouded within her; a bright candle locked in a storage box. She thought it over and then thought it over again. She questioned herself a thousand times, from a thousand angles. Ultimately, she decided it was time to take the candle out and fan its flames for just a moment.

Breathing and focusing on the core of being, she felt the Fifth Magic there. A warm pulse beneath a silk veil. She breathed in, feeling her lungs fill with fresh, chilled air. The veil rippled, and as she breathed out she felt the air leave her lungs and the veil slipped away. The warm glow of the magic spread in her body like she'd sipped warm tea on a freezing day.

Once the shimmering sensation of the Fifth Magic coursed within her, she reached out with it. The essence of the Fifth spread from her like misty strands of diamond dust, catching the barest rays of light and reflecting it in her mind's eye. She stretched it out as far as she could but felt the magic spreading thin. The glistening light dimmed. Soon, she felt it grow so faint she could barely sense it any longer. She couldn't control it enough to reach far enough and feel for anything within the walls of Storm's Pillar.

She sighed and resigned herself to waiting until she could find a way to get into the castle. She'd already tried skulking about at night, but the gate remained guarded too diligently. Trying to climb the walls was impossible and they were well-maintained, so despite their age there was no safe way to sneak through. The cliffs posed another problem. The walls and gate-houses ran clean to their edge; just thinking about maneuvering her way along that severe drop made her stomach shrivel.

Annica once more constricted the warm light of the Fifth within her, covering it, and placing the candle back in the box. She went to bed that night thinking of other ways she may find out more about the mysterious Storm's Pillar and the Courier, possibly a connection between them. Her first instinct was to try the library on the Lord's Pillar, but if Pyotr and Lorna both mentioned that the current state of Storm's Pillar was one of legend even to the Kalthavians, then it was likely someone had already tried researching there and found nothing. She could ask the elders of the community. Any folklore or old wives' tales would likely have some kernel of truth in them.

Before she realized it, sleep had snuck upon Annica.

However, this night was different. Instead of a dreamless sleep, she saw subtle flashes light up the bottoms of dark clouds. In the sheer darkness of sleep, gray-blue strands of illuminated storm clouds spread out in the distance, but no sound came. All was silent. She vaguely realized she was dreaming. Those clouds, they were being illuminated by lightning within them. There was something else, too. Something beyond the clouds, beyond the lightning, shrouded by darkness and cold and the vagueness of a sleeping mind.

WHEN SHE WOKE, the brightness of a clear day shone through her window. She took in a deep breath, thankful the dream was over. She had no lingering sense of fear. The dream itself was rather devoid of emotion, which in itself made her uncomfortable.

That was her first time dreaming since she came to Kalthav. Why did it start now? Perhaps her using the Fifth Magic connected her to the town or its people in some way, so she dreamt, naturally, of a storm that night. It made sense and would explain the lack of unease that tended to follow most of her dreams.

When the day proved to be slow and fruitless for Pyotr's business, Annica decided to see if the castle was receiving visitors. She wore her dress and coat just in case she would be allowed in. The gate to the Drottinsvegur bridge was still manned by two guards. They nodded as she approached and waited quietly when she stopped in front of them.

A moment of awkward silence passed and Annica realized that Pyotr always showed his proof of citizenship. Her face turned slightly red and she began looking for an excuse to give them.

"I, um...I'm usually with Pyotr..." she stammered.

One guard smirked. "Ah, yes. I've seen you two come through here a few times. You do not have your own papers?"

Annica grimaced. "No, we forgot to visit the administrator's office on our last visit and he's gone out foraging."

Both guards chuckled at that statement. Pyotr's foraging trips must be known among more than just his friends. They looked at each other, seeming to have a conversation in that brief moment and one of them shrugged.

"You've been here a while, haven't you? You seem a good lass. You can pass this time, but take care of any business because you won't be able to go again until Pyotr returns. You need a Kalthavian to vouch for you for citizenship. Once you're through here, they'll let you go on through to the Lord's Pillar and return with no problems."

Annica was aware of the last bit of information, but the fact that this would be her only chance to get into the castle without Pyotr was troubling. She couldn't even apply for her papers on her own. Somehow, she had to make it into the castle. She knew the Storm's Pillar was where the noble's son wanted to go when he threw himself from the cliff and an entire family had done the same at some point; despite being able to see it from the edge of the farmlands, she wanted to see the actual location behind the castle and get a feel for the area. Literally, in case of any magic imprints that may be there.

She smiled and put her hand over her chest, voicing a genuine "Thank you so much. I'll make the most of it."

The guards nodded and stepped aside, signaling for the iron portcullis to be raised. It creaked open, giving Annica a view of the wide, splendid structure. As had happened every time before, the guards at the opposite gate let her through without question, knowing that the previous guards would have cleared her to cross. They went about their duties with the detached, rote vigilance one would expect.

She made her way straight to the castle entrance, where guards still lined the gate surrounding the elegant bastion of Kalthav's royal family. The statues and greenery of the Lord's Pillar, especially what could be seen through the iron bars that guarded the royal grounds, looked especially beautiful on a day such as this, where clouds still roamed the skies in thick clusters, but were white as snow and the sun shone brightly in a blue sky devoid of any incoming storms.

One of the guards held out his hand as Annica grew near them. Those protecting the castle were dressed differently than the guards at the gates and patrolling the city. They were also more heavily armored. His voice was gruff and stern, "State your business."

Annica gritted her teeth and approached as formally and self-assuredly as she could. "I'm here to visit the castle. Not the royal family necessarily, but I'd like to see the grounds."

The guard returned his hand to his side and gave her a long-suffering look. He must have had to repeat his question and response many times, lately.

"I'm sorry, but the king is ill so none are allowed on the grounds today."

Annica felt her heart drop. She couldn't say she was surprised, but she had hoped it would be something she could try to resolve diplomatically or talk her way into. Illness would be difficult to work around.

That's not true.

The voice was as clear as the sky, feminine, and confident. The guards continued to look at Annica, expecting her to leave. They didn't appear to hear it at all.

"What is?" Annica replied, unexpectedly asking out loud.

The guards' faces scrunched. "Excuse me?" one of them asked.

The king is not ill. They're lying to you. Ask about Haakonsen's son.

Annica hesitated. It wasn't her voice. She wasn't talking to herself. Someone, or something, was communicating with her.

"Um, the king's son, is he alright?" she asked, trying to sound sympathetic but not understanding the situation at all.

A shadow grew over the faces of both guards. One of them stepped forward.

"Why are you asking?"

"I..." she stuttered, grasping for something to say that wouldn't get her kicked out of the Lord's Pillar at best and arrested at worst. "I heard that he was ill, as well. Should we be concerned?"

The guard's face relaxed, but his gaze remained stern and intimidating. "Nothing for you to worry about. Move along and conclude your business on the Lord's Pillar."

That's only partially true. The voice spoke softly, almost sounding amused. *The king is concerned about the Courier.*

Annica bowed her head in deference and backed away. After a few steps, she turned and asked, "Is the king concerned about the Courier coming for his son?"

The guards gripped their spears so tightly that the leather of their gloves groaned. They both began to approach her. Annica stepped up to them confidently, which threw them off. They reflexively raised their weapons slightly, but Annica's defiant face and strong posture gave them pause.

"I might be able to help him. I'm a mage."

"Magic has already been attempted; by others more skilled than you, I'm sure," one of the guards said in a burly, impatient voice. "Leave. Now."

Annica stood there for a moment, looking up at him and into his eyes. They weren't going to change their minds. She lowered her head and backed away, defeated. The guards watched her leave. It seems they expected her to depart back to Cliff's Pillar, though they didn't order it. She felt their glares on her back and left immediately for the Drottinsvegur gatehouse.

Her pace was slow and sullen. She tried to think of other ways she might be able to get into the castle or just to its outskirts. She went to the side of the bridge facing the Lord's Pillar. The castle did have plenty of space for its surroundings and courtyard; unfortunately, the curtain wall surrounding the Lord's Pillar encompassed the whole area. The grand balcony at the back of the castle, hidden from view at this angle, must rise above the wall to provide a view of the ocean and be close enough to leap over it.

She stood there for a while, listening to the waves below and letting the warm sun work its way into her bones. A breeze blew and cooled her; she could smell the salt of the ocean as well as wet, ancient stone. Her mind calmed, but concern tightened the core of her chest.

You'll get there.

The voice returned. It was supportive and motherly. Annica nearly startled when she heard it, so clear was it in her mind.

"Who are you?" Annica asked in a whisper, not knowing if the voice could hear or not.

There was no reply. Annica waited for a while, maybe minutes or an hour—she wasn't sure. When the voice never replied and the sun began to grow hot as it reflected off the stone, she decided to return home and think of another way to get answers.

Two days passed and two more nights of odd, emotionless dreams about silent storms and blue-gray clouds lit by hidden lightning. The voice never returned. No opportunities or genius ideas came to Annica, so she kept her promise to Pyotr to maintain his workshop in his absence.

The morning of the third day appeared to start like any

other. Then, a commotion came from outside. Annica opened the door to hear better and what came from the streets did not sound pleasant. Had the Courier returned? It would be the first time that such a frightened crowd gathered if that was the case.

Annica went to see the cause of the agitated gathering as the collective voices of the city folk buzzed like angry hornets. They pushed and jostled around something but cleared the way as whatever it was moved through the crowd. Annica made use of her smaller size to tuck between the larger bodies and finally saw what caused the crowd to be so riled.

Two men carried a makeshift stretcher, another man writhing in pain between the branches serving to hold a large blanket in place. Annica saw blood dripping to the ground from the side of the man facing away from her. The injured man was yelling to be put down. Finally, after receiving some choice words from those carrying him, he was gently put on the ground.

"It...it...was them..." he said between grunts of pain.

Now that he was on the ground, Annica could see the red wound running from his armpit to his gut, exposing bone and fat. The man didn't have long. She wasn't even sure her current abilities in the Fifth sect could help him, but was hesitant to use it in front of so many people as well. Her conscience was torn.

It wouldn't do any good.

The voice returned, whispering as though it could be heard.

The wound is too deep and the weapon which created it was toxic, coated in things best not described.

Annica grimaced, feeling awful for the man as he grunted and screamed in pain while trying to talk with his last breaths.

"Marauders...came at dawn...killed two...two families. Edge of...farmlands. Took...wives...others dead..."

The man gurgled, blood bubbling and frothing from his mouth, and let out one last, long breath. The people began shouting, some frightened and others angry. One thing remained a common focus: the marauders had attacked, unprovoked, for the first time in many years. Not only attacked but took captives with them.

Annica heard multiple names thrown around and pieced together that they were guessing at which families were attacked and who was taken. A large group left to go see the damage for themselves. Annica went with them.

Past the gatehouse into the farmlands, the farmers and their families had gathered and were alight with both anger and fear just as those within the walls of Cliff's Pillar had been. They took the group to the outskirts and showed them the houses and farms that were attacked. Many refused to step inside the houses when they saw the blood and remains already littering the areas around the houses.

As Pyotr had said, the marauders didn't just murder and plunder; they were butchers. All but a handful of guards were made to stand away from the gruesome scene as pieces of the men and children were matched together as best as possible just so they could be given proper burials. Some could only be identified by those who knew where they lived, as faces were removed or bashed in. Not all the pieces could be recovered. The stench of blood reached even where the crowds were allowed to gather, including Annica. But she was able to see plenty before everyone was forced to stand back.

The insides of the home were literally covered in viscera and stained red. Multiple guards, especially younger ones, emptied their stomachs as the more seasoned ones continued their grim work. Many had left and returned back to their obligations or just to get away from the horrifying sight and smell.

Annica stayed.

She controlled her breathing, but the sight of the massacred farmers and their families made her face grow hot. Her heart hammered inside her. She flashed back to images of innocent townsfolk strapped to tables while some ancient, demonic entity tethered from outside reality fed on them. These Kalthavians' deaths were quicker by comparison, but they suffered no less.

You could stop them, you know. The voice said, its tone matter-of-fact.

"I saw the fortress. There's too many of them," Annica replied, barely whispering or even moving her mouth.

With power like yours, they will receive justice befitting their ilk.

"I can only use the Fifth Sect with any skill. And fire magic. I barely made it out of my last scrape alive."

No. You can do it. We don't even have to wait. Get some food for the trip and we will return with the debt paid in full.

"I don't know who or what you are. I have no reason to listen to you."

The voice, once so sure and confident, was silent once more. Unable to fully clean the homes that were attacked and feeling none would dare move into them, anyway, the remains of the buildings were set ablaze under the watch of the guards. The area would be cleansed by fire then blessed by the local priests. Perhaps then, they could rebuild. Annica finally left, her mind and heart too pained and tired to watch or listen to anything else. After the horrible attack, little happened further that day in Kalthav. Extra guards were set out in the farmlands on patrol. A few were even stationed just within the forest as scouts to provide advance warning. Annica slept that night and dreamt once again. Only this time, the flashes that lit the clouds were deep red, and whatever the ill feeling she was that told her something sat behind those darkened clouds grew worse.

Part V

The next morning, alarm bells rang early. Annica ran from the workshop. Many simply shuttered their stalls or ushered their families into their homes. A few gathered and tried to see what had happened. Annica made her way to the gatehouse that led into the farmlands to find it closed. Guards ordered everyone to stay back; the gate would not be opened. She reached the front of the crowd and looked through. What she saw caused her insides to grow cold and threatened to upend her stomach.

The homes and fields appeared untouched; however, piles of heads were stacked well within sight of the gate. Humans and animals alike had been beheaded and piled on top of each other, all purposely made to face the city. Possibly every person who lived in the farmlands was murdered along with their live-stock. The piles ranged in size and stretched all up the road and along the sides of the adjoining fields. Someone near Annica said something that made her catch her breath.

"They stacked the families together with their livestock..."

Each pile was a gory shrine to each remaining individual family. Annica momentarily remembered Karl and searched, just briefly, to see if she could find him. Thankfully, Hilna would be with Pyotr.

This can't go on, Annica.

It was the first time the voice used her name. She couldn't admit that part of her was afraid of going after the marauders in their tainted fortress. All she wanted to do was wait for Pyotr to return and continue to live here in peace, leaving her magic tucked away, letting the candle burn faintly in its box until she passed from this haunted and angry world.

You can't do that either. These beasts are on the move. The farm-lands are gone. Where will they turn next?

"I'm afraid," Annica whispered shakily.

You shouldn't be. Your power is beyond theirs. You simply refuse to use it. What will those men...those things...do when they get past the gate?

"We don't know that they will. The walls are tall and the gates—"

You know they will. The voice interrupted. And Annica knew it was right. She knew those monsters would get in somehow.

Yes. And there are many women and children in here. What will happen to Lorna? What will Pyotr return to? You know that the nobles and royal family would rather destroy the bridge than be raided. Everyone will be trapped on one side or another. The Lord's Pillar will devolve into a starving mass of greedy people. One atrocity will lead to another until Kalthav is destroyed.

Annica stared out at the field of piled heads. Her heart ached enough as it was, but the empathy was powered further by the Fifth Magic even as it lay tucked away. She gritted her teeth and took a deep breath. She went to one of the guards who stood straight-backed and alert. He put a hand on his sheathed sword when she came within a few steps of him. He didn't say a word, only looked at her and shook his head.

"I need to get outside," Annica said in a stern but diplomatic voice.

"Have you looked outside? No one is going out there until the royal guard gets here."

Annica took one more step toward him, but her face softened.

"I'm not a Kalthavian citizen. I came here and have been living with Pyotr, the man who found me lost in those very woods. I appreciate Kalthav's protection, but I'm neither a prisoner nor are you obligated with my safety. Please allow me to pass."

The guard sighed and frowned, but his eyes showed pity. He

turned and looked over his shoulder as he said, "I just can't in good conscience let a lady out there."

Annica swallowed. She stepped forward and very slowly and gingerly placed a hand on the guard's elbow. He flinched, knowing what he *should* do when someone placed their hands on a guard. But something about the woman before him made him stay his hand.

"Trust me when I say I will be fine. I've taken care of myself long before I came here." She smiled reassuringly.

He huffed, a long puff of air through his nose, as he closed his eyes and lowered his head. Annica knew he had relented.

"Open the gate for this one," he barked off to the side.

There was a moment's hesitation, but the iron portcullis began to lift. Other guards moved in to prevent anyone else from leaving, but no one moved forward. Annica was the only one who actually dared step out into the horrific scene that waited once the actual opportunity arose.

Once she passed the gate, her face became a steel mask. Her heart pounded in anger and fear as she stepped past the piles of heads. The buzzing of countless flies assailed her ears as the stench of death and blood filled her nose. She looked for the most direct route between the pools of dark, coagulated blood that formed beneath the piles. It struck her as odd that no scavenging animals had come for any of this. Perhaps even they were repelled by the sheer evil of the marauder's slaughter.

At the edge of the farmlands, she veered toward a cluster of small homes. The first thing she noticed was the lack of destruction. It was quiet, the chill wind through the wheat fields the only noise around. No pools or streaks of blood could be seen. She walked into one of the empty homes and only a toppled chair and broken vase showed evidence of a raid. She rummaged around and found a canteen and shoulder bag she could use to carry provisions for her trip.

She tried another home, just to see if things were the same. Again, the only sign that something was wrong was a small line of blood on the wall next to a bed. The other houses were all similar. The only disturbing trait they all shared was the lingering essence of dark—wretchedly dark—magic.

Annica gathered some food and water for her trip. She made sure to take enough so that she wouldn't have to risk foraging for anything since she was still unfamiliar with the surrounding area. She did still remember how to get back to the path where Pyotr pointed out the direction of the marauder's fortress, though.

The thought of what she was wearing didn't matter at the time she heard the alarm bells. She did remember to grab her coat, but the thinner work clothes made her legs cold on the trek through the forest. Thankfully the work boots were well insulated and the trees sheltered her from most of the wind. She remembered the walk with Pyotr was long, but it was her first time coming along that way. Hopefully, this time it would feel shorter. She tried remembering if they'd had to stop for the night, but the time between meeting Pyotr, journeying to his old village, and then coming to Kalthav had all blurred together.

Don't go that way. Head west here.

Annica stopped in her tracks. The voice, as usual, came from nowhere. She looked to where it instructed her to go and there appeared to be nothing but forest and snow-speckled, rocky terrain.

"I don't wish to get lost," Annica said flatly.

You won't. And you'll get to the fortress within the day.

Annica finished taking a drink from the canteen and huffed as she put it away. "I still don't know who you are, what you are and every time I ask, you—or whatever you are—stop speaking for days on end." She shook her head in frustration. "And here I am talking to myself in the woods. I've gone crazy, haven't I? I'm mad."

The silence hung for a moment. Annica expected to be on her own once again, but then the voice spoke softly and with the same level of confidence it always had.

You are not crazy. I have seen crazy. I've seen true madness. I'm someone who understands your power and your burden. The Fifth Magic binds us. Let me help you.

Annica closed her eyes and breathed. The true test would be the marauders and finding their location. If this voice truly led her to a shortcut, it would prove more trustworthy. Just in case, she began tearing strips from her shirt to tie around tree limbs. At least that would lead her back to the path. Then, she took off into the route suggested by the voice.

You're a smart girl. The feminine voice cooed as she tied a strip around the third tree on her walk. *But, I'm not going to lead you astray.*

Everything was quiet, including the voice, for several hours. When the sun began to get low on the western horizon, Annica saw the break in the treeline. It didn't stop suddenly nor drop down a steep hill like at Kalthav; rather, the trees thinned out over a long, flat plain. It was far less rocky and the land greener, signifying they were nearing the boundary of Carnelia. The location of this fort made more sense now. It was probably a staging ground and watchpoint during the days before the Rupture.

The roads around it had become long since overgrown and the fortress stood in the middle of a wide valley where the trees of the forest had finally all but dissipated entirely. It looked, from this distance, to be old but still formidable. A few crumbling sections of the wall stood out like old wounds, but not enough to topple the formidable structure.

Be careful. The voice warned. *They will be watching.*

Annica stuck to the trees as much as possible, watching for any signs of the vicious butchers. Pyotr said they hadn't been attacked by Kalthav in years, so if there were no other threats in the immediate area it would make sense if they let their guard down. They should at least have some sort of patrol, though.

Annica had a much better view of the fort and what the marauders had done to it. Strange, unfamiliar symbols had been crudely drawn in blood on the stone walls. Pikes stuck out of the ground and from the battlements, bearing what remained of some of the beheaded villagers. She felt bile rise into her mouth, burning her throat.

That's when she saw them. Two pairs of men in dirty armor and helmets covering the upper half of their faces circling the fortress in opposite directions. One pair was on the battlements of the second story while the other walked the grounds.

Even their movements looked off. They walked stiffly, without purpose, almost meandering with their lazy gait. Annica waited for the right moment when they were each the furthest away from her to move from one bunch of trees to the next, eventually having to move quickly from a single tree to another. The fortress was designed not to be snuck up on, after all. She was a single person, though, and should be able to get close without being noticed.

At one point, her foot kicked up a large, loose stone and sent it tumbling across the ground. She dropped, trying to hide just behind a rise in the ground. She could still see just the top of the second-story guards' heads, but they didn't seem to hear what had happened. They simply continued their patrol.

What's wrong with them? Annica wondered.

You're about to find out. The voice replied. Stand.

"Are you insane?" Annica whispered. Talking to the voice using her own inner thoughts made her feel even madder than talking to it out loud somehow.

Stand. The voice repeated, still confident and with no tone of impatience.

Annica took a breath and prepared to conjure her fire magic. She also thought herself insane for following a voice out to the home of these butchers. She probably deserved whatever fate awaited her, but if she could slim their numbers or if the voice was somehow correct and she could stop them, it would save a lot of people and she could go back to living her life with Pyotr and Lorna without fear of these monsters.

She stood to her feet, waiting for what would happen next. As soon as she did, both sets of guards turned their heads toward her. They stopped, then their bodies turned so they were fully facing her. One reached down slowly with his black-gloved hand and removed a horn from his belt, cracked down the middle with a strap that was barely holding together.

He put the horn to his mouth, again in a slow, deliberate fashion. A shrill, broken, and ominous sound came from it. He returned the horn to his belt. He moved with all the speed of one completely unconcerned with her presence.

After a few moments, more of them walked out of the fortress, both on the upper battlements and the ground floor. She counted fifteen, all in dirty armor with black gloves. Some had the half-helmets of the guards, while others wore the kind that covered their entire faces. Some wore cloaks so filthy she couldn't tell if they were naturally brown and black or were covered in layers of grime. None of them appeared to be the leader. They all looked and acted similarly.

Annica simply waited. She couldn't reach them from here with any of her magic, save for the Fifth, and she certainly didn't want to help them in any way. The marauders, in turn, simply stood there making no movement towards her, hostile or otherwise. They didn't even draw their weapons. It was eerie and unsettling as their faceless gazes continued to look silently at her.

Use the Fifth Magic. Reach out to them. Hear them.

"Why?" Annica replied, confused.

Because they will not call out to you. They cannot.

"How do you know this?"

Because I know whom they serve.

Annica's whole body tensed. Her fear turned even sourer, intensified by terrible memories.

"Is it Bac'thule?"

Have you ever known a follower of Bac'thule to behave in such a manner?

Annica didn't reply immediately. "I only have limited but very personal knowledge of them. I wouldn't put pure butchery above them."

The voice didn't reply. Annica shook her head slightly in irritation, then she began slowly pulling away the veil that covered her powers of the Fifth Sect. Much like when she tried to reach out and sense any presence on Storm's Pillar, she spread her senses out with the magic. In Nel Aldyri, when she'd first done this, she could feel the presence of people, their emotions, and sometimes even hear them. This is what she tried now. The marauders and their fort were well within her range of capabilities.

She closed her eyes and focused on the sensations the Fifth Magic provided her. The marauders remained in place. When their presence became felt, Annica shuddered. She began to sweat and felt like her insides were on fire. She almost cried out but forced her mouth shut by clenching her teeth together almost painfully. As more and more the blistering hot presences came into focus, she finally let out a pained gasp. It was like white-hot coals burned within the comfortable warmth of her own magic.

She reached further into the fort and felt no one else there. They must have all come outside at the sound of the horn. Fighting through the pain, Annica felt there was more below the ground level. She sensed something different down there. Focusing her magic into some kind of basement area, she felt two other presences. They were in pain, their minds screaming out. The wicks of their lives were flickering out, barely holding on. The core of their being was also glowing white hot like the marauders themselves.

Pain.

The word came to her like a whisper. It was not the confident, feminine sound of the mysterious voice. It hissed and spit like a cup of water thrown onto a raging fire.

Gut them. Rip them.

More sinister, angry whispers joined in. They became a cacophony of harsh, guttural cries that sounded as though they came from men being strangled: shouting as loud as they could from broken throats.

Burn them. Maul them. Rape them. Rip them. Bleed them. Scorch them. Sear them.

Annica dropped to her knees. The magic recoiled back within her and she breathed in heavy, wheezing gasps. The essence of those men, if that's what they still were, was saturated in evil magic. It felt similar to what infested the belly of Nel Aldyri: old, vile, and inexplicable. It was also different; the sensation burned hotter than anything she could have ever imagined. It was angry with a rage that made her heart want to explode and caused her to sweat; such was the fury that crawled through her blood.

The marauders radiated wrath and hate. She could feel their abhorrence for the city and any every living thing they had ever and would ever come across. The influence over them was complete. The voice said that it knew whom they served; it had to be another Inheritor.

"They worship one of Them, don't they? Those men worship an Inheritor."

Her words punctuated the long, deep breaths she had to take. Though her lungs no longer burned, they still felt as though some source of extreme heat had sucked the air from her.

I wouldn't say worship, although they certainly serve One. The Baleful Forge of the Obscured Throne. These men serve it, their lives coals forged for Its use.

Annica's heart continued to pound, in part from sensing the presence of this other Inheritor and also from the panic she began to feel. If these men were bound to an outside entity that was literally some sort of living forge, and that would make perfect sense given her experience with these Inheritors and their servants, it made her doubt they could even be hurt with her fire magic. If that was the case, she would have to flee from here immediately.

They are still human. They can be hurt by many things—including fire.

Annica stood again and shrieked reflexively when she saw two of them almost halfway to where she stood, walking in their strange, casual manner. She also saw that they weren't wearing black gloves, it was their hands and forearms themselves that were blackened like they'd been covered in soot or shoved in a fire until their skin cooked. Charred bone exposed itself in places, especially near the fingers. Her heart shuddered.

Now, Annica. You need to destroy them before they reach you!

She gritted her teeth, her eyes wide with fear, and remembered suddenly how difficult it was in this cold weather to even conjure enough power to light a campfire, let alone enough to kill two grown men. Annica remembered the heat radiating from within the men themselves. She focused on that heat and commanded it to grow. The white-hot aura within the marauder's bodies grew until it engulfed them. The men themselves, their flesh, armor, and clothing, combusted into a roaring flame. They took a few more steps before falling to their knees and then collapsing to the ground.

Annica caught her breath. Perhaps she could destroy these monsters down to the very last one, after all. It was her turn to approach them. She slowly stepped closer to the marauders, gathering all the confidence she could muster. They drew their weapons silently, patiently; all the while, their terrible desires repeated in her head: *Gut them. Burn them. Rip them. Rape them. Scorch them.*

The heat continued to radiate with them. She reached out to stoke that burning aura and light the closest of these monsters aflame. The magic stalled. She could feel it, but it wouldn't cooperate with her commands. Her concentration flickered, and her breathing quickened. The marauder began walking towards her with his sword, caked in dried blood, drawn and held at his side.

You need different magic.

"I don't know what's happening," she said in a low, harsh tone.

Use the First Sect. Raw magic. Practically any mage can.

Annica grimaced. "Not me. I've tried."

Then let me help you, the voice said without hesitation. *Focus on the one coming toward you. Look at him. Stare into him, through him. Reach out, palm open, and then ball your fist like you wish to crush him like rotten fruit while using the words* Pondux Monde*. I'll channel the magic. Do it now.*

Annica followed the instructions, not expecting much to happen. Her talents with the First Sect were all but non-existent. Her time at Nel Aldyri proved that.

She stuck out her hand, palm outward, then recited the

words while balling her hand into a fist. She imagined crushing the fiend before her like a ripe tomato. A tingle vibrated in the back of her mind. The sensation was different than the Second Magic she had been using. Her hand felt like she had fallen asleep on her arm and woken up to feel it tingling and throbbing, though this wasn't painful and she had full use of her fingers.

She heard a sound like a giant suddenly inhaling sharply. What happened next was hard for her to describe. The man simply collapsed in upon himself. His limbs contorted in unimaginable ways. His armor buckled, creaked, and groaned as it crumpled in on its wearer. Blood sprayed from wherever it could before the magic grabbed hold of every part of the former marauder and crunched him into a ball of collapsed metal and flesh.

Annica gasped. The marauder didn't even have time to scream. Her closed fist before her began to shake, but she was too shocked to move.

Move as though you are throwing that grotesque chunk along with the incantation, Ikineti. *Now.*

Annica stuttered at first, still recovering from the shock of the former spell. The next closest marauder began stalking toward her, followed closely by another.

Now! the voice barked.

Annica cast another unknown spell, letting the voice channel the power needed to fuel the First Sect magic. The melon-sized ball of bloody metal flew toward the closest marauder and struck him so hard in the head that his helmet flew off. He staggered, nearly dropping to his knees. His neck was now permanently bent at an odd angle, but he continued forward.

She stared in horror when she saw them up close. The one who'd lost his helmet sneered, and she saw blackened teeth that oozed a dark substance from his inflamed gums. His eyes were surrounded by something that looked like soot, while the sockets themselves were empty save for a burning, furnace-like glow. She wanted to scream, but it caught in her throat.

The first spell, use it again. Pondux Monde *is the incantation.*

The voice was stern but neither frightened nor hurried. Annica repeated the movements, said the words, and felt her whole body tingle with the strange sensation. The foreboding, sharp, inhaling sound returned. This time, both of the men before her were immediately crushed into gore-coated orbs of rusty metal. Some of the copious amounts of blood splattered onto Annica, and she nearly emptied her stomach.

There are still many left, the voice commented.

"I can't keep using that spell," Annica said, practically vomiting up the words.

It's ok; it's quite draining. Try using the Third Sect again.

Annica desperately wanted this to be over. The last time she felt this way, she ignited an entire room, followed by a whole city. Perhaps that's why the fire magic worked so well for her; her desperation and passion drove it to incredible limits. She didn't know and thought to ask the voice about it after leaving this place forever.

Nearly a dozen damned souls stared at her, no doubt with those burning, hateful, and empty eyes. The men on the battlements continued their horrible mantra while the ones on the ground drew their weapons and began their approach.

Annica pushed away the tingling sensation in her body and focused once more on the burning auras surrounding her. Tears welled in her eyes at the thought of being taken alive, at joining in whatever unthinkable fate awaited her within those tainted walls along with the other two women. Her anger rose as she remembered the piles of heads—men, women, children, young and old, and all their animals—left as threats and blood-soaked promises to the people of Kalthav. These are the men that did it. Why did she feel sorry for them when the spell the voice helped her cast crushed them before her? They were no longer men but servants of another Inheritor; the Baleful Forge. Just like Black Gnarl. Just like Gideon.

She screamed, finally letting her anguish and anger out. All that she'd held in and tried to hide in front of strangers-turned-friends had been released. She tried to be strong in a different way but now unleashed that strength in the form of her barely contained Third Magic; her innate talent with fire. She smirked at the thought: fighting fire with fire. Let hers burn stronger.

The remaining marauders ignited, the flames catching as though they were doused in oil. Still, they refused to, or were incapable of screaming or crying out. They simply fell where they stood or dropped to their knees before collapsing as they walked. Their armor blackened from the ferocity of the flames. The last of the marauders, the servants of the Baleful Forge, had been consumed in fire.

As the dreadful bonfires burned around her, Annica remembered the women still held captive in the fortress. She swallowed hard, trying to find her courage. The halls of that small but corrupted structure waited for her. Her mind flashed back to the tunnels and the true temple of Bac'thule below the surface of Nel Aldyri. The darkness and the lingering stain of the potent Fourth Magic that saturated the place still resonated within her.

She kept her magic ready, drawing on the fires around her to prepare another conjuration of flame just in case any marauders lay in waiting. Although, that would be very unlikely given she didn't sense any before. Only the two prisoners should be left.

The gate to the fortress remained open, a small structure just big enough for a man and horse to enter through. The marauders either lacked the martial knowledge to keep it closed or, more disturbingly, didn't care. The fort was little more than a square wall surrounding a small two-story keep and stables. Stairs led up to the wall's battlements where a few of the human-fed fires burned alongside the beheaded bodies hung up like grisly banners.

The wooden double doors to the keep were cracked open. Death itself seemed to seep from within. Annica pushed the door open slowly. Inside, there was nothing to provide any light. The burning eyes of the marauders probably didn't need light to see, if they truly saw anything and weren't just puppets of this Baleful Forge, led around on infernal strings.

She opened the doors fully, letting in as much light as possible in the waning hours of the day. She could just make out the decrepit remains of tables, chairs, shelves, and other things one would expect to find within a small outlying military structure. Torches sat in sconces around the walls, while a few candelabras sat unlit on some of the tables. She approached each of them and lit them using her magic, a simple flick of her hand. The room became illuminated in a yellow glow, which seemed to only enhance the dreariness of the place. Skeletons lay against the wall in the clothes or armor they died in, likely the original inhabitants before the marauders came.

Annica remembered that the women were held below in some lower areas. She didn't want to reach out with the Fifth Magic again, so she grabbed a candelabra and looked for a stairway. Her search revealed a few grisly surprises when she found more skeletal remains. Also, there was no food or signs of fresh water anywhere. The true nature of what the marauders became began to trouble her even more.

She found the stairs to the lower areas in the rear of the fortress at the end of an L-shaped hallway. The structure was laid out very plainly, with nothing but efficiency in mind. The stairs led down to a second floor that looked to be a barracks of some kind. After lighting a few more sconces, it was revealed to be a single, open floor filled with beds. Annica's heart began to pound; memories of bodies on tables and root-covered walls crawled back to the front of her mind. This, thankfully, appeared to be nothing more than a dirty, unkempt room full of normal beds.

She didn't see anyone on this floor. It was quiet, dark, and empty. After looking around, she found another set of stairs in the opposite corner of the first set. The darkness below radiated with something familiar to her, something old and terrifying. It came upon her so strongly that she stopped in her tracks. The dark almost seemed to taunt her.

We have to go down, Annica.

The voice was right. She had to collect herself, shrug off the fear as she had done so many times, and confront what waited in the darkness. There were two people suffering while she stood there afraid.

Her footsteps echoed on the stones as she descended. She steeled her nerves against the darkness that hung at the edge of the candlelight like a living thing, much like it had under the Temple of the First Son. The darkness here was smothering, a cloying thing that despised the light and the living.

A torch, unlit like all the others, sat in a sconce half-fallen from the wall at the base of the stairs. She lit it and looked for others. After lighting two more, there was enough visibility to see two bodies lying naked on a pile of rags, banners, bedsheets, and other random pieces of cloth. They were covered in scars, bruises, burns, and fluids.

Tears ran suddenly and unexpectedly down Annica's face. She let out a stifled cry and covered her mouth. Her body went numb and she nearly dropped the candelabra before running over to be next to them. They lay perfectly still, their chests barely moving. Annica unveiled her Fifth Magic again, reaching out to find their life essences barely clinging on. She also felt pain, so much physical and mental pain that the tears flowed even harder.

"Why are they here? Did those monsters just want to torture them?"

They were going to serve some purpose, surely, if those marauders were puppets of an Inheritor, the voice said in a calm, flat tone.

The presence of the women's life energies continued to grow dim. They were slipping away.

"I have to save them," Annica said in a desperate whisper.

You can't, Annica. I can feel their presence through you. They're dying.

"No, I can't let them die here," she said, kneeling down and taking one of them by the hand. It felt cold and clammy to the touch.

You can tell, the voice commented. *She is dying. A merciful death is all you can offer now. They deserve peace.*

Annica clenched her eyes shut. "I...I can't kill them. What can I do? Slit their throats? *Burn* them? Crush them like those beasts upstairs? Gods, no...I won't do it."

There are gentler ways, Annica, the voice said softly. *The Fifth Sect, its magic connected to the life of this world, you can gently snuff a light out. No pain. No suffering. Just slip into the dark of eternal sleep. Their families are already dead. Let them be together.*

Annica sobbed. She thought about what the voice, with such empathy and assurance, had said. She knew it was probably the best way. That's when she wept. The aura of life belonging to the two women grew dimmer and dimmer, but Annica knew it would be a long night or more of suffering before they passed on their own. She felt echoes of their pain and they would suffer for long hours before coming to their eternal rest on their own.

She held each of their hands as she sat between them. At least they could feel one gentle touch as they left this world. She wrapped the warm glow of the Fifth around their life energies, and sent soothing sensations to them. The painful echoes dulled. Then, giving their hands a soft squeeze, she snuffed out what was left of them. It happened in an instant. The room, despite the torches being lit, felt suddenly much darker.

Their arms were already limp, but after Annica's act of mercy, what was left of their strength disappeared and she felt their arms go heavy with the added weight of death. Annica wept louder, tears falling from her face as she doubled over, nearly touching her head to the floor. It felt wrong. Her whole body trembled. It felt like the world trembled with her.

Annica felt a cold, stale-smelling breeze ruffle her hair. She choked back her tears and looked behind her quickly. Nothing was there but a deep, black hole staring back at her. She must not have noticed it in her shock and grief at finding the prisoners. It also blended into the dark stone quite well. It was roughly dug out, with some broken stones, rubble, and dirt at its base.

She put the candelabra in front of her and approached it slowly. The light did nothing there. All she could tell was that a tunnel ran sharply down into the earth. That old and vile essence amplified within that dark tunnel and Annica recoiled immediately.

"Who did this? Or...what?"

Dwarves, the voice answered quickly. *Well, what used to be dwarves. You do not want to go down there.*

"No," came Annica's sharp reply. "No, I don't."

She returned to the prisoners, regretted not knowing their names, placed their arms over their chests, and situated them in a more appropriate funerary manner. She covered one in a banner and one in a bedsheet, both that she'd found on the floor. Then, she lit the pile of cloth with one of the torches, giving them the decency of a funeral pyre and leaving nothing behind for any Inheritors, monsters, or beasts.

Annica tossed the candelabra on the floor unceremoniously

on her way out. She grabbed a torch, knowing that daylight was disappearing and night would soon come. It was a full day's walk back to Kalthav using the route the voice had provided, but she wouldn't travel at night. She'd have to camp out tonight and return tomorrow. She wouldn't linger near this place, however. She'd return to the forest first.

"Something should be done about this fortress," she said, addressing the voice. "Especially with that strange tunnel in the basement."

Inform the guard upon your return. They'll handle the old Kalthavian fort however they see fit, and are better equipped to do so.

Annica silently agreed and made her way for the trees. She only had about an hour of daylight left and went immediately to work, looking for a suitable spot to spend the night. The terrain on this secret route was quite rocky, and she found an overhang surrounded by a particularly thick gathering of fir trees to take shelter under. She started a fire and settled in for the night.

Sitting close to the warmth of the flames and wrapped tightly in her coat, Annica tried to put the events of the day out of her mind. The morbid state of the marauders and the horrible suffering of the prisoners was enough to weigh her soul to the ground. Worse still, she learned of the existence of another Inheritor. It didn't surprise her that there were more of Them, but the level of Their wickedness and creativity in pain and suffering did.

"Why does that...thing, the Obscured Throne," she said, hesitating to even mention the name of It out loud, "why does it need a forge of any kind?"

Gideon had revealed much to her about what the Black Gnarl knew of the fearsome entity, but every bit of knowledge only raised more questions. Each answer was also more terrible than the last.

The Baleful Forge, the voice said, seeming to reminisce, *It's another extension of the Obscured Throne. All Inheritors are. After all, are children not some sort of extension of their parents with wills and minds of their own? That's a rudimentary explanation, of course, as the Obscured Throne and its Inheritors are simply beyond our comprehension, but, well, the Throne both creates and destroys. The Baleful Forge represents that part of the Throne.*

Annica rubbed her face with her hands, feeling sleep coming on quickly.

"The Throne isn't a single entity, then?"

Yes and no. The Throne is indeed a cosmic miasma of sentient malice, pain, hate, creation, destruction...but the Inheritors are, to a degree, a tangible representation of Its many traits. Although, even They are only so tangible.

Annica groaned, her mind and body tired. The more she thought about the greater beings that tore at the world, the more she simply wanted to let it all be. Live her life in Kalthav and then leave the world to its fate. She'd tried being something special, someone with a rare magic that could help others, but all that had brought her and those around her was pain and suffering.

She felt bad about thinking such things, given the nature of her magical potential with the Fifth. Now that her mind had turned to such thoughts, however, something felt off. Her connection with the Fifth Sect felt just slightly different. Perhaps it was the trauma of having to do what she did to end the suffering of those women. The trauma and essence of their pain still lingered within her.

Annica decided to get some sleep. The next morning she would return to Kalthav and report that the marauders would murder no more of their people. Perhaps Pyotr will have returned. She smiled at the thought of seeing the old man and Lorna again, returning to some sense of normalcy. Annica let her mind linger on these thoughts as she drifted off to sleep.

Part VI

When Annica breached the treeline facing Kalthav and looked down the steep, rocky slopes of the hill before the farmlands, she saw a sad, quiet countryside. The Kalthavians made quick work of gathering the gruesome piles of heads. The land had been cleansed of the blood as much as possible.

Only a handful of people worked the fields as Annica passed the gray-blue wheat along the road to Cliff's Pillar. Likely, they were the family of the slain who lived behind the walls and wanted to tend their crops as best they could. Each of them that was near enough stopped and stared at Annica as she passed. She walked almost trance-like to the gate, feeling a dark presence amplified along that road.

The guards at the gate looked at her with wide eyes and gripped their weapons. Annica stopped and furrowed her brows. She expected heightened security and nerves, but this seemed a little hostile for someone who'd come and gone from this gate before.

"Miss, are you alright?" one of them asked.

Annica wasn't sure how to answer. Why would they ask? Her clothes may have seen better days since she'd been traveling for two days and camped overnight, but nothing too extreme. Then, Annica remembered the blood. The splatter from one of the crushed marauders was still on her clothes, possibly still on her face. She put a hand over a large patch of the dried blood on her coat, now ruined, and sighed.

"I'm fine. This isn't my blood." The guards took a step back, gripping their weapons tighter. "It's the marauders'."

The two men looked at each other. When they turned back to her, they were obviously incredulous. Then one scratched the side of his nose and nodded his head.

"You ran into them and escaped; how did his blood get on you? And so much..." he said, assuming he'd solved the mystery.

"They're dead. All of them. So are the two women they captured a few days ago. The fort is empty and they'll bother the town no longer. I would recommend sending someone to demolish it and let it stay buried."

The guards looked at each other again. The one who hadn't spoken yet shook his head in disbelief. "A waif like you killed a fortress of marauders where a whole platoon could not?"

"Go see for yourselves," Annica replied flatly. "It makes no difference to me. I would like to be let back in, though. I'm hoping Pyotr's returned."

"He hasn't," the one on the right said. "But, firstly, we'd need to see your papers to get through the gate and that's without considering that we'd need to investigate your claims. If true, the royal family would be very interested."

Annica crossed her arms. At first, she was annoyed but realized this may be her chance to finally get into the castle.

"You'll take me to the royal family, then?" she said expectantly.

Both guards were quiet for a moment, then one of them said, "Wait here."

He motioned for the gate to be opened, left, and was gone for some time. The remaining guard offered her a seat, bringing out a stool from the gatehouse along with a mug of water. He stood at his post, not saying a word to Annica. They both waited what felt like hours for the other guard to return. It seemed no one was interested in leaving the city today as not once did a citizen leave through the gates, nor did one of those working the fields come in during the time she waited.

When the gate started to squeal and complain again, she turned to see the guard return along with four of the more heavily armored royal guards. The gate guard simply returned to his post, casting Annica a curious glance as he did so. One of the royal guards, his red beard jutting beneath his half-helmet, looked at Annica and spoke in a stern tone, "We're to escort you to the Haakonsen Castle. Ask no questions as you'll receive no answers. The king and queen will see you after you've been prepared."

"Prepared?" Annica questioned with a slight sneer.

The guards, as promised, didn't answer her. They took positions around her and ordered her to walk. Feeling little room for argument, she followed them through town, passed the gate to the Drottinsvegur, and through to the Lord's Pillar. People stared along the way, curious as to the new excitement following yesterday's dreadful events. The nobles of the Lord's Pillar were particularly interested. Whispers followed her all the way to the castle gate.

The guards posted at the gate's entrance pivoted to the side without hesitation. The two at the front of the procession opened the gate, with the guard on the left inserting and twisting an old, ornate key into a large lock and both pushing on the large iron-wrought doors. Annica frowned as they walked through. She'd tried for weeks to get into the castle using every means, but force and now was quite literally being walked in.

She made sure to look at the statues as they walked past, her head whipping around to see each one. They were carved from stone heavily veined with white quartz. The detail was such that the visible wrinkles made their smooth carved eyes look eerily alive. They were all majestic and powerful to behold.

The procession continued up a flight of wide stairs that narrowed as it drew closer to an archway that led into an enclosed courtyard. Cold-resistant ivy climbed up the walls and over the edges where a clear sky opened the space to light during the day and the stars at night. Shrubs and small evergreens placed in patterns around the courtyard proved the talent of the architect who designed the castle so long ago. Annica felt lingering traces of the Third Sect here. Whoever built the court-yard or tended it must have used magic to some degree.

The ornate doors to the castle's entrance were further guarded, and they opened the way for the procession to enter. The first room was a visitor's chamber, decorated with red and blue banners that Annica recognized as belonging to the Haakonsen family and a different set that she assumed to be the banners of Kalthav itself. A thick red rug covered most of the floor. Plush chairs and couches and fine furniture filled the room. Golden candelabras provided light. All this was intended to keep waiting guests of the royal family comfortable. Annica wondered how often it was actually used. All the furniture, banners, and the massive rug made Annica feel stuffy and uncomfortable.

The guards offered Annica a seat in one of the nice chairs, which she accepted. It seemed she wasn't under arrest as they treated her sternly but kindly; their orders were spoken in a manner meant to be followed, but they never shouted and they didn't once raise their weapons or fists at her.

She didn't wait long before a man in fine robes stepped through the door opposite the entrance and said that the king and queen would see her now. He retreated back through the doors, leaving them open. The guards instructed Annica to stand and follow.

They passed through the open doors into an intersection of two hallways. The same color and style of red rug—now long, narrow runners rather than a single, room-enveloping square— also covered the floors here. The corridor to each side led to stairways, where the one before them, where they continued to walk, held another set of double doors, more guards, and was opened to what looked like a large room beyond. The man in the robes stood beside one of the doors as they entered the Haakonsen throne room.

Where the rest of the castle had so far felt slightly claustrophobic, this room sought to swallow anyone who entered its grandness. The second story of the castle also fed into this room, with balustrades lining all four sides. Pillars held the balconies of the second floor aloft, and the red runner from the hallway led all the way to the dais where the four thrones of the Haakonsen royal family sat. Large windows interspersed the pillars and ran from the floor to the ceiling below the balustrades, letting light flood the room.

Sitting before the dais was a chair for Annica. It wasn't as plush as those in the visitor's chamber but still made of finely carved wood with a cushion set on it for her comfort. It appeared to be more of an interview than an interrogation, she hoped.

Sitting on the two central thrones were the king and queen. They looked as royal as one would expect, though the hard years seemed to be worn clearly on their faces and expressions. At the right of the king sat a young man, likely in his early twenties, wearing rich clothes; the prince. A young woman, older than the prince, wearing a dress similar to the one Lorna made for Annica but red in color with blue accents and gold trim, sat to the left of the queen: the princess of Kalthav. Annica was officially meeting the current line of Haakonsens. She took a deep breath. At this moment, she wasn't sure what was more intimidating: when she first met Helen, the archpriestess of Nel Aldyri's doomed and treacherous temple of the First Son, or this royalty.

The guards stopped, along with Annica, a few feet from the chair. Annica clasped her hands in front of her and looked towards the royal family, gazing at all of them at once and none in particular. She nodded her head in a slight bow, not quite sure what else to do.

"You're polite," The king said, his voice nasally but resonant and thick with the Kalthavian accent. He sounded like someone you wanted to listen to. "There are more unpleasant ways to start a conversation. Please, take a seat," he continued.

As Annica sat down, the king tilted his head and made a motion with his hand. The sound of the doors closing echoed behind her, followed by the sounds of the guards' footsteps fading and then stopping. She didn't turn around, fearing to look rude, but assumed the guards remained in the room.

"Please, give us your name," the king asked politely.

Annica took a small breath. "Annica," she replied firmly.

"Just Annica?" the queen asked, her voice breathy and also calming and motherly in its tone and inflections. "No family name?"

"Just Annica, I'm afraid. No need for family names where I come from," Annica answered plainly.

The king smiled. "So says most who come our way from the outside world. Many would say the same of kings, anymore."

Annica shifted in her seat. Not one to mince words, she asked as politely as she could, "May I ask why you've brought me here, Your Grace?"

"Well-spoken. And you know how to address royalty, still. Articulate and beautiful, just like a young lady our guards at the outer gate said has visited us several times recently to see the castle grounds." The queen said as she regarded Annica with curiosity.

"But where are *our* manners?" the king interjected. "I'm King Trajolf Haakonsen," he said, then placed a hand on one of the queen's own. "My wife, Queen Vorna Haakonsen. Beside us is my son: the prince, Lavdor, and my daughter, the princess, Larna."

"It's a pleasure to meet you," Annica said nervously. "But, that still leaves my question..."

"Of course," the king replied. "We are obviously curious about your story involving those bestial men in the fortress and their alleged demise," he continued, as the princess lowered her head uncomfortably and the prince glowered at the mention of the marauders.

"Kalthav lost many good men and women to them, especially the soldiers we've sent to clear them out. But...you? A young woman, all alone, returns covered in blood," he said while motioning his hand towards her, "and says you have destroyed them to a man?"

"I told your guards they could send someone to see for themselves. I'm not lying."

"We're not saying you are," the queen answered reassuringly. "We've dispatched riders to investigate your claim. They should return tomorrow; we told them to ride through the night if they have to. We want to get to the bottom of this quickly."

"I understand," Annica said. "What will you do with me until then?"

"You will remain here as a guest of the royal family. You will be placed under guard, of course. I hope you understand," the king explained.

Annica let out a soft sigh. "I do."

"Until then, you will be allowed to bathe, provided clothes and food, and given a room until the scouts return, whereupon we shall have another conversation depending on what they report."

Annica simply nodded in reply. The king tilted his head again and motioned for the guards.

All four of them returned, inviting her to stand. The fine-robed gentleman was also present among them.

"Sfen, here, will attend to your needs," the queen said kindly.

This man is a mage. The voice said, returning suddenly.

Annica made no visible reaction to the revelation. She simply followed the guards and did as instructed. They led her to a room where she could bathe and clean herself, and where clean clothes were available to her. Sfen was waiting with one other guard by the time she came out of the bathing room, and told her he'd be escorting her to the chamber she could eat and sleep in.

On their way to her temporary room, Annica asked Sfen, "You're a mage, aren't you?"

Her tone was casual and she continued to face forward. She wanted to be non-threatening but was now in unfamiliar territory surrounded by armed men and another wielder of magic, if the voice was correct.

"Very astute," Sfen replied, his voice old and raspy. His mouth barely moved when he spoke. His wispy gray beard not moving at all. "How did you know that?"

"You have the look of one," Annica replied carefully, not revealing the whole truth.

"You've seen many magi in your travels?"

"Very many," Annica said flatly.

"I would certainly like to know more," he said, his inflection betraying his piqued curiosity. "But I suppose that can wait until the scouts return. I also will not keep you from your meal. Enjoy the food; wine has also been provided for you. There are books you are free to enjoy in the room, as well, as you seem to be literate."

They reached a door at the end of the hallway and stopped, Sfen unlocking and opening it for her. He bowed his head and motioned for her to enter. She thanked him quietly and walked into the room. The door closed and she heard a soft click as it was locked behind her.

Heaving a deep sigh, Annica looked around. It was nicer than any other room she'd been in thus far in her life. Food, still steaming hot, sat next to a bottle of wine on a table in the room's center. A bed so thick it looked to swallow her sat next to the wall. She could see out of a window on the wall to the ocean outside. It was a wonderful view. She tested it and was happy to find the window opened outward. There would be no escape as, from this point on the wall, it plunged straight into the cliffs and sea below. This part of the castle was built into the wall itself. They certainly put her here on purpose so she couldn't flee.

It was fine. The scouts would see she wasn't lying, Annica would explain the situation, and she would begin to find answers so that she could hopefully return to Pyotr and Lorna. Life could go on. She would do anything to make that happen.

She enjoyed the food and the wine. She left the window open to let the chill, salty air flow through the room, and found a book to read while covered with the thick, wonderful blankets of the bed. As night fell, she set the book aside, neither enjoying it nor bored by it, and removed her clothes so she wouldn't wrinkle them in her sleep. They were what she might be wearing to see the royal family again, and she didn't want to appear disheveled. She crawled into bed to listen to the sounds of the ocean as she fell asleep. The muffled sound of the waves, accompanied by a soft wind, caused her to drift off rather quickly. She embraced the warm comfort of the darkness as it overtook her, the bed and sheets embracing her as unconsciousness took hold.

The strange, distant storms continued in her dreams, still tinted red. They seemed to move closer this time, too.

THE NEXT MORNING, Annica awoke to the smell of breakfast. She rose from her bed, light from the window illuminating her room with the morning sun. What disturbed her was the fact that the window was closed. Breakfast was also sitting on the table; ham steak and a bowl of porridge steaming next to a glass goblet of water.

They came in and I didn't wake up? Annica thought to herself.

The first thing she thought was that she slept more heavily because of the comfortable bed. The other possibility caused her to become aggravated; they used magic.

A sleep spell. The voice said as Annica got dressed. *That Sfen fellow likely brought your food after casting the spell. It's late morning already.*

"Damn it," Annica said under her breath. She sat down and ate, making sure to take advantage of the food while she was locked away. After she'd finished, she opened the window again and leaned on the frame, looking out over the ocean. It stretched out forever, heavy clouds rising on the horizon.

She knocked on the door, but no one answered. She hoped they weren't just going to leave her here alone, but supposed there were worst places to be incarcerated. She perused some of the books again for a while, taking an interest in those with maps and other information from the world that was. She often wondered what it was like back then and how closely Kalthavian life resembled it now.

After getting lost in another book for a while, she began to feel tired. She yawned and put the book down. The bed looked very tempting, but it was only midday, judging by the light outside.

Another spell. You might as well lie down before you collapse. You'll either wake up with more food or in a dungeon. Either is likely. The voice said in a matter-of-fact tone.

"I can't stop it?" Annica responded while yawning again.

Perhaps, if I'd trained you. The voice replied in the same tone.

Annica cursed quietly and lay down on the bed. Within moments she was asleep, sure that she'd blacked out before even hitting the cushion. The magic-induced sleep seemed to suppress any nightmares or dreams. She only remembered waking up sometime later, the sun lower in the sky, and her breakfast replaced with a small, whole chicken and vegetables with more wine.

"Son of a bitch," she whispered harshly. It was like they were keeping her mollified until the scouts returned with their report. The food smelled too good, however, and she was hungry after sleeping for the rest of the day.

The chicken was moist, with crispy skin. The seasonings she couldn't even begin to describe. The vegetables were well-prepared and the wine was white and flowery. She was likely the most pampered prisoner imaginable. As she was finishing up the meal, the lock to her door clicked. Her head swung over to see it open slowly, Sfen entering and multiple guards standing outside.

"I hope you've enjoyed the meals," he said. "I apologize for my methods, but the safety of the royal family is paramount, and we are dealing with far too many unknowns."

"I see," Annica answered simply. She didn't want to say much more, especially since it would likely be her giving voice to her frustrations when there was little she could do about it.

An uncomfortable silence hung in the air for a moment when Sfen finally said, "The riders have returned and given their report. The royal family would like to see you again."

Annica nodded. She stood and unruffled her clothing. Sfen stepped aside and motioned for her to exit the room. She stepped out and into the middle of four guards, once again, as Sfen closed and locked the door.

The royal family waited in the throne room. When Annica entered, they were sitting on their thrones and turned to look at her as she entered with the procession. The same chair sat in front of the dais. She didn't quite know what to make of this. She took a seat at the king's insistence.

"It appears you tell the truth. The wicked men of that soiled fortress are all dead," the king said, a note of surprise in his voice.

"As I said," Annica replied politely, "I'm not here to deceive. I've met some wonderful people in your city and wish it no harm. I only wanted to help."

"And we can certainly discuss our gratitude later," the king continued, "but the question still remains: how?"

Annica nervously clasped her hands in front of her.

Careful, the voice warned.

Annica explained that after the attacks on the farmlands, she was angry that such evil threatened what she considered her new home. She'd come from a place that had already been destroyed by malevolent people and didn't want to see the same thing happen here.

The king leaned forward, placing a hand on one of his knees. His face grew stern. "But *how*, young lady? The scouts say that the men were burned until their bones were barely holding together, others were naught but piles of metal and..." he grimaced at the description of what the voice's other spell had done, "other things. Was that all you? Tell it whole and tell it truthfully."

"I'm a mage," Annica answered, hoping that helped explain. She didn't look at Sfen to see his reaction. "I killed them all using my magic. I studied it in the place I came from; there was a temple and academy there and I studied directly under the arch-priestess."

The queen raised an eyebrow. "Strange, a priestess teaching such magic."

"It was a strange place," Annica added. "It was destroyed by a strange group of awful people; I wasn't going to let that happen again. I only wish I had done something before they murdered everyone in the farmlands."

The king nodded, his face softening and growing heavy at the thought. "It's going to take time to replenish what we've lost. Well, no more of them were found in the fortress. We assume you already knew that. Were the women dead when you found them?"

Annica dropped her head slightly. Genuine hurt filled her words as she answered. "There was nothing to be done for them. They were dying. I tried to make their passing as quick and painless as possible."

She took a deep breath, her heart breaking at the memory. The king saw her empathy and shook his head. Life was hard for everyone trying to live anymore. He couldn't blame her for ending the suffering of two tortured captives.

"That is a shame. That must have been hard."

Annica sniffed and nodded her head.

"I can't hold blame over you for showing mercy to the suffering," the king said as he leaned back in his throne. "You must be a powerful mage to have handled them all."

Annica shrugged, happy for the subject to shift. "I have some talent, yes."

"We found a tunnel below the fortress, in the room with the women. Do you know anything about that?"

Annica raised her head. She remembered the voice's warning.

"No, but I, as a mage, felt something awful radiating from it. I wouldn't send anyone down there, ever."

The king shook his head. "We don't plan to. That place is

cursed, always has been. We're already making arrangements to have it torn to the ground, burying everything."

"Good," Annica said, nodding.

"I've had my men asking questions. It seems you have taken shelter with our resident jeweler, Pyotr Kilfersen."

Annica hesitated. She never knew Pyotr's last name; she'd never asked. The same went for Lorna. She smirked. Perhaps last names weren't as commonly used among the common folk as they were nobility and royalty.

"Yes. He's been very kind."

The king smiled. "Good. Very good. We'll summon him to discuss future plans for you. A talented mage should be doing more than polishing jewelry; we can find him a suitable apprentice if he likes."

"Future plans for me?" Annica asked, concern apparent in her voice.

The king raised a hand. "Don't worry. You're going to be well taken care of. Sfen is talented as well, but we have precious few who know how to use magic anymore. As you can imagine, Kalthav's magi received the same horrible treatment as the rest of Alda's around the time of the Rupture. I would like to undo as much of that as possible if I can. I also want you and Sfen working to answer some other questions of mine; deal with some specific concerns."

Annica furrowed her brows. "Concerns? Such as?"

He smiled again and scratched at his brown-and-white beard. "You wanted to see the grounds? Was there any particular part?"

Annica's face scrunched a little further, but she answered with a quizzical, "The grand balcony. Why?"

"Then let us go. You and I. And my escort, of course."

The king stood and bid his family go back about their day. He and the queen shared a kiss on the cheek. The prince and princess took their leave, the prince casting an odd glance Annica's way.

The king beckoned Annica forward. They walked together to the back of the room where Sfen and the four guards awaited them. The guards took the same four-corner formation around the three others and they walked to one of the staircases in the connected halls outside the throne room. Once upstairs, they walked back towards the throne room, where a doorway led to one of the upper balconies. They passed all the way through to the back, where another staircase waited above where the thrones sat.

The stairway led up and turned, where another set of double doors came into sight. The guards opened them and everyone passed through onto the grand balcony. It nearly took Annica's breath away. There was enough room to hold a small party there. Potted plants were spaced around, with tables and chairs on the far ends sitting next to the balustrades.

Annica slowly walked to the edge and placed her hands on the railing. She looked over and saw that, indeed, one could jump from this location and make it over the wall below. Further out to sea, the Storm's Pillar rose from a nest of fog and mist. In the time they'd been inside, dark clouds had been rolling in. The breeze grew stiff and cold.

"A storm moving in," the king commented. "We won't be able to linger here long, unfortunately."

Sfen, standing next to the king, stepped forward with a curious look on his face. "Why did you want to see the balcony so badly, Annica?"

She thought for a moment about how to pose her question. "It has a dark history, from what I hear."

Sfen lowered his head as the king nodded somberly. "It does," the king said. "We try not to let those memories taint our feelings about such a lovely place in the castle. At least, in better weather."

Annica wrapped her arms around herself. The weather didn't worsen, but the warmth of the sun was lost behind the dour clouds. Cold winds from the sea rustled their robes. Annica briefly thought she saw a flash of lightning near the Storm's Pillar.

"Perhaps we should go inside?" the king offered.

They'd already turned away before Annica could respond. She looked out over the churning waters. The whitecaps rolled in from as far out as she could see. The third pillar, another made of natural stone that had survived the weathering of the ocean and time, looked closer here than anywhere else but still so distant. It had an eerie, strange beauty about it.

A sudden gust of wind caused all of them to stagger and grab their robes and clothing that were suddenly flying about. As it died down, a distant sound of thunder echoed all around them. The sound of the guards readying their weapons drew everyone's attention. Annica looked first at the armored men brandishing their swords, then turned to see what they were looking at that was making their hands shake.

At one end of the balcony, the Courier stood in the quickly dying gust. Its robes whipped around it, the breeze seeming stronger just in its presence. Its obscured visage gazed at all of them and none of them, and they all stared back.

"No!" the king yelled as Sfen placed a firm hand on his shoulder. "You shouldn't be here. My son is fine! He doesn't hear the voice anymore!"

"The voice?" Annica said out loud, but no one heard her. Her heart began to pound. *The voice?*

The Courier walked slowly toward them. The guards sheathed their weapons now that they knew who was among them. There was nothing they could do against the Courier. The figure stopped within arm's length of Annica and the king, Sfen behind them, and the guards being off to one side. The king's panicked and heavy breathing had Annica clenching her jaw. She felt the air electrify. She still couldn't get those two words out of her head: *the voice.*

The Courier stopped and its cowled head turned to Annica. Slowly, its right hand raised and was offered to her. Her heart felt like it had stopped beating. The world froze. The Courier had come for her.

Go with him, the voice said flatly. *Now is your chance.*

Annica's mind raced. All she'd learned said that there was no option but to accept the offer lest you come to a horrible end. But the voice was somehow tied to this, too. She didn't want to go. She wanted answers, yes, but only so she could know if Kalthav was a place for her to safely call home. Now, she was once again being called.

She closed her eyes, tears slipping down both her cheeks. She thought of Pyotr and Lorna. In part, wondering what would happen to them if she refused and something happened to her while in their care. Also, she wanted to think of them one more time...just in case. Then, she slowly raised her hand and placed it in the Courier's.

Everything went white, and a deafening peal of thunder cracked. She squinted her eyes, the brightness still blinding behind her eyelids. It only lasted a moment, and when she opened her eyes she was in a different place. A very different place.

THE CHAMBER around her was massive. Stone floors and stone walls, all running seamlessly together. Massive stone pillars held up a ceiling dozens of feet overhead. There were no ornate trappings, no rugs, furniture, banners, or any signs of the place belonging to Kalthav. She first thought she had been taken to the Storm's Pillar, but now she began to doubt.

Before her was a raised section of flooring surrounded by stairs on all sides. Eight thrones of identical make formed a half circle that opened toward her. Seven of the thrones were occupied, those sitting on them glowing silver-white with tongues of ghostly bluish flame emanating around them. They all looked at her intensely, some of them cocking their heads, some leaning forward on their knees, and others simply watching.

She recognized them all instantly. They looked just like their statues in front of Haakonsen Castle. Annica was in the presence of the Storm Kings.

Part VII

Annica froze. Her first instinct was to flee and get out of there however she could. Her eyes wide with terror, she felt the breaths coming in and out of her open lips in sharp, ragged bursts. She couldn't look away from them. Seven bright, burning figures looked back at her with intense interest, but she felt no malice. In fact, she felt no evil at all.

She began to calm down slightly but didn't know what to do. If she was on the Storm's Pillar, then there was likely no way for her to escape. She wouldn't dare attack the ghostly figures, not knowing their power. And, again, there was no sign of malignance or darkness about them.

"You are Annica," one of them said. His voice echoed in the empty room, but also with a supernatural essence.

"I am," she replied meekly. "And you are the Storm Kings."

She tried to rally her courage and confidence.

These people are dangerous. They want to kill you.

Annica ignored the voice. She followed its instructions and came with the Courier; why did it now sound like it was warning her? Or was it simply providing her with their intentions? Did the voice serve them?

"We are," the war queen, Livda, answered.

"We have kept watch over our people for centuries since the Rupture shook the foundations of the physical and metaphysical world," said Sturlsen, the great architect of Kalthavian legend. "We found ourselves able to return after that horrific event. We stayed here to protect our people from its influence."

Annica felt the magic of the Fifth radiating from them. They were practically specters of pure Fifth Magic energy intertwined with some other kind of magic. She felt the magic within her, jostling. It felt strange and uncomfortable, but she assumed it was because she kept it bottled up so near such a powerful source.

"You didn't reveal yourself to your people?"

"At first, we weren't sure what to do. We had to come to terms with our own forms. We decided it best to safeguard our people from the darkness claiming the rest of Alda, as our presence appeared to keep it at bay." Baldyn explained.

"Kalthavians are strong," Hafjor Silford, youngest among them, joined in. "They would need to be stronger and smarter to survive in this new world. So, we kept the worst of the evil from them and let them continue to live and learn in this world; not that we had much choice."

"Much choice?" Annica replied skeptically. "Your power combined could do no measure of damage against what's out there—I've seen it! I've fought it! If I can do that, you must be able to—"

"We can do nothing against Them but bar our doors with our own presence," one of the other kings interrupted sharply. Pyotr never discussed him, so Annica didn't even know his name. "We are wasting time. We need to move on." He was gruff and impatient, waving his hand dismissively.

"Calm yourself, Jaldun," Baldyn subtly scolded. "Remember our promise."

"Promise?" Annica asked. "What promise?"

"To never let one touched by the darkness go without an explanation."

Annica pursed her lips, tears threatening to fall again. "Why am I here?" she asked, genuine confusion and pangs of sadness carrying on her words.

Baldyn, the first king of Kalthav according to Pyotr, answered her, his voice deep and intimidating, echoing in the same manner as the others. "You are here because that darkness has attached itself to you."

Annica's head dropped.

Annica raised her head and looked at them all. "You mean the Obscured Throne?"

"That is what many have come to call it," Livda said.

"Our people have become targeted by something. Some evil attaches to them and threatens to bring destruction here. It's not one of those dread Inheritors, not nearly as powerful, but all we have is being given to fend those fiends off. The Courier was created to find those this lesser evil infects and bring them here."

Annica nodded. "What *is* the Courier? Where are they now?"

The other king, whose name remained unknown, answered her. "The Courier is a creation of ours. A golem of sorts. We constructed it from our connection with the Fifth Magic as well as my skill with the Third Sect."

"You're a mage?" Annica asked.

The storm king nodded his head. "In life, I was Halgr the Spell-touched. I excelled in the Third Sect but knew little of the Fifth Magic until our resurrection in these forms."

"You're all from Kalthav's past, but one seat remains empty. May I ask why?"

She wasn't sure if she was genuinely curious or just prolonging the question she feared to ask. They seemed to take her question in stride, however.

"It remains for the king that will never be. It remains empty in homage to all the kings and history that will be forever lost as a result of the Rupture," Livda explained.

"So you're the saying the world is ending?" Annica asked, fear marring her face.

"That can't be known, at least not by the likes of us. One thing is for certain, the world will never go back to what it was. Our existence, the Storm Kings, we believe we are some sort of fluke in the dark plans set on our world. We only have the means to protect our people for as long as we can, so that is the purpose we serve," Livda said, sitting back in her seat.

Annica felt something boil within her. The Fifth Magic she kept tucked away within her was becoming unsettled. Something was wrong. Her body felt cold and clammy. Her hands trembled. The time had come to ask the question burning on her tongue.

"What will you do with me?"

"The same that we do with all those that the Courier brings us. We cleanse them of the darkness—at the cost of their life," the Storm King Baldyn said, his tone severe but empathetic.

I told you! the voice snapped. *You have to get rid of them, Annica.*

She was torn. Her face contorted with the alternating feelings tearing at her. These vestiges of kings and queens from the past all regarded her with a mix of pity and conviction. There was still one other that had yet to speak, one whose statue didn't reside in front of the castle. Annica's eyes lingered on that individual for a moment. Their eyes seemed to look into her. They wore armor and clothes unlike anything Annica had seen before.

"We've tarried too long," Jaldun began grumbling again. "It's a foul business, and we must get it concluded."

Their eyes turned to the figure seated at the center of the seven of them, at the apex of the half-circle of old thrones. They stood slowly, their ghostly silvery-white cloak flowing as though it were still of physical reality. Their features were neither fully human, dwarven, or elf-kind. Their ears were slightly pointed, but just so. They had the stocky jaw and build of a dwarf but were taller and leaner, like a human. When they spoke, it was without a Kalthavian accent or any accent that Annica recognized. When they spoke, it was a cadence and tone that resonated with age and grace and experience.

"We have tarried because this one is different."

Some of the Storm Kings looked back at Annica.

"The darkness had infected the Haakonsen son. We were prepared to send the Courier when the infection suddenly disappeared. Then, shortly after, it attached itself to you," the figure said, addressing Annica. "It has never done that before. Who are you?"

The question was asked pointedly. Annica felt the weight of millennia upon her. She knew better than to mince words now.

Don't, Annica, the voice said. For the first time, a hint of desperation traced its words. *You need to strike while you have the element of surprise.*

She felt the veil hiding her powers of the Fifth being stretched. Inside that little box where she hid the candle, something was scratching.

"I'm Annica, from a fishing town on the Leen, far south of here. I took a ship to an island in the middle of the Wailing Ocean. I discovered my magical talent there. I'm not very skilled with most sects, other than the fire aspect of the Second, but I do have strong connections with the Fifth Magic."

The figure stood there, observing her for a moment. The

other Storm Kings simply listened and observed. She was conversing strictly with this esoteric being.

"Why do I not feel such power around you? You do not exude a strong essence in the Fifth."

Annica began to sweat. She didn't know if she should simply tell them what she had been doing or remove that veil—take the candle out of its box. The figure began speaking again before she could answer.

"Recently, a strong presence of the Fifth was detected outside the walls of Cliff's Pillar in the farmlands. That was you."

Perhaps they were guessing, but it sounded like an accusation. Annica had to respond.

"Yes. On the island, my powers of the Fifth nearly cost me my life. It did cost my friends theirs. I concealed my connection with it when I knew I was coming to another city."

"That city, it was the site of a powerful outpouring of magical energies, both from the Fifth Sect as well as the otherworldly aspects of the Fourth. You were there."

"I was," Annica said hesitantly. "I discovered a cult controlling the city. I burned the city to the ground, accidentally, when I destroyed the source of the cult's power."

"Bac'thule."

Annica shuddered. "You know that name?"

"And the Black Gnarl. They are certainly connected to the darkness that is after our people. And you did not defeat Bac'thule, girl. Nothing can. You merely burned a dragon's foot and made it retreat, reconsidering its approach."

"I also considered that. Is there anything that can be done to stop Them? The Inheritors and the Obscured Throne?"

The figure's head drew back slightly; it seemed to look through the ceiling to the stars above.

"My kind searched for such an answer for so long. We never

found it. We could only leave it in the hands of our descendants."

"Your kind?" Annica said. Something clicked in her mind. "My gods, you're one of the First Kin."

The figure looked back at Annica. "Close. The First Kin are not far removed from us. I came here, to the north, with thousands more. My descendants sit before me. I am recognized as the first king of Kalthav. I am Kavanthal. My people still have memories of when Alda was sealed from the Obscured Throne. Those memories are so old as to be fading even from me. This threat of that abhorrent Thing's return terrifies me, so that is why we do what we can to stave it off and keep our people safe as long as possible. There is little more we can do as these revenants are held together by the unique magic of this world."

Annica, they're preparing to kill you.

Annica felt her head begin to swim. The veil around her Fifth Magic felt as though it was being torn at, pulled at with thorns and claws. She felt a deep melancholy fill her soul. She wanted to say goodbye to Pyotr and Lorna, but that was impossible. Her death would keep them safe, though, and she could leave this world behind for good. Perhaps the Storm Kings would grant her one last request.

"I accept your offer. I can feel your preparations to end my life. If possible, I'd like to end things on my terms."

All of the Storm Kings rose quickly from their thrones. Kavanthal stepped in front of them and raised a hand. Annica felt a surge of Fifth Magic course through her. It didn't hurt; it felt more like a blanket wrapped too tightly.

"That isn't us," Halgr said, his voice urgent.

"I told you we waited too long! What's happening?" Jaldun shouted.

Annica gasped. The veil over her Fifth Magic was ripped off in shreds. That did hurt. She felt her own magic push against the tight blanket of Kavanthal's spell. Something was terribly awry. Cold onyx veins tore through the warm light and slammed against the enveloping magic Kavanthal used. The veins broke into crawling tendrils and drained Kavanthal's spell until Annica felt exposed.

Her vision began to close in with bright, painful illumination like she'd looked into the sun. She saw Halgr raise his hands, possibly attempting to aid Kavanthal in his spellcasting. After that, everything became clouded in a milky haze. Just before everything transitioned to stark, snowy white, she saw tendrils of utter darkness, glistening with black starlight, wrapping around the Storm Kings. Some were engulfed, their lights being wholly blotted out. Others were torn to pieces, their lights fading as separate pieces. Annica didn't hear any screams. She heard nothing at all until she was standing alone, surrounded by an alabaster nothing.

The sound of her breath was all she could hear. Black stars began to shimmer in the distance, or possibly right next to her; it was impossible to tell. She stood on nothing. She felt nothing.

"That was close," a voice said behind her. It was feminine, sultry, and dangerous. It was the voice that had been speaking to her.

Annica turned and saw a woman in dark robes standing there, robes so red they were nearly black. Her cowl was lowered, and long blonde hair fell around her shoulders. She had strange runes tattooed along her forehead; they were jagged and looked like spider's legs. A pendant hung around her neck. Most notable were her eyes. Annica had trouble looking into them. It hurt in a way that only the worst of her memories could recall.

"You're Black Gnarl," Annica sneered. "Your eyes, your fucking eyes…stay away from me!"

The woman's face dropped. She looked truly hurt.

"Harsh words for someone you barely know. For someone who'll lead you to greatness."

"I've seen what greatness you monsters offer," Annica snarled. "I'll kill you."

Annica had heard the theories of emotions being entangled with the elements. Her rage was such that she tried to draw on it for her fire magic, as she sensed no essence of fire here at all. Unfortunately, it didn't seem to work. She couldn't summon the magic.

"Not here, you won't," the woman said matter-of-factly. "There's no essence of any of the Principle Triad here. Only the purest of the Fifth and Fourth Magics, and they are all expended. Not even I can use much magic here."

"That's fine; I'll use my bare hands," Annica threatened, stalking towards her.

The woman looked at Annica like an impatient teacher. Her eyes, unnaturally blue, gripped Annica's mind and stabbed it like broken glass. Annica gasped in pain and looked away, her eyes burning and moist.

"How can you fight me when you can't even look at me? Stop this, Annica." The woman almost sounded as if she was genuinely pleading with her.

Annica stopped, breathing heavily. She felt the hate burning in her, wanting to cry and scream and lash out while falling to her knees all at the same time.

"Who are you, and what the fuck do you want?" Annica seethed, keeping her eyes lowered.

She heard the woman's footsteps grow near and tensed, ready for the worst. The woman simply knelt next to her and put a hand on top of her head.

"Janesca. In my order, I am the Crown of Night."

"Is that Bac'thule's top whore?" Annica spat.

Janesca chuckled and patted Annica's head.

"I serve the Obscured Throne, which in turn means I serve the Inheritors. All of them. The Black Gnarl serves me."

"I thought that was Gideon."

Annica heard the snarl in Janesca's reply. "Gideon was a prideful, vainglorious old shit who paid the ultimate price for failing in his service. At least, to an extent."

Annica let Janesca talk while she prodded for any presence of the Fifth Magic. If there was anything, she could still kill this woman. It would be painless and more than she deserved, but it may be Annica's solution.

"Stop feeling around for anything you can use," Janesca said practically with a melody in her voice. "You're not going to murder me like you did those two women."

"Murder?" Annica said, her head bouncing up instinctively. She barely managed to avoid Janesca's gaze. "They were dying! I put them to rest."

"We're all dying, you know that old saying. Those two could've been saved, I'm obviously not one in touch with the Fifth, but I could have likely helped you use it to save them. *You're* certainly strong enough in it. Before the Rupture, someone with your connection to the Fifth? You would have been a high priestess before adulthood." Janesca spoke with a strange sort of pride.

Annica's heart pounded. "How many lies have you told me? Why would you make me murder them? The marauders...yes... but the prisoners?"

"A purpose in everything, Annica. I didn't lie. I said they were suffering and dying. You did put them out of their misery; you just technically didn't *have* to. In Nel Aldyri, did that loose-tongued, long-winded old frog tell you about the seals?"

"Fifty-five seals," Annica said, her eyes still wide in disbelief, her heart still breaking. "Eleven for each sect of magic. Four sects had been broken completely, allowing a window for the Inheritors into Alda and exposing it to the Obscured Throne."

"A window, yes," Janesca said energetically. "A perfect analogy. The forty-four seals ripped open a window, cosmically speaking, so that Alda could be seen. The Obscured Throne could find it again. The Inheritors beat on that window until it cracked and their essences flowed through those cracks. They're here, on Alda, where they belong, but only a shadow of themselves. Could you imagine Bac'thule, Ygiddra, Darwolaeth, or the Baleful Forge in their full, glorious forms?

Those eleven seals belonging to the Fifth, though. Those have been quite the conundrum. We had ideas on what had to be done but no clue how to proceed in breaking them. Then, a glorious event occurred that drove us into an entirely new era. Can you guess what it is? I'll give you a hint."

Janesca started stroking Annica's hair lovingly. It made Annica's skin crawl. However, Annica remembered something buried in her mind that she shut away and never wanted to think of again. The flames of Nel Aldyri burned once more in her mind's eye. In that subterranean hellscape, she was tied down in, the smell of death and wet earth and stone overcame her. Desperate to escape, she needed to find a way for her fire magic to affect Bac'thule. She touched that primeval, infinitely dark presence with her own. The Fifth Magic provided a conduit for her fire spells...a conduit.

Annica's mouth hung open. She was barely able to speak and trembled to the point of nearly collapsing. The revelation gripped her heart and her chest felt as though it would explode.

"I fused the Fifth Magic with...something...a being of the Fourth."

Annica felt Janesca's forehead touch her own in some twisted sort of tenderness. "Very good, Annica."

Janesca stood. Both of Annica's hands fell to the ground to

help hold her up. Tears fell silently to the ground. She didn't know any better but still asked herself: what had she done?

"That was one of those pesky eleven seals. At least in our theories. It was unmistakable, though. We all felt it, everyone in the Black Gnarl. It resonated with us. You could practically *feel* the Obscured Throne quivering with malicious delight in whatever starless void it was in. And the world itself certainly has shifted since then."

"In just a few weeks?" Annica said, still trying to gather her composure. "What have I done?"

Janesca smirked. "A few weeks? Annica, the Wailing Ocean is enormous. Half the world fell under its waters. How long do you think it took you to literally float from Nel Aldyri, in the very center of that ocean, all the way to the north here in Kalthav?"

"I should've died. I should be dead," she mumbled.

"Well, yes. But your connection to the Fifth is so strong it preserved you. When you slept, you were out for possibly days at a time. Maybe a week or more. My understanding of the Fifth Sect is through research only, but I know such a thing is possible for those strong enough with it. You just have such an amazing natural connection," Janesca finished wistfully.

"And the prisoners?" Annica asked. She had a feeling she knew what the answer was.

"Another seal. The Fifth is connected to the life of this world, after all. To kill with it?" Janesca chuckled. "That's practically blasphemous, Annica."

Annica launched herself from where she knelt. Her hands reached for Janesca, grasping at her robes and going for her throat. Annica wanted to squeeze the life out of this wretched, evil bitch, even if it meant her own death.

She felt the fingers of one of her hands get a grip on Janesca's throat, but Janesca managed to grab Annica's other arm by the wrist and used a free hand to grab Annica's face around the cheeks. The woman of the Black Gnarl was surprisingly strong and forced Annica's face down, where their eyes fully met. Annica gasped in pain. Janesca glared at her, those blue eyes practically glowing. It almost looked like her eyes were made of cracked glass. Either that or Annica's mind was literally breaking. Her brain, eyes, and even consciousness were screaming in pain. She was forced to let go.

Janesca choked and cursed. She stood up straight and smoothed her robes. "That'll be enough of that, Annica. We can't be arguing. We're going to be spending a lot of time together."

Annica rubbed her eyes. Her hands felt wet and she assumed it to be tears. Then she managed to open her eyes slightly and saw traces of blood smeared on her hands, as well. She blinked away as much as she could, then wiped her eyes with her clothes. Still gasping in pain, she glared at Janesca.

"What do you mean by that? Know I'll never stop trying to kill you so long as we're here."

Janesca smiled. "You won't have to worry about that. Neither of us will. We've found many more seals since your days on Nel Aldyri. I was looking for answers here since the Storm Kings' presence proved so stubborn. I thought there was something useful here or that they were tied to another seal. I was wrong about them, but then I saw this wonderfully bright light...you. When you shone like a beacon on the cliffs, I knew I had to find you. The others after that were just to draw you out."

"You infected the minds of the Kalthavians. You were just looking for a way onto Storm's Cliff. When they weren't working, you drove them to kill themselves." Annica's anger turned inward. When she reached out for Storm's Cliff with her magic, she had indeed revealed herself. She just couldn't imagine what had been waiting.

The dark-robed woman raised her hands and then dropped

them at her sides. "It was worth it. Here we are. There are just a few more seals left. Two, specifically. One will soon be broken, and the other will follow in due time. I feel it coming sooner rather than later. You, however, are key to both. The forty-four gave us a window. Now we need a door. Nel Aldyri was supposed to be that door, but Bac'thule's presence wasn't strong enough there. The door was present but closed. Gideon failed in that. But now I know more. I know how to open that door."

"You need me for that," Annica stated.

Janesca shook her head. "Yes. You are so very important."

"I'll kill myself first," Annica said flatly and with certainty.

A grimace caused Janesca's face to scrunch. "I figured you would try something so foolish and wasteful. Why do you think we're here? We're swallowed by the very flow of the Fifth and Fourth magic combined. Look at the light of the Fifth flickering with the black stars of the Fourth. No magic will work here. I've already said that. You have nothing to kill yourself with. Nothing. My hard-earned gifts from the Inheritors are the only things that will function here."

"Why did you do this? What did you do to the Storm Kings?"

Janesca shrugged and began pacing. "I told you to handle it yourself. You forced my hand. Since you're a conduit for the Fifth and Fourth Sects to flow together, I was able to finally get rid of them. They are no more."

It was quiet for several moments while Annica continued to process all the terrible information. Janesca continued to pace and look at her like a disappointed older sister. When she spoke again, it was like being chided by such a sibling.

"Annica, you're smart. Very smart. Put the pieces together. Kalthav has been awash in the protection and power of the Fifth because of the Storm Kings. How they returned in such a state, gods only know. Perhaps the Fifth was simply stronger here since it first coalesced on Alda. Regardless, within their protective barrier and perhaps because of their magical influence, several individuals gained a connection to Alda's special little magic. However, none were aware of it. Or any other type of magic, really. The king's aide was the only proficient user in the city. I needed someone connected with the Fifth to fulfill my goal, but none of them were strong enough; then you came along. I hoped, I so very much hoped, that when I saw your brightness flash in on the cliffside that it was the same person I'd heard that burned Nel Aldyri to ashes. That person, I told myself, would be perfect. And here you are."

Janesca smiled and opened her arms like she expected a hug. As Annica continued to glare and sneer at her, Janesca lowered her arms again, frowning as though she were hurt.

"You need me to open a door for the Obscured Throne to get to Alda. I will never do that. No matter what you do to me." The look in Annica's eyes was all that Janesca would need to see. However, Annica made sure not to look directly at her. Even a glimpse of those terrible blue eyes caused discomfort.

"Annica," Janesca said, frowning, with a hint of ice growing into her voice, "I assure you that if I wanted to make you do something, there are ways. Bac'thule is powerful; unknowable. But there are other Inheritors with much more sinister and unseemly purposes and methods. I have witnessed them. I have endured them."

Janesca approached Annica slowly, continuing to look to try and look her in the eyes. Annica turned her head away even more. "I wish you could look at me," Janesca said in a low voice. "I wish I could gaze into your eyes and see the unique power you've become."

The Crown of Night gently gripped Annica's chin in her fingers. Annica didn't feel her trying to force them to look at one another, but she showed resistance regardless.

"Fortunately, I don't need your compliance. We are both

vessels. You remember all about Bac'thule and vessels, yes? In the time we've been connected through my magic, the power of the Fourth has crawled into and through your being. Your brief connection with Bac'thule allowed my potent essence in the Fourth to merge with yours in the Fifth. We are the representatives of our magical sects. Now, we are one. As we speak, my body is deteriorating, breaking down into the smallest, basest components as my energies combine with yours. One vessel within another. When the process is complete, I can open the door."

"I don't believe you," Annica said, her voice low and desperate.

"You're a fighter, Annica. You're strong-willed and capable. You have no idea how difficult this was for me. I applaud you, truly, I do. Unfortunately, when you...how did you describe it, in your head? Hid away your candle in a box? You opened it from time to time, and a spider crawled in. Now, its webs are everywhere, unable to be burned by that candle."

"You're lying."

"You know I'm not," Janesca chided like a patient mother. "You can feel it."

Annica wanted to vomit. Her body felt wrong. There was no better way to describe it. Her mind felt tugged in different directions. Her limbs felt like they wanted to move in ways she didn't command them. Both a strange numbness and a euphoric tingling alternated throughout her.

Suddenly, the light and the black stars all faded. Annica was back in the throne room of the Storm Kings. In fact, she was standing in the spot she had been. She could barely see in the darkness of the chamber now that the glowing figures of Kalthav's former rulers were gone. She smelled the rain outside and the wetness of the stones. She felt the chill in the air. She tasted salt on the breeze that made its way into the chamber.

Her eyes went to the raised area where the Storm Kings once sat. Their thrones were all destroyed; piles of unrecognizable rubble. All save for one. The throne of the king that would never be. It remained whole.

Annica began walking toward the raised area, slowly and hesitantly. Of all the sensations she had, control of her legs was not among them. She was not the one in command of her body. She willed herself to stop, to head to the nearest window and throw herself from it. However, her body continued to move toward the empty throne. It was a nauseating sensation. She simply moved.

"We are one, Annica. Opposing elements impossibly combined," she said out loud, but it was not her words. Janesca was speaking through her.

"You have a lovely voice. You could have been a singer in another existence."

Annica felt herself moving. She felt herself smile. She felt hate and joy roiling inside her, turning her stomach into knots. Her feet led her up the stairs to the last remaining throne. Her hands gripped the sides as she set herself down on the cold, hard seat. She wanted to propel herself from the throne and run, but her body moved as though in a dream.

"It's almost time, Annica. My body is almost gone, my essence nearly combined with yours. We will become the door. Through us, through *you*, Bac'thule will complete Its purpose. We will become that passage for the Obscured Throne's arrival... the open door. The existence of something and nothing at the same point in time and reality."

How have you done this? Annica asked, her tone desperate and angry. She was the voice inside her own mind, now. *How can you be controlling me?*

Janesca rubbed Annica's hands together, looking at the tops of them then turning them over to look at the palms.

"Magic," she answered with a hint of a smile. "Why do you think I asked you to use magic you were unfamiliar with to kill the marauders? You allowed me in, Annica. The spider crawled into the box, remember. I was able to merge my essence with your own. When I killed them with my own magic through you, we became bound. Your mind and body entwined with mine."

You killed followers of one of your gods, Annica said accusingly.

"We all have a purpose when it comes to the Obscured Throne. Sometimes, that's just to die. But not you, Annica. Not me. We have a much greater purpose."

Annica felt Janesca's rapturous joy alongside her own grief and anguish. The feeling was unwholesome and wrong. Perhaps that conflict of opposing emotions was the point. Everything the Black Gnarl explained about the Throne and Its existence was conflicting and impossible. Hate and joy. Pain and pleasure. The heat of the forge and the cold of the furthest depths. The light of the stars and sheer blackness in between. Creation and destruction. Reality and annihilation. Everything seemed to encompass the whim and existence of the Throne—and that was the most terrifying thing.

The sense of the Fifth Magic tingled within her. The familiar feeling of slipping into the warm embrace of the magic of Alda should have been comforting, but instead, it brought only dread. As the magic began coursing through her, it screamed out. The malicious power of the Fourth intertwined with her own magic. She felt a smile spread across her face; Janesca's smile, not her own. Her eyes felt strange, like they should be seeing something else other than the dark room around her, as though some other presence was in the chamber. She wondered if her eyes had turned that horrible blue color.

Annica felt the air leave her lungs, but she didn't struggle to breathe. Rather, she no longer needed air. Her head flung back, striking the throne painfully. The pain faded quickly. She no longer felt anything. She saw above her the ceiling becoming a star-filled sky. She knew, inside her through Janesca's knowledge that was merging with her own, that this was not the sky above Alda. It was further into the black reaches of the cosmos. In the middle of other worlds and clouds of space dust and auras colored blue, green, purple, and red was a blank spot. Not just an empty spot devoid of stars, but a spot where darkness and light feared to tread, where neither existed. It was the definition of nothingness.

Her soul trembled, along with Janesca's. Even the Crown of Night, after decades of preparation and learning, was unprepared for a glimpse of the Obscured Throne. It was just that, a glimpse before their conjoined minds pushed the image away and comforted them with madness. What they saw couldn't have been real, and perhaps it wasn't. The Throne is creation and the Throne is annihilation, the sentient, malevolent embodiment of non-existence and existence. How could they look upon such a thing?

Annica's mind reeled along with Janesca's, for they were now one and the same. It folded in upon itself, collapsing in a manner that only one who witnessed the imperceivable could in order to survive. The contrasting powers of the Fifth Magic, the essence of Alda given form, and the magic of the Fourth, the unspeakable powers of the Obscured Throne at only a sliver of a particle of their potential, transformed them.

The dark vessel, Bac'thule, transmuted the physical form of the woman once called Annica into the void, the impossible doorway, that would guide the Throne back to Its creation. Annica's form became a hole in reality. A dark light that drew in all life around it.

Such a transformation activated an immense level of magic, as all the sects of magic were extensions of the world and, thereby, an extension of the Throne's creation. A surge of magical energy exploded from the Storm's Pillar. It washed over the surrounding area, crushing the nearby city of Kalthav under its power. The people scarcely had time to cry out before the wall of power struck them like an earthquake, causing walls to crumble, homes to collapse, and utterly shattering the Drottinsvegur. The bridge collapsed, falling in great chunks of stone and dropping all those on it into the ocean below.

Haakonsen Castle shuddered and its towers fell into one another. The sides of the Lord's Pillar crumbled. Large pieces detached and sloughed off into the ocean with a great rumble. Parts of the castle remained intact, and some rooms became exposed to the elements as large portions of the castle fell along with the pillar.

There was chaos in the streets as buildings and walls collapsed. Terrified citizens were crushed as they fled from their homes and mobbed the gates in their attempts to flee. The crowds surged against the small gatehouse of Cliff's Pillar, crushing people underfoot and against one another in their panic.

When the trembling stopped, the people of Kalthav ceased their panic. They stopped and turned, gawking at the destruction around them. The cries of the wounded and those realizing they had lost loved ones came to replace the screams of panic. No one knew what was happening. The guards tried to keep order, some calling for their captains. They were overwhelmed, the bridge having cut them off from the castle. Most of Kalthav lay dead in the streets or drowned in the fierce ocean waters below.

In the darkened chamber of the Storm's Pillar, a human-shaped silhouette, a void of darkness brimming with cold light, sat on a stone throne. Their shape appeared regal and rigid, but their head turned to the sky above. An aurora of otherworldly energy coalesced from the shimmering glow near their head and shoulder. It grew slowly at first, then shot forth into through the ceiling of the fortress, disintegrating the ceiling entirely and opening the chamber to the sky.

Time had flexed and twisted within the space where Janesca confronted Annica. By the time their conversation had finished and Janesca secured her hold on Annica, it had become morning in the world outside. However, in this chamber, the sky would forever look up at a deep, black part of space. An anomaly of time and reality outside of Alda's existence where the Obscured Throne and Its Inheritors truly resided. The pillar roiled with power. Within its borders, stars and worlds and galaxies shimmered.

When the pillar exploded into existence, another wave of force, a combination of the release of the potent energies of the Fourth and Fifth Magics, burst outward from the Storm's Pillar. It cut through the town like a glistening scythe. All who were caught in its embrace shuddered briefly before dropping to the ground; their life paid in offering to the birth of this dread beacon.

THERE WAS one other who beheld the grisly spectacle from afar. Pyotr heard the quake as he neared the border of the forest. His recent salvaging trip had ended and he was returning home. When the ground shook beneath his feet, he began running. Hilna stubbornly refused, so he was forced to leave her behind. He ran until his feet could carry him no further and he stumbled through the break in the trees to the rocky hillside that overlooked Kalthav.

He gave a breathless cry of grief as he looked upon the remains of the once-great city. Kalthav joined the ranks of all the other city-states that had been ravaged by the forces of the new world. Columns of smoke of all sizes from collapsed buildings and fires rose throughout the Cliff's and Lord's Pillars. The farmlands were devoid of any signs of life; no one running from their homes or gathering to see what happened. Most amazingly, the Storm's Pillar remained whole and a column of dark light, speckled with stars and churning angrily, shot straight into the sky and beyond sight.

He had a terrible feeling about all of it. Huffing and wheezing, gasping for air as he ran and half-stumbled down the hillside, Pyotr didn't stop until he reached the gate to Cliff's Pillar. The portcullis was firmly closed. He looked through and cried out at the sight of all the bodies lying limply on the ground. Beyond, the streets were covered in splashes of blood underneath fallen debris and beneath people half-buried in fallen, crumbled stone. He shouted into the city, calling for Lorna and Annica at first, then for anyone still alive. He shouted until his voice was hoarse. After waiting, weeping at the silence, he slowly collapsed to his knees when he realized that everyone was dead. Kalthav was gone.

PYOTR SLOWLY WALKED BACK to the hillside. When he reached the edge of the forest, he turned back once more. He gave one last look at the ruins of Kalthav, then turned to the Storm's Pillar and the strange, malevolent pillar of light casting out of it. He couldn't possibly begin to understand. The only thing he knew was that this world was filled with awful secrets, and no day was guaranteed one to the next. He returned to where he had left Hilna. The stubborn mule remained in the same spot, flicking her tail.

He patted her muzzle, his eyes moist but unable to release the tears. Hilna blinked and Pyotr told her that it was just the two of them now. He didn't know where he'd go next, but his home no longer existed. The future was truly unknown. He thought of Annica and Lorna, both among the dead in Kalthav, and then the tears finally fell. He quietly wished them goodbye and walked along the rough forest road to wherever fate led him next.

IN THE FORTRESS on the Storm's Pillar, a gathering occurred. The human-shaped void sat motionless, channeling the menacing energies of the pillar. Thousands of souls gathered there, not understanding their fate or the situation as a whole. They looked to the thing on the throne and hoped for answers but had no voices of their own. They filled the chamber, shoulder to shoulder. They stood in such a manner on the remains of the Lord's Pillar; in the streets of Cliff's Pillar, their ethereal forms gathering among the fallen bodies. The farmlands outside the curtain walls and the cliffs facing the Storm's Pillar bore crowds of tens of thousands of specters all watching and waiting silently. A few of those within the chamber looked up forlornly at the silhouette they recognized. Lorna, Sfen, and the royal Haakonsens were among those ghosts in the chamber who saw the familiar shape of Annica on that last remaining throne. Without a voice or answers, all they had left were questions and heartache about the girl who came to them and what had happened to her there on that raised platform and old, stone throne.

PILLAR OF BLACK STARS

THOSE WHO HAD SURVIVED THUS FAR IN THE DARK REMAINS OF
Alda held certain bleak expectations. The monsters of the old
world were once feared and renowned. Fairy tales were written
about feats of bravery and children were warned to beware of
goblins in the night. Mayors and governors hired trained men
and kings sent their armies to clear out more organized creatures like orcs and powerful menaces like trolls and bands of
ogres.

These were distant and near-forgotten memories. The things
that came following the Rupture were beyond the scope of
imagination; worse than nightmares and more real. Stories of
disappearing travelers were no longer told to provide entertain-
ment around fireplaces and taverns. They were whispered in
fear. Legends of creatures in the woods didn't bring men and
women wanting to earn coin or a reputation. They only brought
with them dire warnings, often causing entire gatherings of
survivors to leave for fear of what the reality of the situation
truly was.

Alda had become a place hostile to anyone who dared exist
in it. This is what drove the fear of all who saw the dark pillar on

the horizon that day. Much like the Rupture, which should have been impossible to see from all corners of the world but was, regardless, witnessed by every eye on Alda, the dark pillar was visible to all on their horizons. They knew this was unnatural, though they may not have known why.

In a city covered in the flesh-like vegetation blessed by Ygid-dra, the Inheritor of the Sanguine Garden's children gathered atop buildings and watched the pillar with their milky white eyes. Their multitudinous teeth clacked quietly in admiration. The tender of the garden rose from his seat once more, his mildewed bones bound by sinews of ivy and propelled by muscles of fleshy vines. He traced a loving finger along the moss-covered skull of his beloved, still in her chaise across from him, still crying out among the collective consciousness of the garden. He walked to a point where a building had collapsed from age and beheld the pillar himself. His soul, what remained of it, trembled.

The light of the pillar cut through the foul miasma of the rotting city of Felkirk. The cowled one perched above the streets that crawled with the liquified and empty-husked damned. It offered a bow in the direction of the pillar, patiently awaiting what followed.

In Athyl'glen, thousands of sadistic, shadow remnants gathered in a silent clamor among the boughs of the trees to see the beacon for themselves. They shuddered in delight, impatiently waiting for destiny to unfold.

Among the ghostly trees of the Wilted Groves, a village cowered inside their homes. The appearance of the pillar emboldened the things in the woods and a tall, gangly creature watched them from the trees, daring to barely hide Its presence. A young Sword-Bearer named Grayce polished her blade and prepared to face whatever came for them.

In those towns and settlements that still survived, people

feared it was another form of the Rupture, that the legendary event from centuries past was occurring again. When no terrible quakes or monstrous invasions followed, they tried to return to life as usual. However, the pillar was ever present on their horizon. It overshadowed their every action, some claiming it brought on terrifying dreams. Word began to spread slowly, and it became known as the Pillar of Black Stars.

On the island that held the former city of Nel Aldyri, hundreds of dark-robed Black Gnarl cultists were at work, rebuilding the land and the structures for their own purpose. The leaders of the various sects of the cults worked in tandem as much as they could manage after the ascension of the Crown of Night. They knew that the pillar was a sign of their great vindication. The culmination of all their work was at hand. This island would be their bastion as the Inheritors started to fully reclaim Alda for the Obscured Throne. They worked tirelessly on their new city, sending out ships to bring in new acolytes. Any who came back and chose not to join their ranks was simply put to work as laborers. If they survived, there might yet be a purpose for them, but the Black Gnarl knew their time had come, and their city would be ready to receive all their brothers and sisters.

Two OTHER INDIVIDUALS stared in disbelief at the strange pillar reaching from the horizon until it disappeared into the sky. Victor and Lyra were riding along an old highway when both suddenly felt a jolt deep within their souls. It nearly knocked them from their horses. It felt like they had been struck by a hammer and then struck by lightning. Their skin turned cold and clammy, prickling with gooseflesh.

"What was that?" Lyra asked. "I didn't like it...at all." She was breathing heavily. It hurt both physically and deeply within her mind.

Victor's eyes were wide. He tried slowing his breathing. The pain was endurable, but the dread that struck his chest and wrapped around his heart was exponentially stronger.

"I don't know, but it is very bad."

They stopped their horses. Victor climbed down and stood for a moment, trying to collect himself. Lyra climbed down from her horse as well and came to him, holding her head in her hands.

"My head hurts; it's strange. It's not just physical pain but..."

"Something else. Something supernatural or magical," Victor cut in.

"Yeah," Lyra grunted. She took a drink from her waterskin. "Now my head's ringing. My chest feels weird, too."

Victor shook his head and closed his eyes. He was feeling the same thing. "An echo or...no, a tremor of magical resonance. That pillar has something to do with it; I know it."

Lyra sighed. "Any idea what it is?" She ran a hand over her chest. Victor imagined it throbbed much like his own.

He looked toward it again. Even from here, the malignance of whatever it was could be felt. He took one of Lyra's hands in both of his own. "We're going to have to find out. We've learned practically nothing in the last few months. A development like this would be foolish to ignore."

She looked up at him with chagrin. She smirked and her eyes glistened with determination. He'd come to greatly admire that about her.

"I suppose it is." She frowned and squinted, looking away from him. "We don't know what's there, though. The last time I tried that..."

"You have me with you now. This won't be a repeat of

Felkirk. If we come across something that rings too many alarm bells, we'll turn back and figure something out."

He released her hand and climbed back on his horse. As Lyra did the same, he said, thinking aloud, "I feel like we're losing time, though. I mean, I've always felt that way, but this is different."

Lyra turned to him and furrowed her brow. When Victor became distant and thoughtful like this, it always worried her.

"We've been through worse. We can survive this. What else can we do but keep fighting and searching for answers?" she observed.

Victor offered a weak smile. She practically repeated his own mantra back to him. This felt different, though. The pillar was due north and could be as far north as Kalthav. If that was the case, they had a long trek ahead of them. They could search for what other information they could along the way, but a sense of urgency sat heavily on his heart. Only time would tell what they may be able to do to save Alda—and if there'd be anything left worth saving.

PLEASE REVIEW

We hope you enjoyed *Ghosts of Alda* by Russell Archey.
If you did, we would ask that you please
rate and review this title.
Every review helps our authors.

Rate and Review: Ghosts of Alda

MEET THE AUTHOR

Russell Archey is an author and voice-over talent with a passion for narratives. Fantasy and horror have always been his preferred genres. Some of his favorite stories often combine them–and the grittier the better. His eclectic influences in this genre include Lovecraft and Laird Barron and, combined, create Russell's desire to fashion his own story of cosmic horrors with a fantasy flair. Fantasy often holds many horrific aspects of its own, but Russell enjoys finding ways to take those and kick them up a notch.

Books, movies, TV, manga, and video games are all on the table when it comes to his choice of what series to devour next. He lives in Nevada, with his ever-patient wife who indulges his many hobbies and his unfortunate children who are the victims of his whims as participants in his board game and video game addiction.

OTHER TITLES FROM

OTHER TITLES FROM

www.5princebooks.com

Granting Katelyn *S.E.Reichert*
The Serpent and the Firefly *Courtney Davis*
Raising Elle *S.E. Reichert*
Rom Com Movie Club No.3 *Bernadette Marie*
Rom Com Movie Club No.2 *Bernadette Marie*
Rom Com Movie Club No.1 *Bernadette Marie*
A Crossbow Christmas *Ann Swann*
Hot For Teacher *Felicia Carparelli*
The Happily Ever After Bookstore *Bernadette Marie*
Perfect Mrs Claus *Barbara Matteson*
Princess of Prias *Courtney Davis*
Paige and the Reluctant Artist *Darci Garcia*
A Spider in the Garden *Courtney Davis*
Megan's Choice *Darci Garcia*
Something New *Bernadette Marie*
Something Forbidden *Bernadette Marie*
Something Found *Bernadette Marie*
Something Discovered *Bernadette Marie*